93

THE MORTICIAN'S DAUGHTER

also by
ELIZABETH BLOOM

See Isabelle Run

THE
MORTICIAN'S DAUGHTER

ELIZABETH BLOOM

NEW YORK   BOSTON

Mysterious Press
Hachette Book Group USA
1271 Avenue of the Americas, New York, NY 10020

Visit our Web site at www.HachetteBookGroupUSA.com

Mysterious Press is a imprint of Warner Books.
The Mysterious Press name and logo are trademarks of Warner Books Inc.

Book design by Fearn Cutler de Vicq
Printed in the United States of America
First Edition: August 2006

10 9 8 7 6 5 4 3 2 1

Library of Congress Cataloging-in-Publication Data
Bloom, Elizabeth
   The mortician's daughter / Elizabeth Bloom.— 1st ed.
      p. cm.
   Summary: "A suspended New York City policewoman returns home to a small New England mill town to investigate the murder of her best friend's son"—Provided by publisher.
   ISBN-13: 978-0-89296-786-5
   ISBN-10: 0-89296-786-2
   1. Policewomen—New York (State)—New York—Fiction. 2. Policewomen—Suspension—Fiction. 3. Young men—Crimes against—Fiction. 4. City and town life—New England—Fiction. 5. New England—Fiction. I. Title.
   PS3569.A7882M67 2006
   813'.6—dc22   2005035418

Dedicated to the memory of
Shakespeare the Wonder Dog
1992–2005
a girl's best friend
and finest muse

Many thanks to:

My very patient editors,
Kristen Weber and Les Pockell

Dr. James Terzian
for knowing how the bodies are buried

Brew-Ha-Ha café of North Adams, Massachusetts,
for keeping me fed and caffeinated
and not noticing how many times I reuse a tea bag

And especially my mom, Betty Saulnier,
for hosting Kemp Avenue's locally infamous
Swimming Hole, Feeding Trough,
Canine Spa & Writers' Retreat

AUTHOR'S NOTE

My family has lived in North Adams, Massachusetts, for several generations on both sides; we used to pass my great-grandfather's grave on the way to the supermarket. Although Ginny's hometown is never named, many of the places in *The Mortician's Daughter* are real North Adams institutions: the Fish Pond, Mass MoCA, Angelina's sub shop, Jack's Hot Dogs, and the Mohawk Theatre, just to name a few.

I debated whether to name North Adams specifically, but in the end I decided not to, for two reasons. First, since time marches on, I didn't want to cause confusion resulting from the changes that have occurred in the town between the book's conception and its publication. (For instance, the mill where Danny dies, while actually across the street from a mushroom factory, is no longer a ruin; it has been converted into lofts.) But more important, for dramatic purposes I had to make the local police department something less than competent, and I have nothing but admiration for the real-life NAPD.

Molly's Bakery is real, and such a family favorite that when my father died suddenly, I still had the presence of mind to order several dozen of their whoopie pies to serve at his funeral reception. I have used the name of the bakery with the kind permission of the owners. If you're ever at 27 Eagle Street, a couple of storefronts down from my grandparents' old grocery store, do yourself a favor and buy some cinnamon bread. It's as fantastic in real life as it is in fiction.

THE MORTICIAN'S DAUGHTER

PROLOGUE

She was staring out the window when the phone rang, watching the lights glitter from the bit of Times Square she could see from her apartment. It was just a tiny sliver of a view, but it was enough to get her evicted—the price of Manhattan real estate being what it is.

The phone rang once, twice, three times. She ignored it.

She didn't answer her phone anymore. Why bother? It was always someone telling her she was a lousy cop, and a worse human being.

Especially at two in the morning.

She heard the answering machine click on. It was only through some perverse desire for self-flagellation that she hadn't thrown the thing out her fifth-story window, or at least turned the ringer off.

You've reached Virginia. I'm not home. You know what to do.

Beep.

"Ginny? *Ginny.* Ginny, are you there? It's Sonya. Pick up. *Please.* Please pick up."

She stared at the machine. It was big and boxy, something she would've replaced years ago if she gave a damn. The speaker made Sonya's voice sound tinny and thin even on top of the hysteria, but Ginny would've recognized it anyway. She'd known Sonya since before either one of them had teeth.

"Hello? Ginny, it's me. You've got to be home. *Please?*"

Ginny heard Sonya's voice crack. Three decades of closer-than-sisterhood made her understand. There was only one thing that could have happened, one thing that could have made this rock-solid woman sound so shattered. The next two words.

"Danny's dead."

She reached for the phone.

The Taconic Parkway is a curving brontosaurus of a road, outdated and ungainly. It was built for slow-moving leaf-peepers, not speeding traffic; it has no shoulder and plenty of suicidal deer. It's dangerous enough during the day, but at night or in bad weather it can be more stressful than a Manhattan avenue at rush hour.

Ginny remembered the last time she drove north on the Taconic. Someone had been dead then, too.

That was ten years ago, and in the heart of winter. She'd been driving so fast she nearly skidded off the road, until a trooper pulled her over. She told him she was on the way home for her mother's funeral; he took one look at her NYPD shield and her tearstained face and waved her on. *Slow down,* he said. *You're no use to anybody if you get yourself killed.*

Now the skewed fall sunlight made dappled patterns on the hood of her old Chrysler. She drove the speed limit, partly because the car wasn't up to much more—but mostly because it would delay the moment when she crossed the town line, and her grown-up self would blow away like the crunchy autumn leaves.

It was just after ten when she got to the bottom of Main Street. She'd left her apartment before the sun came up, after a night that included three shots of Crown Royal and no sleep.

Crown Royal. It had been her dad's drink—probably still was—and she'd been vaguely disconcerted to discover that she had a taste for it, too.

She drove up Main Street, not wanting to take in the changes, her training giving her no choice but to notice. The sprawling Kmart, for which a dozen historic buildings had been leveled back in the sixties, had gone out of business. Something had moved into the old Robert's department store, and there was a new card shop where the Apothecary Hall drugstore used to be. The Mohawk Theatre, where she and Sonya had watched badly dubbed Pippi Longstocking movies on many a Saturday afternoon, was still closed.

She drove up the hill without looking left onto Eagle Street. She didn't think she could stomach the sight of whitewashed windows outside Molly's Bakery, where she'd eaten countless half-moon cookies and whoopie pies and nut cups.

And lost her virginity.

Sonya and her husband lived near the top of the hill, on the middle floor of a three-family tenement on a dead-end street. Sonya had grown up in the apartment, so Ginny had spent half her childhood there, eating pierogies and stuffed cabbage and concocting excuses not to go home.

She rubbed her forehead, trying to stave off the headache that was starting to flower from the back of her skull. She'd been in town less than sixty seconds, and already the memories were getting to her.

She parked the Chrysler on the street out front. Her friend was on the porch, sitting in a fraying lawn chair, waiting.

"They found him two days ago. No, three. I'm losing track of time. It was in the big mill down on Union Street—the one across from the mushroom factory. But you don't know about that, do you? It was after you left. There's a mushroom factory now. Fancy kinds they ship all over. They found him there Thursday morning. He'd been missing for three days. Since

Monday. I made him his lunch and he went off to work with Pete and put in his day and clocked out, but he never came home. And then Tuesday he didn't show up at the job site. That isn't like him. He's very responsible. You know he is. Right, Gin? He's a very responsible boy. You know that. Right?"

"Of course I do," she said, and tightened her grip on Sonya's hand. She would've said the same thing if Sonya was claiming Danny could breathe underwater.

"By Wednesday I was going out of my mind. I went down to the police station, but Rolly said he was just off having fun. He said there was no point filing a report, because boys will be boys and when Danny came home he'd just be mad at me for making a fuss. And I told him—I told him Danny wouldn't just disappear like that and make me worry. But that night they found his truck parked over at the Fish Pond. And then on Thursday."

Sonya said it like it was a complete sentence. Her eyes were wide but dry; she wasn't entirely there. Ginny wondered if it was just the shock or if someone had given her a Valium. Even if someone had, she doubted Sonya would've taken it.

"Who found him?"

"Mary Benedetti. She sells real estate now. She was showing the building to some artists."

"Artists?"

Ginny hadn't wanted to interrupt, but she couldn't stop herself. Sonya didn't seem to notice.

"They found Danny lying on the floor. Somebody beat him to death. It was so bad Rolly didn't even recognize him. Somebody who knew Danny his whole life, and he had to identify him by his dental records.

"When they told me what happened, I didn't believe it. It had to be a mistake. An accident. Because I knew something like that could never happen to Danny. You'd have to be so *mad* at somebody to do that to them. And nobody was ever mad at Danny. You know—everybody loved him."

"I know."

"They wouldn't even let me see him. My own son. They said it would upset me. Like it could be any worse. But Pete agreed with them. He saw Danny, and then he said he wanted me to remember him like he was." Sonya focused on the box of snapdragons hanging off the porch rail. They were wild and overgrown, the edges of the few remaining flowers gone to brown. "Did he think I'd forget?"

Ginny squeezed her hand tighter. "He was just trying to protect you."

Sonya clutched the arm of her chair and said, "Obviously."

"And nobody has any idea what happened? None of Danny's friends?"

"Rolly arrested someone yesterday."

Sonya's voice sounded even emptier than before, something Ginny wouldn't have thought possible. She tried to keep her own voice level and low. It wasn't easy. Since Sonya's two a.m. phone call she'd been crawling out of her skin, and the three cups of gas station coffee hadn't helped.

"You mean he's got someone in custody?"

"Yes." Sonya spat the word like a curse. This time it didn't take a lifetime of friendship to make Ginny understand.

"You don't think it's right."

"No." Sonya looked at Ginny like she was only just noticing she was there. Then she stood up. "Can we walk?"

"Where's Pete?"

"At work."

"On Sunday?"

"Job's running behind," Sonya said. "Let's go."

"I gotta pee first."

Ginny stepped inside the ground-floor apartment, the screen door slapping shut behind her. Just the smell of the place made her feel ten years old again—the combination of fried onions and cigarette smoke and Jean Naté perfume that had permeated the walls decades ago. Sonya and her husband had updated the appliances and changed the wallpaper in the kitchen, but the bathroom was the same: olive-green sink and tub, yellowed linoleum floor, daisy-patterned walls. On hot summer days before they were old enough to go to the Fish Pond, Sonya's mother would put them in that tub with their bathing suits on and hose them down.

She smiled at the memory, then wiped the smile off her face before she emerged to find Sonya standing exactly where she'd left her.

"Where do you want to go?"

Sonya shrugged. "Doesn't matter."

"School?"

Her friend nodded, and they started retracing the route Sonya had taken every morning from kindergarten through fifth grade. Sonya was quiet as they went up the hill, by the Little League field, through the scruffy patch of woods. They walked around the back of the low-slung brick building, past classroom windows covered in construction-paper jack-o'-lanterns. A batch of handprint turkeys indicated that some enterprising teacher had gotten a head start on Thanksgiving.

Behind the school was the kindergarteners' Shangri-La, a huge wrought-iron jungle gym shaped like a locomotive and universally referred to as the choo-choo train. Sonya climbed up the side and perched on a top bar, then pointed at the iron outline of a smokestack.

"Remember how everybody used to fight over who got to be in there?"

"Hard to believe we were ever small enough to fit."

Sonya nodded, glancing down at her own body like it was a stranger; she'd gained a good thirty pounds since Ginny last saw her, and it all seemed to have settled around the middle. After a minute she said, "Danny loved to play on this thing."

"Yeah?"

"He used to climb up to the top and hang upside down by his knees. Scared the hell out of me." She stared at the empty space circumscribed by the heavy black metal, seeing the little boy who'd grown up to be the young man, but who would never grow up to be anything else.

"Sonya, sweetie, please tell me what's going on. Who did Rolly arrest?"

Sonya took a deep breath and turned to her. "Jack O'Brien."

"Who?"

"You know. Jumping Jack."

"You mean that crazy guy who used to hang around downstreet? He's still around?"

"Where else would he go?"

It had been nearly fifteen years, but Ginny could still see him: greasy hair, dirty beard, dirtier army coat. A local boy who'd come back from the war with a Bronze Star and a serious case of the shakes, the very stereotype of the shattered Vietnam vet. He used to do calisthenics outside in all kinds of weather—hence the nickname.

"And Rolly thinks he killed Danny? Why?"

"They found Danny's wallet in his pocket."

"That's all?"

Sonya let out a mirthless laugh. "That was enough."

"But you don't think he did it."

"It's ridiculous."

Ginny climbed up and sat next to her. "How can you be so sure?"

"Jack's crazy, but he wouldn't hurt anybody. Much less Danny."

"The two of them knew each other?"

"Everybody knows everybody. You know that."

"I guess I've been gone even longer than I thought."

Sonya bit her lip. "You've been gone forever," she said.

"I'm here now. I can stay as long as you want."

"Don't you have to work?"

"No."

Sonya's eyelids fluttered. The tears were about to come, and with a vengeance. "Thank God," she said.

"I'll do whatever you need. Help you run the house, deal with the arrangements. Anything. Or if you want to get away, we could—"

"There's only one thing I want."

"Name it."

Sonya grabbed her hand.

"I want my son back," she said.

The Shop. That's what the workers used to call it, back when the Northern Berkshire Textile Mill was a going concern. Old-timers still referred to it that way, though the vernacular was disappearing fast; only a few hundred people still understood that "go down shop" meant "go to work"—and every week, more of them took up residence in the Southview Cemetery.

But in its heyday the mill had employed thousands of people, mostly young women who'd emigrated from Quebec in search of work. They'd turned cotton and wool into cloth— nothing fancy, but sturdy goods a person wouldn't be ashamed to buy. The building had hummed with life, three shifts' worth of gossip and frugal lunches; the fabric made there had been whisked by train through the Hoosac Tunnel and sold to the world. Now it was just another hulking brick shell hard by the Hoosic River, padlocked against the predations of teenagers looking for a place to screw.

That lock hadn't been nearly as hardworking as those French-Canadian girls; it had given out the minute some kid smashed it with a handy brick. The scene that greeted Ginny that Sunday afternoon spoke to the festivities that must've followed on that night and a thousand afterward: broken beer bottles, cigarette butts, used condoms, candles, McDonald's bags, an old boom box spray-painted red. The huge multipaned windows were long broken, but chicken wire had kept the shards in place—the poor man's stained glass. Without fresh air for more than a century the vast building smelled of urine, solvents, and age.

It was a lousy place for anyone to die. Ginny still couldn't quite believe that Danny's life had ended there at nineteen, or even that it'd ended at all—she was half expecting him to show up on Sonya's doorstep with a box of doughnuts and a lame excuse. But the evidence was there, on the third floor, in the far corner: a vast pool of blood, splatter marks on the walls and floor. *People never understand how much head wounds really bleed,* she thought, and even though she'd seen plenty of them, they still had the power to turn her stomach.

No weapon had been found. If the killer had used one, he'd taken it with him, or maybe just tossed it into the river. She wondered if Rolly'd had his men search the area, and decided it didn't matter; it probably would've amounted to having a meter maid take a lap around the weed-choked parking lot. She had to get a look at the autopsy report: even a small-town doctor un-used to violent crime should be able to tell whether Danny had been hit by a weapon or a fist.

But even without seeing the report, she could tell that Sonya was right. The attack on Danny had been brutal. She'd seen enough crime scenes—and enough bar fights—to know that for there to be this much splattered blood, Danny must've been hit again and again. He'd fallen to the floor, but the attack hadn't stopped there. Ginny pictured the killer standing over him, smashing his head against the floor, delivering blow after blow long after Danny had stopped trying to protect himself.

Sonya had said that you'd really have to hate someone to do that to him, but in Ginny's experience that wasn't necessarily true. If there was one thing she'd learned in eleven years with the NYPD, it was that human beings could do just as much damage to each other when driven by love or greed or just plain boredom.

She shook her head, wrinkling her nose at the stench. Onto the mill's underlying smells had been added the thick, coppery aroma of blood and the rancid odor of vomit. The latter was fresh enough that it made Ginny wonder if one of the people who'd found the body had lost their lunch at the sight of it. Knowing the local P.D., it could just as easily have been one of the cops.

"What are you doing here?"

Ginny whirled around at the sound of the voice, instinct and frazzled nerves making her half reach for a nonexistent service revolver.

It was just as well she wasn't armed, because she might've taken out a sixty-something man in a pair of sneakers and a sweat suit—color red, size XXL. He was carrying a mop and bucket; Ginny could smell the Clorox from ten yards away.

"Excuse me," he barked at her, "I said, what are you doing here? You're not that reporter from Pittsfield, are you? Because if you are, you're trespassing and I'm gonna hafta call the cops."

Ginny recognized the man, but just barely; it'd been fifteen years and eighty pounds since she saw him last.

"Mr. DiNapoli? It's me. Ginny Lavoie. Mireille's daughter."

The man squinted at her, then put the bucket down. "Ginny?"

"Yeah."

"You had terrible penmanship."

"I still do."

She crossed over and gave him a light hug; it turned out his back was almost as fat as his front.

"What are you doing here?" he asked. "I thought you moved to"—he squinted some more—"North Dakota."

"New York. I came home when I heard about Danny."

He shook his head, chins undulating. "Helluva thing. My Mary just about fainted dead away when she saw. So now I gotta clean up. Promised her I'd do it as best I could. She's gotta show the place again tomorrow."

"You can't do that."

He gave her a withering look. Once a man has been your high school English teacher, she realized, you forfeit the right to tell him what to do for the rest of your natural life.

"I'm sorry, Mr. Dee, but you really can't. This is a crime scene."

"That's all over," he said. "Rolly's got the O'Brien kid locked up. He's not right in the head. Probably didn't even know what he was doing. I guess you didn't hear."

"I did, but—"

"So since it's all settled, Rolly said I could clean up in here so

Mary can show the place to those out-of-towners tomorrow. She really needs the commission. Little Mikey's getting braces for his overbite."

"But . . . don't you need to clean up all that junk downstairs first? The beer bottles and everything?"

"Apparently, that doesn't bother these folks. They think that's"—he cast about for the word his daughter had used—"atmosphere. Blood I gotta clean."

She could tell there was no use arguing with him. She thought about flashing her NYPD shield, then remembered it was presently the property of Internal Affairs.

"Look, can you at least give me time to take some pictures?"

His expression turned to disgust. "What are you," he asked, "some kind of pervert?"

"No. I'm a cop in New York. A detective. I just want to make sure everything's handled right."

"Let me get this straight," he said. "*You* are a police officer?" She nodded.

He scratched his head. "What," he asked, "is this world coming to?"

She did what she could to preserve the evidence, feeling vaguely ridiculous: a Crime Scene Unit of one, minus the training. She took notes, drew a diagram, snapped two rolls of film with Sonya's camera. Last, she scraped up bits of blood and vomit from the floor and sealed them in envelopes labeled according to location. If the fight had been as violent as it seemed, maybe some of the killer's blood was on the floor alongside Danny's. She had no idea how she was going to process it for type— much less DNA—and the chain of evidence had clearly been blown to hell. But she knew one thing for sure: once Mr. DiNapoli and his mop had their way, it was all over.

She went to the photo shop off of Main Street to get the film developed, and found it had been replaced by a beauty parlor, the one kind of business that always seemed to do well in her hometown even in the toughest of times. She'd seen a new CVS near the supermarket—they'd apparently torn down the old nuns' dormitory to put it up—and she took the film there.

Waiting in line at the photo counter, an idea started to form; it was a long shot, but it was worth a try. She went back to her car and divided the crime scene samples in half. Then she brought one set to the post office and put them in an overnight-mail envelope, along with a note laden with apologies and groveling. She sealed it, kissed the cardboard for luck, and dropped it in the slot.

That put her around the corner from Eagle Street, a block from Molly's Bakery. The pull of memory was irresistible. Self-destructive or not, she had to try to peek through the cardboard covering the windows, maybe get a glimpse of an empty display case—assuming all the fixtures hadn't been sold at auction. She set off down the street.

The bakery was open. Ginny shook her head, wondering if she'd landed in the Twilight Zone.

The front door was ajar, the window filled with birthday cakes and puffy loaves of white bread. She stood there so long her eyes stopped focusing on the treats, and she saw her own reflection in the glass—not her adult self, but the Ginny of six or twelve or seventeen.

Without really meaning to, she pushed open the battered screen door and went inside. A bell jangled above her head. The air was heavy with icing and cinnamon, underscored with the clean scents of flour and paper boxes and just a hint of lemon.

She'd read somewhere that smell was the sense most closely associated with memory, and she saw the truth of it: everywhere she went in her hometown, another aroma went straight to her brain stem. This one was the most powerful of all—the scent of the place was so familiar, evocative of so many happy memories, it brought tears to her eyes.

She couldn't believe it. Molly's was exactly the way she remembered it, down to the smiley-face cookies and the ancient cash register.

"Hello?" she called out. "Are you open?"

She heard her voice crack. Whoever'd taken over the place was going to think she was an escaped mental patient—one with a yen for cream puffs and double-chocolate brownies.

"Be right with you."

The voice came from the back of the store. She recognized it instantly, but she was too shocked to move; so much for the catlike reflexes of New York's Finest.

He emerged from the back room wearing a white T-shirt and a baseball cap. He'd changed with age, but barely.

"What can I get— *Ginny?*"

He gaped at her. She gaped back at him, absolutely no idea what to do or say.

She could hardly blame herself. After all, it's not every day that a girl is faced with an entire store full of her favorite desserts and the only man she's ever loved.

Some towns have one Catholic church; Ginny's had four. They all had proper saints' names, but they were known by the ethnicity of the immigrants that founded them: Italian, Irish,

English, French. But Danny's funeral was held in the next town over, because that's where the Polish church was.

At first Father LeGrand—who was also responsible for two other parishes—had said that he didn't do funerals there on Mondays, that Danny would have to be buried from St. Anthony's.

Sonya insisted, without tears or an inch of compromise. St. Stanislaus was where Danny had been baptized and gone to catechism and served as an altar boy, she said. It was there, and only there, that she would send her son back to God.

The priest refused, with deepest regrets. She reminded him that her family had been worshipping there for four generations—and that her husband's construction company was renovating the rectory at cost.

So Danny's battered young body lay in a casket beneath St. Stan's brightly colored windows, the huge church filled to standing room. Sonya sat with Ginny on one side and Pete on the other—outwardly calm, grief numbing body and soul. Her composure was contrasted by the wailing hysteria of the young woman at the other end of the pew: a petite blonde named Monique, all-state cheerleading champion and Danny's high school sweetheart. Across the aisle, awkward in unaccustomed coats and ties, were six teenage pallbearers.

A chorus of high school kids sang one of Danny's favorite pop songs; a church lady sang "Ave Maria." Father LeGrand spoke of Danny's good nature, his strong work ethic, his varied interests—baseball pitcher, pep band, supporting role in *West Side Story*. The faithful took communion.

The service lasted an hour, but for Ginny it was over so fast she thought there'd been some sort of mistake. The church was a blur of familiar faces, hundreds of people she'd grown up with but hadn't seen in fifteen years: "Ginny Lavoie, this is your life."

Danny Markowicz, this is your death.

She rode to the cemetery in the limo behind the hearse, Sonya clutching her hand so hard it hurt. There were five of them in the back of the shiny black car: Ginny, Sonya, Pete, and Pete's parents.

"Such a nice turnout," his mother was saying, though no one else was in the mood for conversation. "So many people. Even more than when Mayor LeClair passed, imagine that. I hope we'll have enough to feed them."

She seemed to be looking for an answer, so Ginny said, "There's a lot of food."

"So nice of them to come out. But you'd think that they'd have the decency to dress. I'm not saying a coat and tie, though of course they should. But jeans? Is that fitting for church nowadays?" She waited for someone to share her outrage. No one did. "Petey, who were those two young men? The ones all dressed in black. At the back of the church."

Pete kept staring out the window. The funeral director had started to line up the cars, but with so many mourners it was going to take a while to get moving. "I got no idea who you're talking about," he said.

His mother pursed her lips. "It's not as though you could miss them. Two young men, pale-looking, odd-colored hair. Out-of-towners."

Sonya cleared her throat. "They're friends of Danny's. I think he just met them. Two boys from New York City."

"New York City?" Pete's mother said. "Ask me, they look like they came from Mars." When she still didn't get a rise out of anyone, her natural inclination was to keep talking. "Of course," she went on, "the whole town's crawling with them. Next thing you know there'll be more of *them* than *us*." Still nothing. "They're just so *pushy*. And no idea of the value of a dollar.

They'll be lining up to buy those condos on the lake, so nobody who actually *lives* here will be able to afford—"

Pete finally had enough. "Ma," he said, "for chrissake, will you let it alone?" Then the cortege moved, and they passed the trip to the cemetery in silence.

Ginny had been to a Jewish funeral once, and she'd never forgotten the sound of the dirt hitting the plain pine box, the finality of that awful empty thud; she was grateful her people didn't do it that way. She and Sonya and Pete walked away with the casket still suspended aboveground in a shiny metal frame, a demure green carpet draping the open grave. By the time Danny was lowered into the ground, the mourners would be eating finger sandwiches in the parish hall.

The huge room could accommodate five hundred people on bingo night. Now it overflowed with mourners, whose sincere grief at Danny's death didn't keep them from piling their plates high with ham roll-ups and Jell-O salad. Ginny had tried to talk Sonya into eating something—she hadn't seen her ingest anything but coffee since she'd been home—but it was no use. Sonya had just smiled a mirthless smile. "Finally," she said, "a diet that works."

Two hours into the reception, with no end in sight, Ginny wended her way between the paper-covered tables and went out for some air. A clutch of people were smoking outside the door, and although Ginny could have used a cigarette, she didn't think it would be decent to bum one from the lady who used to lead her Brownie troop.

"Virginie."

Her name was pronounced with proper Québécois inflection, in a voice so similar to her father's it made her jump. Never mind that its owner was female; her Tante Lisette always had the lowest voice in the girls' choir, and after five decades of smoking Winstons her words were made of sidewalk slabs. If Ginny had no shame at all, she could bum a butt from her: no question, Aunt Lisette would be carrying.

At sixty-six she was still handsome—with her height and large features, she'd always seemed the embodiment of that word when applied to a woman. She was Ginny's father's big sister, ten years older with only miscarriages in between, and she'd never in her life entertained the idea that her baby brother was anything short of angelic.

She'd always thought the same of his only child—that is, until Ginny had the bad manners to disapprove of his second marriage. Still, family was family; Lisette wrapped her brawny arms around Ginny, who was in danger of suffocating in her ample bosom. When her aunt finally pulled back, she leaned down and planted a bright red smooch on Ginny's forehead.

"Why haven't you called me?"

Lisette spoke in French. Ginny answered in English, which made her aunt purse those fire-engine lips in annoyance.

"I just got here two days ago," Ginny said.

Her expression said that was no excuse; she fired questions at her like Québécois cannonballs. "Well, how are you? Why haven't I heard from you? How is anyone to know if you're dead or alive? How come the only time you ever visit is for a funeral? And why haven't you called your father?"

Ginny opened her mouth to answer—which question, she wasn't sure—but her aunt's formidable brain was already on the next topic.

"Where are you staying? Don't *tell* me you're staying at the Holiday Inn."

"With Sonya."

"That's ridiculous. You'll stay with me and Roger. With all the children on their own there's plenty of room."

"That's very sweet," Ginny said. "But Sonya needs me to be with her. I'm sure you can understand." She'd slipped into French without even realizing it; amazing how easily it came back.

Lisette thought about it and apparently couldn't find a decent counterargument. "You'll come for Sunday dinner," she said, then gave Ginny another hug and kiss and drove off in her Lincoln Continental.

Ginny wanted a cigarette even more than before. No new source presented itself, though, so she wandered next door to the St. Stan's school, a Dickensian building that was nearly identical to the one where she'd gone to catechism class—hating it, arguing about birth control with the infuriated teachers, quitting before confirmation. The door was locked, and as far as she was concerned it could stay that way.

"Why'd you run off yesterday?"

She turned around, and there he was: Jimmy Griffin, wearing a coat and tie, holding a big plastic platter dotted with white icing and chocolate crumbs. Was she going to have to go around town with a bag over her head?

"I asked you a question," he said. "Way I figure it, the least you could do is answer me."

"Jimmy, I—"

"Or maybe you don't think you owe me anything. I mean, why should you? All you did was run off and never speak to me again. Oh, right. And kill my baby."

Through clenched teeth she said, "It was an abortion. That's not the same thing."

"Oh, yeah? Why don't you go in there"—he pointed at the church—"and ask God what *he* thinks?"

"Jimmy, please. People are staring."

"Of course they are," he said, offering a jaunty wave to the smokers clustered outside the door. "The prodigal daughter has returned."

"For chrissake, Jimmy, this is Danny's funeral. Don't you think you should have some respect?" His jaw tightened. Ginny had gotten him, and he knew it. "Look," she said, "I'm sorry I ran out yesterday. Honest, I never even expected the store to be open in the first place. And I sure as hell never expected you to be there. I was kind of in shock."

"Yeah, well, that makes two of us."

She cracked the suggestion of a smile. "You probably thought you were going to sell a couple of half-moons, and there I was."

"A blast from the past."

"I would've thought you might not even recognize me after all this time."

"Fat chance," Jimmy said. Then, "You cut your hair."

Ginny fingered her cropped brown locks. In school she'd had straight hair down to the middle of her back. "Ten years ago," she said.

"Suits you."

People had started to walk past them, the mourners finally making their way to their cars. "I gotta go," she said. "Sonya's gonna have her hands full saying her good-byes."

He shifted the sugary platter to his left hand and extended his right. "Have a safe trip back to New York City."

She shook his hand, an odd sensation. Back in the day, they'd done a whole lot of things to each other's body, but shaking hands wasn't one of them.

"I forgot how everybody up here calls it that," she said. " 'New York City.' Everybody in the city just says 'the city.' "

"Probably in too much of a hurry to say 'New York.' "

"Right."

"Well, travel safe, anyway."

"I'm actually sticking around for a while," she said. "Sonya needs me."

"That's big of you. I mean, I'm sure you've got an important life down there." She gave him a look. "I mean it. I wasn't trying to be smart."

"Right," she said. Then, "Take care of yourself."

"You too."

"And maybe wipe that lipstick off your face."

Ginny went back inside the church hall, in time to see two slight, black-clad men walking away from the table where Sonya was still sitting, the untouched plate of food congealing in front of her. Pete was off in the corner, surrounded by burly men she guessed were workers on his construction crew, each toting a bottle of Budweiser and a grim expression.

"Who was that?"

It took Sonya a minute to wrap her mind around the question. "Danny's new friends. Those boys from New York. They stopped by to pay their respects."

"Did you get their names?"

"I don't remember."

Ginny disposed of Sonya's plate and said, "Let's get you home."

"I should stay until everyone leaves."

"To hell with that. You look like you're about to keel over."

"I'll be all right. I ought to—"

Ginny took Sonya's hand and pulled her upright. She signaled to Pete, a strapping guy with thinning hair and a thickening middle. He drained his beer and followed them. They were halfway out the door when Sonya stopped.

"Where's that picture? The big blowup of Danny we had by the altar—I don't want to lose it."

"I'm sure someone got it," Ginny said, nudging her toward Pete's truck. "Otherwise, I'll pick it up tomorrow."

Sonya was silent for a minute, then said, "He was so handsome. Sometimes I used to kid myself into thinking he had my eyes."

"Maybe he did. I heard people today saying how much he looked like you."

"They were just being nice," Sonya said. "Or maybe after all these years they forgot. Sometimes I forget, too. Isn't that crazy?"

"No."

"I raised him," Sonya said. "I loved him. Now that he's gone, it's like a part of me is dead, too." She stopped in the middle of the parking lot and faced her friend. "Danny was the only child I'll ever have," she said. "And he wasn't even mine."

Growing up, Sonya had always been the kind of girl you'd hope your son might marry. Her sister, Paula, was the kind you'd hope your son would steer clear of, for fear he'd catch a disease.

Promiscuous, truant, an expert manipulator—Paula had been every mother's nightmare. The fact that she'd been strikingly gorgeous since the day she was born only made it that much easier for her to get away with murder. Until the day he died, in fact, her father blamed her for driving his wife into an early grave. He always said that Paula only did two good things in her whole life: giving birth to Danny and getting the hell out of town.

She was nineteen years old when she left; Danny was one. She'd asked Sonya to babysit one night and never picked him up. Sonya was fifteen, already dating Pete but saving herself for marriage. At times when her black sense of humor bubbled up through the good-girl topsoil, she'd joke that Danny had something in common with Jesus: she became his mother while she was still a virgin.

Ginny laughed at the memory, sweat trickling down her neck as she did laps around the high school running track. For someone who was trying to escape her past, she was behaving perversely—coming back to her alma mater, the scene of so many adolescent crimes.

She was on her third mile, loose, feeling like she could go on forever. The high school track was hardly the Central Park reservoir, but it had the advantage of reminding her that she was in damn good shape: at thirty-four she could run faster and longer than she had as a teenager.

She kept going despite the light rain, still thinking about Sonya—how she'd so willingly taken responsibility for Danny, a little boy whose mother was gone and whose father was a blank space on his birth certificate.

Sonya could have left him with her parents, could have gone off to school and had her own life like Ginny had, but she didn't. She took a few classes at the local state college, married Pete, feathered their modestly decorated nest. Then she settled down to wait for Danny's brothers and sisters to arrive, and when waiting didn't work, she tried prayer. But the baby she so longed for never came, and the church didn't allow in vitro.

Danny was the only child I'll ever have. And he wasn't even mine.
Poor Sonya.

"Lavoie. How many times I gotta tell you to keep your knees up? You doing laps or running away from a mugger?"

She turned to see a man in his mid-forties, trim, Boston Bruins cap pulled down low against the drizzle. "Coach Hank? Oh my God."

"I saw you at the funeral," he said. "Damn tragic. How's Sonya?"

"Not good."

"Right. Stupid to ask. So how are you?"

"Not bad."

"Well, I see you still know your way around a track. But then, I guess you gotta keep fit in your line of work. Otherwise . . ." He made a gun out of his thumb and forefinger and shot her dead.

"That's mostly in the movies."

"Nah, your dad showed me a picture of that medal you won right out of school. Bravery in the line of duty, he said. He was real proud of you. So how's he doing down in Florida?"

"Fine," she said, though she was just guessing. Ginny hadn't spoken to her father since her mother's funeral.

"You sticking around for a while? If you're still here, you oughta come to the game on Friday night. Quarterback's got a shot at Division A." He was smiling at her, and although nearly twenty years had passed, she bet the high school girls still called him Hank the Hunk behind his back.

"I'll try. As a matter of fact, I was hoping to talk to you."

"You don't say."

"It's about Danny. I promised Sonya I'd try to find out what happened to him."

His bushy eyebrows came together. "I thought Rolly had Jumping Jack down at the jail."

"Yeah. Sonya doesn't think he did it."

"You don't say," he said again. "And what can I do for you?"

"I don't know. I'm going to talk to folks who knew him. And since you were his coach—"

"Hold on a sec. You saying you think this wasn't a random thing?"

The rain was coming down harder. Ginny pulled the hood of her sweat jacket over her head. "I don't know what it was," she said. "But when somebody gets killed, odds are it wasn't a stranger. So rule number one is, get to know the victim."

The coach shook his head, raindrops flying off the brim of his cap. "I find it hard to believe that anyone who knew Danny would want to hurt him."

"So do I," she said, watching a freight train pass beyond the outfield fence. "So do I."

Ginny would never forget the first time she visited the local police station. She was seven years old, and her Brownie troop spent a Saturday getting behind-the-scenes tours at what were arguably the four most interesting places in town: the police station, the fire station, Jack's Hot Dogs, and Neville's Donuts. Most of the other girls had been enraptured by the french-fryer or the gizmo that put the filling in the Boston crèmes; a few begged for a chance to slide down the shiny fire pole or climb on the big red engine.

When they got to the police station, only Ginny wanted to linger. It was she who raised her hand when the officer asked who wanted to be fingerprinted; who actually took pleasure when the whole squealing troop was locked inside an empty cell.

That same cell was now home to one Jumping Jack O'Brien— once the town's harmless lunatic, now its resident pariah. Ginny had gotten in to see him, but only after twenty minutes of wheedling with the cop on duty. She appealed to his loyalty as a brother officer, and when that didn't work, she threatened to expose the fact that when they were in the second grade, she'd let him try on her polka-dotted miniskirt. Finally, he succumbed to bribery in the form of a dozen Neville's crullers, grabbing the box with one hand as he tossed her the keys with the other.

Ginny smelled the prisoner before she saw him. She opened the gate and walked the few steps to the last of the three cells. He was facedown on the floor, doing one-handed push-ups.

"Jack?"

He stopped, looked up, shifted to a sitting position. His face was shiny with sweat, graying hair matted to his skull above a pair of reddened gray-blue eyes. He was still wearing his army surplus clothes—as far as Ginny could tell, the same outfit he'd had on the day she went off to UMass.

"Virginie," he said. "Virginie Lavoie."

Ginny was thrown; she'd hardly expected him to recognize her. "That's right," she said. "But I go by Virginia now. Or just Ginny."

"You ran the five-hundred in 1 minute 16.02 seconds. High school record."

"That was a long time ago," she said. "I'm sure it's been broken by now."

"Hasn't," he said.

She smiled in spite of herself. "Really?"

He nodded. There was something strangely solemn in the gesture. Then he nodded again, this time toward the waxed paper bag in her left hand. "What ya got in there?"

"Doughnut from Neville's. Chocolate frosted."

"Glazed or . . . c-c-cake?" he asked, tongue tripping over the final word.

"Cake."

Jack O'Brien licked his lips. "My favorite."

"I know. I asked around." She handed it through the bars.

"You're nice to me," he said, his smile revealing a railroad track of blackened teeth. "You were always nice to me."

He opened the bag and inhaled a long sniff; he liberated the doughnut and took a surprisingly dainty bite. He savored it, carefully put it back in the bag. Then he looked up at her and said, "I'm a goddamned murderer."

Is that true?"

Jack nodded yet again, but this time his gaze never rose above his duct-taped army boots. "Chief Rolly says."

"Forget what Rolly says. Can you tell me what happened?"

"I beat poor Danny Markowicz' head in. I beat him and beat him till he was dead."

"That's what Rolly *said* you did? Or what you did for real?"

He shrugged. "What's the difference?"

Ginny stifled the urge to reach through the bars and snatch the doughnut back. "There's a big difference," she said. "Forget what Rolly told you. Can you just tell me about Danny?"

"Danny pitched a two-hitter against Pittsfield last year in the Western Mass finals."

"I mean, what happened the night he died?"

He stared at her, like she was very stupid. "There was a fight," he said.

"I know. There was a fight and Danny got hurt. But what makes you think you did it?" He opened his mouth to speak. "I mean, besides what Rolly said." He closed it again. She took a step toward him. "You had his wallet in your pocket. Do you know how it got there?"

"Danny was nice to me, too. Never bought me a doughnut,

though. An Egg McMuffin one time. Came with two packs of ketchup."

"Listen, Jack, you gotta focus here. I want to help you."

"How come?"

"Danny's mom sent me. Sonya. She doesn't think you killed him."

His look, of all things, struck her as slightly wounded. "I killed lots of people," he said.

"You mean here or in the war?"

He shrugged again, suddenly the very picture of nonchalance. "I'm a goddamn baby killer. That's what they told me when I got home."

The memory must've made him hungry, because he pulled the doughnut out of the bag and took another tiny bite.

"Sonya told me you wouldn't even talk to the public defender," Ginny said. "But you've got to have a lawyer. Somebody to—"

"Do not."

"Yes, you do. Believe me."

He shook his head. "A real man doesn't hide behind some bastard lawyer."

"Did Rolly tell you that?" He didn't need to answer. "Christ, Jack, you gotta listen to me. Nobody wants you in jail for something you didn't do, okay? Now, just tell me how you got Danny's wallet."

"Stole it," he said. "Stole it like a goddamned thief."

Ginny tried to keep her temper in check. After all, it wasn't Jack's fault he was a babbling mess. He'd been a professional psycho for the past three decades: the town, which'd had no idea what to do with him when he got back from the war, had cast him as its local loon. You could hardly blame the man for being good at his job.

"I'm gonna get you out of here, Jack, okay? Just sit tight."

He nodded, though Ginny got the feeling he was only half listening. When she was most of the way down the hall, he called after her.

"You know what goes real good with a chocolate-frosted? A nice cold glass of milk. You could bring me one of those next time. 'Kay?"

After eleven years with the NYPD, Ginny thought she'd seen and done it all. But this was a first for her: sleeping in a murder victim's bed.

Sonya had insisted. After four nights on the living room couch it was time Ginny moved into Danny's room. That was so like Sonya, Ginny thought: letting practicality trump a broken heart.

So, for the first time since her son's death, Sonya had ventured into the small room just off the kitchen—the room she'd shared with Danny's mother all those years ago. She'd stripped the sheets, but after inhaling Danny's lingering scent, she couldn't bear to wash them. She'd sealed them in a plastic garbage bag and hidden them in the bottom of her closet, knowing her husband would never understand.

Ginny had watched her, not wanting to interfere. Despite the guilt, she was grateful to have her own room; between all the stress and Pete's habit of being out the door by five-thirty a.m., she hadn't been sleeping well. But from the minute she dropped her little duffel on the blue shag carpet of Danny's room, she felt like the worst kind of interloper.

Except for the sheets, the room was exactly as Danny had left it that last morning, when he'd gone off to work with Pete and the lunch Sonya had packed him and no clue that he'd never come home again. It was a cozy space, tidy without being sterile; Sonya had raised her son right.

"Cleanliness is next to godliness." Sonya was the only person Ginny had ever met who could actually make the cliché sound like it meant something. To Ginny it always seemed like a phrase ripped off a Hallmark card—or maybe embroidered on the pope's underpants—but Sonya really believed that living cleanly in body and soul brought you closer to God. No molecule of dirt could expect to live long in Sonya Markowicz' home; and though she was no one's idea of a bigot, in her laundry room no white ever mixed with a color.

Ginny's mind flew south to her own apartment in Hell's Kitchen, with its sinkful of dirty dishes and the dust so thick you could write your initials on the microwave. God forbid her friend should ever see it. Then again, at the moment even Ginny couldn't think of a reason to go back. Even her cactus had died of neglect.

She shook her head, reached for the cup of Sonya's strong coffee she'd left atop Danny's bureau. Ginny was self-aware enough to realize that she was in danger of sliding into a genuine funk—a pity party whose invited guests included not only poor Danny's murder but also her failing career, lousy taste in men, and imminent homelessness. The thought of slipping a little something into the coffee crossed her mind, until she realized it was seven-fifteen in the morning. Son of a bitch: she really was turning into her father.

The scream yanked Ginny out of her nasty reverie; it sounded like somebody was being flayed alive. She sprinted out of the room, shouting Sonya's name, reaching for her non-existent gun for the second time in as many days.

6

As it turned out, it was still just as well that Ginny wasn't armed: this time she might have blown the pigtails off a freckle-faced redhead, aged about four, or gut-shot a grave-looking little boy in a Red Sox cap.

Sonya's day-care center was back in session.

"Jesus," Ginny said, "you scared the crap out of me."

Sonya pursed her lips. "Please don't use that language around the children."

"Sorry."

"That lady used a bad word," the redhead said, shrugging out of a backpack emblazoned with a goony-eyed cartoon character. "She said *two* bad words."

"That lady's name is Miss Lavoie, Britney," Sonya said. "And she's sorry."

The little girl looked up at Ginny, eyeing her with undisguised skepticism. For a second Ginny was afraid the kid was about to start howling again. But she just said, "Now you have to wash your mouth out with Palmolive."

"Excuse me?"

"That's what happens to a potty mouth," Britney said. "Have to wash your mouth out with a soupspoon of Palmolive."

The punishment was so specific Ginny had a feeling the little girl had taken the potty-mouth rap on more than one occasion. She turned a horrified eye to Sonya, who waved her off. "Don't look at *me*. She gets that from her grandmother."

"Who is . . ."

Sonya helped the girl take her coat off. "Sissy McShane."

"Sissy McShane from our *class*? Are you telling me she's somebody's *grandmother*?"

"Sure. Don't you remember? She dropped out junior year because she was"—Sonya gave her a meaningful look over the child's head—"P-R-E-G-N-A-N-T. Apple didn't fall far from the tree."

Ginny looked down at the little girl. The kid was smiling up at her with a Machiavellian grin, no doubt trying to figure out whether she could overpower Ginny and jam a can of Comet into her nasty mouth.

"And who's this?" Ginny asked, pointing to the brown-haired little boy. He was watching them with saucer eyes, still wearing his coat and clutching his backpack, not saying a word.

Sonya crouched down and called the boy over. "Tell Miss Lavoie your name, sweetheart."

"Willy," he said.

Sonya patted his back, kissed him on the top of his head. An expression flitted across her face, so briefly Ginny almost missed it. But she knew that for that half second, Willy was Danny at three feet tall.

"Can you tell her your whole name?" Sonya prompted him.

"William Patrick Griffin," he said.

Ginny's heart skipped a beat, then another—to the point where she was starting to hope Sonya had a defibrillator.

"Jimmy's nephew," Sonya said, putting Ginny out of her misery. "One of six, actually."

"Oh."

Sonya stood up and swept the children into the kitchen. She'd just gotten each of them perched in front of a bowl of Froot Loops when the front door opened and another pair of kids came blazing down the short hallway. They were girls, blue-eyed and blonde, long hair braided down their backs. Identical twins.

"Meet Cynthia and Melinda Meeks."

"As in Coach Hank? No wonder they're so damn gorgeous." At the sound of the word "damn," Britney's eyes instantly went to the bottle of dish detergent on the kitchen sink.

"You know what?" Ginny said before the girl could read her the riot act. "I think I'm going to go out for a while."

"Sorry," Sonya offered.

"It's okay," Ginny said, distracted by the children's open-mouthed munching. "I'm just not used to being around kids, that's all."

"Sorry," Sonya said again. Her gaze took in the kids eating cereal, then the two others who were settling down at the table. "I wasn't going to start minding them again so soon. But their folks have to go to work, and I just . . . I needed to get things back to normal. To start to, anyway." Her eyes were beginning to fill up, and she blinked furiously. Ginny knew she'd never want to cry in front of the children. "So we're going to have a real nice day, aren't we? It'll be just like it was before. We'll have a real supernice day."

Ginny started the car, no destination in mind beyond getting out of Romper Room. The CHECK ENGINE light was on, as bright as it was meaningless. Ginny gave the dashboard an open-palmed whack, and it flicked off. She really was going to have to get a new car one of these days; holding on to this one had passed *cheap* and was quickly moving into *perverse*.

She drove down the hill, took a left at the river, and half a mile later passed the abandoned mill where Danny had died. There was an identical building across the street, the two massive structures giving the two-lane road the claustrophobic feel of a deep canyon. Not for the first time, Ginny recalled a line from a hymn she'd once heard in someone else's church—the one about Jerusalem being built among some dark satanic mills.

It was a melodramatic thought, especially for her, and she couldn't help but laugh it off—especially when she saw the sign on the building across the street. It was bright purple and white, affixed to the bricks; it said CRITICAL MASS MUSHROOMS—SHII-TAKES, CRIMINIS 'N' MORE!

So that was the mushroom factory Sonya had mentioned when she first told her about Danny's death. Ginny had chalked it up to some grief-induced confusion; it was hard to imagine the mills being anything other than gloomy monuments to the city's long-gone prosperity. But there were a few cars lined up along the rusty barbed wire in the employee parking lot, and a brand-new delivery truck was parked outside the loading dock. Maybe things really were changing.

She pulled into the lot across the street and parked next to the abandoned mill, the scene of Danny's demise. She hadn't been able to search the rest of the building before, what with her former English teacher standing over her, tapping his sneak-ered toes in impatience.

This time, though, both the front and loading-dock doors were locked. Luckily, someone had left a first-floor window open, probably in the hope of airing the place out. Ginny climbed onto a Dumpster, reached for the brick windowsill, and hoisted herself up and over. She found herself in a pile of garbage, laden with Dunkin' Munchkin boxes and cigarette butts and not a single clue.

Danny had died on the third floor; she'd already searched that much. Now she tossed the rest of the building, pawing through several decades' worth of detritus—not only all the crap the ado-lescent invaders had left over the years but broken machinery and rotted bolts of wool that dated back to the mill's heyday.

She hardly expected to find the murder weapon; surely, even

Rolly and his boys would have come across it if it was right there under their noses.

And she didn't find it, or anything else particularly useful—until she got to the fourth floor. There, neatly stashed under the shell of a now-drawerless filing cabinet, was a battered backpack containing everything one man owned in the world.

Back in the car, half a mile into town, through the front door of the police station. The cop at the desk was no one she knew, but when she asked to see Jack, he just shrugged and unlocked the door to the cellblock.

This time she couldn't smell him from a distance; when she got closer, she saw that he'd had a shower, and his army fatigues were nowhere in sight. He was wearing a gray jumpsuit, and although his uniform had been all rags and filth, it had clearly given him some sense of belonging. He still looked crazy, but now he seemed diminished and lost, to boot. No more one-handed push-ups, either; Jack was sitting on the edge of the bed, staring at her through the bars.

"I found your stuff," she said. "At the mill. Right where you left it."

His eyes lit up; it was just about the most pathetic thing she'd ever seen. Still, he didn't say anything.

"I think it's all there," she said. "I don't think anybody messed with it."

She'd looked through the pack and its attached sleeping bag—wearing gloves, though she couldn't imagine why any of it would ever get printed—and hadn't found anything tying Jack to Danny's death. Except, of course, the fact that everything he owned was at the crime scene.

"Can I—" His voice caught, and he had to clear his throat and start again. "Can I have it?"

"I'm sorry, Jack. I had to leave it there. It's evidence. But I'll talk to Rolly about getting it back to you once he's through with it."

In fact, she'd been torn about what to do about Jack's things. She knew there was nothing relevant in his ratty clothes and old magazines—and she definitely didn't want to incriminate him more than he'd already done himself. But although the locals had botched the investigation plenty, she wasn't going to tamper with evidence for no good reason. Never mind that the NYPD thought she was capable of that much, and more.

"They took my clothes," he said, looking down at the jail-issue jumpsuit.

"I'm sorry," she said. "When I get a chance, I'll go to the army surplus and find you something, I promise. But right now I've got to ask you some questions. Okay?"

He considered the request, then nodded.

"You were living in the mill, weren't you?" He shook his head. "Come on, Jack. I won't tell anybody. I'm not going to get you in trouble."

"Wasn't," he said.

"Look, I can't help you if you—"

"Only when it rains," he said.

"Huh?"

"I like to sleep outside." His empty eyes raked the cell's cinder-block walls. "Inside, I don't sleep so good."

"You mean you just used the mill to hole up when the weather got bad? And as a place to stash your stuff?" He nodded. "So that's how you found Danny's wallet. Right?"

Jack's eyes narrowed, like he was really thinking about it. He rubbed a hand across the grayish stubble on his cheek, bit his cracked lower lip.

"Took it out of his pocket," he said. "He didn't need it no more."

"You mean you found the body?"

Jack shrugged. "Kind of."

"What do you mean, kind of? You either found it or you didn't."

He cracked the hint of a smile. "Before you're a body you're a man."

"Christ, Jack, talking in riddles isn't helping me. Can you please just give me a straight answer?"

"First you're there and then you're not," he said. "Then they send you home in a box. Your mom gets to hold the flag, though. So that's pretty good."

"Hold on," she said. "Are you telling me you were there when Danny died? You witnessed it?"

He shook his head. "Heard it."

"What did you hear?"

He shrugged again. "Guys yelling. Real mean. 'Liar, bastard, son of a bitch. I hope you rot in hell.' Like that."

"And did you recognize the voices?" He shook his head. "But you didn't kill him. You know that, right?" Yet another shrug. "So why the hell are you letting Rolly railroad you?"

"Maybe I killed him. Rolly says."

"Oh, fuck Rolly," she said. "You're not guilty of anything but pickpocketing a dead man."

Jack shook his head, suddenly grave.

"I'm guilty," he said.

"How's that?"

"If you hide when your buddy's under fire," he said, "it's like you killed him yourself."

7

Ginny ran down the long hill at the end of Sonya's street, trying not to think about the fact that she'd eventually have to run back up it again. She passed the mill where she'd found Jack's stuff—was it really just a couple of hours ago?—and kept going, past the Dunkin' Donuts and a sub shop that used to be Ginny's favorite place to hang out after school.

She took a left and looped around toward the far end of Main Street, taking in more changes. What used to be the Newberry's five-and-dime was some cutesy ice-cream-slash-gift-shop, its window filled with scented candles and painted wooden bird feeders. There was a new coffee shop on Marshall—and, to Ginny's utter astonishment, it was advertising a special on cappuccinos.

A left at the minuteman monument—a replica, as the original had been flattened by a drunk driver when Ginny was in junior high—and she found herself in front of Lavoie's Funeral Home. It hadn't been her destination, but her feet had taken her there automatically: she was a homing pigeon in sneakers.

Ginny stood outside the massive Victorian house, surrounded by its neatly trimmed lawn. The building looked exactly the same: painted a crisp white with black shutters, a green awning covering the entryway so the mourners could enter their limos without getting rained on. If she'd gone around the right side of the house, she half imagined she'd find a certain three-speed bike, complete with flowered basket and tiger-striped banana seat.

She'd spent her entire childhood in that house. Other than

her apartment in the city, it was the only home she'd ever known.

Ginny's father had been a mortician, the third-generation owner of the town's biggest funeral home. The fact that Ginny had precisely zero interest in following in his footsteps was just one of the many ways she'd disappointed him.

Ginny had never been in therapy—the whole idea of it struck her as too stupid for words—but in the course of her thirty-four years, she'd wondered from time to time whether growing up surrounded by all that death had screwed her up. She tended to doubt it. Her mother had always had a pragmatic view about sharing her home with a casket showroom and an embalming suite, and she'd passed it on to her daughter from the time Ginny could talk.

A dead body is just an empty thing, her mother would say, *like a carton after all the milk's gone.* You didn't fear it; you just retired it with respect, and that was that. It wasn't for nothing that Ginny had been the only recruit in her academy class not to lose her lunch during their mandatory tour of the medical examiner's office.

Ginny picked up the pace, thoughts of her mother bringing up all sorts of memories she didn't feel like thinking about. The last time she was in her childhood home was for the funeral— her mother laid out in a lavender satin dress, decorated with a hideous lily corsage whose fragrance had clogged Ginny's throat when she bent down for a final kiss.

Six weeks later her father moved to Florida, accompanied by his new fiancée: the cosmetician who'd been beautifying the corpses even longer than she'd been banging her boss. And as for the business? He sold it to a corporation so fantastically un- ethical it eventually landed on *60 Minutes* for swindling old ladies out of their burial accounts.

So much for dear old Dad.

She got back to Sonya's in a filthy sweat from sprinting up the hill. Light-headed with thirst, she stuck her head under the kitchen tap and let the cool water run down the back of her neck. She toweled herself off and chugged from a bottle of Gatorade, just then noticing a note on the fridge: Sonya had taken the kids to the playground. She was just about to strip down and jump into the shower when the doorbell rang.

She tossed the kitchen towel around her neck and went to answer it. And immediately wished she hadn't.

"What are you doing here?"

Jimmy Griffin stood on Sonya's porch, arms laden with bakery boxes and waxed paper bags.

"Delivering some stuff," he said in a voice about as welcoming as her own. "What does it look like?"

"Right. Sorry. Come on in."

Ginny stood back to let him pass. She crossed her arms in front of her, trying to cover her sweat-stained running top. Somehow it hadn't seemed nearly as skimpy on the sidewalk as it did in the narrow hallway.

Jimmy looked around. "Is Sonya here?"

"She took the kids down to the Fish Pond."

His mouth broke into a half-smile. "Willy probably talked her into it. He likes the swings."

"Cute kid."

"You met him?"

"Sort of," she said. "He didn't say much."

"He's kind of shy, but once he gets to know you, forget it. You can't get a word in edgewise."

He set the boxes on the kitchen table—which, predictably, bore not a trace of breakfast. Even in her grief Sonya wouldn't let the kids go to the park without making them clean up their Froot Loops.

Jimmy stood there, shifting from one foot to the other like he always did when he was nervous. Finally, Ginny couldn't take the silence.

"What's in there?" she asked.

"Huh? Oh. Sometimes I bring treats over for the kids—day-olds and like that."

"But what's that smell?" She followed the aroma to one of the bags and felt it; it was warm.

"I brought Sonya a prosciutto-cheddar loaf. It's her favorite, and—" He cut himself off, like he was suddenly embarrassed. "I doubt she's been eating much since it happened. I was hoping it might give her an appetite."

Ginny held the bag up and sniffed it; the smell was amazing. "Prosciutto-cheddar? I don't remember your parents making that."

"I've been trying some new stuff. The city people seem to like it." He reached for a knife and sliced her a piece; he did it in the air, without a cutting board, and somehow managed not to lose a finger. "It's sourdough wrapped around the filling. I do a sun-dried-tomato pesto, too, that's real popular." She took a bite and veritably groaned with pleasure. "See?" he said. "I told you the city people like it."

There was a nasty edge to his voice—but it didn't keep her from savoring the bread, which was fantastic.

"So now I'm a city person?" she asked, still chewing.

He shrugged. "I don't know what you are."

"Welcome to the club."

"So . . . are you back in town for good?"

"No way," she said in a tone that even she thought sounded too vehement. "I mean, I'm only staying until I figure out what happened to Danny."

"Don't you have to work? I thought you were, you know, some high-powered cop down there."

Ginny opened her mouth to lie to him. Then, for no reason she could fathom, she decided to tell the truth.

"I'm on suspension," she said. "No gun, no badge, no pay. Maybe no job." *And maybe,* she thought to herself, *a big fat felony indictment.*

"I'm sorry," he said.

"Aren't you going to ask what happened?"

"Only if you want to talk about it. Which I figure you don't."

She nodded, leaning back against the kitchen counter. He could still read her like a drugstore paperback.

"I did something stupid," she said.

"Hard to imagine."

Ginny couldn't tell if he was being sarcastic; his inflection was impossible to read.

"I trusted somebody I shouldn't have," she continued, though she wasn't sure why. "Turned out he was on the take. Got me to do his dirty work for him." She took a deep breath, felt the Formica counter hard against the small of her back. "I helped him destroy evidence in a rape case."

Jimmy's eyebrows came together. "On purpose?"

"Of course not on purpose. But it doesn't make any difference. I'm still screwed."

"I'm sorry."

"You know," she said, "my mom used to say everything happens for a reason. If I hadn't totally fucked up and gotten myself suspended, I wouldn't be able to be up here with Sonya. Maybe it's fate."

"You actually believe that?"

"Hell no."

She thought she saw him stifle a smile. "About Danny," he asked. "How's it going?"

She shrugged and recrossed her arms, again feeling naked in her running clothes. "Jumping Jack didn't do it. I can tell you that much."

"I thought they found him with Danny's wallet."

"I'm pretty sure he swiped it after Danny was dead."

"Then why is Rolly pinning it on him?"

"Because," she said after a long swig of Gatorade, "Rolly is a lazy son of a bitch and Jack's the easy answer."

Jimmy's mouth curved back into his patented half-smile. "Cops in this town must seem like Barney Fife to you, huh?"

She shook her head. "We've got plenty like him on the NYPD, believe me."

He seemed to consider what she'd said, then nodded. "So what are you going to do?"

"Right now I'm just gonna try and ask around, I guess. It's not like I've got any official standing. Just about any way I stick my nose in is guaranteed to piss off Rolly."

They stood there for a minute, Jimmy shifting back and forth. "It's so weird," he said. "Thinking you're a cop. I mean, I remember you were always into that stuff. But cops are the guys who used to try to catch us smoking dope under the bleachers. You know?"

She smiled, too; she couldn't help it. "I'm not Narcotics," she said. "I'm Special Victims."

"What's that?"

"Sex crimes."

Ginny wasn't sure, but she thought she'd actually made him blush. "Well . . . I better go," he said. "I've got deliveries."

"I'll try not to eat everything before Sonya gets back."

"There's a couple nut cups in there," he said. "If you still like those."

"Tell me you didn't change the recipe."

"Never," he said. "So . . . bye."

"Bye."

He took a step toward the door. She took a step toward the shower.

But then, in acts so simultaneous an observer would've thought they'd rehearsed it beforehand, they grabbed each other and kissed so hard they drew blood.

Ginny wasn't sure how long they stood there, devouring each other like a pair of—well, frankly, she wasn't sure like what. Later it all seemed pretty ridiculous. But in the moment, she could no more have let go of Jimmy Griffin than she could've taken a vacation from breathing.

Jimmy hadn't been the first boy she ever kissed, but he'd been her first lover. Even as a pair of awkward sixteen-year-olds, their bodies had fit together so well they'd both found it vaguely scary. Their attraction was so strong it was like a third person in their relationship—a chaperone whose job it was to make sure your clothes stayed *off*.

When kissing in the middle of Sonya's kitchen was no longer enough, they groped their way to the bedroom. They misjudged the direction, overshot the door, and slammed into a shelf filled with cookbooks and ceramic figurines: one of Sonya's Precious Moments dolls sailed down five feet and met its eternal reward on the linoleum. It broke into three pieces; then, as Ginny ran her hands up Jimmy's shirt and admired an array of back muscles that hadn't been there at eighteen, she ground the little angel to dust under her running shoe.

Not that she noticed it—or, frankly, anything beyond the feeling of Jimmy Griffin's body against hers. There was something so damn elemental about it, something so perfectly right. If she'd been halfway self-aware, and willing to risk feeling like a moron, she might have admitted to herself that touching Jimmy Griffin felt like coming home.

Somehow they finally made it through the doorway. Jimmy slammed her into the wall, the faux paneling cool and smooth against her back. Even the skimpy running top now felt like too much; she tried to pull it off, but it got tangled and he had to help her. He was wearing a T-shirt with the bakery's new logo on it, a ridiculous smiley face that matched the store's signature frosted cookie. The silly sight of it might have brought her to her senses, but he took it off too fast. They kissed again, their bodies sticking together where the sweat had pooled between her breasts. Jimmy had always been an athletic guy—he'd even started a cycling team back in high school—and his body was still taut and wiry. Her nipples rubbed against the light fuzz of his chest hair—another thing he hadn't had much of at eighteen, but a damn nice surprise.

His lips moved to the side of her neck. That, more than anything else Jimmy used to do, had always driven her insane. He covered her breasts in both hands; it was an irresistible triple threat. She grabbed him, kissed him harder, and again tasted the coppery flavor of blood in her mouth. She had no idea whether it was his or hers.

"Close the door," she said. "Sonya and the . . ."

She couldn't finish the sentence, but he got her meaning. He drew away long enough to close and lock the bedroom door.

By the time he got back, she was already on Danny's bed,

lying against the freshly laundered sheets Sonya had just laid out. He sat down on the corner and ripped off his sneakers, a gesture so familiar it took Ginny right back to all those nights in his family's bakery. Some things did change for the better: Danny's bed was a lot more comfortable than an eighty-pound sack of flour.

He pulled off her own sneakers and socks, then ran his hands up her legs from ankle to thigh. All she was wearing were her running shorts, not even anything underneath. He reached his hand up farther and discovered that fact for himself.

She wriggled out of the shorts until she was lying naked in front of him. He hadn't seen her like that since she was eighteen years old. Even in the moment, it occurred to her to wonder if her thirty-something body was a letdown. But if it was, he hid it well; or maybe he was too preoccupied with the button fly on his jeans to notice. She helped him get them off, along with the same kind of white briefs he'd worn all those years ago.

Before he tossed his jeans to the floor, he reached into the back pocket and fumbled with his wallet.

"I hope to Christ you've got a condom in there," she said.

He nodded and pulled out the little blue packet. It was wrinkled, but it would do.

She took it and put it on him. Just like old times.

Then she rolled over on her back and reached for him. Just as he was sliding inside her, in that perfect fit she'd tried not to remember for the past fifteen years, she was dimly aware of the sound of the front door opening and closing, of tromping feet, of a chorus of children's voices demanding a snack.

She didn't give a damn.

"You slept with Jimmy Griffin in my *house*? In my son's *bedroom*? You screwed him with four little kids on the other side of the *door*? Are you completely *nuts*?"

"I'm sorry, Sonya, really. It just kind of . . . happened."

"Happened, my *butt*. Did you ever hear of a little thing called self-control? Or getting a room maybe?"

Ginny couldn't remember the last time she'd seen her friend this mad. No, wait; she could. It was the day she realized her older sister had left Danny on her doorstep and was never coming back.

"I'm sorry. Please don't be mad at me. We just kind of couldn't help it."

"Spare me," Sonya said.

"I don't know what happened," Ginny said. "One minute he's delivering some nut cups, and the next I know we're in bed."

"Yeah," Sonya said half under her breath. "I hear Jimmy runs a full-service operation."

"What's *that* supposed to mean?"

Sonya stared down at her fingernails, suddenly seeming ashamed of herself. "Nothing," she said.

She exhaled a long breath; Ginny hoped some of her anger went out with it. Her friend had been lecturing her ever since her last two charges—Coach Hank's daughters, those miniature supermodels—had been bundled into their parents' minivan.

Sonya doused a tea bag with water from the kettle and sat down at the kitchen table, still shaking her head. "Jeepers, Gin," she said. "You sound like you're fifteen years old."

The use of the word "jeepers" struck Ginny as a good sign; it meant that Sonya was slightly less furious.

"Tell me about it," Ginny said, flinging herself into a nearby chair. "It's some pretty screwed-up math. Put two thirty-four-year-old people together, and you get a couple of adolescents."

"So what *happened*?" Sonya asked.

"Damned if I know. We were talking. And then we were kissing. And then we were . . . you know."

Sonya was silent for a minute. Then, as though she were giving in to an irresistible force of her own, she asked, "So . . . how was it?"

Ginny tried to keep a straight face; after all, she had just desecrated the bed of her best friend's dead son. It was perfectly awful of her. She ought to have at least a molecule of decorum.

But she couldn't manage it. A grin blossomed on her face, and she covered her mouth to hide it. "Fantastic," she said. "Goddamn fantastic."

Sonya melted; God bless her. "Like it used to be?"

"Better," Ginny said. "Jimmy's picked up a few tricks."

"But what happened, you know . . . afterward?"

Ginny flashed back to the two of them tangled in Danny's sheets, breathless, sweaty from head to toe. Not saying a word.

"Awkward," she said. "We both pretty much wanted to flee, but we were trapped."

"By me and four kids."

"Right. We had to wait it out."

Sonya's mouth formed the hint of a smile. "The kids kept asking about Jimmy. They saw his truck outside, so they knew he was around somewhere."

"Oh."

"So you holed up in there for an hour, waiting for me to get the hint and take the kids out? And you didn't even talk to each other? What the heck did you *do*?" The look on Ginny's face was answer enough. "Oh, no. You *didn't*."

Her head dropped into her hands. "He found another rubber in his wallet."

"Oh, for God's sake. Ginny—"

"I'm sorry, okay? I couldn't help it."

"Right, right. I got it. You're a slave to your passions." Sonya uttered a few disapproving clucks, then crossed her arms. "So what's going to happen now? Are you getting back together?"

Ginny felt a surge of affection for her friend; leave it to Sonya to be so old-fashioned.

"No," she said. "Jimmy and I are not getting back together. We're ancient history."

"Ancient," Sonya said, "as of an hour ago."

Enough screwing around, Ginny thought. *Literally and figuratively.* She was a grown woman, and a cop, and she had a job to do. She hadn't come home to nail her high school sweetheart; she was here to find out who murdered Danny Markowicz.

What happened with Jimmy was a big mistake, sure, but there was no point in beating herself up about it. No one could be expected to resist her first love, could she? Especially when he's standing right in front of you, wrapping his arms around your—

"Jesus," she told herself. "Get a grip already."

Sonya had gone to the supermarket to buy their dinner groceries. Ginny needed to search Danny's room, and Sonya had decided she'd just as soon not be there.

Tossing the room proved to be a perfect antidote to thinking about Jimmy. Never mind that this was the scene of their crime; Ginny's training took over, and she was all business. Methodically, wearing Sonya's kitchen gloves, she worked her way through Danny's bureau drawers, under the bed, inside each CD case and shoe box and duffel bag.

What she found was nothing more telling than the detritus of a normal teenager's life. He had some notebooks filled with poetry; music mixes he'd burned on his computer; a half-empty box of Marlboro Reds; a set of dumbbells; a fifth of Jägermeister; stacks of men's magazines, none more raunchy than *Maxim.*

In his closet, tucked inside the zipper of his gym bag, she found a stash of Trojans; Ginny preferred not to think about how long she and Jimmy would've stayed holed up in the room if they'd known about *those*.

The phone rang; Ginny stopped what she was doing and picked up the receiver next to Danny's bed.

"Markowicz residence."

"Virginie?" *Oh, hell.* "You bad girl. Why haven't you called me?"

"I'm sorry, Tante Lisette," Ginny said, answering in French in an attempt to mollify her. "I've been really busy helping Sonya."

"We're expecting you for Sunday dinner."

"I can't promise," Ginny said. "I'd really like to, but—"

"Nonsense."

"Sonya doesn't believe that Jack O'Brien killed Danny. I told her I'd find out what happened to him."

She was hoping the pronouncement would get Aunt Lisette off her back. But if she was impressed, she didn't show it. "That's hardly an excuse to ignore your family."

"I'm sorry," Ginny said again. "I swear, I'll come over as soon as I can. Okay?"

It wasn't okay; her aunt made that perfectly clear. She kept her on the phone for a while, grilling her about her estrangement from her father and her life in New York and her prospects for matrimony and reproduction, until Ginny finally convinced her she had to get back to work. She picked up the search, which was turning out to be even less satisfying than the phone call.

There was no diary, nothing that would give her Danny's every thought and deed in one convenient package. That sort of thing rarely happened in real life, anyway; only on those stupid cop shows that made Ginny want to throw something at the television. She did find a pair of photo albums—not family pictures, which Sonya probably kept, but snapshots showing Danny cavorting with his friends.

Ginny recognized some of them from the funeral: the young men who would be Danny's pallbearers were dressed in baseball uniforms or grilling burgers at the lake or beaming in front of new pickup trucks. There were plenty of shots of Danny's girlfriend; that blonde slip of a thing who'd been sobbing her heart out at St. Stan's sure looked great in a bikini.

She put the albums and a few other items aside; she'd take a closer look at them later.

The easy part of the search was done. Now Ginny set about moving the furniture—checking behind it, removing each drawer to make sure nothing had been secreted underneath.

That's when she found it. It was hidden behind Danny's bookcase, a piece so heavy it had put two-inch dents in the shag carpet.

A .38-caliber handgun.

The revolver was tucked into a makeshift holster—a strip of cardboard taped to the back of the bookcase. It slid out easily; Danny had clearly put some effort into keeping it accessible. If Ginny had known it was there, she wouldn't have had to move the bookcase to get at it, just reached her arm into the slice of space between the bookcase and the wall and plucked it out.

She held it gingerly, trying not to smudge any fingerprints—though how she was going to print it in the first place was anybody's guess. She instinctively checked to make sure the safety was on; it wasn't. *Jesus.* She clicked it on, then checked the cylinder. It was fully loaded.

She sniffed the muzzle. It had been fired recently—though, she noted upon further inspection, not cleaned for weeks, months maybe.

Ginny was no firearms expert, but from looking at the revolver, she could tell that Danny wasn't, either. This gun hadn't been treated well; from the oily grime and the fact that the safety had been off even when it was hidden, she figured its owner didn't really know what he was doing.

But it *had* been fired. Had Danny been the one to shoot it? And why? Was he just fooling around, using it for target practice? It was possible, but Ginny tended to doubt it. She remembered that Pete had tried to interest Danny in hunting as soon as he was old enough to hold a rifle, but according to Sonya, it had been a disaster. Danny was afraid of guns, a fact that Pete had found deeply unmanly. So what was he doing with one hidden behind his bookcase—and a handgun, no less?

She checked for a serial number. It was there, not filed off; at least that was something. Maybe she could call in a favor and have it traced.

"What are you doing with that thing?"

Sonya was standing in the doorway, toting a plastic bag from the Price Chopper. Ginny hadn't heard her come in.

"I thought you said you left your police gun in New York City," she said. Ginny hadn't told her about her suspension; she figured Sonya had enough on her mind. "I'd just as soon not have it in the house, if you don't mind."

"It's not mine," she said after a half second's debate about whether to spare her friend the truth. "I think it's Danny's."

Sonya put the groceries down with a thud. "That's ridiculous."

"I found it taped behind his bookcase. I can show you if you want."

Sonya shook her head, very slowly. From the expression on her face Ginny could tell that her brain was in overdrive.

"Are you sure it's real? It's not a toy? Maybe left over from one of his high school plays?"

"I didn't test-fire it," Ginny said, "but I'm pretty sure it's functional."

"You mean *loaded*?"

Ginny nodded, feeling like a sadist. Just about every word out of her mouth was making her friend feel even worse. She took a deep breath. "Yes, it's loaded. Come to think of it, though, I didn't find any extra rounds. Just the six in the chamber."

A flicker of hope crossed Sonya's face. "What does that mean? You think maybe it didn't belong to him? Maybe he was holding it for someone?"

"I don't know," Ginny said. "I guess that's possible."

Sonya shook her head again, then looked Ginny in the eye. "You think this has something to do with what happened to him, don't you? I mean, it must. Don't you think?"

"Do you want to sit down? You don't look so—"

"Just answer me. Please."

"I don't know," Ginny said. "It's possible. Maybe Danny was involved in something you didn't know about."

"I'd say he obviously was."

Sonya did sit down then, perching on the corner of the bed; it was a good thing, Ginny thought, because she looked like she might keel over.

Ginny moved the gun from the bedspread to the bureau, then took off the thick rubber gloves. Her hands were sweaty and pruned; she was going to have to invest in a box of latex gloves from the CVS.

"I want to ask you what else you found," Sonya said. "But now I'm afraid."

Ginny put a hand on Sonya's knee, but the gesture felt woefully inadequate; as though patting her leg through its practical brown stretch pants was going to impart a whole world of comfort.

"There was nothing," Ginny said. "Nothing you wouldn't find in any nineteen-year-old guy's room."

"Booze, butts, rubbers, and porn," Sonya said, cracking a smile.

"And not even much porn," Ginny offered.

"Well," Sonya said, "he *was* an altar boy."

She started crying then, sobbing and laughing at the same time. Ginny reached out and hugged her, and they clung to each other on the corner of Danny's bed, where Ginny had so recently been clinging to somebody else.

Monique St. Cyr lived in a trailer park on the road to Williamstown—not the kind of place that brings to mind white-trash images of giant satellite dishes and abandoned cars, but a cozy development guarded by two huge stone lions. It had a reflecting pool out front, its aging fountain spitting water in unpredictable streams, and just inside the entrance was a community building decorated with tiny white lights that hung down from the rain gutters like icicles.

Ginny maneuvered her Chrysler past the neatly tended lawns, their flower beds faded and scraggly in the autumn chill. There were occasional bursts of color, but they didn't come from nature: plastic pinwheels in the shape of bright yellow sunflowers, concrete garden gnomes wearing cheery red hats.

Some older people were outside, retirees whiling away the day with yard work and card games, and they eyed Ginny's muffler-challenged car with suspicion. Even by the standards of this working-class town, her twelve-year-old Chrysler was a wreck. With her luck, it was leaving a trail of antifreeze wherever she went, like bread crumbs in a fairy tale.

She chuckled as she got the fisheye from a supersized old lady in a polyester housedress—pondering the fact that in New York, where status was everything, people weren't generally judged by what they drove. Even professionals kept a "city car," a four-wheeled ruin you could park on the street and not care if it got broken into—or, in the case of one of her neighbors, set aflame by a bored crackhead.

She drove to the end of the lane, then took a right, following the directions Monique had given her. Ginny had called the girl an hour before, once she'd assured herself that Sonya was okay. She'd left her friend browning ground beef over the kitchen stove, making goulash for Pete's dinner; it was a dish Danny couldn't stand, and these days those were the only things Sonya could bring herself to cook.

Ginny walked up the front steps of the blue double-wide trailer, but before she could ring the bell, the front door opened. Monique had been waiting for her. She got a quick glimpse of a living room filled with cheerleading trophies before Monique ushered her outside.

"My *mémé* fell asleep in her chair," she said, using Québécois slang for "grandma." "It's better if we don't wake her up."

"You want to take a walk?" Ginny asked.

The girl shook her head. "I gotta stay close, in case she . . ." She cast a glance toward the rounded bay window protruding from the trailer like a blister. Ginny couldn't tell if she was worried for the old lady or just plain terrified of her.

Monique led her to a pair of white plastic chairs, carefully removing the fallen leaves from her own before sitting down. She was a tiny little thing, five-one at the most, maybe not topping a hundred pounds; the plastic chair seemed to swallow her. She was wearing a pale pink turtleneck sweater and tight white jeans. Her blonde hair was feathered back from her face in a style that had apparently never gone out of fashion in her hometown; her eyes were accented with arcs of blue-frosted shadow, her lips with a glistening swath of gloss.

"Like I said on the phone," Ginny said, "I need to talk to you about Danny."

Monique's eyes instantly filled with tears. She dabbed at them with a Kleenex, which she produced so fast Ginny suspected she'd had it at the ready.

"Danny was the love of my life," Monique said, sobbing carefully into the tissue. "I don't know if I can live without him."

Justly or not, Ginny was suddenly overcome by a desire to smack her: she could tell that no matter what happened to anyone in this girl's life, it was all about her.

"I'm sorry," Ginny said. "I know this is hard for you. I'd really appreciate anything you could tell me."

Curiosity trumped drama, if only briefly. Monique stopped crying and looked up at her. "About what?"

"I'm trying to find out what was going on with Danny before he died."

"But . . . why?"

"Because his parents need to know what happened to him."

Monique screwed up her dainty nose. "But everybody knows," she said. "That awful man killed him for his money."

"He's innocent until proven guilty."

"So what are you," Monique asked, "some kind of private investigator?"

"Something like that."

"Oh."

"So will you help me? So Danny can rest in peace?"

The melodrama appealed to the girl, as Ginny had guessed it would. "Sure," she said, straightening up in her chair. "Of course."

"Thank you. Now, how long did you and Danny know each other?"

She ran a hand through her hair. "Like, forever. We both went to East." She named the elementary school Sonya and Ginny had also attended. "Then sophomore year of high school Danny asked me to Winter Carnival, and I got elected queen, even though nobody from my grade ever did before. We were together ever since. We were gonna get married and everything."

The tears started again, and Monique dabbed at her eyes. Ginny noticed that the tissue had not a trace of eye shadow on it; Monique was being careful not to ruin her makeup.

"You mean you were engaged?"

"Not, like, officially. More like engaged to be engaged. I'm getting my associate's degree at State and Danny was gonna go to college once he got enough money together. It was tough, though, 'cause his folks wouldn't help him at all."

"What are you talking about?" Ginny said, instinctively springing to Sonya's defense. "Of course they'd help him pay for college."

"Nope. His dad said he wouldn't pay good money for Danny to study some pansy-ass crap. And that's a quote."

"You mean, he wanted Danny to stay and work for him?"

Monique shrugged. "I don't know how much he cared about that. The thing was, Danny wanted to major in fine arts or drama—he loved that stuff."

"But his father wouldn't go for it?"

"He thought it was a waste of money. If Danny went to college, he wanted him to study engineering or science. They had a big blowup about it fall of senior year, when Danny was looking at schools. His mom was on his side, but his dad wouldn't budge. Danny hardly talked to him since—outside of work, I mean."

Ginny felt a surge of guilt. Sonya hadn't said a word about it—probably because Ginny had been so out of touch, so obsessed with her life in the city, they'd rarely had more than the odd ten-minute phone chat over the past couple of years.

"So Danny was saving up to pay for college?"

"Yeah," Monique said. "He was holding down three jobs—doing construction and waiting tables at the Skillet and working down at Café des Artistes."

Ginny knew the Skillet was a popular local diner; she'd never heard of the other place. "Café des Artistes?"

"The new coffee shop near the museum."

"What museum?"

"That thing they put in the old electric plant." Monique's tiny nose screwed up again. "My art appreciation class made us go. But the stuff's all pretty ugly."

"What was Danny's schedule like?"

She thought about it, her eyebrows scrunched up in concentration. "He'd work with his dad from six to three. Then he'd catch a nap and work at the café from five to midnight. He was at the Skillet on the weekends. He was so busy we hardly ever got to see each other. But we didn't know we didn't have much time left . . ."

Her eyes filled up yet again. Ginny dug in her pocket and offered the girl another Kleenex, asking herself why she'd taken such a knee-jerk dislike to her. Did she have a valid reason, or was it just that she'd instantly decided Monique wasn't good enough for Danny?

"Thank you," Ginny said. "This is all really helpful."

"I'd do anything to help Danny. I wish I'd died instead of him."

Ginny didn't disagree with her.

"Let me ask you something else, okay? And I want you to think really hard." Monique offered a solemn nod. "Did you ever get the feeling that Danny was frightened?"

Those pencil-thin eyebrows came together in obvious confusion. "Of what?"

"I don't know. Of someone or something."

Monique shook her head. "No way. Danny was the bravest person in the whole world."

"As far as you know, was Danny ever involved in something he shouldn't have? Something illegal?"

"Danny would *never.*"

"Was he into drugs? You can tell me, Monique. It won't hurt him, and it might help me figure out what happened."

"No. He was *not* into drugs. He hardly ever even smoked weed."

Monique appealed to her with those huge frosted blue eyes. If she was hiding something, she was good at it. "Okay," Ginny said. "One other thing. Did you ever see him with a gun?"

"You mean, like, for hunting?"

"I meant a handgun."

"Are you *crazy?*" Monique shot up out of her seat so fast the flimsy plastic chair fell over backward. "What are you trying to do? Make Danny out to be some kind of criminal?"

"No. Of course not. I'm just trying to find out what happened to him."

"Everybody knows what happened to him. That crazy person killed him for his money, and he'll go to jail and get the death penalty."

The tears were streaming down Monique's cheeks, which had turned the same shade of cherry as the frozen slushie drinks Ginny and Sonya used to get at the corner store on their way home from school.

Ginny had no idea why that particular analogy sprang to mind; just being in her hometown was conflating past and present, jumbling the timeline so it took effort to recall if something had happened that morning or twenty years ago.

And sleeping with Jimmy Griffin hadn't helped.

"Calm down," Ginny said. "I'm not trying to bad-mouth Danny, I swear. His mother and I have been best friends practically since the day we were born."

Monique sniffled, eyed her warily, then righted the chair and sat back down.

"Well," she said, "why didn't you say so?"

10

Ginny got back into her car, meaning to start the engine but letting her head fall back against the worn burgundy upholstery. She closed her eyes, just for a minute, trying to stave off the headache that was encroaching upward from her knotted shoulders.

God damn Pete Markowicz. Making his only son work three jobs to pay for college because he didn't like what the kid wanted to study? It was utterly Neanderthal, exactly the kind of narrow-minded garbage she'd left this town to get away from.

Sonya had never said a word about it. When Ginny had asked her about Danny's college plans, she'd always brushed her questions off with vague answers about how he was still figuring out what he wanted to do. If Ginny had been halfway aware of anyone but herself, she would have realized that her best friend had troubles of her own.

And Ginny knew Sonya well enough to predict what must be going through her mind now. If she'd pushed harder, had dared to contradict Pete and send Danny off to school, he wouldn't have been hanging around his hometown. And he'd still be alive.

She opened her eyes and started the engine. On the passenger-side floor was a bag from Molly's, some of the treats Jimmy had brought over—was it really just yesterday? She'd meant to offer them to Monique as an icebreaker, but she'd left them in the car.

Oh, well. She opened the bag and drew out a jack-o'-lantern cookie, thick orange frosting beneath a gap-toothed grin of chocolate piping. One bite sent crumbs cascading all over the seat; it was slightly stale but still tasty. She examined the rest of the contents: lemon square, whoopie pie, walnut-covered brownie, chocolate-frosted doughnut.

The latter gave Ginny a rush of guilt, and a mission. She put the Chrysler in gear and was about to pull out of her parking spot when her cell phone rang. She checked the caller ID, stifled an urge to let it go to voice mail, and answered. Her partner deserved better.

Although they didn't have much in common on paper, Samantha Salgado wasn't just Ginny's partner; she was her closest friend on the force. And Ginny had to admit it: she didn't have that many.

After all her romantic notions about brotherhood and the thin blue line, it had been quite the letdown for Ginny to discover that she didn't buddy up to her fellow cops that easily. She wasn't sure why, though she'd spent the early part of her career trying to figure it out.

It couldn't just be that she came from a small town and

most of them were New York natives; or that her penchant for reading novels (nothing too highbrow, just the kind of thing Oprah recommended to her book club) got her razzed as a big brain. No, it probably had more to do with temperament. Or maybe—and this was something Ginny preferred not to think about—she'd be a fish out of water no matter where she swam.

"Hey, Sam."

"Ginny? Where the hell are you? I've been trying your apartment for—"

"I had to come home to the Berkshires for a while. My best friend had a death in the family."

"Sorry," Sam said. "So when the fuck are you coming back?"

In terms of upbringing, Ginny and Sam couldn't have been more different: Sam grew up in a huge, adoring Dominican family in Upper Manhattan. Her father had been on the force, as were two of her brothers; another, the black sheep of the family, was in the fire department. The woman was tough as hell, with rock-hard abs and a mouth that would shame a merchant seaman. But she could dance till four a.m., and she loved to play matchmaker: she'd tried to interest Ginny in each one of her single brothers, in descending order of age.

"I don't know when I'll be back," Ginny said. "I've got a lot of stuff to take care of."

"Well, get your ass down here and deal with this shit," Sam said. "If I gotta partner with Jackson one more day, I'm gonna cut his balls off."

"Might make him a better cop."

"Seriously, *chica,* things ain't good. IAB took my statement yesterday."

Ginny felt a cold fist whack her in the midsection. "I'm sorry you got dragged into—"

"Fuck it. I didn't give those rat bastards a damn thing. What's your delegate say?"

"I haven't talked to him since I've been up here. I'm sure he'll call if he needs me."

Sam was quiet for a minute, something so unlike her it gave Ginny the creeps. "I got a bad feeling," Sam said finally, "you're just gonna roll over and let 'em fuck you."

"No, I'm not."

"Mike Scott is spilling his guts to anybody with a gold shield. You gotta get your story out there."

"It's a little late for that."

"The hell it is."

"Listen, Sam, I really gotta go. I'm sorry. I'll call you later."

"You goddamn well better," Sam said, and hung up.

The conversation ran on a loop in her head as she drove back downtown. There was a car outside the police station, which made it a busy day. Ginny pulled into one of the angled slots, grabbed the bakery bag, and went in. There was no one at the front counter; she hollered, and eventually, a uniformed officer came to the front, smoothing his tousled hair.

"You again," he said. "Back to see Jumping Jack, huh?"

It was the same man who'd let her in the first time, the childhood acquaintance who'd so admired her polka-dotted miniskirt; this time he didn't even hit her up for a doughnut.

"Yeah," she said. "Thought I'd see how he's doing. You holding down the fort by yourself?"

He shrugged. There was lipstick on his neck, along with a sizable hickey. Whoever owned the car parked next to Ginny's was obviously here on serious police business.

"You wanna bring him his dinner?" the cop asked. "I, um, didn't get to it yet."

"Been busy, huh?" Ginny asked, deadpan.

He rubbed his neck. "Um, yeah. Lotta paperwork." He held

the door for her, proffering a set of keys and a paper bag. "Cheese sandwich from the Skillet," he said. "Get this. Now Jack's a *vegetarian*."

"You don't say."

He rolled his eyes. "Weirdo."

With that, he went back to his high-level law enforcement meeting. Ginny noticed that as he walked away, his uniform pants didn't quite hide the fact that he took an *intense* interest in his work.

She laughed under her breath, shifting the two food bags to her left hand while she unlocked the cellblock door with her right. Jack was still the only prisoner: the first two cells were empty.

"Hey, Jack," she called. "It's Ginny Lavoie. I brought you dinner. Sorry I didn't get you some clothes yet. But I got a bunch of stuff from Molly's, okay?"

He didn't answer. Two steps later, when she was standing in front of his cell, she found out why.

It wasn't an easy suicide. Jumping Jack O'Brien must have worked hard at killing himself: it had taken both determination and ingenuity.

Even the hometown cops had known enough to take the laces out of Jack's army boots; he needed to find something else to hang himself from. So he'd taken off his jumpsuit and turned the bed frame upright just so, to make sure it wouldn't fall over under his weight.

He'd twisted the clothing into a noose and tied it to the

top of the frame: that was the ingenious part. The determination had come when he slipped his head into the ring of drab gray cloth, leaned forward, and let his own body weight strangle him.

There must have been at least a few seconds, Ginny thought, maybe even a minute, when he was still conscious, struggling for breath. All he would have had to do was stand up and release the pressure on his neck, and he'd be able to breathe. It took a serious act of will to make yourself die like that.

"What the *hell*?"

It was the uniformed cop—eyes wide, hand clutching a bottle of Yoo-hoo. It crashed to the floor in an explosion of glass and chocolate milk.

"I—uh, I forgot to give you his drink . . ."

"He's dead," Ginny said.

He kept gaping at her, not making a move toward the body. "We gotta—somebody better call an ambulance."

"I checked his pulse already," she said. "He's dead."

"I gotta call an ambulance," he said, still not moving.

"Good idea," Ginny said, looking around the cell. There was almost nothing in it, just an out-of-date copy of *Rolling Stone* and a well-worn Boy Scout manual. Jumping Jack had been an Eagle Scout.

She thumbed through the pages of the manual, automatically checking to see if something was hidden between them. There was nothing. But the inside back cover was obscured by line after line of handwriting, surprisingly neat schoolboy script.

Last will & testament of Cpl. Jack V. O'Brien.
To Donny at the Pizza House, I leave my 3 National Geographics.
To the library, I leave my Bronze Star for meritorious service.
To—

"What are you doing?" the cop asked, finally snapping out of his fugue. The look on his face was one of terror—as though he could see the line, and his ass was on it. "You have to get out of here. You're not supposed to be here."

"Just let me—"

"You have to get out," he said again. His face was turning red, Ginny saw, but it still wasn't nearly as dark as Jack's. What it resembled most closely, she thought, was the shade of lipstick on his own hickey-covered neck.

Ginny couldn't make herself go back to Sonya's. She knew it was lousy of her to leave her friend alone, but she needed some time to herself. It'd been a hell of a day, and it was only six-thirty.

And she really needed a drink.

She drove around for a while, eventually making her way to Union Street. Up the block was the empty mill where Danny had died, but Ginny didn't go that far. She parked in front of a bar, a ramshackle place she'd passed by for years but never actually entered. It was dimly lit, with a sticky floor and an aura of not having been aired out since the Eisenhower administration. It was exactly what she was in the mood for.

The bar was half-full, but she was the only woman in it. It didn't bother her. In her line of work she was used to being one of the boys. Out of habit she sized up the crowd—mostly guys in dirty work clothes having a quick one on the way home, plus a few hard-core boozehounds stapled to their stools.

She took a seat at the corner of the bar. Every eye in the place was on her, but she didn't give a damn.

"What can I get you?" the bartender asked, making a token effort to wipe off the counter with a dirty rag.

"Beer and a bump," she said.

He nodded with something like approval, popped the top off a bottle of Michelob, poured her a shot of Jack Daniel's. She tossed it back, felt the delicious heat work its way down her insides, then took a long swig of beer. If her mother knew where her little girl was right now, and what she was doing there, she'd have died of shame. If she weren't already dead, that is.

Ginny bought a couple of packages of Beer-Nuts; they were more appetizing than the pickled eggs and pigs' feet at the far end of the bar, floating in their respective jars like some science experiment gone awry. She finished her beer, then ordered another round; she was close enough to Sonya's to walk home if she got too loaded.

She did the second shot, only slightly less satisfying than the first. Ginny carried her beer to a booth and stretched out with her feet up on the opposite seat; the cracked leather was nearly as sticky as the floor, but she was past caring.

The tension flowing out of her body as the booze flowed in, Ginny's mind wandered back to the reason she'd come home in the first place. Danny.

What did she know about him? He was nineteen years old, beloved by all—except, presumably, the person who had beaten him beyond recognition. He was handsome and athletic, liked to act and sing and write sappy poetry. He had a beautiful girlfriend who, though hardly the sharpest knife in the drawer, had been sloppy in love with him. He took meticulous care of his forest-green pickup truck, which had been found parked at a local lake the night before his body was discovered.

He wanted to go to college, and he was willing to work his ass off to get there. He smoked the occasional cigarette, drank the occasional drink, toked the occasional joint, employed the occasional rubber; nothing scandalous there. So what was he doing with a .38-caliber handgun? And why would someone want him dead?

"Well, I'll be damned," said a voice above her head. "What do we have here but a real live Angie Dickinson?"

Ginny looked up; the last person on earth she wanted to see was standing over her. Chief Rolly had a massive gut hanging over his belt buckle, and a surly expression on his face. She'd thought he'd been talking to somebody else, but as it turned out, he was alone.

Ginny took a deep breath. She was still sober enough to get pissed off, and fast. "Excuse me?" she said.

"You know," he said. "Like that TV show. *Police Woman*."

"That's a little before my time," she said.

"Mind if I sit down?" he asked, and proceeded to do so. The old seat groaned under his weight. "You want another drink?" He turned to the bartender and shouted his order. "Get Angie here another round, huh, Frank? Catching bad guys is thirsty work."

Ginny was about to wave the bartender off, then decided what the hell; she might as well let the fat bastard buy her a drink.

She'd known Rolly her entire life: he'd been police chief since she was in grammar school, a position he reportedly got because nobody else wanted it. Rumor had it that he'd gone into law enforcement after a failed career as a junior high teacher in Pittsfield, where he'd been so fantastically lazy he'd taught entire classes without ever getting out of his chair. The kids had eaten him alive.

As chief of police, Rolly had done a passable job; it was hard to screw up in a place where there was almost no crime beyond the odd break-in or bar fight. But it was also an open secret that anyone who drove through town while committing the crime of being Hispanic or Asian (or, God forbid, black) would find themselves pulled over, grilled, and ticketed for something or other. At least that's the way it was when Ginny was young; maybe Rolly had mellowed with age.

"A big-city cop like you must be pretty bored around here, huh?" Rolly said, draining half his beer and helping himself to her nuts.

She tossed back the shot, looked at Rolly with the critical eye she usually reserved for perps in the interrogation room. He was wearing a windbreaker over a tan sports shirt—at least he wasn't drinking in uniform—and his hair had fallen out to the point where it was only able to cover his scalp through the most meticulous comb-over Ginny had ever seen. And during eleven years in the NYPD, she'd seen quite a few.

"But in the city," she said, "you can't get a shot and a beer for three bucks."

Rolly smacked a hand on the table. "I bet you damn well can't," he said, chuckling so his gut undulated like an unkindly Santa. "Probably cost you an arm and a leg down there. Huh?"

"Most things do," Ginny said. Rolly's odd jocularity was throwing her; had he somehow not been informed about Jack? And did he have no idea she'd found the body?

"How are things down at the station?" she asked.

Rolly didn't just take the bait; he opened wide and gobbled it. "Not too shabby," he said. "Matter of fact, today the taxpayers saved a bundle of money."

She gritted her teeth. "Oh, yeah?"

"Jack O'Brien did himself in. Crazy son-bitch hanged himself in his cell."

"So you're on your way over there?"

He shrugged, his gut lifting the tabletop. "What's the hurry? Guy's not gonna get any less dead."

She yearned to crack her beer bottle over his head. "Listen, Rolly, since we're talking cop-to-cop . . . what makes you so sure Jack killed Danny? From what I've heard, there was no evidence he did anything worse than steal Danny's wallet."

"Guy was his own judge, jury, and executioner."

"Did it ever occur to you," she asked, "that maybe after living on the streets for thirty years he just couldn't stand to be locked up?"

He looked at her, squinting like he was trying to make out the letters of a faraway eye chart. Then he drained his beer, tossed back the rest of her nuts, and stood up.

"Well, I guess I better shuffle off. Got a little mess to clean up."

He winked at her—actually winked—and ambled his way out of the bar, slapping backs all the way to the door. Ginny returned to her drink, wondering whether a fourth round was going to be required to get Jack O'Brien's purple face out of her head.

"Well, I'll be *damned.*"

She looked up again; this time the man standing over her was about five years her senior, wearing a bushy black mustache and a polo shirt from the cable company. He stuck out a hand and she shook it, contemplating the fact that if she was ever going to get to drink in peace, it was going to have to be on the opposite side of the county line.

"You better buy me a beer," her new companion said, "or I'll tell my ma you were sitting down someplace that isn't her living room."

She smiled at him. She'd never been close to her cousin George, but he was always a decent guy. "Aunt Lisette's been trying to get me to come over."

"No shit." He shook his head. "None of us are gonna get a

minute's peace until you come eat her pot roast. So just do it, okay?"

She gestured toward the empty seat; she didn't feel like company, but George didn't deserve the cold shoulder. "You want to sit down? If you promise not to rat me out to your mom, I'll cover your tab for the rest of the night."

He smiled back, revealing a set of crooked teeth; Uncle Roger wouldn't spring for braces. "Okay," he said, "but just a quick one. If I'm late for dinner again, my wife'll have a fit."

He sat down, the booth seeming much less traumatized by his body weight than that of its previous occupant. They spent half an hour catching up—George rhapsodizing about his son's Little League record and the his-and-hers snowmobiles he'd ordered for his fifteenth wedding anniversary, Ginny offering up a few NYPD war stories. It was an odd sensation, sitting there talking to him: George was her first cousin, just about the closest living relative she had beyond her dad, and he was practically a stranger.

"Well, I better take off," George said, draining his second beer. "It's been real good—"

He was interrupted by a commotion from the other end of the bar—angry voices, the whack of a fallen stool, the crash of breaking glass. Ginny stood up to see what was going on. The place had cleared out considerably since Rolly left, and there were only a handful of guys left at the bar.

"You lying little creep," the bartender was yelling, "I *saw* you take the twenty off the bar. I told you last week to stay the hell out of my place. If your mama and me didn't go back—"

"Fuck you," said a voice from the floor. "I didn't take *shit*."

Ginny took a few steps closer and saw a whip-thin man in the process of picking himself up off the ground. There were sweat stains under the armpits of his dirty white T-shirt, and his

Levi's hung on him like the waist was six inches too big. The look in his eyes—half-manic, half-vacant—told her he was on something.

"Get out of here, Bobby," the bartender said. "Before I call the cops."

"Fuck you."

"I said get *lost*."

The man glared up at him. "You're out to get me. You set me up. You—"

He grabbed a piece of broken glass off the floor and leaped to his feet. He waved it in the bartender's face, slicing an angry red line down the man's cheek, then turned and slashed the jagged glass toward the spectators. Everyone hesitated for a second—everyone, that is, except the elderly drunk at the far end of the bar, who seemed not to notice that anything was going on.

Ginny reached for her gun; realized it wasn't there; cursed herself.

Then, when the junkie's attention was momentarily focused on the bleeding bartender, she took two quick steps forward and knocked his feet out from under him with one smooth kick. He landed on his back, still clutching the shard of glass. She stepped on his wrist until he let it go, and when he tried to get up, she clocked him in the jaw. Then she rolled him onto his stomach and held his hands behind him, keeping him still with a knee to the back.

It had taken all of three seconds. The men stared at Ginny in silence. Then her cousin George let out a low whistle.

"If my mom asks," he said, "I'll tell her you left town."

For the first time in ten years, Ginny stood inside her childhood home—not the bedroom with its Duran Duran posters and purple carpet, but the work space in the basement. Its decoration was less whimsical: steel tables, plastic tubing, vats of chemicals. The smell of embalming fluid, acrid but strangely sweet, brought her back to a more innocent age.

How many people, she wondered, could say *that*?

Laid out on a table, without so much as a towel to cover his nakedness, was the late Jack O'Brien. At her side was Bernie Collier, the mortician whom Ginny's father had trained right out of high school.

"Thanks for this," Ginny told him. "I don't want to get you in trouble."

"Screw the bastards," he said.

The bastards in question were his employers, the national corporation that had bought Lavoie's, kept the name to make people think it was business as usual, and promptly fired all the staff. But when it came out that the company was maximizing profits by sending bodies out of town for embalming—trucking them to Springfield and back in the middle of the night, like slabs of beef to the packing plant—the community had gone crazy, and the company had been forced to rehire everyone. Bernie, with two kids in college, had no choice but to accept their offer, pay cut included.

But when Ginny came knocking on the back door, asking if Jumping Jack's body was inside, he let her right in; he didn't give a damn that his boss would pop a vessel if he found out. Screw the bastards.

"You looking for anything in particular?"

She glanced at Bernie, his thick black mustache now speckled with gray. He'd always complained that it trapped the chemical smell, she remembered, but he was too vain to shave it off.

"Honestly, I don't know," Ginny said. "I just can't believe they're not going to do an autopsy."

"Autopsies cost money. Besides, what's the mystery? Coroner already signed the death certificate."

"I remember the coroner," Ginny said. "His other gig is in animal control."

"And he does a damn fine job at both."

Ginny stared at the body, painfully thin without its layers of surplus fatigues and secondhand jackets. Jack had tattoos up and down both arms—most of them military symbols, but one a red heart containing the name Barbara.

"What do *you* think?" she asked.

"Well, I've seen my share of suicides by hanging." He traced the angry line of a ligature mark around Jack's neck, just under the chin. "And they all looked just like this."

There was a wheeled stool next to the table; she kicked it across the room, and it slammed against the wall. "God *damn* it."

"Excuse me, but why are you so worked up about him?"

"Because I told him I'd get him out," she said. "And I should've known this would happen. The guy was a mental case. Any moron could tell he wouldn't last long cooped up in a cell."

"Maybe he wouldn't have lasted long, anyway."

Bernie lifted Jack's left arm to expose the inside of his wrist. It was crisscrossed with scars—some faded, some a year or so old. "From the looks of it, he tried to off himself before. More than once."

"Jesus," Ginny said. "Poor bastard."

"I thought he killed Danny Markowicz. Wasn't his mom your best friend in school?"

"Jack didn't do it. You knew him, Bernie. The guy was loony tunes, but he wouldn't hurt a flea. He was just the easiest mope to pin it on. Case closed."

"Well, I'm no doctor, but I don't see nothing on Jack here tells me he didn't do himself in. No bruises, no nothing."

"Which proves my point," Ginny said, stepping closer to the body. "Look at his hands. If he'd beaten Danny to death a week ago, his knuckles'd still be scraped up. Or even if he used a bat or a pipe or something, he'd have to have some marks on him, wouldn't he? I mean, Danny wasn't a huge guy, but he was strong. He would've gone down swinging."

Bernie opened his mouth to say something, then seemed to reconsider. She watched him stroke his mustache and change his mind again.

"I don't think Danny fought back too much," he said. "There was just the one scrape on his right knuckle."

It took Ginny a second to get his meaning. "Oh my God. You embalmed him."

A grim nod. "I did."

"I didn't even know this place did the funeral. I was so worried about Sonya, and the only service was at the church—"

"Couldn't have a viewing," Bernie said. "Not the state he was in."

"I had Sonya request the autopsy report from the county, but it hasn't come through. Can you tell me . . . what he looked like?"

Bernie shook his head, ruefully rather than in refusal. "Trust me, Gin. You don't want to know."

"You're right," she said. "Tell me, anyhow."

He gave his mustache another thoughtful stroke. "In all my years I've never seen anybody beat up so bad. There was hardly a mark on him below the neck, but above it—*Jesus*. It was like whoever did it wanted to erase his face."

Ginny's jaw tightened. "The official cause of death was massive head trauma."

"Yeah, well, that don't do it justice."

"Perp must've gotten bloody," Ginny said, more to herself than to him. "And there were no other marks on his body?"

"Some old bruises, like you'd see on an active guy. Nothing too bad. The only fresh wound below the neck was on his forearm, like you'd get if you were trying to protect yourself." He raised his own right arm and rubbed at a spot below the elbow. "Bone was broke. Must've hurt like a son of a bitch."

"Yeah," Ginny said, "but not for long."

Ginny walked out of the funeral home into the golden light of a brilliant fall morning. The nights had been chilly enough to make the leaves start to turn, gleaming orange and yellow and red against the still-green grass. It was a picture-perfect New England day, autumn in all its glory. It was the kind of weather that always made Ginny a little sad: everything was so beautiful, and pretty soon it would all be dead.

She shook her head, laughing under her breath. *Don't be such a sourpuss.* That's what her mother used to say to her when she'd get into the sort of mood where she could transform even the nicest thing into a trial. *There she goes,* her mother would say in a voice at once affectionate and exasperated, *Little Miss Cranky Pants.*

Ginny walked toward Main Street, where she'd parked her car for fear of getting caught in funeral traffic. Her route took her within a few paces of Jack's Hot Dogs, another culinary blast from the past. The smell was as intoxicating as ever, but Bernie's description of Danny's wounds had killed her appetite.

It was like whoever did it wanted to erase his face. Bernie had described an attack driven by so much rage the killer seemed to want to erase Danny's very existence. A crime of passion.

But there were no defensive wounds to speak of. That told Ginny that Danny had trusted his attacker, or at least known him. Danny's truck had been parked at the Fish Pond, unlocked as usual but seemingly undisturbed.

So did he and his killer travel to the mill together? And what was Danny doing there? Although establishing time of death wasn't an exact science, the medical examiner thought Danny had died on Monday, the same day he'd disappeared. His body had lain there until Thursday morning, when it was discovered by a pair of New York artists in the market for a bargain-basement loft.

"Ginny," a voice called. "Goddamn Ginny Lavoie. I don't believe it."

She turned to see a woman in her fifties, accompanied by a girl of about twelve and a boy a few years younger. The woman was painfully thin, all elbows and pointy parts—so scrawny she made Jumping Jack look like a candidate for Jenny Craig. Ginny stopped and looked at her without a flicker of recognition.

"Doncha remember me? Belco. From Girl Scouts and shit. Ginny Lavoie. I don't freakin' believe it. I ain't seen you in a hundred million years."

Ginny squinted at her, the name and the memories not jibing with the person standing in front of her. Belinda Cooper—Belco was her nickname on the high school track team—had been a year behind Ginny. Which meant that she looked two decades older than she actually was.

The years had not been kind. Belco's eyes were sunken in their sockets, underlined by brownish-black semicircles of exhaustion. Her spiky blonde hair showed an inch of gray at the roots, and her stained clothes hung on her like a scarecrow's. Her whole manner was twitchy and disjointed; Ginny didn't have to be in Narcotics to know she was on something. Just like the guy in the bar.

"Hey, kids," the woman said to the children, who'd wandered down the block to look in a store window. "Come on over and meet Mommy's old buddy." They acted like they hadn't heard her, which instantly made her pale face flush with anger and embarrassment. Belco had a hair trigger if Ginny'd ever seen one. *"I said get your asses over here,"* she shrieked at them.

The boy cringed, but the girl didn't so much as flinch—just took her brother's hand and walked him back to where the two women were standing. From the resigned expression on the kids' faces, Ginny got the feeling that their mother couldn't do anything worse to them than she already had.

This is Ginny," Belco said. "She was a real big track star back in the day. We had some good times, hey, Gin?"

"Right," Ginny said. "Listen, I'm kind of in a hurry, so—"

"Can you buy me a hot dog?" It was the little boy, looking up at Ginny with pleading eyes and a dirty face. He sounded younger than he looked. "Ma don't got no money."

"Joey." The girl elbowed her brother in the side.

"Shut your stupid mouth." Belco grabbed the little boy by his shoulder and yanked, fingers digging into his flesh. He yelped in pain. Ginny seized the woman's wrist and pulled her hand off him. The action was instinctive: Special Victims detectives also investigate crimes against children, and Ginny was constitutionally unable to watch a kid get hurt.

"Not a good idea," Ginny said.

Belco opened her mouth to sass her, but something in Ginny's eyes must've given her pause. She yanked her arm away but didn't make another move toward the boy—just ran her fingers through her greasy hair in a pathetic effort to act casual.

"Anyways," Belco said to her grimy flip-flops, "we gotta get goin'."

"Wait," Ginny said, pulling a five-dollar bill from her pocket. She expected the ghostly remains of Belinda Cooper to tell her she didn't need her charity, but the woman snatched it out of her hand like a bullfrog after a fly. *Great,* Ginny thought; *it's going to go up her nose or in her arm.*

"I'm going to stand right here," Ginny said, "and I'm going to watch while you walk down to Jack's and get these kids something to eat. Sign said two dogs and a Coke for a dollar ninety-nine."

Ginny could see the woman struggle to do the math: with tax, she'd have maybe seventy-five cents left over to put toward her next fix. She nodded, then grabbed the little boy by the wrist and headed toward the hot dog place. The little girl followed, pausing only to look over her shoulder at Ginny, through empty eyes.

Ginny got into her car, now in an even worse mood than when she'd left the funeral home. Belinda Cooper hadn't been a shining star in school, but Ginny had hardly predicted she'd end up like *that.* She tried to summon up memories of her, but there wasn't much. Girl Scout troop meetings, track practice, diving off the raft at the Fish Pond. On summer nights a bunch of kids would pile into the back of somebody's pickup and hide under a blanket to get around the six-per-car limit at the drive-in; she thought Belco had been there once or twice. That was about all.

She started the car, shaking off the memories. They were a tide that had been threatening to drown her ever since she drove back into town, and the pull was strong. The fact that she hadn't thought about those days in years—had sealed them off when she went to UMass and found any excuse to avoid coming home for vacations—only made them seem that much more vivid, less like memories than flashbacks.

She'd forgotten about so many things, or at least pushed them aside. Not the least of them, she realized as she sat in the idling car, was the fact that the summer before college was the last time she'd actually been happy.

Get out of your own head. Concentrate on the case. Nail the bastard who killed Danny, give Sonya some peace, and get back to the city so you can try to salvage what's left of your life.

It was a mantra Ginny had been repeating for days. It still didn't seem to be working.

She pulled out of the parking space, drove to the end of Main Street and around the corner. She passed Café des Artistes but decided not to stop; it would be better to go later, when she'd have a better chance of talking to Danny's regular customers.

She was debating whether her mood might be improved by an Angelina's double-meat sub when her cell phone rang. The caller ID said PRIVATE.

"Hello?"

"Virginia? Art here."

It was Art MacAfee, an investigator for the Massachusetts State Police. Ginny had met him at a conference in Atlantic City when she gave a talk on techniques for interviewing adolescent rape victims. Art had been newly separated from his wife, Ginny was single; nature had taken its course, but only the one time.

"Hey," Ginny said, pulling over to the side of the road. "You manage to trace that serial number for me?"

"Yeah," he said, his voice sounding strained, remote; Ginny had a feeling it was more about his mood than the poor connection.

"Is there a problem?"

"I don't appreciate getting screwed over."

"What are you talking about?"

"You mighta told me you were in hot water with the department before you had me running down gun owners for you."

Ginny felt her stomach twist; it was just as well she hadn't had that sandwich. "I'm sorry," she said, and meant it. "One thing didn't have jack to do with the other. I didn't think."

"I'm looking at a promotion here," he said. "I got bills to pay. Last thing I need is to be consorting with a dirty cop."

That hurt. "Nothing like convicting a person without a trial."

"Shit," he said after a five-second pause. "I know you're not on the take. It's just—"

"How'd you hear about it, anyway?"

"Grapevine," he said. "Least it hasn't hit the papers."

"Department's had enough bad press lately. They want to make sure they have all their ducks in a row before they crucify me on the steps of One P.P."

"You wanna tell me what the hell is going on? All I heard is, you took a bribe to get some rich kid off the hook for rape. And then the vic went and—"

"Not now," she said. "Can you just tell me who the gun was registered to?" An annoyed groan, followed by silence. "Please?"

After another beat he said, "One .38-caliber Smith & Wesson Chiefs Special revolver, registered to the same owner since 1981." She heard him flip a page in his notebook. "Philip Marchand, date of birth 4-8-41. Address on Chantilly Avenue. Ring a bell?"

"Plenty of Marchands around here."

"Listen, uh . . . I'm sorry about before. That was out of line."

"Don't worry about it," she said.

"But in terms of favors . . . I'd appreciate it if this was it for now. Okay?"

Ginny thanked him and hung up. Then she dialed Sonya, who answered over the roar of a Disney video. "I need to ask you something," Ginny said. "Did Danny know anybody named Marchand who lives over on Chantilly Avenue?"

There was a pause while Sonya thought; it was filled by a singing mermaid. "Doesn't ring a bell," she said. "Why?"

"That's who owned the gun."

"So how did Danny get it?"

"I'll let you know as soon as I figure it out."

The drive took all of ten minutes; it would've taken five if she hadn't been stuck behind a boat-sized Buick driven by an old man in a porkpie hat. She pulled up in front of the address on Chantilly, a well-tended saltbox with a garage nearly as big as the house.

She was about to get out of the car when the front door opened. A man and a woman lingered in the entrance; he was nodding, she was handing him something that looked like money. He tucked it into his pocket; she poked him in the chest and shut the door. He made his way down the landscaped path, turning left in front of her car and continuing down the sidewalk.

Jimmy Griffin.

Jesus Christ, Ginny thought. *What are the odds?*

She waited until Jimmy had turned the next corner before she got out of her car. She hadn't heard from him since that afternoon in Danny's room, and frankly, that was fine with her; she had no idea what to say.

Ginny rang the doorbell, and a fiftyish woman answered the door in a rose-colored robe. "Naughty boy! Back for another game of—"

She cut herself off at the sight of Ginny, gathering the robe to cover her décolletage. The woman's face was flushed, not from embarrassment, but from whatever she'd been doing earlier. And from the musky smell wafting from her person, Ginny had a pretty good idea of what that was.

"Can I help you?" the woman asked.

"Are you Mrs. Marchand?"

"Yes," she said. "Why?"

On the interminable drive over, Ginny had given some thought to what she was going to say. Since she couldn't just flash a badge and start asking questions, she needed another approach. After contemplating different strategies she'd finally settled on the truth.

"I was hoping you could help me," she said. "I'm an old friend of Sonya Markowicz." She waited for the name to mean something, but it obviously didn't. "She's the mother of Danny Markowicz. The young man who was killed last week."

"Killed? You mean like a car accident?"

The woman seemed genuinely confused.

"It's been all over the paper," Ginny said.

"I've been down at Foxwoods with my girlfriends," she said. "Made a bundle on the slots. What did you say happened to this person?"

"They found his body in one of the old mills. He was beaten to death."

Mrs. Marchand genuflected, an action that also seemed genuine—if a bit out of context, considering she was clad in a silk robe that reeked of sex. "How awful," she said. "Did they catch whoever did it?"

"They did," Ginny said. "But what they don't know is why. And like I said, I'm an old friend of his mother's. She asked me to look into his . . . final hours."

"I can't imagine how I could help."

"If I could just talk to you for a few minutes, it would mean a lot to his mother."

The woman nodded and stepped back, leading Ginny into the kitchen. There was a pot of coffee on the counter—right next to two loaves of cinnamon bread.

Ginny knew better than to ask. But she couldn't stop herself.

G inny lifted one of the loaves off the counter; it was heavy and cylindrical, still slightly warm to the touch. Their little interlude must've been a quickie.

"Are these from Molly's?" she asked. As if she didn't know.

"Sure are," Mrs. Marchand said. "Just delivered fresh half an hour ago."

"Gee," Ginny said, trying to keep her voice even. "I didn't know they delivered right to people's houses."

"Not to everybody," she said with a wink. "Only to *special* customers. You want some?"

Ginny shook her head, feeling nauseous. It served her right for opening her big mouth. "I'd love some coffee, though, if you don't mind."

The woman poured her a cup and put two slices of cinnamon bread into the toaster. Within seconds a sweet-spicy aroma filled the kitchen; Ginny's mouth watered despite herself.

"I'm sorry to drop in on you out of the blue," Ginny said, forcing herself to focus. "It's just, we're trying to find out what Danny was doing in the time he was missing, between when he disappeared and when his body was found." She produced a photo and laid it on the kitchen table. "Are you sure you don't recognize him?"

Mrs. Marchand squinted at the picture, then held it at arm's length, like she needed reading glasses but didn't want to admit it. "You know," she said, "that's funny. I *have* seen him somewhere. I'm just not sure . . . Wait a minute. Maybe he was one of the boys who worked on my garage."

Ginny felt a tingle at the base of her spine. It was a sensation she hadn't had in way too long—the thrill of being in the thick of an investigation and actually getting somewhere.

"You recently had some construction done?"

She nodded, getting up to retrieve the toast and slather it with margarine. "Before, we had this ridiculous carport and a couple of rusty old storage lockers. My husband always said it got the job done. But he never let me park *my* car there, now, did he? So after he passed, I took some of the insurance and put up the garage. It's good for the property value, don't you think?"

"Do you remember what company you hired?"

Mrs. Marchand searched her memory. "It was a Polack name. I could look in my checkbook."

"Libanski?"

"That's it," she said. "Is that where the boy worked?"

Ginny nodded. "How much time did he spend here?"

"It took them about two weeks from start to finish. That boy worked with two other fellows. They did a real good job—nice and neat, too. Didn't go tromping sawdust and mud all over the house."

"They spent some time inside? Did you have another job for them?"

"No, but a guy's got to use the john once in a while. And they helped me carry some things once—boxes going to Goodwill. They saw me trying to cart them myself and they helped out. Like I said, they were nice boys."

"Now, this is just a routine question," Ginny said. "Do you keep any firearms in the house?"

Ginny was worried the query would put the woman on edge, but it didn't; she was always amazed at what the use of the word "routine" would let her get away with.

"My husband bought a gun once, back when there was a rash of burglaries around here. Must've been twenty years ago. I told him to get rid of it, or I'd get rid of *him*. I'd never want that sort of thing around the house. So he took it right back to the store."

Sure he did, Ginny thought. *Sure he did.*

They buried Jumping Jack O'Brien the next day, on a rainy morning that transformed the occasion from bad to perfectly miserable. There was no family there: Jack's father was dead, his mother was in a nursing home with Alzheimer's, his sister had moved away. The only mourners at the grave site were the three aged American Legionnaires who offered final honors at the burial of every local war veteran. And Ginny and Sonya.

Sonya had insisted on coming to the ceremony, had asked her upstairs neighbor to watch her day-care kids, and had donned the same black dress she'd worn to bury Danny. It was a statement—her way of telling the world, *Jack O'Brien did not kill my son*. It was important, she said. Even if nobody else was around to see it.

The service was mercifully short. When it was over, Father LeGrand—the priest who had presided over Danny's funeral, as well as Ginny's own first communion—signaled one of the Legionnaires. The old man pushed a button on a boom box, apologizing that their bugler had recently passed away. To the tinny strains of taps, the other two men took the flag from Jack's casket and folded it into a smart triangle, working precisely despite their palsied hands.

When they were done, they seemed confused about which woman to give it to. Sonya reached out and took it, prompting the priest to put a hand atop her head as he walked to his car. "Bless you, my child," he said.

"Thank you for coming, Father," she called after him. "I know how busy you are."

"Of course," he said, and slammed the driver's door shut.

Ginny and Sonya stood at the side of the damp grave for a few minutes after everyone else had left. Jack's casket lay in the family plot, next to his father's. An adjacent patch of earth awaited his mother, whose birth date had already been inscribed: her date of death was just waiting to be carved into the blank granite.

"'Your mom gets to hold the flag, though,'" Ginny said into the silence. "'So that's pretty good.'"

Sonya turned to her. "What are you talking about?"

"It's something Jack said to me, about dying in Vietnam. He said they send you home in a box, but at least your mom gets the flag."

"That's horrible," Sonya said.

"I know."

Sonya looked away, gazing out over the field of headstones. "Danny's over there," she said, "past those two big trees and down the hill."

Ginny took her hand. "You want to go?"

"Not yet," she said. "I can't visit his grave until I know who put him there." She turned to Ginny. "Do you think that's stupid?"

"No."

Sonya turned and walked toward the car, clutching her umbrella. With a final glance toward Jack O'Brien's grave, Ginny followed.

She'd suddenly been struck by a memory of Jack, something from her childhood she'd forgotten until now. It was after school, crowds of kids walking home, Jack doing his usual calisthenics by the fountain across the street from McDonald's. Sometimes the older ones taunted him, but for some reason that day they'd decided to copy what he was doing. More and more kids joined in, and for a couple of minutes he was leading a miniature platoon in sit-ups and knee bends. He had no idea they were making fun of him; his eyes were shining, and he was happy.

"I need you to think harder, Sonya," Ginny said. "Are you sure there was nobody Danny was having problems with?"

"I already told you," Sonya said over her shoulder. "There was nothing. Everything was fine."

"You didn't tell me Pete wouldn't pay for college." Sonya stopped walking. "Or that they had a huge fight, or that he and Danny were barely speaking."

There was a long silence. When Sonya finally answered, she spoke to the neatly mown grass. "That didn't have anything to do with what happened to him."

"How do you know that?"

Sonya turned on her. "What are you saying? You think Pete beat his own son to death to keep him from going to art school? How awful is—"

"No, of course not. That's ridiculous. But you asked me to find out who killed him. That means you don't get to hold anything back."

"I still don't see how—"

"Danny was desperate for money. Who knows what he might've gotten himself mixed up in?"

Sonya shook her head, eyes blazing. "He'd never do anything illegal. You know he wouldn't."

Ginny took a deep breath. "I need you to decide," she said. "Do you want to find out how Danny died, or don't you?"

"Of course I do," Sonya said. "You know I do."

"Even if you find out things about him that you didn't want to know?"

"I can't believe he'd do anything wrong."

"I know you don't. You're his mother. But every perp I ever busted had a mother who swore up and down he was innocent as the day he was born." Sonya opened her mouth, but Ginny cut her off. "And I'm not saying Danny hurt anybody. But he was nineteen years old, Sonya. He had his own life. And unless he was the victim of some random attack, that life had something to do with why he was killed." Sonya stood in silence, thinking, again looking out over the rows of graves. "Now, if you want me to, I'll go back to the city and forget about it. But if I'm going to find out who killed him, I'm going to dig and dig, and I have no idea what might turn up."

Sonya was quiet for a while longer. Then she turned and looked Ginny not quite in the eye.

"There's something else," she said.

Ginny waited for Sonya to speak, but she just stood there—jaw trembling, hands balled up into fists. "What?" she asked finally.

"I didn't say anything because I didn't think it mattered. And I didn't want to . . . I was afraid you'd think badly of him. And maybe it wasn't even true."

"Tell me," Ginny said.

"I'm afraid," Sonya said, "that Danny might have gone to hell."

15

Once upon a time, the Sprague Electric plant had been the town's biggest employer—a defense contractor that had helped put men on the moon only to become a postindustrial ghost town. The place had closed down for good when Ginny was in elementary school, the last hearty shove on her hometown's slide toward economic ruin.

Growing up, Ginny had always thought the abandoned complex—two dozen decaying buildings, dotted with catwalks and smokestacks—would make a great setting for a horror movie. But Hollywood never came calling, and the property lay dormant, frozen in time behind wrought iron and chain link.

Now it was something called Mass MoCA, the Massachusetts Museum of Contemporary Art—the place that Monique had described and dismissed in the same breath. Ginny vaguely remembered hearing rumblings about the project when she was in college, but the promises to extend Boston's largesse farther west than Springfield had always vanished before the ink was dry on the reelection ballots. Somehow, though, it had happened, and the sight of the museum, its name spelled out in artfully lit metal letters atop the once-decrepit buildings, struck Ginny as no less fantastic than the Emerald City rising up from the hinterlands of Oz.

Astounding as it was, the museum wasn't Ginny's destination. That was across the street at Café des Artistes, the coffee shop where Danny had worked. The place seemed to be doing good business: all the stools in the window were full, and people had spilled out onto benches on the sidewalk, clutching paper cups in one hand and cigarettes in the other.

Ginny walked in and was instantly transported two hundred miles south. The café had an urban vibe that made her feel at home—which, ironically, made it wildly out of place in her own hometown.

Who *were* all these people? The men had goatees and interesting eyeglasses; the women had cropped hair and nose rings. Not all of them, of course—but enough to make Ginny feel like she was in the East Village, not just off Main Street. She'd heard that artists were buying the old mills and turning them into lofts; Danny's body had been found during a Realtor's tour. But knowing was one thing—and seeing these hipsters sipping their lattes across the street from a modern art museum was another.

Ginny made her way to the counter, laden with glass jars bearing chocolate-dipped biscotti. She was figuring they were imported from Little Italy—until she saw a handmade sign that said ALL BAKED GOODS MADE LOCALLY BY MOLLY'S OF EAGLE STREET. She looked into the glass case below and saw the usual assortment of smiley faces and half-moons, along with some flavored croissants and miniature loaves of that prosciutto-cheddar concoction Jimmy had fed her in Sonya's kitchen.

Was she never, ever going to get a break from him?

The girl at the counter was wearing a cropped pink tank top that said MISTER BUBBLE. It was skintight, revealing a well-muscled stomach along with the fact that she wasn't wearing a bra. Ginny ordered a cup of coffee—plain coffee, just to be contrary—and asked to speak to someone named Topher.

The counter girl raised a pierced eyebrow. "You looking for a job?" she asked. "'Cause I think the opening's been filled already."

"No," Ginny said. "I just need to talk to him."

She cocked her head in the direction of the back corner. Ginny carried her coffee toward the rear table, debating what she was going to say to the man who may or may not have been Danny's lover.

I'm afraid that Danny might have gone to hell.

That's what Sonya had said. What she'd meant was that Danny might have been gay.

Or bisexual. Or—Sonya didn't have the words for it. All she knew was that her son hadn't been the same since he started hanging around with those boys from New York City. In the months before he died he and Pete could hardly say a civil word to each other; the college argument had just been the beginning of their estrangement. Danny was still cheerful, still hardworking and polite, but there was something different about him. He hardly brought Monique around anymore, stayed out late with no explanation of where he'd been or whom he'd been with.

Sonya didn't hate gay people; she'd said this to Ginny over and over, squeezing her hand as their shoes got soaked in the grass of Southview Cemetery. It was just—it was a mortal sin.

She knew Danny hadn't been to confession in months. What if he'd been doing things with those boys, things she couldn't bear to think about, and had died with them on his conscience? Without absolution his soul couldn't be in a state of grace. What if, when *she* died, he wasn't waiting for her in heaven?

Ginny had held her, stroked her hair, tried to say something comforting. She couldn't say what she felt, which was that it was all a bunch of crap: she didn't believe in hell, and even if there were one, she *definitely* didn't believe that being gay was a one-way ticket there.

But the pope did, and so did Sonya. The church had been her bulwark through sudden motherhood, the absence of her own children, the deaths of her mother and father and adopted son. Ginny wasn't about to try to shake her faith now.

So she'd offered her the only thing she could: the truth. She couldn't say whether Danny had wound up in heaven or in hell, but she could find out who'd taken him from her. And Sonya, being as practical as she was bereft, said that was enough.

"Excuse me," Ginny said. "I'm looking for Topher."

There were two men at the table—both in their mid-twenties, lanky, very pale. They were once again dressed in black, with gelled hair and an assortment of piercings; clearly, fitting in with the local populace wasn't much of a priority.

"That's me," said the one on the right. "But if you're here about the job—"

"No. I'm a friend of Danny Markowicz' mother," she said. "I'd like to talk to you for a few minutes, if you don't mind."

"About what?" This from the other man, who was drinking a café au lait out of a cup the size of a fishbowl. He seemed a few years older than Topher and much harder-edged. This might be Topher's place, she mused, but his friend was clearly the one in charge.

"There's still a lot of confusion about what happened to Danny," she said. "I'm trying to piece together what he did in his last couple of days."

Topher nodded. She was about to drag a chair over when the other man stood up—an act she took for old-fashioned good manners until he said he had to get back to the museum.

"I hope Topher can help you, *Officer*," he said.

Ginny sized him up through narrowed eyes. "Excuse me?"

"You *are* a cop, aren't you?"

"What would make you think that?"

He cracked a nasty smile. "Lucky guess," he said, and walked out.

Topher followed him with his eyes, an amused expression on his face. He turned back to Ginny.

"Sorry about Geoff," he said. The way he pronounced it, the

name rhymed with "off." "He gets a kick out of playing the bad boy."

"I've seen worse."

"So," Topher said, "you really a cop?"

"I'm a detective with the NYPD."

"Yeah? Can I see your badge?"

"I left it in the city."

"What kind of cop doesn't carry a badge?" he asked. "How're you gonna get out of a speeding ticket?"

"Drive slow," she said.

He smiled, revealing a set of lupine teeth, straight and very white. "So what do you want to know about Danny?"

"I'm not here as a cop," she said, for what felt like the hundredth time. "Like I said, I'm an old friend of his mother's. I'm trying to find out what happened to him."

Topher shrugged and took a sip of his coffee. It left a line of foam on his mustache, which made him look ridiculous. "I heard some crazy dude beat him to death."

"That's the official story."

"But you don't buy it." He acknowledged her nod, then leaned back in his chair. "What do you want to know?"

"For starters, what was your relationship with Danny?"

He ran his fingers through his hair, which stood up in shiny, cactuslike spikes. "You don't screw around, do you?"

"No," she said. "Do you?"

16

Topher eyed her from across the table. "Danny was a good kid," he said. "He deserved better."

"Better than getting killed?"

"Better than living his life like he was already dead. Like his parents wanted him to."

Ginny tried to keep her voice even. "And how's that?"

"Those people think the world ends at the county line. That the universe is five miles wide and two inches deep."

She leaned back, gave him an assessing look. "You think you're pretty clever, don't you?"

He shrugged. "I'm just saying."

"You didn't answer the question. What was your relationship with Danny?"

"Are you asking if we were screwing? Is that what you want to know? Whether Danny was taking it up the—"

"Were you?"

"None of your business."

"Look, I'm not trying to invade your privacy for my own amusement. It's important that I find out as much about Danny as I can. I know you paid your respects to his mom at the funeral. So please, just answer the question."

"Oh, man . . ." His voice trailed off; his eyes searched the room, like he was trying to retrieve a memory. "I don't think anybody knew what Danny was. Least of all Danny."

"But the two of you were involved?"

He shook his head. "I'm with Geoffrey."

"Was Danny seeing anyone?"

"You mean other than Princess Skipper?" He grinned at her confusion. "You know. Barbie's little sister."

"Her name is Monique."

"Whatever. She's dumb as a bag of hammers. Danny was getting fed up—high school was fading in the rearview mirror. For him, at least."

"She seems to think they were getting engaged."

"In her dreams."

"Did he tell her that?"

Topher shrugged. "Danny hated to hurt anybody's feelings. He wanted everyone to like him. Like I said, he was still a kid."

"And as far as you know, he wasn't seeing anybody else?"

"What difference does it make? You think Danny got gay-bashed? Or is his mama just terrified her little boy would've turned out queer?"

She tightened her grip on her coffee cup. "Maybe you didn't hear, but Danny got beat so bad they couldn't even have an open casket. So you bet your ass I'm wondering if it had something to do with him being gay, if that's what he was. This town isn't exactly what you'd call a bastion of tolerance."

Topher looked genuinely abashed; maybe there was a nice guy under all that hair gel. After a minute he said, "Danny was questioning, that's all. I can't tell you for sure whether he would've wound up gay or straight or bi. I know he was attracted to men. I could tell the first time he came in here, which was way before he figured it out himself. But whether he ever acted on it, I couldn't tell you."

"Was he close to anyone else in the café?"

"Like I said, Danny was everybody's buddy. When he found this place, he was like some poor starving kid who'd walked into an all-you-can-eat buffet."

"Of what? Good-looking guys?"

"No, you moron. *Ideas.* Art, culture, conversation, books. Films more interesting than what was playing at the mall. Did you know, before he came in here, Danny didn't even know there was an art house cinema right over in Williamstown? He'd never even been to the museum, and that's in his own home-town. Geoffrey's an assistant curator, and he gave him some free passes, and it was like the whole world opened up. The two of them would sit here and argue about art and music and whatever until I closed the place. So no, it was *not* about Danny getting his rocks off. It was about him finding out who he was. And I doubt those two hicks who raised him were going to be much help."

"Watch it," she said.

The look in her eyes must have told him that he'd gone too far. "Sorry," he said. "It's just—I guess I felt kind of protective of Danny."

"Why? Did you think he might be in danger?"

He gazed into his coffee cup, shaking his head. "It was more like we were the first people who ever really understood him. It was sort of addictive, feeling like you're somebody's Obi-Wan. You know?"

"You cared about him," she said.

"Yeah. And you know what else? I envied him."

"Why is that?"

"Because he was still young enough to think people are fun-damentally good."

"Maybe he was just a small-town boy. People here grow up trusting their neighbors."

"Bullshit," Topher said. "If it's such a paradise, what the hell are you doing in the city?"

"And if it's not, what are *you* doing *here*?"

"Love. When Geoff got the job at the museum, I decided to tag along and try opening my own café." He drew out a pack of

American Spirits and a heavy metal lighter. "Had to move to the sticks to find a place where you can still have a butt with your cappuccino." He winked at her, lit a cigarette, and extended the pack. "You want one?" Ginny shook her head. "You know where Danny used to work afternoons before he got this gig?"

"At the Wal-Mart."

"Yeah," he said through a veil of smoke, "and don't that just say it all?"

Ginny walked out of Café des Artistes half an hour later—no closer to finding out who killed Danny, but feeling like she was finally getting to know him.

She was starting to realize something: she and Danny had a lot in common. They'd both yearned for a life beyond this small town, had chafed at the shackles of their families' expectations. Like her, Danny had been an only child, had had a problematic relationship with his father, had wanted to carve out his own future rather than take over the family business.

Guilt hit her, a stabbing pain. Why hadn't she gotten to know Danny better while he was still alive? Maybe if she'd taken more of an interest in her best friend's only child, things would have turned out differently.

She shook her head; now she was acting like Monique, as though Danny's death were her tragedy instead of his. She stood under the awning, chronicling the questions that Topher had brought her no closer to answering. Why did Danny keep a loaded gun in his bedroom? What was he doing in that abandoned mill? And who could possibly have hated him enough to beat him to death?

She ran down the street, sprinting from awning to awning to escape the rain. It was the kind of downpour the town fathers hated, because it stripped the leaves from the trees; the foliage season could be over before it started, and the tourist dollars along with it.

Sure enough, the awful weather was the chief topic of conversation at the Golden Skillet, the diner that rounded out Danny's employment trifecta. It was located on Main Street, just around the corner and down the block from Café des Artistes, but it felt like another world: the pressed-tin ceiling coated in decades' worth of grease, the local businessmen in their shiny suits and military haircuts, the blue plate specials that actually came on a blue plate. The menu, which hadn't changed in living memory, featured chicken-fried everything and a fifties-era diet plate consisting of a hamburger patty, cottage cheese, and a side of canned peaches served on a leaf of iceberg lettuce.

Ginny walked in, scanning the crowd for familiar faces. The place was packed, the Main Street professional crowd having the small-town version of a power lunch. There was Judge Sweringen, digging into a bowl of Cool Whip–laden Jell-O in the company of a pair of local lawyers. Mr. Dulaine was there, eating a turkey club; Ginny couldn't remember his first name, but she knew he was president of the local bank who'd married into the family that owned Letour Motors. She also recognized Bob Gianelli, owner of the town's biggest insurance agency and the father of one of Ginny's high school classmates; he was eating with Chief Rolly himself.

She'd picked a lousy time to try to talk to Danny's coworkers, who were run off their feet with the lunch rush. Ginny should have known better: her father had eaten here almost every workday, and when school was out, he sometimes brought her along.

She took the only empty seat at the counter and ordered the poison of her youth: a Skillet Burger and an orange soda. The former consisted of a vast slab of ground beef, sautéed onions, bacon, Muenster cheese, and the omnipresent leaf of iceberg lettuce. She downed it, along with a slice of homemade strawberry-rhubarb pie—both for old times' sake and for the simple pleasure of eating a dessert that Jimmy Griffin hadn't had his paws on.

She made her bloated way back to the car, moving markedly slower than she had on the way there. She'd go back to the Skillet when it wasn't so busy—and when she'd regained some dietary self-control.

She started the car, wipers swatting lamely at the cascading rain. The Chrysler groaned as it made its way up the steep slope of East Main Street, but it held the curves; trusty steed. The hill crested, and she took a left, the street angling sharply back down toward the river. But when she hit the brakes to make another left into Sonya's street, nothing happened.

She slammed the pedal to the floor. No good.

17

The car was picking up speed. Desperately, lamely, she kept pumping the brakes. Still nothing. She yanked the hand brake. It slowed her down, but not enough to do any good.

Uh-oh.

She was trying to keep the car under control, dodging the few vehicles parked along Gallup Street. At the bottom of the hill was a busy road—and on the other side of that was river.

She fumbled over her left shoulder for her seat belt; like some idiot civilian, she hadn't buckled it for the short trip up the hill from Main Street.

She managed to pull it across her chest and snap it shut just as the Chrysler careened into the intersection at the bottom of the hill. There was a pickup truck directly in front of her. She yanked the wheel to the right and managed to miss its rear fender by inches.

She had no idea how fast she was going—thirty, maybe forty miles an hour—but it was enough to flatten the chain-link fence that ran along the edge of the river. The car flew over the rim of the flood-control chute and into the Hoosic—black and churning, swollen by the summer rain.

The car went in nose-first, then leveled out. Then started to sink.

Manhattan is surrounded by water. Ginny had taken a rescue course once, and there had been some instruction about what to do if you were suddenly faced with the fact that you do, indeed, live on an island.

With water flooding in—freezing cold, filling up faster than she would have thought possible—she tried to remember what the instructor had said to do if you were trapped in a sinking car. There was a tool you could use to break a window with one blow; she didn't have it. She tried the door. The water pressure was too strong, and it wouldn't budge. Neither could she roll the windows down: electric windows were just about the only upgrade she'd gone for on the Chrysler, damn it all.

The cold water was like a hundred little razor blades on her skin. *Think,* she told herself, *think. Or you're screwed.*

First you were supposed to let the car fill up with water; that part was taking care of itself. She unbuckled her seat belt, following the level of water, scrambling to keep breathing. Then you have to check which way the bubbles are going, so you know which way is up. Once the car gets filled with water, the pressure equalizes, and you can open the door.

She waited until the last remaining sliver of the air pocket had all but disappeared. Then she took a desperate breath and reached for the door handle. She shoved with all her strength, and it gave. Lungs exploding, she kicked her way out of the car and followed the bubbles to the surface. She took a choking breath, mouth full of the river and the rain.

The current was stronger than she'd expected; it drew her along as she tried to tread water, scanning the bare cement walls for a way to get out. Did she drag herself out of a sinking car just so she could die of hypothermia?

Finally, after drifting downstream for another quarter mile, she spotted a ladder embedded in the cement. She swam over to it, the current knocking her off course; she made a desperate swipe at it, managing to hook two fingers onto a rung and hold on. She pulled herself up out of the water, hanging there for a minute, catching her breath. Jamming a toe onto the slippery metal rung, she hoisted herself up—nearly losing her grip, forcing herself to go slowly. She got to the top and heaved herself over, rewarded with a chestful of mud and gravel.

Later it occurred to her to wonder what a sight she must have been when she walked into the Dunkin' Donuts—soaking wet, covered in mud, gasping for breath, and half-drunk with adrenaline. Someone shouted for help, and a girl in a paper hat came from behind the counter; the world swam before her eyes, a kaleidoscope of pink frosting and chocolate sprinkles.

Sonya made her go to the hospital. Ginny didn't want to—told her she was fine, just a little scraped up and freaked out—but Sonya insisted. Ginny finally agreed: anything to get her friend to stop berating her for driving a rusting old death trap and nearly tearing her heart in half for the second time in two weeks.

So she let Sonya take her to the emergency room, where the doctor who examined her proved to be another alumna of Ginny and Sonya's Girl Scout troop—and its champion cookie seller, no less. Lizzie Erickson, that mouthy little girl in French braids and Coke-bottle glasses, had grown up to be an MD.

The doctor checked her out, diagnosed her with no major damage, bandaged Ginny's scrapes with her own hands. She told Sonya how sorry she was about Danny, extended an invitation to dinner with her and her husband and their three perfect children. Ginny told her she'd love to, though she wasn't sure that she actually meant it. At any rate, she wasn't thinking straight: her back was killing her, and the pills Lizzie had so obligingly handed out hadn't done the trick.

"Anyway," she said, once Sonya had gone to bring the car around, "thanks for patching me up."

"Good to see you after all these years," the doctor said. "Especially since you came in on your own two feet. One kid from East getting wheeled in flat on her back is enough for one day."

"How do you mean?"

Lizzie wiped at her brow, ruffling the sensible brown bangs. "Girl we used to know came in OD'd on crystal meth this morning. You probably wouldn't remember her. I hardly recognized her myself."

"Belinda Cooper."

Lizzie stared at her, like she'd just guessed the next day's lotto. "How did you know?"

"I ran into her on Main Street a couple days ago. Do you know what happened to her kids?"

"No idea." The doctor shrugged, taking off her glasses and cleaning them with the hem of her white lab coat. "They weren't with her, anyway."

Ginny ran her tongue along her bottom lip. It was split; she must've bitten it in the crash. "Crystal meth. So *that's* what she was on. And then there was this guy who flipped out in a bar the other night, screaming that everybody was out to get him."

"We get a lot of that. Crystal makes you paranoid."

"Jesus. Where's it all coming from?"

Another shrug. "Beats me. All I see is the fallout."

"What happened to Belco?" The doctor squinted at her; without the glasses her eyes seemed oddly small. "Belinda Cooper."

"She'll make it," she said. "This time."

Sonya put Ginny to bed; by then her back hurt so much she didn't even resist. She stretched out against the sheets, which Sonya had so mercifully washed since her afternoon tussle with Jimmy, and closed her eyes. She tried to sleep, but the pills were no match for her brain; it was racing like a Thoroughbred on uppers.

Crystal meth had moved into town, apparently with a vengeance. Danny was desperate for money to go to college. He was hanging out with a new crowd—urban, fast, into God knows what. He'd lifted a gun from the house where he was working. Did he steal it because he was selling drugs and needed a firearm like a carpenter needs an electric drill?

The thought made her back hurt worse. Sonya had sworn she wanted Ginny to find out the truth, no matter what. But as much as she loved her friend, Ginny didn't believe her. Anything would be better than finding out her son had been killed in some kind of botched drug deal—even never knowing. Ginny would just as soon pin the murder on poor Jumping Jack O'Brien; the law couldn't do anything worse to him than it already had.

She shook her head, tossing back and forth on Danny's pillow. She really was one hell of a cop, wasn't she?

Ginny rolled over on her stomach, trying to get comfortable. It didn't much help. She gave up, rolled over onto her aching back, stared up at the ceiling. When Danny was little, Sonya had put little stickers on the ceiling—stars that glowed in the dark so he could sleep beneath a twinkling sky. They were gone now, but the ceiling hadn't been repainted; Ginny could make out the outlines of some of them, tiny star shapes where the paint was less faded.

Crystal meth. It was a drug Ginny had run into plenty of times—both in uniform and as a detective. Over the past five years or so, it had come onto the Special Victims radar as a party drug, especially for gay men who used it to fuel all-night encounters. It lowered inhibitions, made you feel like you were king of the world. But like most drugs, once you got hooked, the highs got shorter and the lows got deeper.

She knew that although crystal had its urban aficionados, it also had a reputation as a white-trash drug, cooked up in trailers from easy-to-shoplift ingredients like cold medicine and the sulfur from matches. So was it being made locally? And, more important, had Danny been involved?

Ginny hadn't found any drugs in Danny's room—or paraphernalia or wads of cash. Sonya hadn't said anything that hinted he'd been using; neither had his girlfriend or his boss at the café. But she knew perfectly well that dealers didn't necessarily use; in fact, the best ones wouldn't dream of it.

She rolled over again, desperate to get comfortable. Was she off on some idiotic tangent here—tagging poor Danny as a drug dealer just because she'd found out crystal meth had joined the menu of locally available stimulants? Maybe. But she couldn't stop thinking about the gun. He'd stolen it either because he was afraid someone wanted to hurt him or because he wanted to hurt someone else.

The door opened a crack, and Sonya peeked in. Ginny felt

instantly guilty, as though her friend could tell she'd been mentally convicting her dead son without a trial.

"You awake?" Sonya asked. "I could hear you tossing and turning."

"Yeah," she said, trying to sit up before deciding it was a bad idea.

"Want something to eat?" Ginny shook her head; that Skillet Burger was still parked in her gut, heavy as a bowling ball. "Some tea maybe?"

"Sure," Ginny said.

Sonya put the kettle on, then came back and sat on the edge of the bed. "You don't look so good."

"I probably caught typhus from swimming in the Hoosic."

"Nah. I think there's just some PCBs in there."

Sonya pushed Ginny's bangs away from her face. It was a consummately gentle gesture, one that reminded Ginny what a good mother she'd been.

"How's your head?" Sonya asked.

"Fine."

"Are you sure you're not hungry? There's a quiche in the refrigerator. One of Danny's city friends brought it over earlier when he paid a condolence call."

"Topher?"

"That's right. He seemed nice. But pierced like a pincushion."

"Yeah."

"I just talked to Pete. He's getting your car hauled out of the river."

"Might as well have left it there. Given it a burial at sea." Ginny smiled, then winced when it made her split lip start to bleed again.

"Town frowns on that kind of thing," Sonya said. "Especially once the water level drops."

"Right."

"I hope you want Lipton," Sonya said, suddenly fighting back tears. "'Cause that's all I've got. None of those fancy teas."

Ginny put a hand on Sonya's arm. "Are you okay?"

"Sure," she said, with no conviction whatsoever. "Sure."

"It's okay, sweetie," Ginny said. "I'm fine."

She watched Sonya battle the tears, blinking and sniffling with gusto. "Good," she said. "Because if you—"

"Don't think about it," Ginny interrupted. "It was just a stupid accident. It's my fault for being too cheap to stop driving a wreck."

"A wreck," Sonya said, "would be trading up."

Ginny hugged her. It hurt, but she did it anyway. "I'm sorry I scared the crap out of you."

Her friend cracked a small smile, hugging her tight. "I guess you've been punished, huh?" She patted Ginny's head, then got up to get her tea.

"Hey," Ginny called after her, "there's something I need to ask you." Sonya poked her head back into the bedroom. "What did you mean," she asked, "when you said Jimmy ran a full-service operation?"

Sonya didn't answer right away. Ginny heard her puttering in the kitchen, just outside the bedroom door—pulling down a mug from the rack, ripping open a tea bag, pouring water from the kettle. Finally, she came in and put the steaming cup on

Danny's bedside table. She perched on the corner of the bed, exactly as she'd been before, but this time she seemed utterly fascinated by the pattern of the checkered spread.

"That seems like a funny thing to ask right now," she said.

"Yeah," Ginny replied.

Sonya looked over at the mug, as though it offered a reprieve. "You still like sugar in your—"

"Just tell me, okay?"

"I don't get why you're worrying about Jimmy when you practically just drowned."

Ginny slumped back onto the pillows. "Maybe because I doubt I can feel any worse right now. Or because when I went over to this Mrs. Marchand's house the other day, Jimmy came out, and any idiot could tell he'd been screwing her. I think she might even have paid him for it."

"I see." Sonya took a deep breath, rubbing a hand over her eyes like Ginny's headache was contagious. "I'm sorry I said that before. It was mean. It's just—I don't want you to get hurt again."

"Last time, I think it was the other way around. I walked out on *him,* remember? And I—"

Ginny had been about to mention the abortion, but she cut herself off. She'd never told anyone but Jimmy that she'd been pregnant, not even her mother or her best friend. Sonya loved her like a sister, but Ginny knew that her choice to have an abortion was something Sonya could never understand, maybe never forgive. Indeed, when Ginny had once asked why Paula carried Danny to term, Sonya seemed shocked: although her sister had her faults, she said, she'd never do something as awful as killing her unborn child.

"I didn't want to marry him," she said instead. "He got down on one knee and gave me the smallest diamond you ever saw, and I turned him down. So it's not like he owes me anything. I just need to know."

Sonya looked up at her, brow twisted in concern. After a long pause she said, "He's just kind of got a reputation, that's all."

"For what? Screwing older women in the afternoons?"

"Yeah. That exactly."

"So you're saying he's . . . what? Some kind of gigolo or something?"

"I don't know what you'd call it. It's just kind of an open se-cret that there are these lonely ladies he sees. He's supposedly delivering stuff, but everybody knows his truck is parked out front way too long."

"Married women, too?"

She watched as Sonya did a mental inventory of all the women Jimmy was banging; she wondered, with rising humilia-tion, whether she'd been his only visit of that particular day. "I don't think so," Sonya said. "Just widows and divorcées, I think."

"Oh, Christ, Sonya. Why didn't you tell me?"

A flicker of annoyance crossed Sonya's face; for her it con-stituted major aggression. "I'm sorry if I didn't take time out from mourning my son to fill you in on Jimmy Griffin's love life. I hardly thought you were going to jump in the sack the minute you were alone with him."

"I'm sorry. Please—you're right. I'm a selfish bitch."

The anger went out of Sonya as fast as it had gone in. "No, you're not," she said. "You came up here because I asked you to. I know it's not easy for you to be back."

Sonya looked ashamed of herself. Ginny hated to think what she must look like: between the bruises and the humiliation, she was deeply grateful that Danny's room had no mirror.

———————

Libanski Construction was headquartered in a building that was, in itself, no advertisement for its services. The business was run out of a small vinyl-sided cottage on the road to Williamstown; the plain, squat little house was so dwarfed by the parking lot that surrounded it, it had always reminded Ginny of a Monopoly marker.

Sonya's father had founded the company, hoping to pass it on to his son someday. But the boy died in infancy. Left with two daughters—and not of a mind to utter the words "female" and "contractor" in the same sentence—Mr. Libanski set his sights on an appropriate son-in-law. Sonya's older sister, of course, was a source of shame practically from the time her mother took her to downstreet to buy her first training bra. That left Sonya to attract the right man, and as in every other aspect of her life, she'd made her parents proud.

Pete was passably smart, and a good Polish boy, to boot. He'd grown up in the next town over but had started working summers for Sonya's dad during high school, impressing him with his strong arms and even stronger work ethic. Mr. Libanski himself made the match, offering Pete a deal in the unspoken language of men: you can't have her virginity until after the wedding, but you can have the business before I die.

It wasn't that Pete and Sonya weren't in love or that theirs was less of a marriage than a merger. They'd been genuine high school sweethearts, had slow-danced at their respective proms and steamed up the windows of Pete's pickup on nights when Sonya barely made curfew. They carved their initials in the lifeguard chairs at the Fish Pond, along with those of every other adolescent Romeo and Juliet—Ginny and Jimmy among them.

Ginny and Jimmy. Their names had been linked since freshman year—the assonant pairing as sweet as a half-moon cookie, as cute as a poundful of puppies. Back then, when she was fifteen and crazy in love, she'd taken it as a sign that they were meant to live happily ever after: their names, like their hearts, were a perfect pair.

She winced, both at the memory and at the pain in her shoulder as she reached for the door handle. It had taken her a few minutes to find Danny's truck in the construction company's lot, where it was parked in a sea of nearly identical pickups. Once again, Sonya had chosen sense over sensibility, insisting that Ginny drive Danny's beloved Dodge Ram until she got another car. The truck was doing no one any good just sitting there; it was silly for Ginny to waste money on a rental.

She climbed into the driver's seat for the second time—the first having been when she searched the truck the same day she tossed Danny's room. Pete had since moved it from their street to the company lot, once Ginny had hinted that maybe Sonya didn't need to face it every time she walked out her front door. Now, thanks to Ginny's lack of automotive maintenance, it was going right back where it came from.

Pete was a tall guy, and the seat was set way back; even at five-nine, Ginny had to move it forward. She backed out carefully, determined not to make things worse by dinging Danny's most prized possession. But instead of going back to Sonya's, she headed to where Danny himself had driven it last: the parking lot at the Fish Pond.

The place was officially named Windsor Lake, but nobody called it that; for reasons lost to history, it was universally referred to as the Fish Pond. Where Ginny grew up, such things weren't unusual; even if a store changed hands three times in the past fifty years, people still doggedly called it by its original name. The local state college, for instance, had tried to raise its profile by renaming itself the Massachusetts College of Liberal Arts. But everybody still called it State, and fell over themselves buying the old T-shirts and coffee mugs before they got pulled off the shelves.

Ginny had the parking lot to herself. School was in session, and since it was after Labor Day, there was no one around to collect parking fees. She cut the engine and was again struck by the sheer weight of silence. The city was never quiet: there were always neighbors, sirens, car alarms, bus engines, squealing brakes, boom boxes, honking horns. It was a constant cacophony, so loud and unrelenting it could be hard to think straight.

She'd forgotten how just incredibly *silent* it was here. Maybe that was why she was feeling so discombobulated: there was nothing to drown out that inner voice telling her what a mess she'd made of her life. Since she was staying at Sonya's, she hadn't even been drinking much; she could hardly curl up in Danny's bed with a fifth of Crown Royal. So no background noise, no chemical anesthesia: for the first time in a long time, she was alive to how bad things really were.

She got out of the truck, looking out over the lake. The rain had stopped the night before, but the sky was still clogged and threatening. The leaves were changing, though, and there was something undeniably beautiful about the melancholy mood.

It was the first time she'd been back to the Fish Pond—scene of so many childhood hijinks and adolescent rendezvous. The playground equipment had been replaced, but it was essentially the same: swing sets, slides, that rotating thing that had always made her nauseous.

She had no idea what Danny had been doing here the night he died; neither did Sonya. She'd come there for no other reason than to walk a mile in Danny's shoes—or, rather, drive in them.

With the grounds entirely empty, it also seemed a good place to take a closer look inside the truck. When she'd searched it, she hadn't been thinking about drugs; although she still hoped she was way off base, she knew she had to toss the truck properly. There were all sorts of places dealers hid their stashes: inside the doors, in the wheel wells, in false compartments under the floor. She had to rip the truck down to its constituent parts, and do it where Sonya couldn't see. She hung her leather jacket on a jungle gym and went to work, searching the truck using Danny's own tools.

Two hours later no one had so much as driven into the parking lot—and she had found next to nothing. Danny, being his mother's son, had kept his vehicle fantastically clean; even the capped bed seemed sterile enough for surgery. The only thing she found, stuck in the crack where the seat bottom met the back, was a piece ripped off the top of a navy-blue condom wrapper. There was nothing else in any of the nooks and crannies, no secret compartments, nothing hidden under the hood.

Having saved the worst for last, she lay on her back and shimmied under the truck, shining a flashlight over the undercarriage. She saw no new welding, nothing to indicate that anything had been added after it had been driven off the dealer's lot. With a resigned sigh she reached for a wrench and started to take off the spare tire suspended underneath; it was covered in mud, probably caked on since its fastidious owner's death. She was going to get filthy.

The nut turned with surprising ease; it must have been removed recently. She spun it until the housing came free and the tire landed on her stomach.

And finally, there was something: a plastic bag, wrapped in tape, sealed up tight. Exactly as Danny had left it.

19

It wasn't crystal meth; that much she could tell right away. The package was thin and pliable, weighing no more than a few ounces. She crawled out from under the truck, examining it in the skewing afternoon light. It was a stack of papers, wrapped in a Ziploc bag, reinforced with electrical tape.

Before she opened it, she cleaned her hands with the Handi Wipes Danny kept in the cargo bin next to the Armor All and Turtle Wax, and put on a pair of latex gloves. Then she sliced the tape with a knife and unzipped the bag. Inside was a small stack of documents, folded in half and squished at the corners from having been jammed inside the spare tire.

On top was a photocopy of Danny's birth certificate, his tiny footprints forming a pair of black smudges at the bottom. Daniel Michael Libanski had been born on January 8, weighing in at 7 pounds 11 ounces; he wouldn't become a Markowicz until five years later, when Pete and Sonya formally adopted him.

Beside MOTHER was the name Paula Marie Libanski; FATHER was listed as unknown. Ginny remembered that the local hospital usually decorated its birth certificates with gold seals and pink or blue ribbons, but there was no sign of either on the photocopy. She wondered if the lack of them was due to some long-ago clerk's moral outrage: no curlicues for the bastard children.

She turned to the next page and realized with a start that she'd seen this paper before—had even held it in her hands. It was an original, worn and stained, folded and unfolded umpteen times until it threatened to fall apart.

Hey, Sonya,

Don't be mad at me but I gotta go. I gotta have a life, OK?
Your real good with Danny and he likes you a lot and mom can
help so its no big deal. OK? It will just be for a couple months or
whatever and he's so litle he wont even know I'm gone. I'll send some
$ to pay for his food and stuff if I can maybe. OK?
                              Love ya lots—yer big sis

Ginny remembered when that letter had arrived, two days
after Paula had asked Sonya to babysit and never returned. The
fact that she didn't come home that evening had surprised no
one; although Sonya's parents had given her the basement apartment rent-free once the baby was born, where Paula slept on
any given night was anybody's guess.

By the next day her absence was remarkable only in that she
hadn't shown up for a free meal, or to filch another five from
her mother's pocketbook. It was only when the letter came in
the mail the following afternoon, in a plain white envelope with
no return address, that the family had any inkling that Paula had
left town.

Sonya alone had waited for the promised money to come,
had watched for her sister to show up on their doorstep two
months later. After nearly a decade of disappointments her parents had learned to expect the worst. They might have tried to
find her, might have hired the sort of mustachioed private detective they enjoyed watching on prime-time action shows—but
to seek her out would have increased the risk that she might actually come back.

Ginny fingered the note, recalling the desperate look on
Sonya's face when she told her what her sister had done. *How
could she?* Sonya asked. *How could she leave him without a mom when
he doesn't even have a dad?*

The letter itself was as infuriating as Ginny remembered,

and twice as pathetic: the awful spelling, the little heart that dotted the "i" in the word "sis." But, now as then, it was the repe-
tition of "OK?" that really pissed Ginny off. It was as though
Paula was begging Sonya to condone what she'd done—not
only abandoning her year-old child but foisting him on her
teenage sister. Even back then, Sonya's mother had a heart con-
dition; she was no more capable of raising her grandson than
doing cartwheels down Main Street.

I gotta have a life, Paula had said—blithely ignoring the fact
that by leaving Danny on Sonya's lap, she was forever altering
the way her sister would live her own.

She put the letter aside. Beneath it was a small memo book,
spiral-bound and bought from the CVS. It was filled with notes
in Danny's handwriting. Ginny had a hard time deciphering them
all, but from skimming through it she knew one thing for certain.

Danny had been looking for his mother.

It was starting to get cold, but Ginny didn't want to go back to
Sonya's yet. She drove to Main Street and entered a near-empty
Café des Artistes, where she hunkered in a corner with Danny's
notebook and a café mocha. The coffee was extremely good—
far better than anything she could have gotten at Dunkin'
Donuts or the Golden Skillet, which were her other options.
You could take the girl out of the city, but you couldn't take the
city out of the girl.

She opened the notebook, imagining Danny hunched over it,
recording the scant details of his mother's life in slanted, sloppy
handwriting.

Shoplifting arrest Newberry's age 15 (warning from judge)
Drop out of H.S. March 6 Jr. yr.
Work @ Pizza House April fired May

Disorderly conduct age 17—beer in park (comm. service)
Work @ car wash June-July

It went on like that for a few pages, Danny chronicling his mother's sins and shortcomings. She had no idea how he'd gone about gathering all the information; surely, Sonya would have mentioned it if Danny had been asking about his mom.

Other than some innocuous details about Paula's meager childhood accomplishments—she'd won some sort of kiddie beauty pageant the Elks sponsored when she was in the second grade—the cheap blue-lined pages contained few bright spots. Ginny did smile when she got to a line that said *Me—Born Jan. 8!* But the year during which Paula was actually present in her son's life passed with little comment. On April 6, when Danny was just shy of fifteen months old, she left him for good.

In retrospect, Sonya had said, she should have known something wasn't right. Paula used to leave Danny on her lap without so much as a wave. But that day, that last day, Paula had bent down and kissed her son on the forehead—had hugged him so hard he started to whimper, had told him Mommy loved him three times when she usually didn't bother to say it at all. Looking back, Sonya said, she could see that Paula was saying good-bye.

There it was in the notebook, recorded in stark first-person: *April 6, 9 p.m.—leaves me with Mom.* At the bottom of the page was a notation about Paula's letter arriving in the mail. But between the two was a line Ginny didn't expect: *10:15—hitch ride to Fish Pond w/ B. McSheen—big suitcase.*

So Danny had somehow traced the first leg of his mother's trip out of town. Ginny could picture it: Paula toting a suitcase that she'd snuck out of the downstairs apartment without her family catching on, hauling it up Gallup Street hill, old Bob

McSheen passing by in his baby-blue Oldsmobile and offering her a lift.

A lift to the Fish Pond—the very spot where Danny's truck had been found the night he disappeared. Was there some connection? And did his search for his mother have anything to do with the loaded gun in his bedroom?

"Hey, whaddaya know? It's the fuzz."

She looked up from the notebook. There was a man standing over her, scrawny and stubble-faced, with black-framed rectangular eyeglasses and a silver ring piercing his left brow. It was the guy who'd been sitting with Topher—his boyfriend, the assistant museum curator. What was his name? Something pretentious. Geoffrey; that was it. Pronounced *Joff*-rey.

"Hello," she said, closing the notebook and sliding it into her pocket. "Would you like to join me?"

The invitation seemed to take him by surprise. But he shrugged, sat down, and lit a cigarette, tossing the pack on the table without offering her one. His bad manners pissed her off enough to make her pluck out one of his American Spirits and light it without a word. The expression on his face was a mixture of surliness and curiosity.

"You're the cop who was asking about Danny."

"That's right. I was hoping to talk to you about him."

"You're a friend of his old lady."

"His old lady," she said, "is thirty-four."

One corner of his mouth curled up. "Fossilized."

"Oh, yeah? How old are you?"

He smiled, exhaling smoke through his teeth so it dispersed in a wide nimbus. She got the feeling he'd practiced it. Everyone needs a talent.

"Twenty-seven," he said.

"Where'd you grow up?"

"Brooklyn Heights."

"Topher tells me you're a curator at the museum. Did you go to school for that?"

"Majored in art history at Bard."

"Is that where you met Topher?"

He shook his head. He was starting to look annoyed. "I thought you wanted to know about Danny."

"Just being polite. But we can cut to the chase. I hear you and Danny were hanging out a lot."

"Not a lot," he said. "Some."

"Talking about art, that sort of thing. Is that right?"

"Yeah," he said. "So what?"

"I want to know what was going on in Danny's life in the weeks before he died. If you were spending time with him, maybe you can help."

Geoffrey took another long drag on his cigarette, held it in like it was smoke from a bong, finally exhaled. A snake tattoo wended its way around his right forearm. "What do you want to know?"

"Did Danny ever mention he was looking for his mother?"

She watched as he thought about it. She got the idea that he wasn't contemplating the question so much as whether he wanted to answer it in the first place.

"Yeah," he said.

"Did he get very far?"

Geoffrey shrugged. "He asked around. Seemed like he hit a dead end. But the kid wanted to know where he came from."

"Can't blame him."

He took another long drag, exhaled. "I told him fuck it, just get out of town and live your life and don't look back. But I guess he needed—I don't know. Validation or whatever."

"Do you know if there was anybody he was having problems with? Anybody he was scared of?"

Geoffrey shrugged. "Nothing too serious."

"How about you let me be the judge of what's serious?"

Another shrug. "He and some guy got into it one time, that's all."

"Who?"

"He didn't say. Danny could be pretty closemouthed sometimes."

"When did this happen?"

"Couple months ago."

"And you have no idea what the fight was about?"

"I guess the guy just jumped him. I told Danny he ought to get himself some protection."

"You mean a gun?"

"No," he said, rolling his eyes, "I mean a box of rubbers. If the guy came back, he could throw them at him."

"And do you have any idea what he might have been doing up at the Fish Pond the night he died?"

Geoffrey leaned back in his chair and gazed at her, eyes wide behind the geometric glasses. "No idea at all," he said.

Ginny returned his stare, certain of two things. The man wasn't nearly as charming as he thought he was. And he was lying.

onya's voice came through Ginny's cell phone, harried and distracted. The Meeks twins had strep throat, and she'd spent the day simultaneously tending to their demands and chasing the other two healthy but bored children around the house.

Ginny offered to pick up a pizza for dinner, but Sonya reminded her that it was Pete's birthday; even though she was in no mood to celebrate, he deserved a home-cooked meal. His parents were coming over, along with Monique, who'd been attending family events for so long Sonya didn't have the heart to snub her. She was making chicken à la king, another recipe from the Danny-hated-it cookbook.

"Hey, could you—," Sonya began, then cut herself off.

"Could I what?"

"Nothing."

"Come on," Ginny prodded. "What?"

"I was going to ask if you could pick up the cake. But it's no big deal. I'll do it."

"Meaning you ordered it from Molly's."

"I usually make it from scratch, but—"

"I'll get it."

"Don't worry about it. I can skip down there as soon as—"

"For chrissake, Sonya, I'll get it. I'm a big girl. Do you need me to pick up anything else?"

"Just some snowflake rolls," she said. "Oh, and I almost forgot. Your Aunt Lisette called. She thinks you're avoiding her."

"Imagine that."

"And one other thing. Your car's over at Marty Mangino's

place out on State Road. Pete thought there might be some stuff in there you'd want."

"Doubtful. But I appreciate it."

"Maybe you can go over and check it out today," Sonya said. "I don't think Marty's got a lot of space in his lot."

Ginny said she would, pulling out of her parking spot in front of Café des Artistes and heading out of town. It was a good thing there wasn't any traffic—not that there was ever much traffic in the first place—because she was only half concentrating on the road. The rest of her brain was replaying the brief conversation with Geoffrey, which had ended when Topher walked into the café carrying a case of flavored syrups. Geoffrey had leaped up and kissed him long on the lips, an act that Ginny suspected was designed to make her uncomfortable, and didn't.

Every instinct was telling her that Geoffrey knew more about Danny's last hours than he was willing to admit. Back when she was an actual cop, she could have picked him up for questioning, plunked him down in an interrogation room, and used the usual bag of tricks to convince him to talk: deception, persuasion, threats of prosecution for hindering the investigation. But how was she going to get him to spill his guts?

She pulled into the garage's lot, negotiating the truck among the cars parked in various states of repair. There was no one in the office; she found the owner in one of the two service bays, examining the underside of a PT Cruiser. She introduced herself, and he asked after her father; apparently, Lavoie's had done a nice job on his grandma's funeral once upon a time.

"Too bad about your car," he said.

"Thanks," she said. "Guess I should've taken it behind the barn and shot it a while ago."

"Nah. She probably had another fifty thousand miles on her. Don't make 'em like they used to."

She followed him into the other bay. It didn't have a lift; there were two legs sticking out from beneath her car. Considering that it had gone over a fence and into the river, it was in surprisingly good shape.

"Wow," she said. "Can you actually fix it?"

"Nah," he said again. "She's a goner."

"Then what are you—"

"Hope you don't mind," Marty Mangino said. "Since she's on her way to the boneyard, I let Stu here tinker with her." He pointed to the legs, clad in dirty jeans and work boots. "He's an apprentice mechanic from the trade school. I wouldn't let him get his hands on somethin' belongs to a customer."

"Aw, come on," said a voice from under the car. Marty mouthed the word "imbecile."

"Sure," Ginny said, surveying the sad remains of the only car she'd ever owned. "I guess it doesn't matter."

Marty left her alone, in the company of the totaled car and the unseen imbecile. She opened the door, and a trickle of water came out. There really wasn't anything to salvage; the sodden box of Kleenex and ruined cassette tapes could go the way of all flesh.

"Hey," said the disembodied voice. "You got any enemies?"

"Um . . . excuse me?"

The apprentice rolled himself out from under the Chrysler. He looked to be all of sixteen, face covered in black grease and angry red acne.

"Somebody out there don't like you."

"I know," she said. "It was really lousy luck."

"Luck ain't got nothin' to do with it," he said. "Somebody cut your brake line."

The pizza-faced apprentice wasn't such an imbecile, after all. He'd caught what many people would have missed—a jagged slash in the brake line that was nonetheless too clean and perfect to be accidental.

"Ask me," he said after he'd had her go under the car to see for herself, "somebody wanted to make it look like a rock did it or somethin'. But weren't no rock." His boss took a look for himself; though it clearly pained him to admit it, the kid was right.

"Who'd know how to do something like that?" she asked them. "Would it have to be a trained mechanic?"

Marty shrugged. "Seems to me any fool knows where the brake line is."

"I don't," she said.

"That don't count," Marty said. "You're a lady."

It wasn't something she'd been accused of before, but she was too distracted to argue with him. "How long would it have taken from the time the line was cut until the brakes went?"

The kid opened his mouth to answer, but Marty cut him off. He'd been shown up enough for one day. "Maybe twelve hours, if she was leaking out real slow. Didn't you notice you were losing fluid?"

"No," she said. "It was pouring rain. And besides, it was always leaking something or other."

"Indicator light didn't go on?"

Jesus, she thought, *nothing like blaming the victim.* "It was a goddamn wreck. Warning lights went on and off like a Christmas tree. It always ran just fine, anyway."

The older mechanic made a harrumphing noise, a single grunt that contained a universe of censure. The kid echoed it, clearly desperate to get into his good graces.

"I hope," Marty said, "you're gonna take better care of that truck."

The fact that someone had tried to kill her seemed to have escaped them both. She thanked them—for what, she wasn't entirely sure—and asked them to tow the car to the construction company lot. Now it wasn't just a wreck; it was evidence of attempted murder.

She drove back to Sonya's, unconsciously holding her breath every time she stepped on the brakes. What the hell was going on? If the crash had really been no accident—and Abbott and Costello back there seemed positive it wasn't—there was only one possible reason why someone would want her dead. Whoever had tampered with her car must be trying to stop her from investigating Danny's murder. It had to be; unless, of course, someone she'd wronged in high school had been nursing a grudge for fifteen years, biding their time until she happened back for a visit so they could wreak their revenge. Ha, ha.

Maybe she was an idiot, but it had never even occurred to her that the crash had been anything but an accident. And it wasn't just that her Chrysler was a wreck. She'd been working cases for years, and no one had ever come after her before. New York's criminals did plenty of bad things, but the premeditated murder of an investigating officer was practically unheard-of. She was used to facing danger on the street. But some perp tampering with her car? You had to be kidding.

If the mechanic was right that the brake line had been cut about twelve hours before, that meant it had been done overnight, while the car was parked in front of Sonya's house. It made sense: theirs was a short, dead-end street, with only a few houses on one side and a sheer banking on the other. If Ginny had wanted to sabotage someone's brakes, she couldn't have picked a better place. If you knew what you were doing, you could probably be in and out in two minutes, and no one the wiser.

Son of a bitch. She'd spent over a decade on the streets of New York without getting seriously hurt, and she hadn't been back in her hometown for a week before nearly getting killed.

Not for the first time, she longed for her service revolver. Her gun was two hundred miles away—but she was damn well going to start carrying Danny's. She had no way of printing it, any-way—not that the gun was even connected to any crime—and at the moment protecting herself seemed a hell of a lot more important.

She drove over the overpass, took a right, parked the truck in front of Molly's. Her pulse was racing, her flannel shirt getting wet at the armpits. Nerves. Understandable, since she'd just found out that somebody wanted her dead.

That had to be it, didn't it? If she was more anxious about the prospect of facing Jimmy Griffin than getting offed, she was well and truly a moron.

Better not think about it.

She walked into the store; the bell jangling over her head felt less like a welcome than a taunt. For half a second she held out hope that he might not be there—might be out servicing his sta-ble of menopausal honeys—but she should have known better. She didn't deserve that kind of luck.

There he was, wearing that idiotic T-shirt with the bright yel-low smiley face. But the expression above his neck wasn't nearly as jolly: he seemed as uncomfortable as she was. There, at least, was some satisfaction.

"What can I get you?"

A bus ticket to Port Authority, she thought.

"Pete's birthday cake."

"Right." He pulled a chocolate-frosted confection out of the case and laid it on the counter for her inspection. Shockingly, it said HAPPY BIRTHDAY PETE. Was he waiting for her to applaud?

"Looks fine," she said. He boxed it up, wrapping it in twine from a dispenser dangling above his head. "Oh, and Sonya wants some snowflake rolls."

"How many?"

She shrugged. "I don't know. Half dozen, I guess."

"How many people's she feeding?"

"Six."

"Take a dozen," he said. "Nobody eats just one." She reached for her wallet, but he waved her off. "Tell Pete happy birthday."

"You don't have to do that."

"That's what friends do," he said.

He counted the rolls into a waxed paper bag and laid it on top of the cake box. She picked the items up, and he came around the counter to get the door for her. He reached for the handle, then paused.

"You want a dip for the road?" She stared at him, trying to decipher the words. "Upside-down cupcakes. You know. With the frosting all over."

"Oh, right. I forgot."

"Raspberry-coconut ones didn't move today," he said. "And you look kind of pale."

"I guess I forgot to eat," she said. "It's been a hell of a day."

"Yeah?"

"Yeah."

He took that for an assent—though why he was suddenly being nice to her, she had no idea. He lifted the box out of her hands and set it back down on the counter, then went around and fished a pair of cupcakes out of the case. "Here," he said as he put them into a bag. "I'm about to close up, anyway."

He extended the bag. She took it. Then he grabbed her and kissed her, and two perfectly good cupcakes lay forgotten on the floor.

21

She got to Sonya's just in time for dinner—half-witted, messy-haired, sans birthday cake. Her back, which had been aching since the crash, had taken a marked turn for the worse. It had been a long time since Ginny had sex on an eighty-pound sack of flour, and she wasn't a kid anymore.

Sonya didn't say a word. One look at Ginny told her exactly what had transpired, but this time she couldn't bring herself to criticize. After all, she was the one who'd asked her to stop at Molly's—had sent the proverbial rummy to the liquor store. She couldn't help but feel partly responsible. She'd just have to stick some candles in a Freihofer's coffee ring and endure her mother-in-law's disapproval.

Ginny had forgotten about the cake entirely—never mind the snowflake rolls. She was too busy kicking herself, both mentally and with toe to ankle under the table. She had no idea what postadolescent *whatever* was being played out between her and Jimmy, but she knew one thing for sure: they couldn't be alone together five minutes without jumping each other. Which meant that they shouldn't be alone together at all.

"So I told him," Pete's mother was saying, "go ahead and ask for top dollar. You know they're just going to come back and lowball you. Those people always do."

Sonya had a beleaguered look on her face, her standard-issue expression when Rhonda's lips were moving. "It's not right to generalize," she said. "Isn't that true, Ginny?"

Her friend clearly needed a wingman; Ginny forced herself back into the conversation. "What people are we talking about?"

Mrs. Markowicz blinked at her, owl eyes enlarged by the matronly frames of light pink plastic. "Jews," she said. "New York Jews. A pair of them bid on the Bernardos' place next door. They want it to be a *weekend* house. Can you imagine? Owning that great big house and only living there on the *weekends*? What is this town coming to?"

Sonya looked like she was getting a migraine. Pete and his father looked like they weren't listening, which was absolutely true.

"You know," Ginny said, "lots of people in New York have weekend houses. It's kind of a thing down there, if you have the money."

She'd meant to mollify the woman. It didn't work.

"Well, who do they think they are?" Rhonda demanded. "Coming here and throwing their city money around like this isn't a place where people *live*. And have you seen some of those characters down on Main Street? In my day you'd give them a smack and tell them to get a haircut and that's that."

Pete and his father kept eating. Sonya rubbed at her temples, while Monique sat there with a vacuous smile on her face. Ginny was on her own.

"Just so I understand," she said. "You don't like them because they're from the city? Or because they have money? Or—because some of them are Jewish?"

An uneasy silence filled the room. Then Monique piped up. "Jesus loves everyone," she said. "Even them that murdered him."

Sonya stood up like a shot. "Who wants more chicken?"

Pete's father held out his plate, accepting the third helping without a word. Sonya had just sat down when the doorbell rang; she leaped back up like a prisoner under reprieve.

It was Jimmy, bearing the cake and the bag of rolls. Ginny stared down at her plate, where the chicken and sauce and egg noodles lurked in a cold yellow mound beside a limp pile of tomato salad. She hadn't had much of an appetite.

"Sorry this is late," he said. "When Ginny came to pick it up, I wasn't finished decorating it. Told her I'd drop it off."

It was, of course, a total lie—and much less embarrassing than the truth, which was that after they'd screwed half-clothed on the very spot where they deflowered each other all those years ago, Ginny had fled as fast as she could pull up her Levi's.

She made herself look up at him, to listen to what he was saying, to avoid thinking about what that mouth had been doing to her less than an hour ago. "Thanks," she said.

"And what have you got there in the bag?" Rhonda asked, plucking it from his grasp. "Snowflake rolls! My favorite! Aren't you *sweet*! Are you hungry? You must be hungry. A man's always hungry after a long day's work. Sit down, Jimmy. Have some dinner. Sonya, set another place. It's the least you can do after he brought the cake over special. Aren't you sweet! Now, sit down and have some chicken à la king. It needs salt and the noodles are a teensy bit overcooked, but you won't mind. A man never notices. Ooh, these rolls are so flaky. Petey, pass the butter dish, will you? Now, Jimmy, what do you want to drink? A Coke? Sonya, get Jimmy a nice cold Coke."

He tried to beg off—even Ginny had to admit it was a valiant effort—but in the end he gave in. She couldn't blame him: Rhonda Markowicz was a force of nature, the kind they show leveling trailer parks on the evening news.

Sonya set him a place, and Monique was sent to retrieve an extra chair, and the next thing Ginny knew she was having dinner with Jimmy Griffin. Sonya, ever the diplomat, steered the conversation toward the innocuous: Pete's latest building project, Jimmy's new pastries, Monique's classes at State. At one point Rhonda tossed some conversational grenades—noting that a nice boy like Jimmy shouldn't still be single, and wasn't it cute to see him and Ginny back together just like old times—but Sonya threw herself on them faster than her mother-in-law could pull the pins. For the millionth time Ginny pondered the fact that she loved Sonya more than anyone in the world.

The cake turned out to be fantastic, even better than Ginny had remembered. Jimmy accepted the compliment—it was the only thing she said directly to him the whole night—and mumbled something about how he'd upgraded to a finer baking chocolate than his parents had used. The seven of them devoured it, leaving nothing but crumbs and frosting on a gold paper doily. Ginny had to give him credit: it was hard enough to be really good at even one thing in this life, and Jimmy Griffin was expert in at least two.

She listened to him making small talk with their tablemates—about the weather, the high school football team, the criminal price of gasoline. She paid attention to the way he spoke, tried to have something approaching an impartial opinion of him, but it was impossible; she'd met him too early and known him too long. There was no way even to summon up the memory of first impressions.

Back then, if someone had asked her why she was so nuts about him, she would have said he was smart and hunky and nice and funny. He definitely hadn't lost his looks, and he was smart enough to run a thriving business. But his niceness was an open question, and lately when she was around him, laughing was the last thing on her mind.

Pete's father was scraping the frosting off his plate when his beeper went off. Although retired from the buildings and grounds department over at Williams College, he was still a volunteer fireman. He got up and used the kitchen phone, an old-fashioned affair with a long curly cord.

"I gotta go," he said, shrugging into his windbreaker. "Good dinner, Sonya."

Ginny rose from the table, desperate for the party to break up before Rhonda said something too obnoxious for Sonya to deflect. "What's up?"

"Car accident over on Kemp. I gotta go direct traffic. Guess Rolly's short-handed."

"You want some help?" Ginny asked.

He looked at her like she'd sprouted a third limb out of her back. Then he shrugged and said, "Guess you're qualified. What the hey?"

They left the others with open mouths, their expressions ranging from annoyed (Rhonda) to amused (Jimmy). No sooner were they out the door than Mr. Markowicz—Pete Senior—confessed that his eyes weren't so great at night, so maybe Ginny could drive. They took Danny's truck for the mile-long trip, passing Ginny and Sonya's elementary school before reaching the site of the accident: the hairpin turn where Kemp Avenue met Bradley Street, right outside the entrance to the Fish Pond.

Two police cruisers and an ambulance were already there, red and white flashers lighting up the dark night. Cars were lined up, trapped at the blocked road because the P.D. hadn't had the manpower to set up a detour. Ginny parked on the shoulder, and they hiked downhill toward the accident scene. As they got closer, she saw the car—a silver Dodge minivan that had gone off the road and whacked a utility pole, which had toppled over into the middle of the street. The fallen power line was sparking, the streetlights were out, and all the houses nearby were pitch-black.

"Helluva mess," said Pete Senior.

The minivan's air bags had deployed, and although its front end was badly mangled, it looked like the passenger cabin had held. The driver seemed to have gotten out under her own power: she was sitting in the ambulance, blood trickling down her face but apparently coherent.

"He came out of nowhere," she was saying. "I looked up and

there he was—just lying in the road. Just *lying* there. But I didn't hit him. I *tried* not to hit him. You don't think I hit him, do you?"

Ginny walked up farther, giving the power line a wide berth. In the middle of the road was a white sheet, covering what was unmistakably a human body.

No one was around—no one who seemed to be in authority, anyway—so she raised the sheet. She'd expected to see the broken body of an accident victim. But she hadn't expected to see someone she knew.

22

Ginny went back to the ambulance and eavesdropped while the police officer took the driver's statement. She'd been on her way home from hockey practice in Williamstown, she said, toting three rowdy boys and a vanful of pads and sticks. She'd just dropped off a fourth boy and was heading down Kemp Avenue hill, about to turn the corner onto Bradley Street, when she suddenly saw a person lying in the middle of the road. She slammed on the brakes, jerked the wheel to the right, and the next thing she knew, some nice man was helping her get out of her smashed-up car and there was blood all over her new fall coat.

The body still lay beneath the sheet, ten feet in front of where the van had gone off the road. Ginny stopped lurking by the ambulance; the driver just kept saying the same thing over and over. And from what she could divine, the woman was telling the truth. By the time she and her van of aspiring Wayne Gretzkys had come down the hill, the victim was already dead.

Ginny shined Danny's flashlight around the body, still wait-ing for someone in command to come and tell her to get lost. But no one did; Rolly was nowhere to be found, and the cops and firemen had their hands full with the traffic and the wrecker and the banged-up kids. The power company had arrived, and a man in a hard hat was simultaneously shaking his head at the damage and salivating over his impending overtime; at least he'd gotten the line to stop sparking, though the outage now ex-tended to every house in sight.

On the asphalt, a few feet away from the sheet-covered corpse, was a dark red splotch: blood. There was another nearby, and another, and another, headed away from the van and toward the lake. Ginny followed them—up the driveway and into the parking lot, where they ended in a crimson pool. It was diffuse, smudged, as though someone had lain there and wallowed in it. At one end of the blood pool was a pair of rectangular eye-glasses, one lens shattered; at the other was a human tooth.

Whatever had happened to the victim happened here, in the lake's pitch-black parking lot. Somehow, despite the blood loss and the pain, he'd managed to crawl down the driveway and halfway across the road. He must have been desperate for help. And died waiting.

Parked in a corner of the lot, not far from where she'd searched Danny's truck, was a new Cooper Mini. She knew she ought to leave it alone, but she couldn't stand to let Rolly screw up another crime scene. He'd already bungled the investigation into Danny's death—and cost poor Jack O'Brien his life. She'd just check it out, not disturb anything. What could it hurt?

She donned a pair of gloves and tried the door; it was open. Flicking on the overhead light, she made a cursory look through the car. The registration in the glove compartment listed the owner as Geoffrey Dobson.

So that was his last name.

She searched the car's interior, then popped the trunk. It was a tiny space, and her search didn't take long, but it garnered a lawbreaker's bonanza: secreted in spots clever but not ingenious were a roll of hundred-dollar bills; a brand-new semiautomatic handgun; colorful sheets of what Ginny assumed was LSD; and small glassine bags of what law enforcement types liked to call a suspicious white powder. Maybe coke, maybe crack—maybe crystal meth.

She left everything where she found it. A sneaky search was one thing, but she could hardly justify tampering with evidence.

She went back to Geoffrey's body, still unattended. She lifted the sheet and took a closer look, touching nothing. His body was lying on its side, right leg twisted at an odd angle. He'd been wearing black jeans, and there was a sandy line at midthigh. As a patrol officer, Ginny had been at the scene of enough car-versus-pedestrian accidents to recognize the classic injury: she'd bet her confiscated shield he'd been hit by a vehicle, a high one with a dirty bumper. She thought of the blood pool she'd found in the parking lot, the tooth, and the shattered glasses. With all those injuries he'd somehow managed to crawl back to the road. He must have been in agony.

"What in the hell do you think you're doing?" She let the sheet drop and turned to face Chief Rolly, who seemed more perplexed than annoyed. "Hey, Angie, it's you," he said with a crooked smile and a hard whack on her aching shoulder. "Guess you New York City police just can't resist a dead guy, huh?"

She took a step toward him. The odor of beer was faint but distinctive. "I came to help direct traffic."

"Always gotta be in on the action, eh?" He mimed a one-two punch, then another. Then he looked down at the body, not making a move to lift the sheet. "Guess the poor bugger never learned to look both ways before he crossed the road."

She cocked her head toward the lake. "He didn't get hit

here," she said. "It happened in the parking lot. I think he made it down here on his own power before he died."

He stared at her, like he was waiting for the punch line. When he didn't get one, he asked, "And how would you know that?"

"Blood trail leads that way. And his car's parked up there."

Rolly scratched his head, perfect comb-over flopping like a hair-sprayed trout. "Christ Jesus. You want to tell me who his next of kin is, too, while you're at it?"

"I have no idea. But I did recognize him. His name is Geoffrey Dobson—he's a curator at the museum. Buddies with the guy who owns Café des Artistes down on Marshall."

"Out-of-towner."

"Yeah."

Rolly seemed relieved, an instinct Ginny could understand. He wasn't going to have to knock on some local family's door and tell them their son was dead. After all, it had only been two weeks since he knocked on Sonya's.

A second ambulance showed up, and Geoffrey's body was loaded inside. Ginny donned an orange vest and made good on her offer to direct cars around the detour, something she'd never done before, the NYPD having its own dedicated traffic bureau. It was late, nearing midnight, and there weren't many cars; this was a residential neighborhood.

As she watched a pair of taillights disappear into the dark, she thought back on everything that had happened in the past twenty-four hours. First finding out that Danny had been looking for his mother, then learning that someone had tampered with her brakes. She distinctly recalled standing in Jimmy's store and telling him she'd had a hell of a day—and that was before they'd screwed like rabbits in the back room and she'd found Geoffrey's mangled body in the middle of Kemp Avenue.

Geoffrey Dobson. It had only been a few hours ago that she

sat across from him in the café, convinced he was lying about his ignorance of Danny's last hours. Now he was dead.

Was it because he'd talked to her? That seemed far-fetched—but if someone was really willing to kill *her* to keep her from investigating Danny's murder, then anything was possible. Maybe Geoffrey had known something—maybe even everything—and the killer had to silence him before he talked.

Then there was the stash she'd found in Geoffrey's car—a cornucopia of sins that practically advertised membership in the drug dealers' credit union. Although she'd joined the force after the height of New York's crack epidemic, she'd still seen plenty of dealers killed in turf wars. But in her hometown? The idea seemed absurd. Until she remembered the scene in the bar and the sight of Belinda Cooper and her sad, dirty children—and it didn't seem so ridiculous, after all.

The story missed the deadline for the local paper. But it was all over the radio, the announcer's voice heavy with hyphens: out-of-towner dies in hit-and-run. Never mind that Geoffrey had been working at the museum for nearly a year and his car had Massachusetts plates; this was a town where having a grandparent born outside the county made you fresh blood.

It didn't help, of course, that the circumstances of Geoffrey's death made him something considerably less than a martyr. By the time the breakfast crowd had trickled out of the Golden Skillet, everyone in town knew that the victim's car had been found to contain a gun and more drugs than the local CVS.

Ginny waited for the news announcer to mention the wad of cash, but no one seemed to have heard about it. She was confused, but only briefly: that very same day, Chief Rolly hired Pete to renovate his hunting lodge.

She'd been on the verge of going in to talk to him about her sabotaged car, on the principle that even an incompetent cop was better than none at all. But now he was incompetent *and* corrupt; she decided she'd just as soon have him as far away from the case as possible.

She could picture Rolly searching the car, finding the drugs and the gun and the cash, drool running down his jowly chin as he realized he was holding half a year's salary. She imagined him rationalizing that Geoffrey was nothing but a drug dealer, not even a homegrown one at that, and what use was all that money going to do shut up in some evidence locker? She saw him slipping the wad of bills into his coat pocket, next to the Tootsie Rolls and the Tums, and marking it a victory for justice.

Someone sworn to uphold the law, twisting it for his own gain. As far as she was concerned, that made him the lowest of the low.

It was with a nauseating start that she realized that this was exactly how her colleagues saw her: a cop on the take. And she had no idea how she was going to clear her name.

Ginny swiped the rain off her jacket, shook her head like a wet dog. The weather hadn't been improving, and the leaf-peeping season was getting blown to hell.

She walked into the Skillet and surveyed the crowd, zeroing in on her lunch date. Coach Hank was sitting in a narrow two-person booth, nursing a can of Sprite. He stood up when he saw her approaching the table, because that was the way he'd been raised.

"Lavoie," he said. "Glad to see you're not drowned."

"You heard about that, huh?"

"Front page of the *Transcript*," he said. "Hard to miss."

She took a seat opposite, the hard Formica booth a medieval torture device for her aching coccyx. "Thanks for meeting me," she said.

He nodded his *You're welcome*. "I figured you wanted to talk about Danny."

"Yeah." She shifted, trying for a more comfortable position. "Hey, I met your little girls at Sonya's. Pretty gorgeous pair."

He rolled his eyes in mock horror. "God help me when they're sixteen."

"Maybe they'll be angels. Just like me."

He let that one pass. "You know we've got three older girls, too. The Good Lord's idea of a joke."

"Huh?"

"Three kids would've been plenty, but I talked my wife into trying for a son, male chauvinist pig that I am. Wound up with twin daughters." He smiled at the memory. "And you want to hear the kicker? We only have one bathroom."

"Wow."

He looked at his watch. "Do you mind if we go ahead and order? I gotta be back for practice in an hour."

Ginny consulted the menu, flirted with the idea of ordering a salad that would doubtless turn out to be a gummy tomato slice on iceberg, and wound up asking for another Skillet Burger. She waited for Coach Hank to reprove her, until he ordered the same.

"Okay to eat it," he said to her raised eyebrow, "long as you burn it."

"Amen."

He popped open his second Sprite and took a long drink. "So what can I tell you?"

She leaned forward, hoping to relieve the pressure on her tailbone. "Well . . . did you get the idea that Danny was in any sort of trouble?"

The coach thought about it, running a hand through a thick shock of graying blond hair. He was definitely showing his age—his face had the lines of a fair-skinned person who spent too much time in the sun—but he was still a handsome guy. When she was in school, though, he'd been movie-star gorgeous: half the girls' running team started wearing their uniform tops a size too tight, just in the hopes he'd notice.

"You gotta remember," he said, "I hadn't seen much of him since graduation. It wasn't like he was still on the team. But I gotta say, the last couple times I saw him, he didn't seem like himself."

"How so?"

"Can't put my finger on it. It was more like, you know how sometimes kids are different with one set of friends than another? Like they can be real polite around some people and little smart alecks around some others?"

"You saying you think Danny was getting in with the wrong crowd?"

"Yeah, maybe. And I don't want to come off like some old fogy. It wasn't just that he needed a shave. It was more like an attitude shift, you know? Like he was always on the straight and narrow, and suddenly it was like, screw the world."

She looked him in the eye. "Did you ever think he might have gotten mixed up with drugs?"

"It crossed my mind. Town isn't the same place you and I grew up in, believe you me." A shadow crossed his face, like the subject was hitting close to home. She wondered whether he was thinking of a student—or one of those golden-haired daughters. "But I don't know for sure," he continued. "I never caught him stoned, nothing like that."

"Did he ever seem scared to you?"

The question seemed to surprise him. "Scared? Danny? Nah. Why would you ask?"

"Just standard."

"Well, there *was* one thing. I didn't think anything of it at the time."

"What happened?"

"The last time I saw Danny was a Sunday afternoon—a few days before he died. The girls wanted subs, so I scooted down to Angelina's to pick them up, and I saw Danny standing by his truck in the parking lot by the overpass, looking like he'd just lost his best friend. So I pulled over, and it turned out somebody'd let the air out of all four of his tires while he was working at the Skillet. I asked him why didn't he get his folks to pick him up, but he said he didn't want to bother them. I offered him a ride, but he said he was gonna call one of his buddies who had an air pump."

"And he didn't say who he thought might have done it?"

Coach Hank shook his head. "He downplayed the whole thing, said it must be some kids having a joke, but naturally, he was mad as hell. Like I said, I didn't think anything of it till just now."

"What about his social life? Was he dating anybody besides Monique St. Cyr?"

"I thought the two of them were practically engaged."

"I was just wondering. Anything else?"

The coach seemed to debate something in his head, then come to a conclusion. "Well," he said, "it probably doesn't matter, but a while before he died he did ask me something out of the blue."

"What's that?"

He paused to wave at the two men who were being seated at a nearby table: Father LeGrand and Mr. Dulaine, bank president and church deacon. Ginny had gone to school with his kids, whom she recalled as the sort of uptight prigs who ratted when the teacher forgot to assign the homework.

The two men hung their overcoats on poles between the booths and stopped by to shake hands. Mr. Dulaine—his first name, she now recalled, was Arthur—praised one of Hank's daughters for winning an ice-skating medal. Still holding his hand in hers, Father LeGrand told Ginny he hoped to see her in church on Sunday.

"It was good of you to attend Jack O'Brien's burial," Father LeGrand said.

"It was good of you to bury him," she said, and meant it. "I thought suicides couldn't have a church funeral."

Arthur Dulaine opened his mouth to say something, then apparently thought better of it.

"Jack was a very sick man," the priest replied. "As I saw it, he wasn't capable of making any rational decisions, least of all to end his own life. His illness killed him."

"That's one way of looking at it," Dulaine said. His voice was even, but his jaw was clenched.

"The man's only sin was refusing help," said Father LeGrand.

"What about the sin he was in jail for?" Dulaine asked through a tight-lipped smile. "What about the Sixth Commandment? Thou shalt not kill?"

"Danny's own mother doesn't think Jack was guilty," the priest said. "That's good enough for me."

They said their good-byes and sat down at their own table. Ginny's eyes widened. "Tough customer," she said.

Coach Hank shot a glance in Dulaine's direction, then leaned toward Ginny. "Thanks to him," he said in a lowered voice, "they took *Macbeth* out of the high school library."

"*Macbeth?*" she whispered back. "What for?"

He rolled his eyes, shook his head, and said, "Witches."

"*No.*"

"And don't get me started on the abstinence-only health class." He looked at his watch again. "Sorry. Where were we?"

"You said Danny asked you something out of the blue."

"Right. He wanted to know if I remembered anything about his mother."

"You knew Paula?"

"Not really. I started coaching the year she dropped out, and she wasn't the type to play sports. But she got into plenty of trouble, so all the teachers knew who she was."

The food came then, and Coach Hank further endeared himself to Ginny by giving her first dibs on the ketchup.

"So what did you tell him?" she asked after downing a hefty bite.

"Well," he said, "first off, I asked him why he didn't just talk to his parents about it."

She dunked two fries and popped them into her mouth. "And?"

"He was afraid it'd upset his mom. Made sense to me. Personally, I always wondered why they told him the truth about his birth mother."

"Sonya struggled with it," she said. "But she always figured Paula'd come home someday. She didn't want it to be some awful shock. When Danny was old enough, she even gave him the letter Paula sent after she took off. So what did you say to him?"

"There wasn't much I could tell him. Just gave him some names of folks she used to hang around with, that's all."

"Can you remember who?"

"Phil McCoy, works over at the welfare office. Andy Draco—he tends bar down at the Legion. Steve Pecor. Not sure he does much of anything. He's on disability, I think."

"All men."

"I don't recall that Paula Libanski had any girlfriends. But like I said, I didn't know her."

"Was there anybody else?"

He thought about it. "Just those three," he said. "Oh, yeah. And Jimmy Griffin."

The Skillet Burger, so tasty on the way down, threatened to come right back up. But she managed to finish the meal without puking in Coach Hank's lap, thank him for his help, and make it back to her truck in the driving rain.

Jimmy? Messing around with Paula Libanski? It didn't seem possible. For one thing, the logistics didn't make sense. Paula left town when she was nineteen; she and Sonya and Jimmy were all fifteen. As far as she knew, Paula had always gone for older guys. Would she really rob the cradle with the boyfriend of her sister's best friend?

She remembered overhearing an argument between Sonya's parents shortly after Paula had left town; even at fifteen and as in love with melodrama as any adolescent, she'd been glad Sonya was out of earshot. Heaped on top of her sister's abandonment, the conversation would have laid her flat.

It's just as well she's gone, her father had said. *That girl poisons everything she touches.*

Don't say that, his wife had replied. *She's your daughter, for God's sake.*

God wants nothing to do with her, and you know it.
Ronnie!
It's as though she can't stand it if something's good and pure and clean.
She's got to go and ruin it, like a normal person needs to scratch an itch.

So would she have gone after Jimmy? Of course she would, if she damn well felt like it. But would Jimmy have given in? She never would have even considered such a thing; she'd always thought of him as the most morally upright person she knew, after Sonya. Now that she knew he was taking his love to town with every lonely divorcée in the zip code, though, she wasn't so sure.

She drove down Main Street and around the corner. She slowed down when she passed Café des Artistes and saw a sign on the door: CLOSED DUE TO DEATH IN THE FAMILY. She took another right, then another, and before she knew it she'd parked the car behind the back entrance to Molly's. She flung open the screen door, scaring the living hell out of a pimply-faced kid bent over a trayful of half-frosted brownies. She stalked past him and went through the connecting door that led behind the counter.

"Did you screw Paula Libanski?"

Jimmy turned to her, mouth agape. There were similar expressions on the faces of two little girls who were counting out quarters to pay for cookies shaped like vampire bats.

He put the coins in the cash drawer and slammed it shut, then handed each girl her cookie, carefully cradled in waxed paper. Without a word, just a pair of cautious glances at the crazy-scary lady, they went out to the sidewalk where one of their mothers was waiting.

Jimmy turned toward her slowly. "What did you just ask me?"

"You heard me."

"Are you out of your mind?"

"Possibly. Just answer the question."

"It doesn't even deserve an answer." He crouched down and pushed the cookie tray back into its perch inside the display case. "What would make you come barreling in here to ask me *that*?"

She bit her bottom lip. "It's a long story."

"Well, make it short."

"You know I'm trying to find out what happened to Danny. It turns out right before he died he was trying to track down his mom."

He lifted both hands palm-upward; she couldn't tell whether he was more angry or confused. "And what does that have to do with me?"

"Coach Hank told me Danny went to him wanting to know about Paula. He gave him some names of guys she used to hang out with."

"And one of them was me?" She nodded. He stared at her, long and hard. "Holy shit," he said. "You're jealous."

"No, I'm not."

"Oh. So then you probably already went running over to where those *other* guys work, yelling like a crazy person. *Right?*" She chose that moment to take an intense interest in the display of refrigerated custard puffs. "I didn't think so."

She turned back to face him. "Would you please just tell me the truth?"

"What difference does it make? It's not like you ever really loved me."

There was something petulant in his voice; he sounded all of fifteen years old.

"Of course I did," she said. He looked away. "Come on, Jimmy. You know I did."

"I wanted to have a life with you—get married, the whole thing. But you got rid of the both of us like we were nothing."

"The both of who?"

His look said she was profoundly dense. "Me and the baby."

"Son of a bitch, Jimmy. I am *not* going to have this conversation with you again."

"What do you mean *again*? We never had it in the first place. You ran off so fast I couldn't tell which way was up."

She squeezed her eyes closed, pressed her fists to her forehead. "I did *not* come in here to talk about us."

"No," he said, "you came in here to ask me if I cheated on you with the town whore. Imagine my delight."

"Well, did you?"

He slammed a hand on the counter, making the bread loaves leap in unison. "If you think you have the right to ask me that, you're out of your mind. But just for the record, just so you don't make yourself sleep better at night by deciding the father of your child was screwing around on you—no, I was damn well not messing with Paula. I don't know what Hank thinks he remembers, but the only time I was even alone with her for five minutes was when she was working here."

"*Working* here?"

"Her folks asked my folks to give her a job. Guess they thought getting up at four in the morning to make crescent rolls would put her on the path to righteousness. She lasted three days."

"Oh."

"Yeah," Jimmy said, voice dripping with sarcasm like frosting off a half-moon. "*Oh.*"

She let his answer sink in. "Hank said he didn't really know Paula," she said after a minute. "Maybe he got mixed up."

Jimmy took a long look at her. She could tell he was still furious from the way the tips of his ears were glowing bright red. Just like when he was a teenager.

"Jesus," he said finally. "You're really not much of a cop, are you?"

There was a folding chair behind the counter, where Jimmy's mom had sat to do word-search puzzles when business was slow. Ginny fell into it heavily, cradling her head in her hands.

"No," she said. "I guess I'm damn well not."

"Is this honestly how you do business down there? Get some half-baked tip and go running in with guns blazing? No wonder so many innocent black guys get shot to death."

It was a low blow, but at the moment she was hardly in a position to argue with him. "I'm sorry," she said. "I'm usually not like this, I swear. Time was, people actually thought I was good at my job. But lately, I've kind of just . . . lost it."

"Really," he said. "You don't say."

Jimmy took her out for a drink. It was the last thing she'd expected, but the nice guy in him must have taken pity on her. He'd put the startled brownie-froster in charge of running the counter and led her to his pickup and practically lifted her into the passenger seat. She had no idea where they were going as he drove up the Mohawk Trail, a winding mountain road that had started off as an Indian path centuries ago. He pulled into a package store and told her to wait, and when he came out, he was carrying a six-pack of Michelob and a bag of pork rinds.

"My God," was all she could summon up at the sight of them.

"Old habits," he said, and kept driving until they got to an overlook. He pulled in backward, and they sat in the bed of the truck and stared out at the Berkshire valley, the dark purple mountains dotted with the red and gold of the few remaining leaves.

In the distance she could just make out the three narrow cascades of Trinity Falls. Like any teenagers, Ginny and Jimmy had spent their share of time at the falls, smoking cigarettes and worse. But she'd never really liked the place, had always found it too creepy. Legend had it that if you went there and listened long enough, you could hear the voices of the dead, whispering to you beneath the rush of water.

They didn't say anything until they were halfway through their first beers. Eventually, when she couldn't take the silence anymore, she asked, "What are we doing up here?"

"Hell if I know," he said.

"I'm sorry I flipped out back there. It was just . . . When Hank said your name and Paula's in the same sentence, I totally lost it."

"Gee," he said. "I hadn't noticed."

She cracked a small smile, and they were both quiet for a long time.

"Jimmy," she said finally, "what the hell are we doing?"

25

Out of the corner of her eye, she saw him shrug.

"Don't ask me," he said. "You're the sophisticated city girl."

Her laugh was more of a snort. "Yeah," she said. "That's me."

"All's I know is, when I'm around you, I can't think straight."

"I know the feeling."

"Good," he said.

"Good?" she shrieked at him. "Are you *nuts*? I don't have the luxury of acting like some kid all drunk on hormones. I came up here to help Sonya. I swore to her I'd find out who killed Danny, and so far I've done such a great job that two more people are dead and somebody practically had me drowned in the river."

Her rant was enough to make him stop staring out at the mountains and look at her. "What are you talking about? I thought you had an accident."

She told him about the sabotaged car, news that shook him so that he drained his beer and opened another. She went on to say how guilty she felt over not doing more to get Jumping Jack out of jail, for not realizing he wouldn't be able to stand being cooped up in a cell. Then, after a moment's indecision, she took a deep breath and told him about Topher and Geoffrey, about the open question that was Danny's sexual orientation, how she was convinced that Geoffrey knew way more about Danny's death than he'd admitted—how just hours after she'd spoken to him, he'd wound up dead.

"What are you saying?" Jimmy asked. "You think this Geoffrey guy killed Danny?"

"I don't think so—not alone, anyway. Danny had six inches and fifty pounds on him at least. Geoffrey was clearly dealing, but my gut tells me he was no killer."

"I thought you said you found a gun in his car."

"I know," she said. "But I don't think it had ever been fired—I only saw it under my flashlight, but it looked new right out of the box. Maybe he just had it for protection over his drug deals."

"What a prince."

"Okay, I know I'm not at the top of my game right now, but my instinct is that Geoffrey didn't do it himself—but maybe he knew who did. When I asked him what Danny was doing up at the Fish Pond the night he died, he said he didn't know. But I was positive he was lying."

Jimmy opened the bag of pork rinds and offered them to her.

They used to be one of her favorite snacks, but she waved them off. "You think this Geoffrey was there with Danny?" he asked.

"Maybe. Or maybe he knew who was—and that somebody might very well be the person who beat Danny to death."

"But how does he end up getting hit by a car in the Fish Pond parking lot?" He looked up from the pork rinds. "Why are you smiling?"

"I don't know. It's just . . . There's a reason cops have partners. It really helps to have somebody to bounce stuff off of, toss scenarios back and forth."

"And you've been trying to figure this all out in your own head."

"Can't talk to Sonya about it. Practically everything I find out would blow her image of Danny all to hell. At first I thought the best approach was just to tell her everything, but now I'm not so sure."

"Does she know Danny might have been dating guys?"

"She told me she's afraid his soul is burning in eternal damnation."

He shook his head. "Narrow-minded crap."

"I thought you were such a good Catholic."

"At least I go to church."

"Yeah? How many Hail Marys do you have to say for servicing lonely divorcées with your giant loaf of cinnamon bread?"

She hadn't meant to say it; it just popped out. The question, idiotic as it was, seemed to float in the air between them. Like a toddler who's taken a tumble and is debating whether to laugh or cry, neither one of them was sure which way the moment was going to go.

But after a few seconds of silence they burst into simultaneous laughter—Jimmy clutching his ribs, Ginny chuckling so hard beer came out her nose.

"Jesus," he said once he'd caught his breath, "maybe you're not such a lousy detective after all."

The rain stopped that night, symbolism that even Ginny was self-aware enough to find ridiculous. She got up just after dawn the next morning, made coffee for Sonya, and asked her if she'd had any inkling that Danny was looking for his birth mother.

Her friend took the question better than she'd feared. But the subject still had weight and heft; Sonya sat down at the kitchen table, as though it were too much to deal with standing up.

"You know, he used to ask about her all the time when he was little. He always wanted to know if she was coming back, and for years I'd always tell him she was. Even when my folks said it was cruel to keep his hopes up, I still kept saying she'd come home, 'cause that's what I really believed. Finally when he got older, like in junior high, he didn't ask about her anymore."

Ginny covered Sonya's hand in hers. "You can't blame yourself, sweetie. This is all on Paula. I know she was your sister, and Danny's mom, but she never cared about anybody but herself."

Sonya shook her head. "That's not true. Paula wasn't all bad. I know she loved me. And she could be so charming when she wanted to—she had this way of making you feel like you were the most important person in the whole world. I know she had her faults, believe me. But she was still—*irresistible*. She was so beautiful, you know? Men were just drawn to her. I guess in the end Danny was, too."

"I went through this whole stack of papers he had hidden in his truck. He kept a notebook with facts about her life. Like did you know the night she ran away she hitched a ride to the Fish Pond with Mr. McSheen? I looked him up, but he's in a nursing home—he had a stroke two months ago and he's pretty gonzo. Danny must've talked to him before that."

"Fish Pond? What for?"

"She was carrying a big suitcase. Maybe she was running off with somebody, and that's where they were meeting up."

A memory flitted across Sonya's face, brief and bittersweet. "That was our place, you know. Paula and I weren't that close once she was older and she couldn't stand sharing a room with me. But when we were little, like when she was ten and I was six and trailing around after her all the time . . . we spent a lot of time down there."

"I remember."

"We'd run around and play little games and hide things in secret spots. When I look back on it, it was the only time I really felt like I had a sister. You know?"

Ginny squeezed her hand tighter. "I'm sorry to dredge all this up. I know it's not easy."

Sonya reached for her coffee cup, raised it with a shaking hand, put it back down. "What you said about her meeting somebody down at the Fish Pond," she said, "it makes sense. I think she always felt like the queen of that place. She'd traipse around in her bathing suit, and all the boys would look at her."

"Do you have any idea who she could have been meeting? Any particular guy she was involved with around the time she left?"

"What difference does it make now?"

"Maybe nothing. But if this is the trail Danny was on, I think I have to follow it."

Sonya thought about it. "I really can't remember anyone in particular. I know she had more money than usual—at least she wasn't hitting up my folks as much. I didn't think about it at the time, but looking back, I wonder if she was into something illegal. Sometimes I wonder if she skipped town to keep from getting busted."

"Coach Hank mentioned a few guys." Ginny summoned up the names. "Phil McCoy, Andy Draco, Steve Pecor. Could one of them have been who Paula ran off with?"

"Honestly," Sonya said, "one guy just blends into another. Did you talk to them?"

"Not yet. I got kind of sidetracked." Ginny hadn't told Sonya about the scene she'd made in Jimmy's store—how she'd run in howling about him screwing Paula and scaring the spit out of two little girls buying Halloween treats.

"Do you think she's still alive somewhere?" Ginny didn't answer. "Come on. Paula was a beautiful girl with awful judgment. Of course it's crossed my mind that she might not have made it to thirty-eight."

Ginny started to say something comforting, then decided there was no point. "I have no idea," she said. "She could have OD'd or God knows what else. Or maybe after she was gone for a while, she figured nobody wanted her to come back."

Sonya stood up and walked to the bedroom doorway, running a toe along the seam where the carpet met the kitchen linoleum. "Sometimes when Mom and Dad weren't home, she'd ban me from the room. She'd say I had to stand on the other side of this line. Remember?"

"Sure. I always wondered why she didn't just shut the door."

"She liked to have an audience. So I'd keep my toes on the line and hang on to the door frame and lean in as far as I could." Sonya shook her head. "But I never told on her."

"Let me ask you something else. Did Danny ever mention to you that somebody deflated the tires on his truck?"

"What? When?"

"On the Sunday before he died. Coach Hank told me he ran into Danny, and all four tires got flattened while he was working at the Skillet."

Sonya shook her head again. "No," she said. "He never said a word."

"And did he ever mention that some guy jumped him?"

"What? No. Do you think—"

Ginny's cell phone rang. Reluctantly, she let go of her friend's hand and went to her room to retrieve it.

"Hello?"

"Virginia, right? Is this the right number?"

The man sounded familiar, but Ginny couldn't place who it was. It didn't help that the voice was thick with what she thought were tears, punctuated by sniffles. She didn't recognize the number, but it started with 917, a New York City cell phone area code.

"This is Detective Lavoie. Can I help you?"

"I need to see you right now. Can you come down here?"

"Who is this?"

"Topher Malkovich. From Café des Artistes. Remember?"

"Of course. I'm sorry. What's going on?"

"I was going through Geoffrey's stuff," he said. "And there's something *horrible*."

Ginny's definition of "horrible" included many things, such as severed human body parts and the collected songs of Air Supply. What Topher Malkovich proffered across the café table didn't quite qualify. But considering what he'd just lost, what he was continuing to lose, she could understand why he held out the manila envelope like it was filled with spiders.

It was a stack of photographs. Nude pictures of a young man

posed in a variety of artsy but erotic positions on a geometric-patterned sheet. Photos taken by Geoffrey. Of Danny.

"That's our bed," Topher said. That pretty much said it all.

Topher's face was tearstained, nose red from blowing. He lit a cigarette with shaking hands that immediately reminded her of Sonya's from half an hour before. Some days, she thought, this world doles out so much pain there's more than enough for everybody to get a second helping.

"Are you sure you want to be here?" She indicated the busy coffee shop, where the latte line was six deep.

"I can't go home," he said. "That was our bed."

"You said you found these in Geoffrey's things?"

The tears started up again, and he swiped at them with a napkin. "His mom called. She wanted him to be buried in his grandfather's cuff links. Like he ever wore a French-cuff shirt in his life. But I guess it mattered to her." He blew his nose again, a deafening honk. "Not like she's thinking straight. She's totally freaked out. Like it wasn't bad enough her kid was a fag. Now he's a dead fag."

"Topher, I—"

He recoiled as if she'd reached for him, though she hadn't moved a muscle. "Don't try to console me, okay? You're not my friend."

She tried to keep her voice even, afraid he'd spook if she said the wrong thing. "Then why did you call me?"

"I don't know," he said. "I didn't know what else to do. All my friends—they're his friends, too. And you wanted to know about Danny, so I—" He cut himself off, body shaking with sobs. "How could he? How could that bastard do this to me?"

Ginny wasn't sure to whom he was referring—his unfaithful boyfriend or the guy he'd cheated on him with. "Hold on a second," she said. "Maybe you're jumping to conclusions. Geoffrey was an artist. Couldn't these just be—"

"You ever seen art with that big of a hard-on?"

He was right; it was porn. And covered with suspiciously sticky fingerprints, at that.

Topher shook his head, an ugly expression parking on his face. "You know, I gave up my whole goddamn life to come up here with him. I had a restaurant job I totally loved and this kick-ass apartment in the East Village. Went out every night of the week. Tons of friends. But I chucked it all, because I loved him. So what the fuck am I supposed to do now?"

"I'm really sorry," she said, putting a hand over his. This time he didn't push her away.

"It was bad enough he was dealing like he was the fucking Ronald McDonald of crystal meth. I told him it was too much, it was gonna get him killed. But no—he loved the money, but he jonesed for the goddamn thrill even more. I think that was why—" He shook his head again, slammed a snotty fist on the tabletop.

"Why what?"

She watched him debate whether to answer. Then he glanced down at the photos, and they seemed to help him make up his mind.

"I heard him on the phone the day after they found Danny's body. He didn't know I was home. But I think he was threatening somebody."

"Who?"

"I don't know. I only caught part of it, but I think he was saying he'd go to the cops if the other person didn't do what he wanted."

"Which was what? Money?"

"I don't know. I don't think so. That's why I say he got off on the thrill." He took a drag of his cigarette, hands still shaking. "Motherfucker."

"I'm sorry, but there's something else I need to ask you. Do you have any idea if Geoff was with Danny the night he died?"

Topher squeezed his eyes shut, stayed that way for a while, then opened them. "He never told me," he said. "And at the time, nobody knew anything had even happened to Danny, you know? He did come home pretty late that night, and he seemed riled up. But I was afraid to ask too many questions."

"Because you suspected there was another guy?"

Topher shook his head. "I figured it had something to do with his dealing, and I didn't want to hear about it. Back then I thought that was as bad as it could get."

He stared at the photos, so intently Ginny got the feeling he couldn't look away. The Danny captured in black and white was muscular and beautiful. And though he was trying to affect an air of worldly sensuality, the expression in his eyes was strangely innocent.

26

The autopsy report finally came in the mail that afternoon. She hid it under a Lillian Vernon catalog and snuck it into the bathroom, where she read it behind a locked door.

It didn't tell her much. The autopsy had been done by a local physician—not the dogcatcher-slash-coroner, but not the board-certified medical examiner in Pittsfield, either. She flipped through the meager pages, translating the doctorspeak into English.

Danny's wounds indicated he'd been beaten by a cylindrical object such as a pipe or baseball bat. In the city the M.E. would have scrutinized the wounds for evidence that could narrow it down, like wood slivers or metal shavings. No such luck. The doctor had noted the weight of Danny's brain, that his heart appeared healthy, and that his tox screen was negative for drugs and alcohol. It helped her not at all.

Ginny had also ordered, and paid for, a complete set of autopsy photos. She set her jaw and opened the envelope, flipping through them quickly; there was a limit to how long Sonya was going to believe she was in the john.

She thought she was beyond the power of such things—spending your childhood in a funeral home and your adulthood as a cop ought to have inoculated her by now. And she wasn't freaked out by the medical part: the infamous Y-incision, the exposed tangle of internal organs, the skull sawed open and the scalp folded back to reveal the brain. That was all standard procedure.

No, what got to her was Danny's face. Sonya had told her Danny's wounds were so severe that he had to be identified by his dental records; Bernie had warned her the damage was among the worst he'd ever seen. But it still didn't prepare her for the reality of it. Danny's face wasn't just brutalized; it was gone.

Ginny stuck her head under the tap and took a long drink of water, splashing some of it on her face. It would be different if this were just any victim. But this was Sonya's baby, and someone had beaten him beyond belief.

If this were any other case, she would have had the body exhumed and the autopsy redone by a pro. But pulling Sonya's son from his newly sodded grave was unthinkable. She hid the report in her duffel, where she'd already stashed the naked photos of Danny; if Sonya ever happened upon that bag, she was going to end up in the hospital.

Her cell phone rang as she was zipping the bag shut. It was her union delegate, calling with an update on the case against her.

Ginny listened, tried to ask the right questions, managed not to toss the phone across the room at the news that the department might convene a special commission to investigate the extent of the corruption. She hadn't been charged with anything yet—but she was afraid it was just a matter of time.

After twenty minutes on the phone she made the rounds of Paula's long-ago beaux: Phil at the welfare office, Andy at the American Legion; Steve she found on the porch of his apartment, a dingy affair on River Street that had started out as millworkers' housing and gone downhill from there.

Their reactions were so similar that Ginny found it profoundly depressing. It was as though Paula had only ever had one relationship, and she'd repeated it with one man after another—just change the name, repaint the pickup truck, shuffle the background music, add or subtract a mustache.

All three of them remembered Paula with great nostalgia and zero concern; she was a very nice piece of ass, and when they'd been with her, they couldn't get enough—but she wasn't the kind of girl you brought home for Sunday dinner. None of them had any idea whom she might have run away with—but if she showed up again, and still looked half as sweet as she did back then, they'd be more than willing to give her a tumble.

But there was one way they were helpful, this trio of potbellied ex-Romeos: each reported that Danny had come calling with the same questions.

The interviews put Ginny in a bitch of a mood. She tried to burn it off by running all the way to the high school and back, but it wasn't enough. She got to the bottom of Bradley Street, with its hill so brutal as to be nearly perpendicular. She didn't have to go home that way, but the physical punishment was perversely attractive. She chugged her way up, lungs bursting and legs on fire, and when the road leveled out, she bent over and took great gulps of air and tried not to throw up.

She stood up, head still spinning but stomach out of danger, and realized where she was: the entrance to the Fish Pond. The site of Geoffrey's murder; the place Danny had parked his truck the night he died. Her psyche was a lot of things, none of them subtle.

She followed the driveway to the deserted parking lot, the bloodstains visible despite all the recent rain. The police still hadn't found the car that had run Geoffrey down, and Ginny didn't have much faith that they would—short of a confession or a miracle. She'd heard that Rolly had actually made the rounds of the local body shops to see if anyone had brought in a car whose front fender bore a dent roughly the shape of a short, gay New Yorker; amazingly, though, no such damage had been reported.

What had Geoffrey been doing there that night? The most obvious answer was that he was pursuing his second career as a drug dealer and had crossed the wrong person. But what self-respecting criminal would leave a stash of drugs and money behind? She took various scenarios out for a spin, including the idea that the killer had been interrupted before he could rip Geoffrey off. But if someone had happened by, why did Geoffrey have to crawl to the street half-dead in search of help?

No, it made more sense that the drugs weren't the point. She was almost positive that Geoffrey had known something about Danny's last hours. What if—

Her train of thought was cut off by a voice coming from the woods on the far side of the beach: a child's, high-pitched and terrified, calling for help.

27

Ginny sprinted in the direction of the cry—past the swing sets and the teeter-totters, across the beach, around the corner, and through the woods. The voice had gone silent, and she had to stop and get her bearings.

"Hello?" she called. "Where are you? Are you okay?"

She peered through the trees, looking for movement. After a few seconds the child cried out again. "*Help!* Please! Over here! *Please!*"

She ran another twenty yards and found a boy of maybe eight, crouched over the body of another about the same age. The first boy's eyes were somewhere beyond hysteria; the second's were closed, his breathing so imperceptible Ginny first took him for dead. His friend was trying to pick him up, to scoop him into his puny arms, but he was too little for the job. The unconscious boy's head was lolling back, blood pouring from a gash in his forehead, more seeming to pump out with each attempt to lift him off the ground.

"*Stop!*" she shouted.

When her warning didn't seem to register, she ran over and forcibly removed the boy's arms from around his friend's back. "You can't move him," she said. "It might make him worse." The boy gazed down at his bloody hands, rubbing them together like a third-grade Lady Macbeth. "Give me your shirt."

"Wh-what?" His expression was even more alarmed; he was clearly wondering whether his savior was turning out to be a pervert.

"I need to try and stop the bleeding," she said. "Now, give me your shirt."

He shrugged out of the plaid flannel, revealing a T-shirt underneath. Ginny took the flannel shirt and pressed it to the boy's head. He gave a soft moan, which she took as a good sign. *Responds to painful stimuli. Not brain-dead.* Gently, she wrapped the shirt around the boy's head, tying the sleeves to form an ersatz bandage. His friend stood there, stock-still, hugging himself with his arms.

"Listen to me," Ginny said when she was done. "What's your name?"

It took a while for the question to sink in. Just when she thought she was going to have to grab him by the shoulders and start shaking him, he said, "Charlie. Charlie B-B-Bombardier. Likethehardwarestore."

The phrase popped out, incongruous and nearly incomprehensible, and Ginny got the feeling he'd identified himself that way a thousand times: Bombardier, as in the hardware store his family owned on State Road. Just like the way people used to refer to her when she was growing up: Ginny Lavoie, the mortician's daughter.

"Okay," she said. "I think I know your dad. Mark, right?" The boy nodded. "My name's Ginny. Now, tell me what happened."

"Tommy and me were riding bikes. He fell off and hit his head."

She rose from her crouch and turned to see a pair of bicycles: one lying in the dirt, the other jammed nose-first into a sharp dip in the ground. When she turned back, she realized the boy was pointing a trembling finger in the direction of a white birch.

"He hit his head on the tree?" she asked. Charlie nodded again. "He wasn't wearing a helmet?"

The boy shook his head and said, "Helmets are for s-s-sissies."

"Okay, you gotta listen now. I don't have a phone with me, and I need to stay here with Tommy. So what I want you to do is run over to one of the houses across from the lake and tell whoever's home to call an ambulance. Tell them exactly where we are, okay? Just keep trying houses till you find somebody." For a second she thought he was going to protest, but the boy nodded once more and headed for the park entrance with a wobbly gait. "Wait," Ginny called after him, the image of Geoffrey's broken body still vivid in her memory. "Make sure you look both ways before you cross the street. Okay?"

She watched him shuffle off toward the parking lot, then looked down at Tommy. He was still out cold; if anything, his breathing was even shallower than before. She summoned up her first-aid training: stabilize him, keep him warm, call for someone who knows what the hell he's doing. So far she'd managed two out of three.

She left his side long enough to see if there was anything useful on the bikes: nothing but a bag of Funyuns lying next to one—and a helmet swinging impotently from each set of handlebars. She stripped off her tank top and laid it across the boy's scrawny chest; it wasn't much, but it was the best she could do.

Ginny knelt back down by his side. His skin seemed awfully pale, but then again, she had no way of knowing how it usually looked. The chilly evening air was prickling at the drying sweat on her newly exposed skin; she wished she had some better way of keeping the boy insulated. Up close, he looked even younger than his friend: delicate eyebrows, girlish lashes, a pair of buckteeth that jutted out past half-open lips.

She stood up, hugging herself, as Charlie had been doing moments before, rubbing her palms over her biceps for warmth. She surveyed the scene, picturing what must have happened: the two boys bored between school and supper, riding through the deserted woods like a pair of skinny bats out of hell, dodging trees, whoever slowed down getting called names like "sissy" and "wimp." She saw Tommy's wheel getting stuck in a rut, his small body flying over the handlebars and striking the tree, his friend slamming on the brakes and vaulting to his side. At that age, she recalled, odds are you'd be equally terrified that your friend was going to die—and that even if he didn't, you were going to be in a heap of trouble, anyway.

The two bikes lay where their riders had left them: Charlie's on its side, Tommy's jammed into the dirt. She stepped closer and noticed that Tommy's hadn't wound up in a rut so much as a hole in the ground, one that had been dug and only loosely filled back in.

Keeping an eye on the boy, she walked a wider circle around the scene. It turned out that the hole Tommy had ridden into wasn't the only one: she counted three others in the immediate vicinity, places where the soil had been disturbed and replaced with varying degrees of success. She couldn't tell how recently the holes had been dug, but it seemed to her that they predated the rainfall: all the water had made the loose soil congeal into mud and sink slightly below ground level, making the disturbances easier to see.

She returned to Tommy's side; he didn't seem to have improved in the two intervening minutes. She stroked the boy's arm and mumbled something soothing, trying to make up for her lack of maternal experience by imitating what Sonya might do. She told him that everything was going to be okay, that help was on the way. The boy seemed unconvinced.

Ginny stood back up, too anxious to stay still. She paced around the woods, ears straining for the sound of a siren headed her way, but hearing nothing but the wind. Maybe she'd made the wrong call; maybe she should have left Charlie with his friend and gone for help herself.

Well, it was too late now, damn it.

She pulled Tommy's bike out of the mud, laying it on its side next to his friend's. The hole it had been stuck in was the deepest of the four; it was no wonder the poor kid had gone ass over teakettle. Whoever had been digging around here obviously hadn't spared a thought that somebody might break an ankle, or worse. What were they thinking?

She went back to check on Tommy again. The bandage had held; the bleeding from his head wound had stopped. An image came into her mind, as vivid as it was unwanted: Danny lying on the floor of the empty mill, face bashed in, surrounded by a vast pool of blood. She hadn't seen Danny for years before his death—her fault for not coming home—and even though she knew he was grown-up, she couldn't help thinking of him as a kid, about the same age as the boy lying in front of her.

Danny. Danny had been here the day he died—the very spot where his mother had been last seen the night she ran away. Geoffrey, who probably knew too much about Danny's death for his own good, had been here the night *he* died. And now someone was digging in the woods, looking for something or hiding God knows what. Could it have been Danny or Geoffrey—or both? Or was it just some—

The sirens derailed her train of thought. She stood up and peered through the trees: an ambulance had reached the end of the parking lot and was speeding across the grass. It stopped at the edge of the woods, and she yelled and waved at the two EMTs. They loaded Tommy onto a stretcher and carried him to the ambulance, light as a sack of white bread, and since she wasn't a relative, they wouldn't let her ride along.

So she stood in the parking lot and watched the flashing lights disappear down the hill, siren quickly fading away. Her tank top was on its way to the emergency room, and in an effort to keep warm and ignore the image of Danny's broken and bloody face, she ran all the way home.

The headline was in the next day's paper: VAN FOUND IN FISH POND HIT-AND-RUN. Sonya brought it to her in bed, along with a cup of tea and a Pillsbury sweet roll still warm from the oven. What with all the running and the exposure and the lingering effects of her car accident, Ginny could barely move.

The story described how one George Baldessarini, retired electrician and volunteer at the senior citizens' high-rise, had arrived at the parking lot at nine the previous morning prepared to ferry the elderly to their doctors' appointments and such. But when he went to start the van, an unmarked Dodge recently donated by the family of a dearly departed resident, he found that the keys weren't above the visor where he always left them. He'd found them soon enough, on the carpet between the two front seats, but the deviation from the regular order of things perturbed him enough that he gave the van the once-over. He found that the front end, which had been parked against the building, had been damaged—with dried blood and bits of flesh jammed into the grille.

Mr. Baldessarini was a hunting man, and he knew what deer skin looked like: this wasn't it. Neither was it the remains of some unfortunate dog. With news of that New York City drug dealer's demise in the paper every day, and his mind sharp as ever no matter what his wife said when he forgot to turn off the electric blanket, it only took him the duration of a cup of coffee to put two and two together. So he'd called the cops, and they'd come down and surveyed the damage, and that very afternoon Rolly had called a press conference to announce that the offending vehicle had been identified. Quote and unquote.

Ginny closed the paper, stuffed the last of the sweet roll into her mouth, settled back against the pillows. So Geoffrey had been killed by a van stolen—or, rather, borrowed—from the high-rise parking lot. That limited the suspects to whoever knew that the van was kept unlocked, with the keys inside—which probably translated into half the town.

The fact of the van being ripped off seemed to her less important than its being returned. That bespoke an even higher level of premeditation: an untraceable weapon, taken not in some drugged-out haze, but with malice aforethought, put back exactly where it was found so the damage might not be discovered for days. Again, she felt sure that no dealer or user would have left a trunkful of drugs and money in Geoffrey's car. Someone had already tried to hurt her to keep her from finding out what had happened to Danny. What if Geoffrey really did know too much—and someone had made sure he kept his mouth shut for good?

She heard the phone ring. Sonya answered it, then told Ginny to pick up.

"It's Jimmy," Sonya said, not even bothering to keep the amusement out of her voice.

Ignoring both the ache in her neck and the fluttering in her stomach, Ginny reached for the phone.

"Hi," she said. She pawed at her hair, momentarily surprised it was so short; she felt that much like a teenager.

"I'm calling," he said, "to ask you on a date."

"A what?"

"A date," he said. "It's what people do when they want to get to know each other."

"That's ridiculous. I've known you my whole life."

"Minus fifteen years. So how about it?"

She twirled a lock around her finger. It was silly, but she was getting into it. Later, when she was back in the city, she could feel like a fool for indulging in these high school hijinks; for now she was in no shape to resist. "What did you have in mind?"

"Dinner and a movie."

"That's original."

"We eat nothing and stare at snow on the TV. Is that better?"

She laughed. No, she might as well admit it: she giggled. "I'd rather go for what's behind door number one."

"Fine. I'll pick you up at six-thirty."

"You have to have me home by midnight," she said, "or I'll miss my curfew."

They went on like that for a while, jabbering like a pair of adolescent morons, until Sonya stuck her head in the doorway and made like she was strangling herself and puking at the same time. Ginny got off the phone; she'd no sooner gotten up in search of another sweet roll than it rang again. Sonya answered it and handed it to Ginny.

"It's for you," she said. "And don't get excited. It's not Prince Charming."

Ginny made a face at her, but in truth she was more relieved than annoyed: for the first time since Danny's death, Sonya was acting like something less than the weight of the world was on her shoulders.

The disembodied voice turned out to belong to Elsie Bombardier—mother of Charlie, the terrified boy she'd found in the woods. Through the small-town grapevine she'd figured out who this Ginny was who'd helped her son, had tracked her down to Sonya's to tell her that both boys were going to be fine. But it had been a close call: Dr. Erickson at the E.R. had told her that without Ginny's first aid, Tommy could have lost a lot of blood and gone into shock and heaven knows what might have happened. In any event, Elsie wanted to know whether someone would be home the following morning; she wanted to bring her a casserole.

Ginny got off the phone, thought for a few minutes. Then, making sure that Sonya was out of earshot, she picked up the receiver and dialed.

"Molly's Bakery."

"Hey, Jimmy, it's me. Can you get off work early?"

"I can do whatever I want," he said. "I own the place."

"Then pick me up at two," she said. "And bring a shovel."

They were covered in sweat, breathing in ragged gulps, clothes sticking to their filthy bodies. But this was nobody's idea of romance—spending four hours in the Fish Pond woods, digging up the dirt and finding nothing.

They'd started with the four holes Ginny had seen the day before, but if anything had been there, it was long gone. Then, at her insistence, they'd started turning up random plots of earth in the general area, on the off chance that someone had been looking for something and hadn't found it.

"You know," Jimmy said, wiping his forehead with his arm and smearing it with dirt, "staring at the snow on TV is sounding awful good."

She jammed her shovel into the ground and leaned against it. "You must think I've gone insane."

"To say you've gone insane," he said, "implies you were sane to begin with."

"Ha, ha," she said, and started on another spot.

"Seriously, how long do you want to keep this up? We've dug up half the woods, and for what? Because you think *maybe* the stupid hole that kid fell into *maybe* has something to do with . . . something or other. I'm so hungry I lost track."

"It's a hunch. Did you ever have a hunch?"

"Sure," he said. "I once had a hunch that provolone and chives would go together real well inside a pumpernickel roll. Worked out for me, too. No digging required."

"Okay, I know it's a little nutty. But like I told you, everything leads back to this place—Danny, Geoffrey, even Paula. And I was thinking, what if Danny got the idea that his mother left something here way back when? Sonya told me she and her sister used to have secret hiding places around the lake when they were kids. Maybe he got it into his head there was something he could find that might lead him to her."

"By digging randomly in the dirt like a crazy person?"

"We are *not* digging randomly. We are digging in the general vicinity of where someone has already *been* digging. That means we're following their trail."

"Assuming there's a trail to follow."

"Okay, all right, I get it. This is not your idea of a date."

He looked at Ginny, her face as dirt-smeared as his. "If it's yours," he said, "then that city of yours is even stranger than I thought."

"Haven't you ever been there?"

"Sure," he said. "A few times. Can't say I see the attraction."

"What are you talking about? There's a million things to do. Broadway and museums and—"

"Yeah, yeah. I took my folks down there to see *Phantom of the Opera* for their anniversary, before they moved out to Arizona, and we had a good time and all. But that place is just—too much."

She leaned on her shovel again. "What do you mean?"

"Too much noise, too much traffic, too much money. *Way* too many people."

"But that's part of what I love about it. There's so many choices. And yeah, it's crowded, but in a weird way it's so much easier to be alone. You know?"

He clearly didn't. "Place makes you be on your guard twenty-four-seven. Like you're one raw nerve, from your hat down to your socks. That's no way for a man to live."

"Jesus," she said, "you've obviously given this some thought."

He shrugged. "A little," he said. His voice was calm, but he was attacking the dirt like it had done him a wrong. "I mean, sure. It was what you left me for, so yeah. I thought about it. Might have been easier if I could've seen the attraction."

His answer left her without one of her own. She went back to digging, wondering if the temperature in the woods had really just dropped ten degrees in the past two minutes.

"You know," she said a few minutes later, "it takes time to get used to the city. They say it's two whole years before you really feel like you—" She cut herself off, exploring the dirt with the tip of her shovel.

"What?" he prompted. "Before you—"

"I think I hit something."

He stopped what he was doing and went over to see. Sure enough, there was something solid under the dirt. He helped her remove the soil, being careful not to damage whatever was underneath. When they got down nearly three feet Ginny jumped into the hole and started clearing away the dirt with her hands.

It was a garbage bag, intact except for the small tear Ginny had made with the tip of her shovel. Carefully, she pulled back the black plastic.

Bones.

And again she was in mourning.

The two arms of Sonya's grief stretched out and embraced each other, like twin cities whose populations grew and grew until they became one. It was impossible to tell where the loss of her son ended and the loss of her sister began.

Ginny tried to console her, but it was no use. It was as though her friend had moved away, had relocated to some vast metropolis of sadness where she couldn't follow. Even Pete, whom Ginny had always considered to be about as sensitive as a donkey with earplugs, could tell that his wife was something beyond devastated.

Losing Danny was bad enough—coming on top of the deaths of both chain-smoking parents before the age of sixty. But to find out that her sister had never lived to see twenty, had never even left town—that sent Sonya to her bed and kept her there.

To think, she told Ginny in one of her more lucid moments, *to think she's been there all these years, rotting under the ground we used to play on. All this time I've hated her for leaving, and she never even left.*

Paula's skeletal remains, identified via dental records, were in the custody of the county medical examiner in Pittsfield. From the second Ginny had realized they'd dug up human bones, she was determined to keep Rolly and his band of jokers from messing up the crime scene. So she'd called the M.E., who brought in the state police evidence-gathering unit. Rolly would probably scream about them invading his jurisdiction, but at least the scene would be processed by the book.

Ginny had stood there as the crime-scene technician worked—taking soil samples, clearing the rest of the dirt from the plastic, giving the all-clear for the body to be removed. It was loaded onto a stretcher, just like the injured little boy a matter of hours earlier, but rather than an ambulance, it was carried to a van. As it turned out, Paula hadn't been buried alone: a large suitcase was in the grave with her, presumably the same one that old Mr. McSheen had reported she was carrying when he dropped her off.

Did that make him a suspect? Ginny had a hard time believing it. If he'd killed her, why even admit he'd picked her up? And more to the point, someone had obviously been looking for the body very recently—and McSheen had been flat on his back in a nursing home for the past few months.

Ginny pondered the subject as she hung Pete's work clothes on the line. Sonya didn't believe in dryers—she thought they ruined fabric and wasted money—so she dried her laundry on a line that stretched from the rear of her side porch to a pole at the far end of the backyard. With Sonya too upset to get out of bed, Ginny figured it was up to her to keep the household going; Pete's mother was already making noises about moving in to take care of them, and if that happened, Ginny was going to have to find herself a cheap motel.

So there she was, clipping Pete's Fruit of the Looms to the line with cheery plastic clothespins, rotating the wheel to move them out over the yard and make room for the next. She was already thinking about what she was going to make for dinner, God help them all. For the past fifteen years Ginny's idea of home cooking had involved a Swanson's Hungry-Man dinner and a microwave.

Despite the circumstances, she couldn't help but laugh. Here she was—back in her hometown, doing the housework, concocting a roast chicken to feed a workingman after a long day.

She'd struggled like hell to avoid it, but there it was: she'd turned into her mother. Thank God it was only temporary, or she'd blow her brains out with Danny's stolen .38.

She patted the gun, tucked into the back of her jeans between her T-shirt and Sonya's borrowed sweat jacket. She'd been carrying it ever since she found out about the sabotaged brakes, but so far she hadn't felt the slightest hint of danger—at least to her. Geoffrey hadn't been so fortunate, though from the litany of sin she'd found in his trunk, she had a feeling he'd made his own luck. And then there was that poor kid who'd gotten hurt in the woods—not on purpose, of course, but collateral damage just the same.

Discovering Paula's bones made Ginny look at those holes in the woods in a new light. She couldn't believe Danny had been searching there for something his mother had hidden—it was too much of a coincidence. No, whoever had been digging there must have been looking for exactly what she'd found: Paula's remains. Could it possibly have been Danny?

But who would have known where the bones were—except the person who'd put them there? It seemed logical that it would be hard to find the grave after all this time, what with new trees growing up and old ones coming down. Which begged the question: *why* was someone trying to find the body? Why not just leave it where it was? No one had found it for nearly twenty years; as far as she knew, Paula would have lain undisturbed for another two decades and more.

But what if it wasn't the body the mystery digger had been after? What if it was something in that suitcase, something that could still implicate the killer all these years later? Ginny had watched while the bag was opened in the crime lab, the friendly young investigator suitably impressed by her NYPD credentials even sans the shield. Although he wouldn't let her touch anything, she took photos of each item, scribbled pages of notes. The suitcase had been carefully packed, the clothes folded neatly; Paula might have been lazy, but she liked to look good.

Ginny knew the contents of that bag so well she could practically recite the list from memory, like the words to the hit songs she and Sonya used to track on *Casey's Coast to Coast*.

Two pairs of Jordache jeans

One pair red leather Frye boots, size 7

Seven pairs of cotton underpants, assorted colors,
    embroidered with the days of the week

Eight pairs of socks

T-shirt decorated with a red and black tongue—the Rolling
    Stones logo

Copy of *Cosmo*

Pink plastic hairbrush

Four bras, all white, size 32-B

A rosary, the silver crucifix engraved with the initials P.L.

White denim overalls

Box of saltines

Bright green sweatshirt with the neck cut out, à la *Flashdance*

Family photos: of herself and Sonya aged around four and
    eight, clad in floral sundresses; of Danny, propped in front
    of clouds and blue sky at the Sears Portrait Studio; of her
    grandmother. Her parents were conspicuously absent.

A plastic toiletry bag filled with drugstore makeup

Denim miniskirt

Cutoff shorts

Seafoam-green babydoll nightgown

Pack of six Hershey bars

Bikini, black with white polka dots

A small boom-box radio and eleven store-bought cassette
   tapes
Toothbrush
Yellow plastic flip-flop sandals
Pink rabbit's-foot key chain

If there was anything revelatory in the inventory of Paula's possessions, Ginny couldn't see it. It had crossed her mind that maybe there could be something on the cassette tapes—something other than the musical stylings of Fleetwood Mac and Steely Dan—and the state police investigator had assured her he'd check them out. Other than that, the suitcase seemed to be filled with nothing more remarkable than the dreams of a nineteen-year-old girl who thought she was going to start a new life somewhere. Somewhere warm, Ginny surmised: it was early April when she left, and the nights were still chilly in New England, but she'd packed no cold-weather clothing. Assuming she was going to stay in the United States—and Paula didn't own a passport—that meant down South or out West.

There was a knock on the front door, a welcome relief from thoughts of death and laundry. It was Jimmy Griffin, looking pale and reeking of cigarettes.

"I wanted to check on Sonya," he said. "Is she okay?"

"She's asleep. Let's get out of here." She scribbled a note to Pete that she was going out, not sure when she'd be back.

"Where do you want to go?" he asked as they climbed into his truck.

"It doesn't matter. Anywhere."

"What happened?"

"Nothing new," she said. "I just need to think."

She rolled down the window and stared out of it. Jimmy was in no shape to handle the silence; he kept talking.

"I thought I was the only one who was freaked out by find-ing . . . what we found. You know, I haven't smoked since high school. But when I got home the other night I just paced around like a dog in a cage, and I finally went down to Pop's and bought a pack of butts. No idea why. Stupid thing to do, probably. Can you believe how much these things cost?"

He lit one and offered her the pack. She took it and lit one of her own and kept staring out the window. Jimmy drove out of town and up the hill toward Clarksburg, glancing her way every once in a while to make sure she hadn't fallen out the door.

"I just can't believe it," he said. "That somebody killed Paula and she's been buried right under our noses all this time. I mean—it seems crazy. That something like that could happen here—"

Ginny slammed a fist against the armrest. "Would you wake up? This is not some paradise. Paula is *dead*. Danny is *dead*. Geof-frey Dobson is *dead*. I already told you somebody cut my brakes. I know you think life is terrible down in the city. But it's not so great up here, either, is it?" His face turned hard, one hand tight on the steering wheel while the other tossed ashes out the win-dow with a violent flick. "Look at Paula," she went on. "She probably thought she was running off with Mr. Right, and he killed her."

"How do you know that's what happened?"

"I don't," she said. "But even if you just run the numbers, when a woman is murdered, the single most likely killer is a man she's sexually involved with."

Jimmy didn't answer, just shook his head and lit another cig-arette. After a few minutes he stared at the glowing ember and just said, "Sad."

"I know. Paula was no angel, but she didn't deserve what she got."

"I wasn't talking about her," he said. "I was talking about you."

"Excuse me?"

Jimmy hit the brakes, pulled the truck over to the side of the road. The sun was setting, the golden light cutting through the trees, reflecting on the signs that said NO HUNTING.

"Living with these awful ideas," he said. "How do you even sleep at night?" The look on her face made him reach out to touch her shoulder. "Don't be offended. I don't mean you're a horrible person. Just . . . To think of what it must be like for you, to look at some tragedy and be able to think like the bastard who caused it." He slapped the steering wheel. "God," he said, "I sound like an asshole."

They looked at each other, then away. Jimmy took a long drag of his cigarette and asked, "What are you going to do now?"

"There must be some reason why the killer didn't want Paula's grave to be found—something worth the risk of trying to dig her up. I'm hoping that if I can figure out what it is, it'll lead me to him."

"Great."

"Christ, Jimmy, after that whole little speech just now, I know you don't think I'm handing out parking tickets down there. I can take care of myself."

"Don't you think you ought to—I don't know, call in re-inforcements?"

"The state police are looking into Paula's death. But as far as the locals are concerned, Danny's case is closed, and Geoffrey's just some drug dealer who got what was coming to him. Who am I gonna call? In case you forgot—officially, I'm not even a cop at the moment."

He nodded, that grim expression back on his face. "I'd say something macho about how I'll protect you," he said. "But at this point in our lives I think you could probably kick my ass."

"You and several of your closest friends," she said. "But hopefully, it won't come to that."

He took her back to Sonya's, and they parted without so much as a kiss; since that afternoon when she'd come charging into his store demanding to know if he was screwing Paula, their rela-tionship had gone from wordless sex to sexless words. That was fine with her—just having someone to talk to was enough. Maybe after all the years and all the water under the bridge, they could actually be friends.

"Ginny?"

Sonya's voice came from the bedroom, so weak it broke her heart.

"It's me," Ginny said. "I'm back."

"You have to give out the candy."

Ginny was worried her friend was starting to hallucinate. "The what?"

"It's Halloween. Have to give out the candy. Can't disappoint the kids."

"Don't worry about that. Where's Pete?"

"Dunno. You gotta do the candy. In the kitchen cabinet,"

Sonya said. *"Please.* Danny always loved to give out the c-c-candy . . ."

Sonya's voice dissolved into sobs; Ginny heard her roll over in bed and muffle them with a pillow. Sonya sounded utterly devastated, a shade of herself. Ginny had briefly flirted with the idea of taking her friend to the doctor, but for what? To give her pills to make her stop feeling what she had every right to feel?

Ginny shook her head and went in search of the Halloween candy. There were eight bags of various chocolate bars, and she dumped them into the largest bowl she could find. Not two minutes later, the first trick-or-treaters rang the doorbell.

Halloween. The unrelenting stream of vampires and ghosts and pointy-hatted witches conjured memories of all those nights when she and Sonya had prowled the neighborhood, plastic pumpkins overflowing with swag. They'd spend the night at Sonya's, gorging themselves till their stomachs ached, Paula helping herself to their stash until Sonya cried for her mom. Although there had been variations over the years, for the most part they'd recycled the same costumes again and again: Sonya was a fairy princess, and Ginny was the cop dragging her off to jail.

Ginny would have thought that Sonya's dual tragedies might keep the trick-or-treaters away, but she should've known better: if your porch light is lit on October 31, you're fair game.

Belinda Cooper's two kids showed up, clad in the lamest costumes of the evening: the little boy had pinned a towel around his shoulders and drawn on fangs with two errant swipes of lipstick; his older sister was wearing a plastic cowboy hat and an oversize vest that looked like it had come from an old three-piece suit. The kids were clutching pillowcases, each filled to bursting as though they'd been at this for hours, but they jammed their hands into the bowl and yanked out as many chocolates as each small fist could handle. She was on the verge of telling them only two per customer, but then she figured, why bother? At least the candy was something to fill their stomachs. Their mother was nowhere in sight.

Then there was Lizzie Erickson and her three kids, all of them wearing lab coats and stethoscopes; Coach Hank and his four younger girls, disguised as a variety of very pretty monsters; even that irksome Arthur Dulaine, shepherding what must be his granddaughter—anyway, she was the only kid who showed up dressed like Mother Teresa.

Dulaine seemed annoyed when she answered the door; she got the feeling that he had a whole speech prepared for Sonya, about the redemptive value of suffering or some such crap. The little girl, who looked to be about six, only had eyes for the candy.

"I'm surprised you approve of Halloween," Ginny told Dulaine as they were leaving. She knew it wasn't nice to bait Grandpa in front of the little Sister of Charity, but she couldn't resist. "All the witches and ghosts and all," she continued. "Isn't it a little too, you know, *occult* for your taste?"

Dulaine looked equal parts confused and annoyed. "I don't know what you mean."

"Well, if you object to *Macbeth,* then all this—"

"That's entirely different," he said.

Now it was Ginny's turn to be confused. "I don't see how."

Dulaine smoothed his neat shock of gray hair, which actually didn't need smoothing. "I'm sure you don't," he said.

"Then why don't you explain it to me?"

"If you can't understand why Jack O'Brien didn't deserve a church burial," he said, "then I doubt you can understand much at all."

And with that, he took his tiny nun by the hand and walked out.

The vultures had descended and wiped her out. Ginny wouldn't have believed she'd see the bottom of Sonya's enormous trove of chocolate bars, but the miniature ghosts and goblins had swept through like an invading army. At nine o'clock she turned out the porch light and settled down on the couch with the sole survivor, a miniature Butterfinger. She was just biting into it when the phone rang; she jumped up and grabbed it, afraid it would wake Sonya.

"Markowicz residence."

"Virginie? It's your father."

She froze—standing there in the kitchen, clutching the receiver, long cord dangling at her side.

"Virginie? Hello?"

"Um . . . yes?"

"It's your father."

She was well aware of that. She still had no idea what to say; all she could come up with was, "Hello."

"How are you?" he asked.

It had been almost ten years since she heard her father's voice. He sounded different than she remembered—less gruff, more relaxed. Florida must agree with him; or maybe there were health benefits to sleeping with a woman young enough to be his daughter.

"I'm fine," she said. She was still standing at attention; at the moment, sitting down seemed to require too much in the way of muscular coordination.

"Why are you still home? Did you lose your job?"

Leave it to her dad to jump to the worst possible conclusion about her—although, she had to admit, this time he wasn't far off.

"I took a leave of absence so I could stay with Sonya. Her son, Danny—"

"Lisette told me. That's how I knew where to find you."

"Oh."

"It's a hell of a thing," he said, "when a man doesn't have his own daughter's phone number."

"Most cops are unlisted."

"That's no excuse." The three words contained a world of resentment. Now, *that* was the voice she remembered.

"How's your wife?"

A pause. "Her name is Suzie. And she's fine. Shaping up to be quite the lady golfer."

"Great."

He cleared his throat. "You could come down and visit us sometime."

"Or you could come up here."

"I'm an old man, Virginie."

"For chrissake, Dad, you're sixty-two. You're probably in better shape than I am."

He didn't take the bait. "You should call your Aunt Lisette. She's worried about you."

"What for?"

"She thinks you're in trouble." Another pause. "Are you in trouble?"

"I'm fine."

"Did you lose your job?"

"I already told you no."

"Why don't you come down here for a vacation? I'll buy your plane ticket. It'll be a late birthday present."

Yeah, she thought. *For the last ten birthdays.* "I'll think about it," she said. "Right now I have to take care of Sonya."

"How's she holding up?"

"She lost her son."

"Terrible thing," he said, "to lose a child."

"I'm aware of that."

Then her father did something she never expected: he said something wise.

"There are lots of ways to lose a child," he said, "besides just dying."

31

Ginny lay in the bathtub, hoping the hot water would unknot her aching muscles. She tried to stretch out, but the tub was too short for her; amazing to think that she and Sonya used to fit in there together, with room to spare.

Her head was still reeling from the conversation she had with her father the night before—not the substance of it so much as the fact that they'd even spoken in the first place. They'd cut off contact so long ago, each furious at the other, their temperaments so alike as to allow no compromise.

Now that her dad had stuck out an olive branch—even offered to fly her down for a visit—she had no idea what she should do. And, more to the point, she had no idea what she *wanted* to do.

She was similarly clueless about how to get through to Sonya. Her friend had barely said a coherent word since learning what had happened to her sister. Ginny had left her alone with her grief; she didn't know what else to do. Pete—who'd gotten home around ten on Halloween night, mumbling about paperwork and a McDonald's burger eaten at his desk—had asked her how his wife was doing, and taken Ginny's stricken expression for an answer. He'd washed up and gone to bed, and through the thin door Ginny could hear him shushing Sonya's cries and telling her that he loved her and everything was going to be okay. Sometimes people surprise you.

He'd left for work that morning a little later than usual, and Ginny had brought Sonya some tea and toast, neither of which she'd touched. Ginny had flirted with the idea of a run, then decided her body ached too much. So she'd drawn herself a bath, curling up into the fetal position to get all four limbs underwater. She'd jammed a facecloth into the safety drain, but the water level was still dropping, so she left the hot tap running.

She tried to empty her mind, to stop thinking about her weeping friend and all those wasted lives: Danny, Paula, even Geoffrey Dobson and Jumping Jack O'Brien. She closed her eyes, but their faces stayed with her. In the water's rush she could hear their voices, like in the cascade of Trinity Falls.

What had Paula set in motion? She'd run away with someone who'd ended her life less than a mile from home. Who could it be? She thought of Paula's trio of suitors, none of them a prize. She supposed any one of them could have tampered with her brakes or run Geoffrey down or attacked Danny. But those three couldn't have been the only men Paula was seeing; her reputation and Ginny's own memories said there had to be others. If Danny had compiled a chronicle of his mother's liaisons, Ginny hadn't found it yet. Neither Pete nor his parents could summon up specific names of men Paula had dated.

"What do you expect?" Rhonda Markowicz had said through a clucking tongue. "A girl like that isn't the kind you'd take out in public."

Ginny suddenly sat up and turned off the tap, water splashing onto the floor. She could have sworn she'd heard someone try the front door. She listened again but heard nothing.

She glanced at the .38, nestled on a towel in the corner, a thing of beauty if there ever was one. She'd cleaned it, bought some extra ammo, taken it down to the county sandpile to test-fire it by picking off a row of innocent soup cans from Sonya's recycling bin. Worked like a charm—if your idea of a charm is blowing something to hell.

She stood up and drained the tub, saving some hot water in case she could talk Sonya into taking a shower. Her friend was going to have to get out of bed sooner or later.

Ginny toweled off and got dressed, took a cup of tea out to the front porch. Sitting on a folding chair outside the door was a waxed paper bag. Ginny picked it up—carefully, like a person who's had her brakes cut and has a stolen .38 stuck in the back of her pants. The bag wasn't ticking; it fact, it smelled pretty good. She opened it up. Inside was a note.

For Ginny—
My giant loaf of cinnamon bread.
—Jimmy

Beneath it was, indeed, Molly's famous bread, but on steroids. It was a good ten inches in diameter; lucky thing Sonya had a toaster oven.

She smiled and carried the five-pound confection into the kitchen. The thing could feed a family for a week. She pictured Jimmy getting up at whatever ungodly hour he did, concocting it while his workers questioned his sanity behind his back, dropping it off on her doorstep. Jimmy always did have a wicked sense of humor. And whatever the state of their relationship, it was damned romantic of him.

She put a slice into the oven—it was the size of a small pizza—and brought a fresh cup of tea in to Sonya.

"Hey," she said, "you awake?" Sonya responded with a groan. "Come on," Ginny said, "you've got to eat something. You won't believe what Jimmy dropped off."

Sonya rolled over, squinting into the light from the open door. The bedroom window shades had been closed for two days straight.

"Thank you," she said, so polite it was scary, "but I'm not hungry just now."

"Jimmy made us a cinnamon bread as big as your whole head," Ginny said. She was trying to be chipper, but even she could tell that she sounded like a cruise director on speed.

"That's nice," Sonya said.

"He dropped it off this morning. With a keg of beer and the Hibernian Men's Marching Band."

"That's nice," Sonya said again.

Enough was enough. Ginny strode to the windows and raised first one shade, then the other. Sonya recoiled, pulling the covers over her head like a sleep-deprived vampire. Ginny sat on the edge of the bed and drew them back.

"You have to get up," she said. "Come on. I made you some tea."

Sonya squeezed her eyes shut, then threw a hand over them for good measure. Ginny could see from the expression on her face that she wanted to tell her to go away, to get out of her bedroom and leave her in peace, but even half-wrecked with grief Sonya didn't have it in her to be rude.

"Please," Ginny said. "I need your help. It's about Paula."

That did it; Sonya opened her eyes. She didn't sit up, but it was a start.

"I have pictures of everything that was in her suitcase. I need you to go over them and tell me if there's anything unusual."

Sonya closed her eyes again. "Later," she said. "Please? Just let me sleep a little more."

Ginny opened her mouth to argue with her, but the phone rang. She took a step toward the kitchen but decided to answer it in the bedroom. She was about to pick up the receiver when she pushed the speaker button instead; anything to rouse Sonya from her stupor.

"Hello?"

"Virginia Lavoie, please."

"Speaking."

"Detective? It's Matt Zeigler from the Berkshire County M.E.'s office."

His voice came through the speaker, tinny and hollow but distinct. Ginny went to grab the receiver so Sonya wouldn't have to hear, but she called out from the bed: "No."

"Detective Lavoie? You still there?"

"I'm here." She gave Sonya a look that said, *Are you sure about this?* Sonya ignored it.

Matt Zeigler was the M.E. who'd collected Paula's remains. Even over the bad connection his voice sounded kind, just as it had that day at the burial site. Ginny had told him she was a cop, asked him to let her know when the results were in. She just hadn't thought it would be so soon.

"I can hear you," she said.

"Do you want all the medical mumbo jumbo or the straight story?"

Ginny cast another sidelong glance at Sonya. "For now let's keep it short."

"All right. You know the remains were completely skeletal, and there's a limit to how much we can tell from them, but my best guess is that Paula Libanski was strangled. The hyoid bone was broken, indicating—" He cut himself off. "Never mind that. She was probably strangled."

Sonya was staring straight up at the ceiling, her face a blank. Ginny was reminded of that cliché about defendants not showing any emotion when the verdict was read.

"Were there—" Ginny's voice caught; she coughed and cleared her throat. "Were there any defensive wounds?"

"Nothing that would have been apparent on the skeleton," he said, "like a knife wound that had nicked bone."

There was a long staticky silence; Zeigler obviously couldn't tell if she wanted him to go on. He seemed confused: what kind of cop couldn't handle an autopsy report?

"Do you want to hear about the body position?" Zeigler was starting to sound annoyed.

Ginny looked over at Sonya; as far as she could tell, she hadn't moved a muscle since the phone rang. "I can get the details later. Thanks, Doctor."

"There's one more thing," Zeigler said.

The static didn't hide his meaning. *If you couldn't handle what I just told you,* it said, *you're definitely not going to like what's to come.*

32

"We found something else with Miss Libanski's remains," Dr. Zeigler said.

Ginny itched to pick up the receiver so Sonya couldn't hear, but she kept her hands balled at her side. "What's that?"

"The skeletal remains of a fetus."

"You mean—"

"The victim was approximately three months pregnant."

"*No.*"

The voice belonged to Sonya, who'd sat bolt upright in bed. Dr. Zeigler's sentence had transformed her. Her cheeks were cherry red, eyes blazing. The news—something that Ginny would have expected to send Sonya spiraling back into grief— had made her utterly, implacably furious.

"*No,*" she said again, and stood up. "*No.*"

"Detective?" Zeigler's voice came through the speaker, more bewildered than before.

Sonya stalked to the phone and stood over it, like it was one of her day-care children who was in a heap of trouble. "This is Sonya Markowicz. Paula Libanski's sister."

"I see." The tone in his voice said he understood what had been going on before.

"Do you mean to tell me that someone murdered her in cold blood and she was *pregnant*? They strangled her even though they were killing an innocent baby, too?"

Ginny was momentarily speechless. The doctor, for whom she was starting to feel genuine pity, stepped into the breach. "It's possible," he said, "that the killer had no idea she was—"

"*Bullshit,*" Sonya said. "*Bullshit, bullshit, bullshit.* Who else would Paula have run away with but her boyfriend—the father of her child? Jesus *Christ.*" She turned to Ginny, eyes a startling shade of blue. Sonya was her best friend, but at the moment Ginny could scarcely have picked her out of a lineup. "God help me," she said. "When you catch this son of a bitch, I am going to use that gun you found and kill him myself. I swear it on my son's grave."

Ginny looked from Sonya to the phone. "Um . . . Dr. Zeigler, would it be okay if I called you back?"

"Definitely," he said, and hung up.

Sonya stalked from the phone to her dresser and started yanking out clothes, jamming her feet into jeans, pulling a flow-ered sweatshirt over her head. She looked in the mirror, saw that her hair was greasy and tangled, and ran a brush through it so violently it left a snarl of strands in the plastic bristles. Then she turned to Ginny.

"Tell me what to do," she said.

"Sonya, I—"

"Enough screwing around. Danny was nineteen. Paula was nineteen. Add those two together, and it still doesn't make a life."

"Let's just slow down a minute and—"

"Tell me what to do." Sonya's voice was calm, but it had an undertone Ginny had never heard before, something steely and vicious. "Tell me how I can help you find the son of a bitch who took them away from me."

It didn't take a detective to figure out that there was no use arguing with her. "Let's go into the kitchen," Ginny said.

She went to her room and retrieved the photos of Paula's suitcase contents. In the few moments she was gone Sonya had raided the refrigerator and was eating leftover chili con carne—cold, straight from the Tupperware—shoving one spoonful after another into her mouth. She stood there and ate, tasting nothing, as Ginny laid the photos on the table.

"She loved those Frye boots," Sonya said through a mouth full of chili. "Seeing they were gone from her closet was what convinced me she'd really left."

"I remember," Ginny said. "Now, just look through this stuff and tell me if there's anything odd."

"What makes you think there would be?"

"Someone was searching for Paula's grave. I'm wondering if there might be something in here he didn't want found."

Sonya's gaze slid over the array of photos: jeans, cassette tapes, day-of-the-week underpants. She ran a finger across the photo of Paula's lucky rabbit's foot, still a garish shade of pink after two decades in the ground.

"Guess it didn't work for her," she said. "Did it?"

Sonya put down the empty Tupperware and reached into the fridge for some milk. She drank straight from the carton, something she would never even have done as a child. Then she ripped open a bag of Oreos and shoved one into her mouth, whole. Ginny was starting to think this new id-of-Sonya was even more worrisome than the version that had spent the past two days in bed.

Her friend was on her fourth cookie, still staring at the photos, when she suddenly stopped chewing. She picked up one of the snapshots and took it over to the sink, where she examined it under the harsh fluorescent light.

"This rosary," she said. "It isn't Paula's."

Ginny consulted her notes. "It has her initials on the back of the cross. P.L."

"I don't care," Sonya said. "My sister never kept a rosary in her life."

"Didn't she get one for her first communion?"

"Sure she did. We both did. But she lost it right away. And it wasn't anywhere near as nice as this."

Ginny watched as Sonya brought the photo to her nose. Then she rooted around in the junk drawer for a magnifying glass, the one her grandpa used to use to read the paper. "I'm not sure," she said, "but I think I've seen this before."

"Really? Where?"

Sonya shrugged, face dark with frustration. "I don't remember. But if I did, it was a long time ago."

"That makes sense. I mean, it's been buried for nearly twenty years. Maybe Paula had it around the time she—"

"No. I'm telling you. My sister and a rosary—it just doesn't compute."

"But she had it in her suitcase," Ginny said. "It was one of the things she took when she ran off, and she didn't take much."

Sonya sat down at the kitchen table, still eyeing the photo under the magnifying glass. "I know."

"What if she stole it?" Ginny continued. "You said yourself it looks valuable. Maybe she was planning on selling it when she got where she was going."

"I guess," Sonya said. "But stealing a rosary that had her same initials on it? What are the chances of that?"

Ginny didn't disagree. "And you can't remember where you saw it before?" Sonya shook her head again. "Well, it obviously belonged to somebody Catholic. Think of who you knew from church back then." She watched as Sonya dredged up the memories. "Was there anybody with the initials P.L.?"

Sonya slapped a hand on the table, magnifying glass landing with a thud. "Oh my God. That's it. Oh, *Christ*. Paula, how could you?"

"What?"

"Just when I thought this couldn't get any worse. Paula took that rosary from Father LeGrand."

"She stole from a *priest*?"

"That's where I recognized it from. I'm pretty sure it's the rosary he had when we were kids at CYO summer camp. All those little silver flowers between the beads are pretty distinctive. And the initials match—Father's first name is Pierre."

"Is there anything else? Anything in the suitcase that catches your eye?"

Sonya examined the photos again, then shook her head. "It's all Paula's stuff. I mean, I don't remember every little piece, but there's nothing else in there that's out of place."

Ginny collected the photos into a stack. "All right. Thanks."

"So what do we do now?"

"I guess I'll go talk to Father LeGrand. Right now it's the only lead we've got."

Sonya grabbed Ginny's wrist, a talon's grip. "You don't think he had anything to do with Paula's death?"

Ginny shook her head, hand rapidly going numb. "Just because Paula boosted his rosary doesn't mean he did anything wrong. But it's the only thing out of place in her suitcase. And there had to be some reason the killer was trying to dig her up after all this time."

"Maybe she didn't steal it," Sonya said. "Maybe whoever *did* steal it was afraid it could somehow be traced back to him."

"Maybe," Ginny said, though she didn't really mean it. "Anything's possible."

She called Father LeGrand and got his voice mail; with all the money going to settle those molestation suits, the diocese had laid off the church secretary. Ginny left him a message saying she'd like to speak to him, then went out for a run. Sonya, who was pacing the apartment like a caged leopard, was starting to drive her out of her mind.

She did three miles, wimped out, and went home for a shower. Sonya was on her hands and knees, waxing the kitchen floor. The priest hadn't called back. To avoid getting roped into Sonya's cleaning frenzy, she told her friend she had some errands to run, and went down to the Golden Skillet for a burger.

It was still early for lunch, and there wasn't much of a crowd. Ginny sat at the counter and ordered her usual artery-slamming concoction. The college-aged waitress was someone Ginny didn't recognize; she hadn't served her before, and she hadn't been there when Ginny trolled the place for useful information about Danny during what would have been his weekend shift.

"Are you new here?" Ginny asked when the girl delivered her lunch, the burger glistening amid a sea of crispy fries.

"Been here a month or so," she said. "I usually work weekends. But I swapped with Wanda last Sunday, so here I am."

The girl had a sturdy build, a long brown braid that flopped down her back, and a moon-shaped face with milky white skin. She reminded Ginny of the farmers' daughters who'd ride in the Fall Foliage parade on the float marked DAIRY PRINCESS. She was smacking her gum and leaning against the counter, coffeepot in hand—like she was auditioning for the role of *waitress,* and she wanted to make sure she had all her clichés covered.

"I was wondering," Ginny asked, "did you used to work with Danny Markowicz?"

"Poor guy," the girl said. "But he's in a better place. You know?"

Ginny didn't know, not at all. But she just nodded and smiled. "Did you know him very well?"

"We worked together a bunch of times." She blew a bubble, popped it, sucked the gum back into her mouth. "Would've liked to know him better. Danny was a *hottie.*" Her eyes widened, like she'd broken some taboo about wanting to bang the dead. "I mean . . . May he rest in peace."

"Did you ever notice anything unusual going on with him?"

She shrugged. "Like whaddaya mean?"

"Was he arguing with anyone? Was there a particular person he had a problem with, something like that?"

"Not really," she said. "Except that time somebody came in screaming about wanting him dead."

33

There was not a trace of irony in her. From her braided hair to her sensible white sneakers, Ginny could see that the girl was utterly without guile. And, she suspected, the better part of a brain.

"Someone came in here threatening his life?"

The waitress looked at her through round eyes. "I never said *that.*"

"You said someone wanted him dead."

"Right," the girl said. "That's not the same thing."

Ginny took a big bite of her burger. She felt like she needed the protein. "How about if you explain it to me?"

The girl shrugged. "People say stuff like that all the time. 'Drop dead, I wish you were dead.' Nobody ever means it."

Ginny wanted to point out to her that, perhaps, if the person on the receiving end of that particular wish *does* end up dead, maybe that changes things an eensy-weensy bit. She decided not to bother.

"Can you just tell me what happened?"

"Danny and me were closing up one Saturday, just the two of us—mopping down the floors and like that. And there was this wicked knock on the front window, like so hard I thought it was gonna break the glass. I went to tell them we were, you know, closed, but it was Danny's girlfriend."

"Monique?"

The girl's bulky shoulders rose into a shrug. "I guess. I mean, *I* was never introduced. I saw her around here a couple times, a little Skinny Minnie cheerleader type, but Danny never really talked about her. I asked him once if he was seeing anybody. And you know what he said?"

She seemed to want an answer, so Ginny said, "I don't."

"He said he was in a *transitional phase,*" she said with a dramatic roll of the eyes. "I mean, what guy our age talks like that?"

Ginny was momentarily distracted by the fact that the girl had somehow taken her for a fellow college student; before she got too excited, though, she recalled that this Dairy Princess was a few ounces short of a full gallon.

"A transitional phase," the waitress said again, waving the pot in the air so the coffee sloshed dangerously toward the spout. "What the heck is *that?*"

Ginny knew exactly where he'd picked up that particular turn of phrase—his new friends over at Café des Artistes. "Did you hear anything she said to him?"

The girl's eyes narrowed. "It's not like I was eavesdropping or anything."

"Of course not," Ginny said. "But if she was yelling, you probably couldn't help but hear."

The waitress paused to put the coffeepot back down on the warmer; Ginny felt her odds of getting through lunch without third-degree burns improve considerably.

"Well," she said, "like I told you, she was pissed. She told Danny she wished he was dead. She said he couldn't humiliate her like that and get away with it. She was the queen of the Winter Carnival or some stupid thing—she said she could have any guy in town and he was a disgusting pig. Or something like that—it was all sort of a rant."

"Do you remember anything else?"

The girl thought about it. "She said something about a rubber—a wrapper she found someplace. I guess it was the wrong brand. I didn't catch it all."

"How long did she stay?"

"Maybe not even two minutes. Danny asked me to finish up, and he hustled her out of here. And the next day he wouldn't say diddly about it, and that was the last I ever saw of him."

"You mean this happened the Saturday before he died?"

"Yeah," the girl said with a shrug. "I thought I told you that already."

More customers were starting to come in, and the girl went off to wait on them. Ginny sat and ate her burger, wondering whether the waitress's story meant anything. If nothing else, it showed that Monique was a liar—or, at best, fantastically self-deluded.

Her ravings about Danny being a "disgusting pig" had one likely source: somehow she must have found out he was involved with Geoffrey Dobson. And although Ginny would never be able to prove it, she was pretty sure she'd just solved the mystery of who had flattened Danny's tires; it had happened the very next day, and that kind of passive-aggressive stunt seemed right up Monique's alley.

But when Ginny had talked to her at the trailer park, she'd seemed convinced that she'd lost the love of her life. So whom had she been lying to? Ginny—or herself?

"Virginie Lavoie." Ginny felt a smack on the back, looked up to see the owner of the booming baritone. It was Judge Sweringen, who'd presided over the town court for even longer than Rolly had been chief of police. "How's your dad?"

"Fine," she said.

"He still playing golf?"

"I guess."

He sat down next to her. The Dairy Princess instantly appeared and filled his coffee cup, bringing him a little metal pitcher of skim milk and two Sweet'N Lows. Judge Sweringen was a regular, and he was on a diet.

"Little bird tells me you're not just up here for old times' sake."

The judge's voice was smooth as caramel, but there was something sharp underneath it. Ginny lifted a fry from her plate, studied it.

"Where'd you hear that?"

"Oh, you know how this town is. Everybody knows everybody's business."

She dipped the fry into a pond of ketchup. "Right," she said.

"I just wanted to let you know, if there's anything I can do, just ask. My name still opens a few doors around here."

Ginny turned to look at him. The judge had a generous mop

of gray hair and a matching beard, cropped so close it was like a fog hovering precisely over his cheeks and chin. His eyes were pale blue, his nose very pointy. As a kid, he'd always scared the living crap out of her—like he was the very embodiment of authority, with a sort of moral X-ray vision that told him whether you'd been bad just by looking at you.

"Thanks," she said.

"Rolly tells me you don't think Jack O'Brien killed Danny Markowicz."

So they were cutting straight to the chase; that was fine with her.

"No, I don't," she said. "Do you?"

"I reviewed the evidence myself," he said. "Case seemed open-and-shut. The O'Brien boy was always a loaded pistol."

It was an interesting choice of words. It was also bullshit.

"Well, it can't hurt to look into it," she said. "Not like I'm wasting taxpayers' money, right?"

The waitress dropped Sweringen's lunch in front of him; she must have put in the order the second he walked in the door. It was the Skillet's infamous diet plate. Sweringen cut into the hamburger patty with his fork; the inside was rare to the point of raw, which appeared to be just the way he liked it.

"I'd think you'd have plenty to take care of down in New York City."

"I took a leave of absence," she said. "I'm staying with Danny's mother."

"Funny how things are different down in the city," he said, sliding a sliver of meat into his mouth. "Up here we'd just call it something simpler."

The hair on the back of her neck snapped to attention. "Oh, yeah? Like what?"

"Hmm . . . suspension, accepting a bribe—that sort of thing."

His tone was light, like he was talking about her father's golf game. She studied his features—the sharp nose, the weak chin, the ice-blue eyes. Ginny put down her orange soda in midsip and thought, *Shit*.

"Small-town customs are so interesting," she said.

"They say all news is local," Sweringen said. "But sometimes it's nice to pick up the phone and find out what's happening in the wider world."

Damn, damn, damn. Sweringen had been checking up on her; small-town judge or not, the man had connections all over the place. So much for *let me know if I can help,* the weaselly bastard.

"At the moment I'm more concerned with what's happening right here at home," she said. "Like who ran down Geoffrey Dobson in cold blood in the Fish Pond parking lot? And then there's the fifty-thousand-dollar question: who murdered Paula Libanski eighteen years ago and buried her in the woods like a *dog*?"

Her little speech seemed to throw him, if only for a moment. Ginny got the feeling he'd expected his implied threat—*stop your digging or I'll tell everyone the local-girl-made-good is a fraud and a disgrace*—to send her running back to New York with her lunch half-eaten and her tail between her legs. Fat chance.

"Dobson was a drug dealer who sold poison to our children," he said. And on that point she could hardly argue with him.

"What about Paula?"

"A tragedy," he said. "But after so many years justice may never be served."

Ginny watched him raise another piece of the ruby-red meat to his lips. It was the thinnest of slices, like he was trying to make it last.

Sweringen obviously had an agenda; he wanted her out of town on a rail. The question was why.

"Did you know Paula?" she asked.

"Everyone knew her," he said. "She was a rather infamous character." Again, she couldn't argue.

"You presided over her shoplifting case, didn't you?"

He reached for his coffee. "I don't recall."

"I do. Paula got busted for stealing some makeup at Newberry's. You let her off with a warning. Which was odd, because you had such a hard-ass reputation." He didn't answer, just took another careful sip of coffee. "Then she got picked up for underage drinking, and even though you could've thrown the book at her, she got community service, which as far as I can recall, she never even did."

He cleared his throat, as though the coffee had gone down the wrong way. "I'm sure," he said, "that Miss Libanski served her sentence."

There was something different in his voice all of a sudden. And Ginny realized: *He's afraid of me.*

34

You know," Ginny said, "there are a few things I remember about Paula—a few things that stand out in my mind. You want to know what they are?"

The waitress had drifted over to top off the judge's coffee cup. She whisked Ginny's empty Fanta glass off the counter with a flourish and poured her another, even though the Skillet didn't do free soda refills. She winked at Ginny, like they were best friends and coconspirators.

When she was out of earshot, Ginny smiled at the judge, all

sugar and spice and everything nice. She said, "One, Paula was extremely beautiful. Two, she'd do just about anything to get what she wanted. Three, she slept around like other people shake hands. And four, she had a thing for older guys." The judge kept his gaze fixed on his plate, where the meat juices had tinged the cottage cheese a nauseating shade of pink. "Maybe you haven't heard," she said. "But Paula was pregnant when she died. Isn't that *sad*?"

He tried to cover himself, but she still caught it: the sharp intake of breath, the reflexive clenching of jaw muscles. Her hunch was right. Sweringen had been screwing her.

"Maybe you don't recall," the judge said. "But the publisher of the *Transcript* is a close friend of mine."

She revived her saccharine smile. "How terrific for you both."

He smiled back. "It would be a shame if those troubles of yours made their way into the paper."

"Tragic," she said.

He opened his mouth for what was doubtless going to be another cagy riposte, but he never got the chance to deliver it. Rolly had walked in and made a beeline for her, all florid jowls and indignation.

"Look who's here," he said. "Detective Buttinski."

Oh, hell. At least he wasn't calling her Angie Dickinson anymore.

"Hi, Chief."

"Don't 'hi, Chief' me," he growled. "Who do you think you are, calling in the staties and the Pittsfield M.E. behind my back?"

Ginny opened her eyes wide, fluttering her lids at him. "I'm sorry," she said. "Wasn't that the right thing to do?"

She thought she heard the waitress snicker, but she couldn't see her anywhere nearby. Ginny was starting to like her. Rolly, for his part, had turned a darker shade of purple.

"Now, listen here," he said. "Just because you're some big-city cop doesn't mean you can run around my town like Perry Goddamn Mason."

"Perry Mason is a lawyer," she said.

"Whatever. I'm not gonna stand here and argue with you." He aimed a doughy thumb at a man sitting alone at a booth, reading the paper. "That's the fellow I'm having lunch with," he said. "You know who he is?"

"Sure," she said. "Bob Gianelli. I went all through school with his daughter."

"Well, now he's *Mayor* Gianelli. Or maybe you didn't hear."

She glanced from Gianelli to Rolly to the judge, who was looking at her like she was the hamburger on his plate. "So what's your point?"

"Mayor pretty much runs everything around here," Rolly said. "The building inspector's office, for instance. And I hear Molly's is up for its certificate of occupancy." He winked at her, and she noted that even his eyelids were fat. "Be a damn shame if it flunked and Jimmy Griffin had to close down."

Ginny looked from Rolly to Sweringen and back again. She wouldn't be surprised if the two of them broke into song, like the chorus of a Broadway musical.

"For chrissake," she said, "did the two of you practice this beforehand? You're one hell of an act. You're the goddamn Ice Capades of extortion." She'd cracked a wide smile, something that seemed to throw Rolly off his game. "But hey, the more the merrier. Maybe Mr. Mayor'd like to come over and threaten to bust Sonya for unlicensed day care."

Rolly was at a loss for words. The judge wasn't.

"You're making a mistake," he said.

"Wouldn't be the first time," she replied. "But hey—I'm an amateur. It's hard to beat building a new hunting lodge with money you stole from a drug dealer." She turned to the judge.

"Or letting the town whore off the hook for the price of a blow job."

Sweringen's fork fell to the plate with a clatter.

"By the way," she told him, "make sure to tell your friend at the *Transcript* that I changed my name. It's Virginia now. With an 'a,' not an 'e.' Virginie just didn't suit me." She turned back to Rolly. "Oh. And one more thing. If you go after Jimmy Griffin, I will well and truly kick your fat ass from here to New York City."

She tossed a ten-dollar bill on the counter, offered a jaunty wave to the newly elected mayor, and walked out into the sunshine. There was sweat under her armpits. But otherwise, she was cool.

"His name," she said, "was Michael Scott. He was a detective in my squad. And he was married."

Jimmy sat opposite her on a folding chair in his office, a tiny space filled out by a desk and his racing bike suspended from a hook in the ceiling. The air around them was thick with the smell of chocolate-chip cookies. Ginny was pretty sure she could also detect another odor—call it *eau de guilt*—but it was probably just her imagination.

"You know," he said, "you don't have to tell me this."

"Seems like I do," she said. "I'd rather have you hear it from me than read it on the front page of the local rag."

"You really think Sweringen'll make good on his threat? Even though you know he was screwing Paula?"

"Maybe," she said. "Maybe not. Either way I think it's time to come clean."

She took a deep breath. It wasn't as though the story hadn't been playing in her head every night for two months. But putting it into words was a whole other thing.

"Mike wasn't my partner," she said. "But we worked together on a couple big cases." She examined her pinkie finger, then started chewing on the nail. "I fell for him. I don't know how to explain it. But I knew he was married, and I didn't give a damn. What I didn't know was that he was dirty."

"Dirty how?"

"You name it. He was on the take practically from the day he graduated from the academy. Nothing big at first—just taking favors from the stores on his beat. 'Keep the street kids away from my shop, and I'll give you a big-screen TV.' That kind of thing. Eventually, he was taking bribes from defense lawyers to help get their clients off the hook—forty, fifty grand a case."

"But how—"

"How did he pull it off? A bunch of different ways. If it was his case, he'd screw up on the stand—not so you could put your finger on it, but he'd give the jury reasonable doubt. Mike's a bastard, but he's not stupid. Or he'd call in a favor, and a material witness would come down with amnesia."

"And somehow you got dragged into it?"

"Internal Affairs had their eye on him for years. One day we're working our cases, and two guys from the rat squad come in and read him his rights. And there I am with my mouth hanging open—I thought the whole thing was a mistake."

"So what happened to you? Guilt by association?"

She shook her head. "Mike's not what you'd call a stand-up guy. The first thing he did was start naming names. He cut a deal for a reduced sentence, and IAB started investigating fifty other cops. One of them was me. And the worst thing was"—she drew in another deep breath, exhaled—"he had the evidence to prove it."

No way," Jimmy said. "There's no way you did something like that. You just don't have it in you."

She felt tears prickling at her eyes, and she blinked madly to send them back where they came from. *There it is,* she thought. *This is why I loved him. Jimmy Griffin always saw my best self, always believed I was worthy of being loved back. Until I proved him wrong.*

But all she said was, "I've been waiting a long time to hear that."

Jimmy's face screwed up in confusion. "But the people you work with—didn't they back you up?"

"Some of them. But you gotta understand, it's a goddamn witch hunt—everybody terrified they're going to be next. If what Mike says is true, it'd make the Rampart scandal in L.A. look like nothing."

"But you don't think it's that big?"

"All I know is, I'm innocent. I can only assume some of the others are, too. But Mike's got the chance to save his ass and settle old scores, and he's having a field day—especially over me. Once I found out what he'd been up to, I didn't want anything to do with him, and that made him furious. Nobody dumps Mike Scott."

"What did he say you did? All you told me before was that it was a rape case."

She ran her fingers through her hair. It was a long, sordid story, and at the moment she barely had the energy for the condensed version.

"There was this guy named Alexander Van Vlick—twenty

years old, from a society family on Park Avenue. He's home from college over Christmas, but his folks are off skiing, so he's got the apartment to himself. He picks up a girl at a club and brings her home along with a couple of his friends, and the two of them go to his room to fool around.

"She's okay with it at first, but it turns out that Alexander likes it rough. He's loaded, and when she won't go along, he gets pissed off. He beats her up and rapes her. It turns out she wasn't the first."

"And his friends had no idea what he was doing?"

"They say nothing bad happened. *She* says that at one point she got away and made it as far as the living room. Alexander dragged her back in, and from the way she describes it his buddies thought it was a lark."

"And you're telling me this guy got acquitted?"

"You haven't heard the worst of it. She was only fifteen. She looked older, but the girl was a sophomore in high school."

There was a bottle of water on Jimmy's desk, and Ginny took a drink. The condensed version wasn't turning out to be so condensed, after all.

"I wasn't the lead detective," she said. "But it was a big media case, what some cops call a red ball, so there were four of us working different aspects of it—me, Mike, and two others.

"Since the girl was so young, even if the guy could convince a jury the sex was consensual, he was still going down for statutory rape. His semen was all over her. The only way he could skate was if something happened to the rape kit."

She paused, ostensibly to take another drink, but really to delay the inevitable. What she did was so stupid it killed her for Jimmy to hear. But better from her than the morning paper.

"The day after we picked up Van Vlick, Mike called me real early. He said he'd made a mistake with the rape kit. He'd gotten the samples mixed up with another case, and it could cost him his job. He begged me to go down to the lab before they processed it—told me he was tied up with his kids, and since I was working the case, too, it wouldn't break the chain of evidence. So like a jerk, I signed it out and gave it to Mike, and he fixed things and brought it back."

"And when they ran the DNA," Jimmy said, "it didn't match the rich kid."

"Of course not. He was exonerated."

"And this Mike blamed the whole thing on you?"

"He had my signature on the evidence log. Plus my bank records. Like a moron, I kept some money for him, supposedly to keep his wife from cleaning him out in a divorce. So I'm screwed. I didn't get cuffed and processed, but I'm on suspension until they figure out which tree to hang me from."

"Don't you have a lawyer?"

"From the PBA, and a union delegate, but with everything that's going down they've got their hands full. And anyway, it all happened a few weeks before Danny died. I haven't really had a chance to deal with it."

"Whatever happened to the girl?"

"Her family filed a civil suit against the Van Vlicks, and of course the papers painted her like some money-grubbing liar. They never printed her name, but it came out on the Internet and she had to leave school. A couple of weeks later I found out she OD'd."

"And *died*?" he asked.

"And died," she said.

They say confession is good for the soul. Ginny had no idea if she had a soul in the first place—or, if she did, where it was bound to end up—but she had to admit that unburdening her-self to Jimmy made her feel a hundred pounds lighter.

When she was finished, as though he couldn't bear to leave her so exposed, he told her he wanted to explain about his af-ternoon delivery rounds. She told him he didn't have to; he told her to shut up and listen.

He was lonely, he said, and so were they; it hadn't meant any-thing, and the women hadn't paid for anything but the pastries. His last stop, he swore, was that afternoon with Mrs. Marchand. Lately, the whole thing had started to feel silly and sordid.

"It was such a crazy coincidence," Ginny said. "I find you coming out of the same house where Danny got that gun."

"It's not much of a coincidence," he said. "You could say I was the reason Danny was ever there in the first place."

"Huh?"

"Lorna—Mrs. Marchand—she was looking for somebody to build a new garage. I recommended Pete's company."

"Oh."

She felt exhausted and clammy, like she'd been doing wind sprints up Bradley Street hill. Jimmy must have noticed, because he got out of his chair and knelt down in front of her and put his hands on her shoulders.

"You didn't do anything wrong," he said, "except fall in love with the wrong guy."

She shook her head, bit her bottom lip. "It wasn't love," she said. "I don't know what it was."

He lifted a hand from her shoulder and stroked her cheek. She started to smile at him, but the whole thing was just too much, and she had to concentrate on not crying like a fool. But he noticed and smiled back at her a little, and then he leaned in and kissed her.

It was different than before—different from when they were

kids and from when they'd been screwing like maniacs the previous week. It was hard for her to describe; all she could think was that the kiss was whimsical and grave both at once. It lasted a long time, and then he pulled back and said, "Spend the night with me."

"Here?"

"No, you idiot. At my house. I want to show it to you."

"I've been to your house a hundred times."

"Not my parents' place. That's where my brother and his wife live. I mean, the place I had built up on the mountain."

"Really? Where?"

"Off the trail, near where we went the other day."

She thought about it for a while. Then she said, "Okay."

"Yeah?" A broad grin had crept across his face. Sometimes he really didn't look an hour over sixteen.

He gave her directions, and she promised to be there by seven. She went back to Sonya's to take another shower and—on the off chance that Judge Sweringen made good on his threat—to tell Sonya everything that she'd just told Jimmy.

Sonya listened, not saying a word until she was finished. Ginny expected her friend to lecture her for getting involved with a married man, to tell her she was disappointed that Ginny had strayed so far from the values she'd been raised with, but something in Sonya had changed over the past twenty-four hours. It was like she'd torn free from her moorings and was rushing along in uncharted waters where there were no moral absolutes. She'd said she was going to kill the man who'd murdered Danny; Ginny was starting to think it was no empty threat.

Nevertheless, by six-thirty Ginny was as giddy as a junior on prom night. She'd come to town with all of three pairs of pants—jeans, khakis, and the black trousers she'd worn to two funerals. She opted for the khakis by process of elimination, and when all of her shirts seemed too mannish, Sonya took pity on her and offered her a pale blue angora sweater pulled from a box in her closet marked SKINNY CLOTHES.

She got into Danny's truck, but instead of starting the engine she first pulled out her cell phone.

"Dr. Zeigler."

"Hi," she said. "It's Detective Lavoie. I wanted to thank you for calling earlier. I'm sorry it was a little weird."

"Next time," he said, "let's keep it off speakerphone."

"I know. I'm sorry. The victim's sister thought she'd run off back then. Finding out she was murdered has hit her pretty hard."

"That's why I'm a pathologist," he said. "The dead are a hell of a lot easier to deal with than the living."

"I was hoping you could do me one more favor. Is it possible to get DNA from the remains of the fetus?"

"Should be. Why?"

"If I send you a sample from the victim's other child, could you tell me if the two had the same father?"

"Are you referring to the Danny Markowicz case?"

"That's right."

"Then there's no need to send a sample. My office ran some tests for your local coroner. There's enough left over to process the DNA. It'll take at least a week, though. We're pretty overloaded."

"I'm grateful for whatever you can do," she said. She made a mental note to send him a bottle of Scotch and started the engine.

Jimmy's house was in Florida, a tiny hamlet known principally for its rutabagas; the locals said there was something about the dirt. The irony of such a name slapped on a town in the snowy Berkshire mountains wasn't lost on anybody: every year the local paper took a photo of the WELCOME TO FLORIDA sign dripping with icicles and ran it on the front page like it was a joke no one had ever told before.

She was glad to be driving Danny's truck as she headed up what passed for Jimmy's driveway, a steep dirt road checker-boarded with rocks and ruts. She parked the truck next to Jimmy's, still a fair hike from the house up a long, steep wooden staircase.

She paused to check herself in the rearview mirror: hair neat, lipstick unsmeared, nothing obvious sticking out of her teeth. It was as good as it was going to get.

She got out of the truck and headed for the house, the dark-ness illuminated by spotlights affixed to the trees. She wasn't sure just what was going to happen tonight, but her gut told her that she was exactly where she was supposed to be.

As it turned out, though, she was wrong. She'd just mounted the first step when she felt the knife at her throat.

Don't move."

It was a male voice, maybe vaguely familiar, *definitely* not friendly. She stood stock-still, assessing the situation. Was he alone? And where the hell had he come from?

"Don't move," he said again. "Or I'll slit your fuckin' throat. Got it?"

He was sounding increasingly edgy. The knife at her throat was anything but steady; the tip of the blade had scraped skin, its trail written in a thin line of her blood.

"I'm not moving," she said. "What do you want?"

"Get back in the truck," he said. "We're going for a ride."

"Please don't hurt me," she said. She was trying to sound helpless; if he thought she was some hysterical female, he might drop his guard. "I'll do anything you want," she said, not moving a muscle. "Just please don't hurt me."

She could feel him breathing heavily behind her, his whole body reeking of tobacco. She cast a careful glance down at the arm around her neck. Even through the flannel shirt she could tell he was one burly son of a bitch. The only reason they were close to the same height was that she was standing on a step six inches off the ground.

"Now step down, real slow."

How had this guy come out of nowhere? There hadn't been a car following her; she was sure of that. She'd been watching her back ever since her brakes were cut. You didn't carry a gun in the waistband of your pants and then go blithely about your business like nothing was amiss—and if you did, you deserved whatever you got.

Had he somehow known she was coming to meet Jimmy? It seemed unlikely. *He was hiding in the bed of the truck,* she thought. *It's the only way. And me so hepped up about my big date I didn't even notice. Christ, maybe I do deserve to get gutted like a fish.*

It all flashed through her brain in a matter of seconds. But it was clearly too long for Mr. Burly Arm; he pressed the knife harder against her throat. "I said step down," he growled into her ear. "And don't even think about yelling for help. I'll cut you open before anybody gets down here."

"Okay, okay," she said. "Just please don't hurt me."

She still had her right hand on the railing; in her left was a paper bag containing a twelve-dollar bottle of Australian Shiraz. She raised both as though in surrender. Then, gambling that bulk and speed didn't mix, she whirled around and smashed it against his head with both hands. She'd aimed blind, and it struck only a glancing blow. But it was enough to shatter the bottle, a shower of bloodred wine raining over them both.

He stumbled backward, not so much stunned as monumentally pissed off. The man's head must be made of concrete. But he'd dropped the knife; that was something.

She reached for the gun at her back, but it was under layers of sweater and leather jacket, and she wasn't fast enough. God damn it; she really ought to have invested in an ankle holster.

He grabbed at her shoulders and called her a crazy bitch, and she kneed him in the groin so hard it even hurt *her*. He gasped but didn't go down, so she punched him twice, a right cross followed by an uppercut, just like on the bag at the PAL gym.

Even that didn't drop him. She finally got ahold of the .38 and aimed it at him, right hand steadied with her left. She cocked it, the click one of the most satisfying sounds she'd heard in her entire life.

"Freeze," she said.

He stood there panting, still partly doubled over from the pain in his gonads. "What the *fuck*?"

The guy was about forty-five—topping six feet, weighing in around two-fifty. His gut was even bigger than she'd imagined when it was pressed against her back. He was wearing an old mesh cap that said JOHN DEERE, a pair of dirty tan Carhartt work pants, leather gloves, a fraying down vest over a red-and-blue-checked flannel shirt. If his voice had been familiar, his round and bushy-bearded face was not.

"Who are you?" she spat out. He glared at her. "If you're

wondering if I know how to use this thing, let me assure you that I'm a cop and I damn well do."

He didn't answer, just kept glaring at her with an expression that said he really, really wanted his knife back.

"Ginny?"

It was Jimmy's voice, coming from the top of the stairs, and it distracted her for half a second—not long, but just enough for the guy to duck into the woods.

She chased after him, trying to follow the sound of his lumbering body as it crackled through the underbrush, but it was no use. There was no moon, and Jimmy lived in the middle of nowhere. She emerged from the trees to find her date at the bottom of the stairs.

"I saw your headlights, but you didn't come up." He took in the gun in her hand, the shards of green glass and wine-soaked paper, the stains on her sweater that looked so much like blood. "What the hell is going on?"

She told him what had just gone down, pausing to don a glove and retrieve the guy's serrated hunting knife from where he'd dropped it, and when she was finished, it took some convincing to stop Jimmy from carrying her up the stairs like an invalid. But she made it up on her own power—Jimmy with an insistent arm around her waist, Ginny reminding him that she'd been the one to clean the other guy's clock, thank you very much.

He took her into his house, a log-cabin–style place with wide windows looking out onto the pitch-black mountain. A table in the corner of the living room had been set for two, all wineglasses and candlelight, but Jimmy sat her down on the couch and made her take off her sweater so he could look her over.

He went away for a minute and came back with a bottle of

alcohol and some cotton balls, which he dabbed at the tiny drops of blood that formed a connect-the-dots across her throat; she sat there and winced, topless except for her black bra. Her khakis were also covered with wine, pungent and damp, and after he had disappeared again, he came back with a T-shirt and a pair of gym shorts.

"So much for all my primping," she said, putting them on.

"You primped?" He cracked the first smile of the evening. "I'll take that as a compliment."

"And I'll take a bag of ice," she said. "I split my knuckles when I clocked that guy." He got her the ice, sat back down, and just looked at her. "What are you staring at?" she asked.

"You said that guy was like twice your body weight."

She rolled back her shoulders, rotating her neck. Her back hadn't really been right since the car accident. "Yeah," she said, "but he was slow."

"You turned into one hell of a woman," Jimmy said. "You know that, right?"

"Oh, sure," she said. "A disgraced cop who can't even figure out who killed her best friend's kid. I'm surprised nobody's thrown me a parade."

"Shut up. You just faced down some psycho in my front yard, and you didn't even break a sweat."

"Yeah," she said, shifting the ice bag from one hand to the other. "But I can't bake for shit."

He shook his head, exasperated and amused. "What are you gonna do about this guy?"

"Report it to the county sheriff. At least we're out of Rolly's jurisdiction." The look on his face told her otherwise. "Hell no. You're *kidding* me."

"Town contracts out its police coverage. Rolly's our guy."

"Oh, crap," she said. "Then I guess I gotta deal with him. I figure I'll look through some mug books in the morning and see if he has a record—if they've even got mug books up here. And I could try tracing his knife. It looks expensive."

Jimmy stood up and headed for the other side of the granite counter that divided the living room from the kitchen. "You want a drink? *I* sure want a drink."

"I brought some wine," she said, "but I used it to split that guy's head open." He called it a worthy cause and got each of them a bottle of Heineken. "You know," she said, "living up here, I'm surprised you don't have a dog. You were so nuts about that puppy you got senior year."

"That puppy lived to fifteen," he said. "Just lost her last Easter. Haven't had the heart to get another one yet."

"I'm sorry."

He acknowledged it with a nod, then said, "You hungry? I was gonna grill us some steaks. There's baked potatoes in the oven. And salad."

"That," she said, "is pretty damn domestic."

He popped open the beers and handed her one. "I'm thinking about opening a café downtown—salads and panini sandwiches and smoothies and like that. Place on Marshall just came up for sale. They don't do meals, but I figure I can expand."

"Café des Artistes?"

"That's the one."

The news made her unaccountably sad. Topher had lost the man he loved, and then he'd lost the dream of him, to boot. Now he was giving up the business he'd built from nothing. What a damn shame.

"Can we hold off on dinner?" she asked. "I'm a little too wound up right now."

"Too wound up to talk?"

There was a different tone in his voice all of a sudden—something weighty and serious, like he'd gone from discussing the weather to debating Middle East peace.

"Um . . . no."

He sat down on the couch, and his beer bottle met the glass coffee table with a gentle clink. Hers she kept on her lap like a shield.

He took a deep breath, and Ginny had the distinct feeling he was gathering his courage. Apparently, he found it.

"I still love you," he said.

Never mind the beer; the wind rushed out of her like she'd been the one to get kicked in the nuts. "Jesus," she said. "You don't beat around the bush."

He shrugged, ran a nervous hand through his reddish-blond hair. "We're too old to screw around. And you know me, Gin. I'm not a complicated guy. I can be a pain in the ass sometimes, but I'm not complicated. The way I figure it, most people are lucky if they find the right person once. Not a lot of them get a second go-round."

She didn't answer—which was no accident, because she had no idea what to say.

"Look at us," he went on. "We're almost thirty-five years old. Neither one of us has had a decent relationship since the day we broke up. You even been close to marrying somebody else?" She shook her head. "Me neither. That's gotta tell you something."

"Maybe it tells me we're both maladjusted freaks."

"Then we better stick together," he said. "Because nobody else'll have us."

She smiled; she couldn't help it. "That's for sure."

"So what do you say?"

"Excuse me," she said, "but have you noticed that we live on two different planets?"

"I know that. Believe me. And there's no way I could ever live in that city, and I know there's no way you want to move back here."

"So?"

"So let's go for it anyway."

She took a sip of her beer, just for something to do, but it tasted bitter in her mouth, and she let it drain back into the bottle. "For chrissake, I'm the woman," she said. "I thought *I* was supposed to be the hopeless romantic."

"We're all screwed up," he said with a laugh. "I bake bread, you beat up guys twice your size. It's a good thing I'm confident in my masculinity."

She shook her head, tried not to laugh, but the serious expression on her face just wouldn't stay put. She looked at him, sitting there next to her on the couch, eyes lit up with nerves and humor and hope. She'd been in love with him since she was fifteen, and old habits die hard. But she also knew that sometimes love wasn't enough.

"I need to ask you something first," she said. "I need to know you understand why I left before." He didn't answer. "Jimmy, I know you were all gung ho about it at the time, but do you really think you were ready to be somebody's father at eighteen? Because I was sure as hell not prepared to be somebody's mother."

She watched him consider it, though he still didn't say anything.

"I'm sorry about the abortion," she said. "I really am. I didn't do it anywhere near as cavalierly as you think I did. But I thought it was the best thing for both of us at the time, and I still do." He looked away, out the big bay window and into the darkness. "Come on. We were just kids, for chrissake. I had my scholarship to UMass, and you were all fired up to get your business degree at State. If we'd gotten married and had a kid that young, God only knows how much we might regret right now."

After another long silence he said, "I know that."

"Yeah, maybe rationally you do. But if you're gonna hold it against me for the rest of my life, then I don't see how this is gonna work."

He didn't answer at first. But after some more staring out at the emptiness beyond the window, he said, "I guess you've got a point."

"I do?"

"I'm still not saying I agree with what you did. But I suppose I can understand why you did it." He finally turned back to face her. "And since I'm still nuts about you . . . I guess I gotta let it go."

"Yeah?"

"Yeah."

She searched his face, trying to make sure he meant it. When she was satisfied, she said, "All right."

"All right what?"

She threw her head back, eyes rolled to the ceiling. "You're just not going to let up until you make me say it like some sappy goof, are you?"

"You bet your ass."

"Fine. You win. I always loved you, and I still love you, and God help us both when the phone bills come due."

He exhaled, like he'd just dodged a speeding truck. "Thank *God*."

She laughed at him, but not unkindly. "So now what?"

"Now comes the part where I pick you up and carry you to the bed," he said. "Before you beat me to it."

His alarm went off at four the next morning. He silenced it and made a phone call and came back to bed. The next thing she knew it was seven, and he was feeding her bacon and explaining that even though she was the Queen of the Amazons, he hadn't wanted to leave her alone in his house in the woods in the middle of the night. But he hadn't wanted to rouse her that early, either, so he'd told his workers to make do without him for a few hours.

They camped out in bed, eating his homemade biscuits slathered in maple butter and listening to the news on the radio. At one point she looked at him and he looked back, and their expressions were identical: *I absolutely cannot believe my luck.* Then she smiled and kissed him, and the next thing she knew it was eight-thirty.

They left together, driving in tandem down the mountain and splitting off when he went to work and she turned left for Sonya's and some clean clothes. The day-care kids were back, and Sonya had them finger-painting at the kitchen table. She left them there, with admonishments about not making a mess, and followed Ginny into Danny's room and closed the door.

"I guess you had a good time," Sonya said. Ginny thought there was a note of censure in her voice, but it might just be stress.

"That depends on which part of the night you're talking about." Speaking low to make sure the kids didn't hear—that little Britney probably had her ear pressed to the door, on alert for potty-mouthed profanities—she told Sonya how she'd been attacked outside Jimmy's house. Two days earlier her friend would have oohed and clucked about her near miss; now she just stood there and took it in, like the world had nothing left to surprise her.

"And you have no idea who he was?" Ginny shook her head. "What do you think he planned on doing?"

"Nothing good."

Sonya nodded, cracked open the door to make sure the kids hadn't run amok, and closed it again. "What about Jimmy?"

"He wants us to get back together."

"And?"

"And so do I."

Sonya hugged her tight, which was the last thing Ginny had expected, given Sonya's brittle mood. But when they pulled away, her friend's face was still in shadow. "Are you going to start sleeping up there every night?"

"He wants me to. I told him I was going to stay here for the time being."

Sonya exhaled a relieved breath. "I'm selfish," she said. "But I really don't want you to go."

"It's okay. Staying out there in the middle of the woods is probably asking for trouble, anyway. I mean, who knows what this guy might try next?" Then something else occurred to her. "You know, maybe I *should* move out. What if I'm putting you and Pete in danger—not to mention those kids?"

"What do you think?" Sonya asked. "He's gonna burn the house down while we're sleeping?"

"I sure as hell hope not. But Rolly already threatened to shut down Jimmy's business. Who knows what else he'd try to pull?"

"You don't think Rolly had anything to do with you getting attacked last night? I mean, I know he's a lousy police chief, but—"

"I already told you he stole a wad of cash from that dealer's car. Once you're dirty, it's a slippery slope."

"What about Judge Sweringen?"

Ginny thought about it. "He obviously doesn't want me to find out who Paula was seeing," she said. "But if he was behind my getting attacked, then why would he threaten me to my face? It's just too obvious."

Sonya took another peek at the kids, then sat down on the edge of the bed. Something was playing out across her face, and Ginny just stood there and watched her. Finally, Sonya said, "I really am selfish."

"What are you talking about?"

"I know I should tell you to go home and forget about all this. I should say finding out who killed Danny and Paula isn't worth it—you might get hurt, or worse. But I just can't."

Ginny sat on the bed and put an arm around her. "You could tell me all that," she said, "but I still wouldn't go."

38

Sonya took it in, the two of them sitting in silence for a couple of minutes. Then they heard shrieking from the other side of the door, and Sonya leaped up to deal with it. "Oh, I almost forgot to tell you. Father LeGrand called for you last night. He said there was no answer on your cell."

"There's no service up at Jimmy's. What did he say?"

"He'll be in his office at the French church all afternoon. It's his day off, but he's catching up on paperwork. You can stop by."

"Did you tell him what it was about?"

Sonya shook her head. "Actually," she said, "I think he's hoping you've decided to get religion."

Ginny laughed that one off and jumped in the shower. She put on her black pantsuit—jeans didn't seem right for meeting a priest—and admitted she was going to have to shop for some new clothes. The idea was about as appetizing as taking another swim in the Hoosic.

Since it wasn't even noon yet, she drove downtown to report the previous night's assault. She was two blocks from the police station when she saw a certain diminutive blonde on the sidewalk, heading into one of the stores on Main Street. Ginny pulled over and parked. She'd been meaning to talk to Monique ever since the Dairy Princess told her about the run-in with Danny at the Golden Skillet. She wasn't sure if Monique had any useful information, but when she interviewed her, the girl had spun a web of lies; who knew what else she might be hiding?

The store she'd entered was the cutesy gift shop that had replaced the old Newberry's five-and-dime. As it turned out, Monique wasn't shopping; she'd taken up residence behind the counter, where she was polishing a display case filled with homemade fudge.

"Oh," she said when she looked up and saw Ginny. "It's you."

"I didn't know you worked here," Ginny said by way of an icebreaker.

"It's my part-time job," Monique said. "Weekends and whenever I don't have class. When the owner's not here, I'm in charge."

The last sentence was uttered with undisguised pride—though Monique's authority was rendered less impressive by the fact that there wasn't a single customer in the store.

"We need to talk," Ginny said, figuring she'd better get to the point before somebody walked in. "About Danny."

Monique's eyes were blue and very empty. "We already did," she said.

"You gave me the fiction version," Ginny said. "Now I need the truth."

"I don't know what you—"

"You and Danny weren't engaged, Monique. I know about the fight you had at the Skillet. I know you know that Danny was seeing other people. Specifically—other men."

Monique's face flushed crimson, such a vivid contrast to her fair skin it was almost funny. She threw the cleaning rag on the counter, her expression suddenly and intensely furious.

"You're a liar," she said.

"Stop it," Ginny said. "Wake up, for chrissake. You and Danny were not going to live happily ever after. I know you found out he had a gay—"

Monique slapped her across the face. Ginny hadn't been prepared for it, and it brought her up short. Cheek stinging, she did the only logical thing: she slapped her back, harder.

"Ow," Monique yelped. She gaped at Ginny, like she couldn't believe anyone would have the gall to do such a thing to her. Then she started to cry—real heaving sobs, not the crocodile tears she'd shed outside her family's trailer. This time her eye makeup was going all to hell.

"Danny was murdered," Ginny said. "I'm here to figure out who did it, and your stupid stories only made my job that much harder. Now I need you to tell me what you know."

Still sobbing, Monique reached for a stack of napkins and used one to wipe her face. When she finally spoke, her voice was small. "I don't know anything," she said.

"You found a condom wrapper," Ginny prodded. "Isn't that right?"

The girl nodded and blew her nose. "It was a weird kind, Seven something. I found it in a jacket Danny left in my car. And when I asked him about it, he got all funny. And then he told me—" She tripped over the words, then started again. "He told me he didn't know who he was anymore. He said he might be in love with someone else. And then when I got all upset, he told me it wasn't even another girl—like that would make it easier. Did he really think it would be better to find out I was in love with some *pervert*? And then he just left for work at the Skillet. Just like that, like I was nothing. Like he didn't owe me . . ."

She started crying harder. Ginny reached out and put a hand on her arm. Monique might not be her nominee for Coed of the Year, but finding out the guy you love is banging a man—that's got to inspire sympathy in women everywhere.

"So you let the air out of his tires to get back at him." Monique nodded, still snorting and sniveling. "Was that all you did? Tell me the truth."

Monique looked up at her with raccoon eyes. Her mascara was obviously not waterproof. "That's all," she said. "I swear. I was just so *mad*."

"You didn't do something crazy? Like talk some guy into teaching Danny a lesson?"

Those black-rimmed eyes widened in unmistakable shock. "What? *No.* I'd never hurt Danny. I loved him. Even though he made a fool out of me, I still loved him." A memory struck her, inspired her to cry even harder. "I told him I wanted him to die," she said. "And then he really *did*. But I didn't mean it. I never ever meant it. I said so many awful things—and I never even got the chance to take them back."

She was telling the truth; that was Ginny's instinct, anyway. Monique seemed far too unhinged to be lying. She kept sobbing and sobbing until Ginny finally put the CLOSED sign on the store, lest a fudge-seeking customer come in and find a hysterical ex-cheerleader behind the counter.

Ginny stayed with her until the owner returned, explained that poor Monique was having a delayed reaction to the shock of Danny's death and was in no shape to work. She loaded the girl into Danny's truck—the sight of which prompted a whole new round of tears—drove her home, and plopped her into an easy chair in the trailer's small but tidy living room.

Then she drove back to town, finally getting to where she'd been going before the detour: the police station. The officer, Mr. Polka-Dotted Miniskirt from her youth, took her statement about the previous night's assault and pointed out that her description could fit half the guys in the county. She flipped through what passed for a mug book, but her attacker wasn't there.

"Funny," the cop said. "Guy didn't even bother to wear a mask."

The thought had already occurred to her. Either the man who'd attacked her was too dumb to think of hiding his face, or he figured it didn't matter: Ginny wasn't supposed to live long enough to ID him.

"He dropped the knife," she said. "I have it. I was hoping you could run the fingerprints."

"Okay," he said, "but we don't do those in-house. If you leave it here, we can send it off to—"

She thanked him, but said she'd just as soon hold on to it; there was no way she was going to let the knife out of her sight. Then, because she couldn't resist, she went from the police station to the bakery, where she and Jimmy made eyes at each other like a pair of fools. After ten or so minutes of that, Ginny left with a complimentary bag of nut cups and walked down a few storefronts to Couture's Sportsman Supply. It had always seemed odd to her that "sportsman" was synonymous with "hunter"—as though the deer were armed and had a sporting chance.

The store was the same size as Molly's—the buildings had been built at the same time by the same developer—but instead of cookies and cakes, the displays were filled with guns and ammo. A row of fishing rods decorated one wall, and in a glass case was a selection of knives, steel polished and gleaming.

Two customers were at the counter, finishing up the negotiation of some taxidermy services. When they left, Mr. Couture smiled at her and asked what he could get for her, and how was her dad doing down in Florida, anyhow?

She displayed the knife, encased in a plastic bag. "Actually," she said, "I was hoping you could help me. I found this in the woods up on the mountain, and I thought maybe you might know whose it is so I can return it."

He picked up the bag and admired the knife. It was seven inches long with the angry serrated blade folded inside the handle, over a foot opened up. The handle had been fashioned from some kind of ivory-colored animal horn, etched in black with the image of pheasants at the edge of a pond.

"She's a beaut," he said. "Nice of you to give it back."

"I figure it probably means a lot to the owner. Did it come from here?"

"Not recently. But maybe last year. Guy from Becket used to make 'em."

"And you're the only store that carried them?"

"Nah. I think he sold 'em all over east of Springfield."

"Is there any way of finding out who bought this particular one? I mean, assuming he bought it here."

He shrugged. "They were all by special order. I could look it up if you don't mind waiting."

She said she didn't; he went into the back and emerged with a plastic file box and riffled through it until he found the right folder. "Joe Preminger."

"That's who bought the knife?"

"Nah. That's the guy who made it." He opened the folder

and pawed through a stack of yellow papers, preprinted order forms that had been filled in by hand.

"Hmm . . . lemme see. Looks like we sold only one of the pheasants. Most people went for the deer or else the trout. Though I never quite figured out why you'd need a blade like this to gut a fish. Or maybe they just liked the picture. Trout were jumping out of the pond real pretty. Okay—here we go." He pulled one sheet from the stack. "Josie Pecor bought it. Christmas present for her son."

"You mean Steve Pecor—lives over on River Street?"

He shook his head. "She's not his mama. And anyway, Steve's no hunter. Since he flipped his motorcycle, he can barely cross the street. It was for his half brother Lance."

"Big guy, maybe six-four, two hundred fifty pounds? Bushy beard?"

"You know him?"

"Not personally," she said. "But I think I was there when he dropped it."

The voice; that was what she'd recognized. Lance Pecor didn't look anything like his half brother Steve—but he *sounded* like him.

It'd taken her all of an hour to find out Lance's particulars: how he'd been laid off when the limestone quarry shut down, then fired from a local auto shop for having a generally miserable disposition. His common-law wife had left him, and he lived in a trailer on his mother's property because the bank had repossessed his house. He had no felony record, just a couple of drunk-and-disorderlies and a bar fight that he'd pled down to a misdemeanor. Oh: and he owned at least three hunting rifles.

It had taken her considerably longer to decide what to do about him. The obvious answer was to call in the local cops, but the idea of them getting a confession out of Pecor seemed absurd. The state police and the county sheriff would say it was Rolly's jurisdiction—and why piss off a brother officer for the sake of collaring some local lout? She thought of recruiting Jimmy, for no other reason than she thought about Jimmy pretty much every waking second that she wasn't thinking about the case, but she dismissed that idea as even more absurd.

No offense to his manhood, but what was he gonna do? Pummel the guy with a baguette?

Then another possibility occurred to her: a man not quite as massive as Pecor, but with a respectable hunting arsenal of his own. So after stopping at Sonya's to change out of the pantsuit, she drove to Libanski Construction and told Pete she might finally have a suspect in Danny's murder. Sequestered in his office, she filled him in on how she'd been attacked the previous night and how she'd traced the knife to Lance.

"So what do you have in mind?" he asked. "Some kind of citizen's arrest?"

The idea seemed to appeal to him. She realized that in all of this, she'd forgotten that Sonya wasn't the only one to have lost a son.

"Not exactly," she said. "But once Rolly gets his hands on him, Pecor's going to lawyer up, and that's going to be the end of that."

"So—what? You want to hold him at gunpoint until he confesses? I doubt that would stand up in court."

"You've got the wrong idea," she said. "I don't even want to confront him. I just want to toss the place for evidence—figure out if I'm headed in the right direction."

"Then what do you need me for?"

"Because only a moron goes into a suspect's house without backup," she said. "Either you've got a death wish or the idea that you're invincible. And I've got neither."

Lance's mother lived out in the hinterlands of Clarksburg, her driveway marked by a decorative wagon wheel and a pair of junker cars. She worked the day shift at the Wal-Mart; at least they wouldn't have to worry about her.

Ginny and Pete parked down the road and walked up, Pete toting his rifle and looking like the hunter he was. She still had the .38 at her waist, because Couture's Sportsman Supply didn't carry ankle holsters.

Pecor's trailer was hell and gone from the one Monique lived in; no birdbaths and plastic-flower pinwheels here. The thing was a ruin, hoisted up on cinder blocks and decorated with rust. There were no cars in sight—at least none that could move.

They emerged from the woods into the weed-choked yard, and Ginny put her ear to the trailer's flimsy side. No snoring, no TV; nobody home.

The door wasn't locked. They entered, and were greeted with the odors of cigarettes and sour milk.

"Come on," Pete said as she started tossing the single space that passed for Pecor's bedroom and living room and kitchen. "Hurry up and find whatever you're after."

"We just got here."

"My heart's beating like a rabbit," he said. "You really do this crap every day?"

"We usually have a warrant," she said. "This breaking-and-entering stuff is what you might call extracurricular."

"Great," Pete said, peering at the driveway through the cracked window. "Could you please do it faster?"

She riffled through the mess: old winter coats, junk mail, greasy chicken buckets, cardboard boxes, dirt-encrusted boots. If Lance ever bothered to cash in all his empty beer bottles, they'd probably be worth more than the trailer itself. She was starting to worry about catching hepatitis from his dirty clothes when Pete interrupted her.

"Ginny."

He was at the window, gesturing wildly. She heard the sound of tires on gravel. *Oh, crap.*

Pecor was driving a ramshackle station wagon—faux wood panels falling off, front fender askew, tires all awiggle, and hubcaps but a memory. She watched him get out of it, the car practically sighing with relief as it was unburdened of his bulk. He stood there under a gray sky, swatting at gnats and smoking a cigarillo, and then made himself even more attractive by taking a leak in the overgrown grass.

"Come on," she told Pete, waving him toward the bathroom. He followed, and she shut the paper-thin door behind them and tried to lock it, but of course the handle was broken. The whole room was no bigger than a phone booth; Ginny was smushed closer against her best friend's husband than she'd ever hoped to be.

They could hear Pecor entering the trailer, the whole thing seeming to shift under his weight like a seesaw. She put a finger to her lips, then tried the window. It was stuck, and she tried to force it and be quiet at the same time. She was only half-successful: the window gave, but in the context of Pecor's rattrap of a home, that meant the whole thing fell out, frame and all.

It landed on the ground outside and shattered with an earsplitting smash. Ginny looked at Pete, and Pete looked at Ginny, and before she could say anything, he'd lifted her up and pushed her through the gaping hole. She cut her hand on the exposed metal, slashed her jeans and the skin underneath, but she made it out— and landed on the broken glass, which cut her up some more.

Pete handed her the rifle through the window and tried to get himself out, but it didn't work: the hole was too small or else he was too big. *Shit.*

She heard Pecor yell, "What the fuck?" and a crash and then him yelling the same thing again. Revolver drawn, she sprinted around the side of the trailer and through the front door, every motion under control. It may have been a couple of months since she went through a door, but she still knew how to do it right.

Pecor was fifteen feet away, meaty right biceps stuck clear through the poor excuse for a bathroom door; Pete must have grabbed his arm when it went through, and the two of them were wrestling like a pair of minks in a cage.

"Freeze!" she shouted, and like Yogi Berra said, it was déjà vu all over again.

She'd clearly surprised the hell out of Pecor, and Pete took the opportunity to reach around the door and knock him a good one in the jaw. It didn't have much of an effect, so she took a few steps forward and pushed the gun barrel against the rolls of fat where his thick neck met his skull.

"Hi, Lance," she said. "Remember me?"

She hadn't planned on interrogating Lance Pecor in his stinking trailer—but you had to roll with the punches. She sat him down in the only good chair and held the .38 on him while Pete stuck him to it with duct tape. When she was done, he looked like a fat, silver mummy—each leg and arm secured to the chair's corresponding anatomy, and a mile of tape wound around his middle for good measure.

Lance swore at them, until Pete punched him again and told him not to talk that way in front of a lady. Never once did their prisoner say anything about them getting in trouble with the cops for their little home invasion, which told Ginny that Lance had plenty to hide.

"What the hell do you want?" he demanded.

Ginny pulled out the hunting knife, still in its plastic bag. "I thought I'd return this," she said.

Lance looked at the knife with puppy eyes; the thing clearly meant a lot to him. "Really?"

"No," she said. "Not really. How stupid are you?" He glared at her but didn't offer an answer. "Talk to me about Danny Markowicz."

"Who?"

"The kid you beat to death."

He turned to Pete, like any guy was better than some crazy lady—even a guy who was standing in his living room holding a hunting rifle. "She's nuts," he said.

Pete aimed the rifle in his direction. "Just answer her."

"But I don't even know the *question.*" The sentence came out in a plaintive whine; Lance Pecor sounded like a big baby.

"Fine," Ginny said. "Let's begin at the beginning. Paula Libanski."

That name, at least, meant something to him. "Who Steve used to bang when we was kids? What about her?"

"Maybe you used to bang her, too."

He shook his head, and a few seconds later his several chins followed. "Did not," he said.

"Sure you did. You knocked her up, and she wanted you to run off with her, but you didn't feel like being anybody's daddy. So you killed her and buried her in the woods by the Fish Pond."

"Did *not*," he said again, and twice as loud.

"Don't lie to me."

"I ain't," he said. "Paula wouldn't give me a go. She said I weren't her type."

Pete and Ginny looked at each other, and they were both thinking, *That's a new one.*

Ginny walked over to Lance and yanked a handful of greasy hairs from his head; he yelped and called her a crazy bitch. It hadn't been a necessary action, but she liked it for the shock value.

"I'm going to send this out for a DNA test," she said. "And it's going to prove you fathered her kid. And *that's* sure as hell going to prove you were screwing her."

"So send it," he shouted. "I'm tellin' you, I never nailed the slut."

Ginny took a good look at him, all clammy sweat and righteous indignation. She was pretty sure he was telling the truth. "Then you've got to be covering for your brother," she said. "Maybe he's not as much of an invalid as he pretends to be."

Lance turned back to Pete, eyes pleading and chin wet with spit. "Will you tell this crazy chick she's way off base?"

Ginny jammed the gun back in her waistband and grabbed the front of Lance's dirty shirt. He tried to look away, but she shook him until he met her eyes. "You put a knife to my throat," she said. "You telling me you just did it for sport?" She held the blade an inch from his face. "You used to work in an auto shop. If I test this against the cut on my brake line, you wanna bet it's not gonna come back positive?"

She was bluffing, or at least grandstanding. She had no idea if it would even be possible to match up the severed hose with the knife that had cut it—but Lance didn't know that.

She let the silence expand; like a shrink, a good detective knows that silence can be her ally. Most people can't handle it, and what they rush to fill it with occasionally turns out to be the truth. Lance glared at her, his two-digit I.Q. struggling to calculate just exactly how much trouble he was in.

"Big deal," he said finally. "You didn't get hurt too bad."

Ginny let go of his shirtfront, and the countervailing force made his head snap back. "It's called attempted murder, you moron."

She quenched a desire to sock Lance again, right in his florid face. The man was utterly disgusting, a bully who lived in squalor, sleeping among piles of dirty dishes and mud-encrusted clothes.

"Ginny?" It was Pete, who'd been rooting around in Lance's putrid possessions for something incriminating. "I think you better take a look at this."

He handed her a piece of paper, white and pristine, probably the cleanest thing in the entire trailer. At the top was the logo for the local Tunnel City Savings Bank. Ginny read it; it was dated two days earlier.

Dear Mr. Pecor,

Per our recent phone conversation, enclosed please find certification that your outstanding mortgage has been paid in full and the foreclosure voided. We regret the error that led to the seizure of your property and are investigating to determine if its source was elec-

tronic or clerical. Again, please accept our sincerest apologies for any
inconvenience.

Yours very truly,
Mary Ellen Montgomery
Loan Officer

So that's what all those packing boxes were for: Pecor had gotten his house back. And not only was it out of foreclosure, the mortgage had been paid off.

Christ, she'd been such an idiot. Lance wasn't after her because he'd been involved with Paula; he was just muscle for hire. The fact that his brother had been dating Paula was a coincidence—and not a particularly big one, since she'd been sleeping with half the town.

She turned back to him, holding the letter three inches from his snout. For the first time, Lance Pecor looked afraid.

"Who are you working for?"

He didn't answer. Even under the rolls of lard, she could see there was a grim set to his jaw. She asked the question a second time, with no more success than the first.

Pete seemed to take his silence as a personal affront. He got right in Lance's face and shook him, twice as hard as Ginny had done before, the legs of the old wooden chair beating a rhythm against the trailer floor. But Lance still wouldn't say anything.

"Attempted murder," Ginny said. "Attempted kidnapping. Not to mention first-degree murder in the death of Geoffrey Dobson."

"*What?*"

"No jury on the planet's gonna believe you didn't run him down on purpose."

"I got no idea what you're talking about."

"Geoffrey Dobson. The drug dealer who knew too much

about Danny's murder. You ripped off a van and ran him down."

"Did *not*," he said. He started to look to Pete for male bonding, then seemed to realize that he might be just as nuts as she was. "Go ahead and beat the piss outta me if you want. But I ain't gonna admit to something I didn't do."

"Then tell us what you did," she said. "That'll do for a start."

Lance gathered all the spit he had left in his mouth and hawked a loogie at her. But it lacked momentum; it fell well short of her and landed on the floor. "Go screw yourself," he said.

Ginny slapped him across the face, hard enough for him to know she was pissed. If Internal Affairs could see her now, roughing up a suspect duct-taped to a chair, it wouldn't help her case one little bit.

"I already got you dead to rights for trying to grab me at knifepoint. The guy who owns the house saw you run away. He can ID you, too." It was a total lie, but again, Lance didn't know that. "And I already told you the cops can match your knife to my car. You're going away for a long time. Only way to shave some time off your sentence is to plead out."

Her speech seemed to shake him, but not nearly enough. Lance shook his head and said, "I ain't tellin' you jack."

"Fine."

She walked the two steps to the kitchen, where a nearly full jug of cheap overproof rum sat among the empty cartons of frozen lasagna. She uncapped it and started sloshing it around the room—over the dirty clothes, the packing boxes, the tin cans filled with cigarette butts. She saved the last bit for Lance Pecor's head. The clear liquid dripped down his cheeks, stinging the red spots where either Pete or Ginny had split the skin.

"What the *fuck*?"

By way of explanation Ginny picked up a stray matchbook

and waved it in his face. "Either you tell me what you know," she said, "or I burn this shithole and let you roast like a fat fucking marshmallow."

"Ginny?"

It was Pete, eyes bugging out of his head. Ginny turned her back on him.

Lance shook his head, rum spraying from it like water off a dog. "You wouldn't," he said, sounding like he was very much worried that she would. "You're a goddamn *cop*."

"You were supposed to kill me, weren't you?" She struck a match and brought it an inch from his hair. "*Weren't* you?"

He nodded. She blew out the match and smacked him again in the face, just for the fun of it. The memory of that giant knife against her throat still pissed her off.

"But that was all I did. Just that and roughing up the Markowicz kid one time. And some digging over at the Fish Pond. But that don't count."

She glanced at the pile of filthy clothes, the mud-covered boots; she should have put two and two together when she first saw them, but with all the squalor, they'd just blended in.

"Bullshit," she said.

There was something in his voice that told her he was lying. Lance may not have killed Danny or even Geoffrey Dobson, but he was guilty of more than he'd admitted so far. She lit another match.

"Okay," he said, pulling as far away from the flame as the tape and the chair would allow. "There was that other guy."

"What guy?"

"The guy today. The one I was supposed to mess up so you'd back off."

A nasty suspicion took up residence in the pit of her stomach. "Who?"

The match burned down and singed her fingers. She barely felt it.

"The dude I ran over on his bike," he said. "The guy who owns Molly's."

She could have killed him. In fact, she might have if Pete hadn't intervened. As they sped along country roads to where Lance had left Jimmy to die not an hour before, she still wasn't entirely sure she'd made the right decision. Well, at least the bastard was damn uncomfortable, trussed up in the truck bed like a prize deer on its way to the taxidermist.

He still wouldn't say who'd hired him. Even when Ginny had murder in her eyes, he wouldn't talk. All he said was that if he did, he'd lose everything and his life wouldn't be worth living, so she might as well go ahead and burn the trailer down around his ears.

"Christ," she told Pete, "can't you go any faster?" They would have called an ambulance—if only they could get a signal on their cell phones. Pete pushed the gas pedal closer to the floor.

It took them forty minutes to find him. There was no evidence on the road; both Jimmy and his bike had flown off the pavement and down a grassy slope at the edge of a cow pasture. Ginny sprinted toward him, tripped over a rock, and lost her footing but stayed upright. She got to his bike first, a spindly, twisted wreck of a thing that didn't bode well for its rider.

Jimmy was lying a few yards away. Her heart and stomach flip-flopped, seemed to change places inside her gut, then righted themselves. He was alive and at least partially awake. He'd been wearing a helmet, which had been bashed so hard it was leaking Styrofoam.

"Jimmy?"

He moaned, eyelids fluttering. Lying there like that, semi-conscious and so goddamn vulnerable, he didn't look much older than the kid she'd found hurt in the woods at the Fish Pond. At least he'd had the good sense to wear a helmet—thank God.

She touched his chest lightly. "Jimmy?"

She was about to tell Pete to get an ambulance, but Jimmy mumbled something and opened his eyes. "What the *hell*?" He groaned, tried to sit up, then thought better of it. "Some ass-hole . . . ran me off the road."

"I know," she said. "We've got him tied up in the back of the truck."

Her answer clearly befuddled him. "You're a freak," he said, and tried to sit up again.

"Don't move." This from Pete, who was standing at the edge of the grass. "I'm gonna call an ambulance."

Jimmy waved him off with his right arm. His left was hanging limply at his side, at something of an odd angle. He sat all the way up and unclipped his bashed-in helmet, the sight of which seemed distinctly sobering. "I think I dislocated my shoulder," he said.

"Which is why we ought to get you an ambulance," Ginny said.

Jimmy shook his head. "Just give me a hand."

He reached out his good arm for support, and although she wanted to argue with him, she helped him up. He looked plenty wobbly, standing there in his skintight biking clothes with his left arm markedly longer than his right, but he managed to stay upright.

Pete grabbed the mangled bike and tossed it in the back of the pickup along with Lance, not making much of an effort to avoid winging him with it. The three of them piled into the truck, Ginny squished up against Pete to keep from touching Jimmy's bad shoulder. He winced over every bump, but he didn't complain about it, and Ginny decided he was a hell of a lot tougher than she'd given him credit for.

Their first stop was the police station, where they marched Lance Pecor inside, still in his duct-tape gift wrapping. Rolly wasn't happy to see Ginny, but Pete was a solid citizen, and that put the chief on his best behavior. She said she wanted to press charges against Pecor for assault and attempted kidnapping, and by way of proof she offered the knife with his prints on the handle and her blood on the blade.

When she was satisfied Rolly was going to lock him up, she and Pete took Jimmy to the emergency room to have his arm shoved back into its socket. After an alphabet soup of tests on his injured noggin, he emerged with nothing more serious than a sling and a prescription for Vicodin. After dropping Pete off, Ginny drove Jimmy home and fed him some soup out of a can, which she somehow still managed to burn.

He ate it anyway, and she sat on the edge of his bed with Jimmy propped up on strategically placed pillows.

"I'm damn glad," she said, "that idiot didn't kill you."

"You're such a poet." He sounded a little dopey; the pills were starting to take effect.

"Seriously, I—"

He waved her off, just like he'd waved off the ambulance. "I know, Gin-Gin."

He hadn't called her that since high school. It had been his pet name for her, and she'd never had the heart to point out that it sounded just like what the girl on *I Dream of Jeannie* called her dog. She leaned over and kissed him lightly on the lips; he reached up with his good arm and kissed her harder.

"I should let you get some rest," she said.

He kept his arm around her. "Don't go yet. You gotta tell me what the hell is going on."

"Don't worry about it."

"You found me in the middle of nowhere, with the guy who hit me taped up in the back of Danny's pickup," he said. "There's gotta be a good story in there."

She told him how she'd tracked down Pecor and interrogated him in his trailer, softening the details so she sounded like less of a psycho. When the drugs finally took over and he was snoring lightly against the pillow, she kissed him on the forehead, made sure the house was locked up tight, and drove down the mountain.

Ginny walked into the church, silent and Gothic and vast, and blessed herself with holy water out of habit. It was a place she'd first entered long before she could speak; she'd been baptized in that marble font, just off to the right of the altar. Although she hadn't given it much thought, she'd half expected the church to seem smaller than she'd remembered, but if anything, it was the opposite. The vaulted ceiling rose high above her head, the crucified Jesus over the altar seeming impossibly far away, looming like a mountain in the distance.

She walked down the aisle, retracing the steps her mother had taken as a bride. She shivered; it was just too weird.

Off to the right, behind the baptismal font, was a door that opened up into a vestry filled with robes, hung on hangers like coats outside a party. The image struck her as vaguely heretical, though she had no idea why; did she expect them to be kept in a golden ark, like something from *Indiana Jones*?

Through the vestry was another door, marked PARISH OF-FICE. Ginny knocked, and Father LeGrand said to come in.

He was sitting behind a dark wooden desk that took up most of the room; for no particular reason, it occurred to Ginny to wonder how they'd gotten it through the narrow door. He told her to sit down and asked if she wanted some tea. She said she did. He poured her a cup from a brown clay pot on the windowsill to his left, flinching when he reached for it. Sonya had told her the priest had a bad case of bursitis.

"So," he said, "what did you want to speak to me about?"

Ginny shifted in her chair like a schoolkid in hot water. She'd never had the occasion to grill a priest; even though it was his day off and he wasn't dressed in clerical garb, she still felt like she was committing some eighth deadly sin.

"It has to do with Paula Libanski."

His face took on a grim cast. But he nodded and pulled out a yellow legal pad. "I'd have thought that Sonya and Peter would make the arrangements. But of course if she's too upset . . ."

"Um . . . arrangements?"

"For the burial. Isn't that why you're here?"

"What? No. The M.E. won't even release her remains for a while yet. I'm here about something we found buried with her."

His eyebrows came together, dainty things that would have seemed more at home on a woman's face. Father LeGrand was a slight man, about Ginny's height but probably weighing less, with small gray eyes and delicate lips. He had small hands, too, and one of them was gripping the silver pen so hard they'd turned white.

She laid a photograph atop the legal pad. "Do you recognize this?" He stared at the rosary with unblinking eyes. "The crucifix is engraved with the initials P.L. Is it yours?"

Father LeGrand nodded, very faintly. He cleared his throat, tried to speak, cleared it again. "My parents gave it to me," he said. "Upon my ordination."

"Do you have any idea how Paula got it?"

He kept his eyes on the photo. But he dropped the pen and folded his hands together, not technically in prayer but with the fingers so tightly interlaced their tips had gone from white to ruby red.

"Father," she asked again, "do you have any idea how Paula got the rosary?"

He opened his mouth as though he'd found the answer, then closed it, like it tasted sour on his tongue. They sat there like that, the hands of the grandmother clock ticking the minutes away, the framed painting of Jesus surrounded by some happy ex-lepers staring down at them both.

Finally, Father LeGrand's mouth opened again. And he said, "I gave it to her."

42

His answer raised a thousand questions, but she kept them to herself—just let the silence float down from the ceiling and hover over them again. She kept her eyes on him, but her mind was racing with possible scenarios. She envisioned Father LeGrand giving Paula the rosary in an act of faith, like the priest handing the silver candlesticks to Jean Valjean at the beginning of *Les Misérables*—the musical, not the novel she'd been way too impatient to read in college.

But the expression on LeGrand's face told her the story was nowhere near that wholesome. He looked like a fox caught with his paw in a trap, drowning in pain and well aware that the only way to get free was to leave something precious behind.

"She said she wanted it," he said, speaking so suddenly it startled her. "Since the initials were the same as hers, she said it was like fate."

"And you just gave it to her? Something with that much sentimental value?" He nodded, hands still clenched tight. "Why?"

"I have no idea," he said.

She could see he was telling the truth; she could also see it was more complicated than that.

"Father," she asked, "how well did you know Paula Libanski?"

He'd had his forearms on the desktop. Now, without unlacing his fingers, he raised them until he was leaning on his elbows, forehead pressed against his clasped hands. After a few moments he raised his head and said, "I won't lie to you." The statement felt like it was directed as much to himself as to her.

"Father," she asked, "were you sexually involved with her?"

Another long silence. Followed by the word "yes."

"Are you Danny Markowicz' father?"

"No," he said. "Daniel was already born."

"Are you aware that she was three months pregnant when she was murdered?"

She saw him flinch as the question struck him—not new information, she thought, more like a blow on a bruise. He nodded.

"Was the baby yours?"

He nodded again, then laid his forehead back down on his clenched hands. She was about to ask another question—*the* question—when he lifted his head, eyes begging her to understand.

"She wasn't in my parish," he said. "Her family went to the Polish church in Adams, and back then I was only assigned here. I don't mean that as an excuse. Just an explanation. When I met her, she was already eighteen."

She listened without interrupting. It sure as hell sounded like an excuse to her.

"I met her at a summer picnic for the CYO," the priest continued. "Sonya wanted to go, and her folks made Paula drive her. I don't think I talked to her for five minutes. But after that she started . . ." He grasped for the word and came up empty. Finally, Ginny took pity on him.

"Pursuing you?"

He nodded—eyes wide, like she'd just performed some neat parlor trick. "At first I thought she wanted spiritual counseling. That's what she said. But that wasn't the case. And she was so *determined.*"

Ginny thought of what she'd heard Paula's father say more than twenty years earlier: *It's as though she can't stand it if something's good and pure and clean. She's got to go and ruin it, like a normal person needs to scratch an itch.*

"Are you saying she seduced you?"

He didn't answer right away. She watched the memory play out across his face. Father LeGrand couldn't be much beyond his mid-forties, but he looked a good ten years older. There were deep lines between his eyes, a blossom of pink veins wending their way across his nose.

"I was—" He started to speak, stopped, started again. "This was my first parish. I was young and . . . inexperienced. I'd gone from a boys' school straight into seminary. I felt my vocation at a very young age. I'd never so much as gone on a date. And she was so beautiful. I couldn't believe she'd want me."

Ginny pictured the priest at twenty-five, awkward and nerdy and pure as the goddamn driven snow. Paula must have eaten him alive.

"And she got pregnant," she said. Another nod, again nearly imperceptible. "What made you so sure the baby was yours? Paula didn't exactly have a reputation for monogamy."

The question seemed to startle him. The idea, she realized, had never even occurred to him.

"She told me the child was mine," he said.

He'd broken into a sweat. The office was stuffy and close, and beads of perspiration were zigzagging down the gray hair at his temples. He took off his sports jacket and undid the top two buttons of his plain white shirt, which had been fastened up to the neck. Then he reclasped his hands, as though they'd been brought together by magnetic force.

"Did she threaten to expose you?" He shook his head. "Did she ask you for money?"

"I took a vow of poverty," he said. "I don't have any money."

You also took a vow of celibacy, she thought, *and look how well that turned out.*

"What did she want?" Ginny asked.

"She wanted me to leave the church and marry her," he said. "She wanted me to prove that I loved her more than I loved God."

The memory made him too agitated to sit still. He stood up and paced behind the desk, turning away from her to look out the tiny leaded-glass window.

"Father," she said, "what *happened* to you?"

She wasn't referring to his moral downfall. When he'd turned his back to her, she'd seen the crisscrossed red lines, angry stripes of blood that had seeped through his white shirt. So that was why he'd flinched when he reached for the teapot.

"Did somebody hurt you?"

He shook his head, back still turned. Finally, in a voice approaching a whisper, she heard him say, "Punishment."

"You did that to yourself?" Something bubbled up in her memory, a long-ago lesson from before she dropped out of catechism, and suddenly, it became clear.

"After they found Paula's body," she said, "you actually whipped yourself." His silence prompted her to cruelty. "What's wrong," she asked, "you couldn't find a hair shirt and a bed of nails?"

He didn't answer—not that she'd expected him to. But it didn't matter; it was time to ask the question.

"Father," she asked, "did you kill her?"

He kept looking out the window. When he finally turned around, there were tears in his eyes.

"I take full responsibility," he said.

"You didn't answer the question."

"Yes," he said. "I killed her. And God help me, I killed my own child."

He walked with her to the police station, where a very startled Chief Rolly took Father LeGrand's confession like it was a case of indigestion. Ginny wasn't in the room; Rolly wouldn't allow it. Before she left him, out of pity or just a sense of fair play, she asked LeGrand if he wanted legal counsel. He said he didn't want a lawyer; he wanted a priest.

She drove back up the mountain. She didn't want Jimmy to wake up alone, and she couldn't face Sonya yet. How was she going to tell her that her sister had been killed by a priest? And not just any priest, but a man she'd looked to for guidance her entire adult life?

She found him already awake, lying in bed, watching some

cycling race on ESPN2. It was a perverse thing to do after what had just happened to him, and she told him so. Then, because she needed his advice, she told him about Father LeGrand.

"Are you sure?" he asked, sounding much more alert than she'd expected. "I can't believe it."

"He confessed," she said. "I'm sure there's more to it—Rolly wouldn't let me sit in on the details. But I know what guilt sounds like, and he's guilty as hell."

"Maybe it was an accident. I don't know—or self-defense or something."

"Are you going to make excuses for him just because he's a priest?"

"No. But the man must be racked with guilt," he said. "To beat himself bloody—"

"Let's keep our eye on the ball here, shall we? Pierre LeGrand is *not* the victim. The guy killed a pregnant woman. The mother of his child, for chrissake. He said so himself."

Jimmy took it in, a stricken look on his face. If *he* was taking it this hard, how was she going to break the news to Sonya?

"Do you think Lance Pecor was working for Father LeGrand?" Jimmy asked. "And would a priest really be able to pay off the guy's mortgage?"

"Not unless he inherited family money. And his parents did buy him that expensive rosary, so maybe—" She cut herself off. "But the letter didn't just say the mortgage was paid off. It said the whole thing had been a mistake."

"So what?"

"So who could do that except somebody who worked at the bank?" She leaped up from the bed, jostling the mattress and making Jimmy groan in pain. "Sorry," she said. Then, "I think maybe I know who hired him. Goddamn Arthur Dulaine. He's president of the Tunnel City Bank. I bet he could pay off

Lance's mortgage on paper without any money ever changing hands."

"And why would he do that?"

"Because he's a big wheel in the church. Maybe he was covering for LeGrand."

"Do you honestly believe that Father LeGrand would let him kill people to cover up what he did to Paula?"

Ginny thought about it. "Maybe LeGrand asked for his help, and Dulaine went overboard. Maybe with all the molestation scandals in Boston he thought the church couldn't take any more bad press. I met him a couple times. He's one sanctimonious son of a bitch."

"Doesn't that mean," Jimmy mumbled, "that he'd be *less* likely to break the law?"

Ginny stifled a laugh; if she and Jimmy had any kind of future, she was going to have to respect his faith just as she respected Sonya's. But she couldn't keep her mouth entirely shut.

"Sometimes those Bible-thumpers," she said, "are the biggest hypocrites of all."

43

She was exhausted—from tangling with Pecor, from taking LeGrand's confession, from the stress of what had happened to Jimmy. But another part of her was so wired she was surprised she didn't get a shock from the knob on Sonya's front door. She walked in to find her friend equally on edge—pacing the kitchen, holding a wooden cooking spoon in her right palm and whacking it against her left. Ginny took one look at her and thought, *She already knows.*

Sure enough, instead of hello, Sonya said, "I can't believe it."

"I know," Ginny said. "I'm so sorry."

"But he's a good man. I know he is."

"He confessed, Sonya."

"I know," she said. "He told me."

"What?"

Sonya stopped pacing and faced her. "You know how on TV when you go to jail you get one phone call? Well, he used his to call me."

"What did he say?"

"That he was sorry." *Whack* went the wooden spoon. *Whack, whack, whack.* "That he knew that no matter how many times he confessed, there was no absolution."

"Did he mention Arthur Dulaine?"

Sonya looked at her like she was speaking in tongues. "What does he have to do with anything?"

Ginny answered with a helpless wave. "It was a stupid question. But I think he's the one who paid Lance Pecor to attack me. And Lance was the one who was digging in the woods at the Fish Pond, looking for Paula's body."

"I don't really know Mr. Dulaine," Sonya said. "I only ever met him when his bank lent us money so Pete could buy some new equipment. But why would he—"

"I think he was covering for LeGrand, trying to make sure the scandal never came out."

She told Sonya about the letter from the bank she'd found in Lance's trailer. Her friend sat down at the kitchen table, still clutching the spoon, dropping into her chair with a thunk.

"Lance killed Danny. That's what you think, isn't it?"

Ginny sat down next to her. "I don't know," she said. "He flat out denied it, and he was pretty convincing. But maybe he's a better liar than I gave him credit for."

"Danny was trying to find Paula," Sonya said. "You think Dulaine was afraid he'd somehow figure out she'd been sleeping with the priest?"

"It crossed my mind. And if her body was ever found, that rosary is a direct link to LeGrand."

"But it seems so unlikely. Nobody knew where Paula was. There's no reason she would've been found."

"I've been thinking about that," Ginny said. "I remembered something your mother-in-law said about how they're building condos on the lake. Maybe Father LeGrand was afraid they'd dig her up, and he went to Dulaine for help."

"I guess."

"Well, did you ask him? Did he give you any details?"

"I asked him a lot of things," Sonya said. "Practically all he would say was he was sorry, over and over. 'Please forgive me, no amount of penance is enough.'" She shook her head, let out a bitter laugh. "He's not wrong."

"Are you okay?" Ginny forcibly removed the spoon from her grip, then took her hand. "Can I get you something to drink?"

Sonya shook her head. The motion made something gray and fine fly off and float down to the immaculate kitchen table. Ginny ran her fingers through her friend's hair; it was coated in dust. For the first time she noticed that her hands and shirt were smeared with it, too.

"I've been up in the attic," Sonya said.

"What for?"

"After I talked to the Father, it made me think of something. About Paula." She seemed lost in thought all of a sudden, only dimly aware that Ginny was sitting next to her.

"What's that?" Ginny prompted.

"I asked him about the rosary. I guess I was hoping he'd say he gave it to her because he loved her. But he told me she had to have it, like it was some sort of a trophy. It was just about the only straight answer he'd give me. But it made me think."

Sonya stood up and led her to Danny's room. Sitting on the pristine bedspread, an island of dirt in a sea of cleanliness, was an old Wisk detergent box sealed with brown packing tape.

"I always thought Paula was coming home. You know that, right?"

"Yes," Ginny replied.

"About six months after she left, my folks decided it was time to rent out the basement apartment. They said Paula wasn't coming back, and we weren't exactly rolling in money. Dad was working two jobs, and Mom was already sick. So they told me to clean the place out and throw all of Paula's stuff away."

"But you couldn't."

"No," Sonya said. "I knew she'd come home. And even if she didn't, I thought Danny might want it someday. But either way, throwing her stuff away just seemed so *mean*. You know?"

"So you saved it."

"Not everything. Some of the household things I gave to the women's shelter. But her personal stuff I packed up and put in the attic."

"Did Danny ever look through it?"

Sonya shook her head. "Like I told you before, he only asked about her when he was real little. And it's been so many years I forgot about this stuff myself. Until just now."

She ripped off the tape. It came away from the cardboard easily, like it had gotten tired of holding on to its secrets. The bedspread was frosted with dust, proof that the box hadn't been touched in years; even if Danny had gone poking around the attic in search of maternal memories, Ginny thought, he hadn't found this.

Sonya opened the flap to reveal a collection of miscella-neous things: a Zippo lighter with the Harley-Davidson logo, a single leather glove, an empty money clip emblazoned with a green plastic dollar sign, a key chain from Green Mountain Dog Track that bore no keys.

"It's just junk," Sonya said. "Stuff I found in a couple shoe boxes under Paula's bed."

Ginny sifted through it. There were dozens of items in there, nothing particularly valuable or revealing. A second-place swim-ming medal; a tin of Skoal; a Rotary Club membership pin; a graduation tassel; a red bandana; a bulky Timex watch; a yel-lowed school-issue paperback of *The Good Earth;* a St. Christo-pher medal on a tarnished silver chain.

"I don't understand," Ginny said. "Why did you go looking for this?"

"Trophies."

"Huh?"

"I remember even back when I found this stuff, I couldn't figure out what Paula would want with it. I didn't even really look through it—just packed it all up and forgot about it. But after I talked to Father LeGrand, it kind of popped into my head."

Ginny looked from the box to Sonya and back again. "You mean—"

"These are all men's things. Either that or they're neutral. But there's nothing in there Paula would've bought for herself."

"And you think she took them off the guys she was dating? Like she took Father LeGrand's rosary?"

Sonya shrugged. "What else could they be?"

Ginny lifted the items out one by one, laying them on the

dusty bedspread. There were so damn many. If Sonya was right about them being trophies of her sister's sexual escapades, then by the ripe old age of nineteen Paula had racked up three times as many notches on her bedpost than Ginny had at thirty-four.

The two of them scrutinized the collection, which proved to include one actual trophy—an award for first place in some Western Mass wrestling competition held during Paula's sophomore year of high school. There was no name engraved on it, no initials on the lighter or the watch or the St. Christopher medal.

Ginny was looking inside the leather glove when she heard Sonya gasp. Her friend was holding the copy of *The Good Earth,* the shocked whiteness of her face even more pronounced against the yellowed pages.

"Oh, no," Sonya moaned. "Oh, God—*no.*"

Ginny tried to take it from her, but at first Sonya wouldn't let it go—as though if she held on to it, this awful thing couldn't be true. But Ginny persisted and got the book out of Sonya's hands and read the name scribbled in pen on the inside cover. And her thoughts instantly echoed Sonya's words.

Oh, no.

44

She spent the night at Jimmy's, switching to the other side of the bed to avoid his injured shoulder. He'd been surprised to see her; he'd assumed she'd want to stay close to Sonya as she dealt with the news about Father LeGrand. And that was when Ginny told him that Sonya had learned something even worse.

The name scribbled in the book, the one Sonya had found amid the trophies of Paula's sexual exploits, was Pete Markowicz.

Her husband had slept with her sister.

Ginny had offered to be there when Sonya confronted him—had begged her to let her stay—but her friend had practically dragged her out the door. She wanted to be alone with him, she said, to look him in the eye and make him swear it wasn't true. But from the time she saw his handwriting in that old high school paperback, she'd known it in her gut: some shard of memory, some wisp of long-ago jealousy or suspicion, told her she was right.

Ginny asked Sonya what she was going to do if he admitted it; Sonya didn't have an answer. And when Ginny called the house to check on her around ten that night, the phone just rang and rang.

She dropped Jimmy off at the bakery the next morning and went straight to Sonya's. There was no one home, no day-care kids in sight. She drove to Libanski Construction and found that Pete, for the first time in living memory, hadn't shown up for work.

Where were they?

She drove toward the jail, practically jumping out of her skin when someone honked at her at a red light, and recalled with a start that around here honking meant *hello* rather than *move your ass*. Sure enough, there was Lizzie Erickson, the E.R. doc from her old Brownie troop, offering a jaunty wave from the next lane.

She parked outside the jail and went in, hoping to have another crack at Lance Pecor, only to find out that his mother had sprung him on a bail bond, using her property as collateral. So she asked to see Father LeGrand and was told that he was with another priest; Rolly seemed to take special pleasure in saying the two had been praying together for hours, and Lord only knew how long they'd go on.

Frustrated and furious, she walked over to the Tunnel City Savings Bank and asked to speak to Arthur Dulaine. His receptionist, a fusty old bag of a woman, said he was in meetings all day but if she left her name, the great man would try to fit her into his busy schedule.

She walked out into the morning sun, looking to her right and her left, desperate for something to put her fist through.

God damn Pete Markowicz. Dating the nicest girl in the world, anointed by her dad to inherit the family business, and still unable to keep his pecker in his pants until the wedding night. And while she was at it, God damn Paula Libanski all to hell for needing to seduce every guy in sight, even her poor sister's lunkhead of a boyfriend.

But of course, Ginny thought, the Paula she'd come to know over the past few weeks would have seen Pete as an irresistible conquest. Frankly, it would've been a miracle if she'd kept her paws *off* him.

She paced the sidewalk in front of the bank, wondering what to do next. She contemplated a bacon and cheese omelet at the Golden Skillet but decided she wasn't hungry; she thought about getting a coffee at Café des Artistes, then remembered it was closed. She could go back to Molly's for some sympathy, but Jimmy had his accounts to do, and one-handed no less.

Ginny felt the weight of the .38, which had probably tattooed its outline into her spine by now. Lance Pecor would have to be an idiot to try something while he was out on bail—which meant she'd better watch her back.

Had Dulaine really been the one who hired him? The letter from the bank was hardly ironclad proof. But there was something so unpleasant about him, so brittle and holier-than-thou. From the minute she'd met him, he'd struck her as the kind of person who saw the world in black and white. She knew the type, the ones who divided people into saints and sinners. The former could do no wrong, and the latter just didn't matter.

If Father LeGrand had confided in Dulaine about what he'd done to Paula, the banker might well have seen him as a good man brought low by some Jezebel; frankly, Ginny wasn't sure that was too far from the truth. Rather than urge the priest to come clean, he might have offered to help cover it up—paid Lance to move the body before the construction crew dug it up, to get rid of the people who'd threatened to expose LeGrand's secret. They were all sinners, anyway: a bastard child dabbling in sodomy, a drug dealer. A dirty cop.

The thought made her head ache and her mouth go dry. She went down Main Street and curved left onto Eagle, past Molly's and the sporting goods store. At the end of the block was a Mc-Donald's, where she ordered a large Coke and sat in a booth to think.

Paula seduces Father LeGrand. She gets pregnant, says it's his. Whether it is or it isn't, who knows? But he believes it. She tells him to meet her at the Fish Pond. But something goes wrong, and instead of running off with her, he kills her and buries her there.

Flash forward eighteen years. Danny starts to look for his mother. Maybe he asks the priest for advice. LeGrand starts to panic. He confesses to Dulaine, who says he'll take care of it. He brings in some muscle to teach Danny a lesson, tune him up a little, but things get out of hand and Danny winds up dead.

Somehow Geoffrey Dobson knows what Lance did, and he threatens to go to the cops; good-bye, Geoffrey. Then Ginny starts sticking her nose into everything—a cop and a native-born daughter and the biggest threat of all.

It was a neat package and made sense. But was it the truth?

Or was she missing something? She thought about Judge Sweringen, whose threat to have her humiliated in the local paper hadn't yet materialized. Was he just afraid his little tryst with Paula was going to come out, or was there more to it? And what about Rolly, who'd so blithely pocketed Geoffrey's drug money? Was he just slightly corrupt—or genuinely dirty?

Ginny did a mental inventory of Paula's tawdry trophy collection: so many men, so many chances for jealousy and revenge. The thought led her to another question. Where the hell were Sonya and Pete?

She tried their number again; still no answer. She finished her soda, decided she was hungry enough for an Egg McMuffin, and ate it as she walked over to the French church. She went past it, the Cyclops eye of the rose window staring at her in un-blinking reproach, as though it knew what she was up to.

She turned the corner to the little brick cottage where Father LeGrand lived. The door was unlocked. She wasn't sure what she was looking for—just had a general idea of finding a link between LeGrand and Dulaine, something beyond normal church business. LeGrand proved to be a fastidious housekeeper, and nobody's idea of a pack rat; there wasn't much to search.

What did she expect? A memo that said: *Dear Arthur, Strangled my pregnant ex-girlfriend twenty years ago. Please cover it up, and merci beaucoup?*

She was pawing through the paltry contents of LeGrand's anal-retentive filing cabinet when her cell phone rang. The caller ID window said UNAVAILABLE.

"Hello?"

"Virginia? It's Sylvia Zweig."

Ginny's stomach flip-flopped. She hadn't spoken to Sylvia for three months, not since the man who raped her had been sprung on appeal. During the long haul from investigation to trial, she and Ginny had gotten to be friends—they hadn't socialized, but there'd been a solid mutual respect. Even after the son of a bitch was released, Sylvia hadn't blamed Ginny for the prosecutor's failings. But the intervening weeks of looking over her shoulder could very well have changed that.

Sylvia Zweig had been raped on her way home from her job in a medical testing lab. She was either calling with information about the samples Ginny had sent—accompanied by apologies for imposing on their relationship—or to tell her to go screw herself.

"Hi," Ginny said. "How are you?"

"I got what you sent me," Sylvia said. Her voice was tinny, like the call was coming from much farther away than Manhattan. It was a lousy connection, and Ginny couldn't get a handle on her mood. "Are you there?"

"I'm here. Did you get a chance to process it?"

"I did. I'm sorry it took so long."

"That's okay."

"It turned out the samples did come from two different individuals."

Her stomach flipped again. She'd been hoping that Danny's killer might have left some evidence behind at the crime scene; how could anyone stay untouched amid all that violence?

"Both donors were males," Sylvia continued. "One had A-positive blood."

"That's the victim."

"The other was AB-negative."

"And you ran the DNA?"

"Yes. There were no genetic anomalies, and no diseases that might help you identify either of them, if that's what you're after."

"Okay. Thanks."

"No problem," Sylvia said. "You know I'd do anything for you."

"I really appreciate it."

"But there was one more thing I noticed. First off, the AB-negative blood came from the same donor as the vomit. And compared with the other, it had a CPI of over three thousand."

"What does that mean?"

"The two donors," she said, "were father and son."

45

She stood in Father LeGrand's humble living room, still clutching the phone a full minute after the call had ended, mind racing.

Danny had been killed by his own father. There was no other reasonable way to interpret the evidence. Sure, maybe in some alternate universe it was possible that the man's blood and vomit just *happened* to show up in the very room where his son had been beaten to death, but the second Ginny took the idea out for a spin it struck her as ridiculous.

Danny's biological father had murdered him. He left some of his own blood behind in the struggle. And when he saw what he'd done, he threw up: the vomit that Ginny so blithely ascribed to the local cops had come from the killer himself.

That spoke of remorse, didn't it? Of conflicted motives, of something less than evil?

Brain still whirring, she forced herself to finish what she'd started; even if Father LeGrand was still refusing bail, it would be just her luck to have someone walk in on her while she was tossing his place. Mechanically, she did a thorough search of the tiny cottage. If there was anything useful, she didn't find it.

On a whim she gathered up all his paperwork—on the desk, in an in-box on the bookcase, in the filing cabinet—and shoved it into a plastic grocery bag for later inspection. She walked over to Jimmy's shop and found him sitting at his office computer, scowling at a spreadsheet program. He smiled at her, but one look told him that something was fantastically wrong. She filled him in about the phone call from Sylvia and about her own hardening certainty that Danny's life had been taken away by one of the people who'd given it to him in the first place.

"How can you be so sure?" Jimmy asked when she was done. "The blood just means his father was *there,* doesn't it? It doesn't—"

"I've been a cop for a long time," she said, "and Danny's autopsy photos almost made me lose my lunch."

"I still—"

Ginny slammed a fist into her palm. "It was like the killer was trying to erase Danny's face. That's what the guy who embalmed him said. I thought it was just plain old rage, but now I get it. This was as personal as it gets—a father trying to erase his own son."

"But I thought nobody even knew who Danny's father was. Even his own mother always said she didn't know. Do you really think Danny somehow figured it out? And his father killed him over it?"

Ginny thought about it. She'd been so blown away by the DNA results that she hadn't even started to consider what the motive might be.

"And hold on," Jimmy said. "I thought you were operating on the assumption that Danny was killed to keep him from finding out what really happened to his mother. So are you saying the same person killed them both—Father LeGrand?"

She sat down in the other chair, rubbing the space between her eyebrows with her thumb and forefinger. "He told me he only took up with Paula after Danny was born, and I believe him. Besides, I can't see any resemblance between the two of them. Can you?"

Jimmy shook his head. "What about Lance Pecor?"

"There's no resemblance there, either. And there was something about the way he said Paula would never give him a tumble—I'm pretty sure he was telling the truth." She kept massaging her forehead, as though the stimulation could make her brain work faster. "Maybe I've been on the wrong track all along. Maybe Danny's murder isn't really connected to Paula's. Unless—"

She cut herself off, staring mindlessly at the glowing computer screen.

"What?"

"Unless," she said, "Father LeGrand is lying."

"Why would he do that? You said yourself you knew a guilty person when you saw one."

"I know he *feels* guilty," she said. "But that doesn't necessarily mean he *is* guilty. Somebody who beats himself bloody with a whip is hardly in his right mind."

He looked at her like she was even loonier than the priest—like he had some rampaging creature in his office, and him without his tranquilizer gun. "Are you saying LeGrand didn't sleep with Paula, after all?"

She ignored him, grabbing the plastic bag she'd dropped on the floor and heading for the door.

"Where are you going?"

"Sonya's. I haven't heard from her since she found out about Paula and Pete. I'm starting to get worried."

"What does that have to do with—"

"Don't you get it? Pete slept with Paula. He could be Danny's father as much as anybody, and God knows they weren't getting along. And Sonya told me he'd done business with Dulaine. What if it wasn't Father LeGrand he was covering for? What if—"

"You gotta be out of your mind," he said. "You honestly think Pete's behind all this? He killed his own son? And now he's done something to his wife?"

She blew out of his office without answering—Jimmy's admonishments not to go off half-cocked ringing in her ears as she ran out of the store and down the sidewalk to Danny's truck. It was only through blind luck that she avoided getting ticketed by one of Rolly's minions as she gunned the engine down Main Street and up the hill.

Sonya's apartment was empty, nothing touched since Ginny had been there last. What was going on? Starting to itch with worry, Ginny broke down and called Pete's parents. But they had no idea where their son was, or his wife, either.

She searched the apartment for evidence of violence, a surreal experience if there ever was one. Was she serious? Could Pete have really hurt his wife—Pete, that big galoot Sonya had been in love with since she was a kid?

Then Ginny remembered something Sonya had said: that when she found out who had murdered Danny, she'd kill him herself. Maybe Sonya wasn't the one Ginny should be worrying about.

Nothing in the house was awry; that, at least, was a relief. She tried both of their cell phones for the umpteenth time and got no answer. She called the construction company again; Pete still hadn't checked in.

Frustrated, desperate for something else to occupy her, she spread the papers from Father LeGrand's office on the kitchen floor. She was flailing, swapping crime theories like they were baseball cards. But even if the priest hadn't been Paula's killer, or even the father of her child, her gut told her he was nowhere near innocent.

She shuffled through the documents: official church correspondence, utility bills, drafts of sermons. He'd been working on something about original sin—an apt topic. She recalled how he'd stood at his office window, shirt stained with blood drawn by his own hand.

Ginny heard the front door rattle. She stood up and sprinted through the living room and into the hall. Sonya was standing there, looking lost in her own home.

"Thank *God*," Ginny said, hugging her tight. "I was so *worried*."

Sonya's expression was as confused as it was exhausted. "Worried? Why?"

"I was terrified something happened to you. Where have you been?"

"Driving around."

"All night?" Sonya answered with half a nod, as though she didn't have the energy for a whole one. "Where did you go?"

"Lake George."

"You drove all the way to the Adirondacks? What for?"

Sonya shrugged. "My folks used to take us to Storytown—that park where they have those fairy-tale characters made out of concrete."

"And?"

"I always liked it there. But it's closed now. The season's over."

Sonya walked past her and into the apartment. Ginny followed, grabbing her arm and making her sit on the living room couch.

"You drove up and turned around and came back?"

"I slept awhile," Sonya said. "In the car."

Ginny's eyes went to the front door. "Where's Pete?"

"I have no idea."

"He never came home last night?"

Another half-nod. "Sure he did."

"So what happened?"

"He asked why his supper wasn't on the table," Sonya said. "I showed him that book. *The Good Earth.*"

"Did he admit he slept with Paula?"

She shook her head, reached for one of the magazines on the coffee table, flipped through it. Ginny was starting to wonder if she was drunk.

"Sonya." Ginny snatched the *Reader's Digest* out of her hands. "What did Pete say?"

Unperturbed, Sonya reached for an old copy of *Good Housekeeping,* studying a recipe for Fourth of July cupcakes like it held the secret of eternal youth. "He denied it," she said. "But it doesn't matter. I could tell he was lying. Sixteen years of marriage, and I get a mouthful of lies."

"So where is he now?"

"I told him I never wanted to see him again."

Sonya's voice was casual, distracted. Still, there was something implacable beneath the air of nonchalance; Ginny had a feeling she meant what she was saying, at least at the moment.

"And you really don't know where he is?"

"What difference does it make?"

Ginny snatched the second magazine away, then took both of Sonya's hands in hers. "I have to tell you something," she said. "It's not going to be easy to hear."

"So? Go ahead." Sonya's attitude said, of all things, that she was annoyed that Ginny had confiscated her magazine.

"I took some blood samples from the mill," Ginny said. "The results came back today. They showed that Danny's biological father was at the scene of his murder."

"Oh."

That was all she said: *Oh*.

"Do you understand what I'm saying?" Ginny prodded. "It's pretty likely that Danny was murdered by his own father."

Ginny had relaxed her grip, giving Sonya the chance to pull her hands free. Mechanically, she started to reach for another magazine but seemed to change her mind; her hands fell into her lap.

"Is that why you keep asking about Pete?" Sonya asked in an odd singsong sort of voice. "Because you think he's Danny's father and he killed him and you thought he killed me, too?"

It sounded absurd when it was dragged out into the light like that. But it'd been less than an hour ago that both she and Pete were MIA; the probability that he'd slept with Paula, layered on top of all those fights with Danny over his future, had made him seem guilty.

But even if Ginny had been way off base—had jumped to the wrong conclusion out of concern for her friend—it didn't explain what Sonya did next. Ginny sat there and watched while she took in great gulps of air, the couch shaking with the motion of her body as she laughed and laughed and laughed.

46

Pete was sterile. That was the long and the short of it and everything in between. Sonya, who seemed very much in danger of going off the deep end, told Ginny the whole story like it was the punch line to a joke.

How, when Sonya had failed to conceive after two years of marriage, a trip to the doctor revealed her husband was shooting blanks. Adoption was out of the question; Pete was already raising one child that wasn't his. Medical interventions were either too expensive or theologically out of bounds. So Sonya had given up the dream of having her own children. But it was okay; Pete was the man she loved.

Now that she knew that he'd nailed her sister, however, all bets were off. By the time Ginny was able to force a couple of Tylenol PM down her throat and tuck her into bed, Sonya was using the word "annulment" and announcing that at thirty-four she was still young enough to have a baby. How it would all shake out was anybody's guess. Sonya had a forgiving heart, but there were limits.

Sweaty and freaked out, Ginny went into the kitchen for a Coke—only to trip over the mess of Father LeGrand's papers she'd left all over the slippery linoleum. She caught herself, got a drink, and settled down on the floor. With Pete off the hook and Sonya safe—and Ginny able to think straight—she might as well sift through them.

She scrutinized the papers one by one. She'd pegged Father LeGrand for a fastidious guy, but this was ridiculous; he even saved his old grocery receipts. The man clearly had a predilection for grapefruit, but that hardly seemed to solve anything. Eventually, after another can of Coke and a foray to close Sonya's bedroom door to stifle her snoring, Ginny came upon something interesting.

It was Father LeGrand's cell phone bill. It told her that on one day alone he'd made a whopping fifty-three calls, all of them to the same place. It was a number that ended in two zeros; probably a business. Ginny rose on half-numbed legs and dialed the number from the kitchen phone.

Good afternoon. You've reached the Tunnel City Savings Bank. If you know your party's extension . . .

So LeGrand had called Arthur Dulaine's workplace—making her initial suspicions about him covering up the priest's wrongdoing seem more likely than ever.

Then Ginny noticed the date: October 30. And the time: the calls came every few minutes, from eight a.m. onward. Each one lasted exactly sixty seconds—probably the minimum increment for the cell company, which rounded up to the nearest minute so it could rob you blind.

She sat back down and flipped through the other phone bills. LeGrand had called the bank a few times here and there, but there was nothing like the morning of October 30, when the priest had mounted an all-out telephonic assault.

There had to be something to it. She pondered the notes she'd found in Danny's truck—his chronicle of his mother's short life—and thought about the attempts he'd made to track her down. Then there was everything that had come afterward: Danny's brutal death, Jumping Jack's suicide, Geoffrey's blackmail threat and murder, the attempts on her own life.

Through it all, Father LeGrand hadn't made more than a few random calls to his supposed guardian angel—unless he'd used the phone in the church office, which she doubted, and since he had three parishes to take care of, it didn't seem likely that he spent much time at home.

But on October 30, after most of the excitement had already happened, he'd phoned the bank fifty-three times in six hours, each call lasting just long enough for him to leave a message. If LeGrand were a suitor and Dulaine the object of his desire, the phone bill was sufficient evidence to charge the priest with stalking. So what was going on?

She traced the days backward. October 31, obviously, was Halloween. She remembered how Sonya had pleaded with her to dole out the trick-or-treat candy. She'd been devastated because her sister's corpse had been found two days earlier.

Son of a—

She flew out the door and into the pickup truck, again risking Rolly's wrath by speeding down the hill and barging into the police station like an avenging angel. The chief wasn't there; thank heaven for small favors. She told the officer on duty that she needed to see Father LeGrand, and though she'd girded herself for an argument, the guy just waved her through.

"You're on the list," he said.

"What list?"

The cop rolled his eyes. "People he's wronged. If they come by, we gotta let 'em in so he can atone."

For a second Ginny thought he was putting her on, but he was entirely serious. "Who else is on it?" she asked.

"How much time you got?"

The officer unlocked the heavy metal door and handed Ginny the key to LeGrand's cell; the priest was hardly a danger to anybody. She went down the short hallway and nearly tripped over a pile of stuff just outside the bars: flowers and candy and mass cards and a literal stack of Bibles. LeGrand didn't hear her approach. He was on his knees, facing the back wall, praying.

"Father?"

LeGrand turned, not seeming the least bit surprised to see her. There was something off about the look on his face, and when he came closer, Ginny saw that his eyes were lifeless and flat.

"What's all this?" She indicated the stack of goodies outside the cell.

He didn't answer, but the explanation was obvious: the priest's supporters were rallying around him. It was either touching or nauseating, depending on how you looked at it.

"I need to talk to you," Ginny said. "About Arthur Dulaine."

Ginny wouldn't have thought the priest could look any more defeated, but he managed it.

"I've been an idiot," she said. "And you've been a liar."

The priest didn't dispute either claim, just took the insult like it was no better than he deserved. She unlocked the cell. There was no chair, only a bed and a metal toilet. Since LeGrand wasn't inclined to get off his knees, she took a seat on the thin mattress and doffed her leather jacket. Then she drew the wireless bill from its pocket and threw it on the floor in front of him.

"Paula Libanski's body was found on October 29th," she said. "The story broke in the *Transcript* the next morning. You started calling the Tunnel City Bank at eight a.m., which is when I figure you got your morning paper and found out that for the past eighteen years you'd been living a lie."

Father LeGrand didn't say anything. He stayed there kneeling on the cement floor, tears pooling in his eyes.

"You called him fifty-three times, Father. *Fifty-three times.* If I hadn't seen those bloody marks on your back, maybe I'd believe it was because after the body was found you were terrified you were about to get caught. But you're not afraid of punishment—in fact, you're desperate for it.

"Cops have a saying about how when you arrest someone, it's the innocent ones who pace around the holding cell and cry all night long. The guilty ones sleep like babies, 'cause part of them is relieved they can finally stop looking over their shoulders."

The priest made as if to say something. But though his mouth hung open, no sound came out.

47

What I'm trying to make you understand," Ginny went on, "is that those fifty-three calls don't jibe with a man so appalled by what he's done that he beats himself bloody and confesses to the first person who wanders into his office and mentions Paula's name.

"So maybe you were calling out of guilt. But that doesn't make sense, either; Arthur Dulaine isn't your confessor. I've seen the two of you together—in terms of morality you're not even reading from the same book. Sonya was right about you, Father. Even if you did sleep with Paula, you're a good man. And Arthur Dulaine is a self-righteous son of a bitch."

LeGrand blinked—he didn't have much choice, physiologically speaking—and the tears slid down his face in two neat lines.

"Tell me the truth, Father. Until you read it in the paper you didn't even know Paula was dead, did you?" Something registered in his eyes. It wasn't much, but it encouraged her to go on.

"That was why you called Dulaine those fifty-three times—because you realized what had really happened to her."

The priest squeezed his eyes shut, sending the rest of the tears tumbling onto his cheeks. His hands balled up into fists, which he pressed against his face, as if the absence of sight could make him disappear. Ginny rose from the bed and knelt at his side.

"It wasn't just now that Dulaine was covering for you," she said. "It was eighteen years ago, when you were young and terrified. You told me how innocent you were back then. I should've known you wouldn't have had it in you to kill a pregnant woman and bury her with your own two hands. But you were so *guilty*."

LeGrand was sobbing, great soul-shattering wails that echoed against the blank cell walls, raw and desperate.

"Listen to me, Father. I am *not* going to let another innocent man die in here. You have to tell me the truth. You turned to Dulaine for help eighteen years ago, didn't you? You told him you'd gotten Paula pregnant, and he said he'd take care of it. Didn't he?"

His only response was another round of wailing cries. Ginny grabbed his arms and pulled his hands away from his face, forcing him to look at her. "What did he tell you? That the baby was being raised by a nice family somewhere? And this whole time you thought your child was alive and well, when all the while it was rotting in the ground in its mother's womb."

The priest pulled away from her and folded himself over his knees, his agony bending him into the oxymoronic attitude of a Muslim facing Mecca. She'd pushed him too far. His arms were splayed out in front of him, sobs convulsing his body against the unforgiving concrete. She touched his heaving back, but if he felt the contact, it didn't make any difference.

"You never meant for this to happen," she whispered. "You slept with Paula. You broke your vows. But it was Dulaine who killed her, wasn't it? Fifty-three phone calls, Father. Fifty-three times you called to ask, *What have you done?*"

The tiny cell echoed with the sound of his misery. Then, layered on top of it, came a man's voice.

"You're wasting your time," it said. "He'll never talk."

She looked up. Standing in the open cell door was Arthur Dulaine, wearing an immaculate black topcoat and a condescending smile.

"Yes, he will," Ginny said. She looked from the banker to the priest. He was still doubled over, but his head was raised, empty eyes taking in Dulaine.

The banker shook his head, eyes smiling behind a mask of feigned regret. "The secrecy of the confessional," he said, "is sacrosanct."

"You smart son of a bitch," Ginny said. "You admitted everything to him. But you did it in church, to make sure he could never testify against you."

The banker inspected the sleeve of his coat, picked off a microscopic speck of lint. Ginny stood and faced him.

"It doesn't matter if he testifies," she said. "I know you hired Lance Pecor to do your dirty work. That's got to be enough to put you away for a long time. And you're what—sixty-five? Might amount to a life sentence."

Dulaine's handsome coat must be made of Teflon; her threats flew across the cell, but they didn't stick. She watched as he shrugged them off, a placid smile on his clean-shaven face. "I don't know what you're talking about," he said.

Ginny looked at him, scanned his face for an iota of guilt

and didn't find it. "You know," she said, "I've never been able to understand people like you. The ones who can justify anything in the name of protecting the church. Like it was better to ruin some poor kid's life than admit that his priest molested him— transferring some pervert to another parish instead of calling the cops."

They stood there glaring at each other in relative silence, LeGrand's sobs having diminished to a pathetic snuffle. The priest was still on his knees, looking so miserable Ginny thought that crucifixion would constitute a major step up.

"You're one hell of a hypocrite," Ginny said. "What happened? Paula wouldn't go away quietly? She shows up at the Fish Pond expecting to run off with her boyfriend and finds you there instead?"

Dulaine's eyes narrowed. At first she thought she'd nailed the truth, but then something in his demeanor told her otherwise. She thought about Paula's skeleton, wrapped in plastic like so much garbage, her favorite possessions buried alongside her as though she were some Egyptian queen—one who couldn't go to the afterlife without a pair of Frye boots. Or a boom box or a lucky rabbit's foot or her boyfriend's rosary.

The rosary.

"Wait a minute," Ginny said. "How did you even know the rosary was in her suitcase?"

Dulaine's eyes searched her face. She got the distinct feeling he had no idea what she was talking about.

"Father LeGrand thought she was off somewhere having his kid," Ginny said. "He sure as hell wouldn't have thought her suitcase was buried in the woods along with her. So if you weren't afraid somebody would trace the rosary back to him, why were you trying to dig her up? What could possibly be worth the risk?"

A tightness had developed around Dulaine's jawline; finally, she was on to something. For the first time she thought she saw a flicker of fear in his eyes.

"Oh my *God*," she said. "I've been such an idiot. It wasn't the stupid rosary you were worried about. It was the *baby*."

Ginny started to laugh—not quite as hysterically as Sonya had a few hours before, but with enough gusto to make both men stare at her like she'd lost her marbles.

"Christ," she said. "Ever since I connected you with Lance, I've been thinking you killed Paula to get Father LeGrand off the hook. I thought you were one misguided son of a bitch. But it turns out I was giving you way too much credit."

Dulaine stood stiffly, his tall body framed by the hard black lines of the prison bars. It was a good place for him, Ginny thought. She turned to the priest.

"Get up," she said. "You don't belong in here." He didn't move. She fixed her eyes on Dulaine. "You took a pretty big risk hiring Lance. Maybe you've got him over a barrel with the mortgage on his house, but he could still turn on you. I should never have believed you'd stick your neck out like that for anybody but yourself."

Father LeGrand was looking from her to Dulaine, eyes wide but dry. Finally, for the first time since she walked into the cell, he rose from his knees and spoke.

"Arthur," he said. "What's going on?"

The priest wobbled, as though he'd been kneeling for so long he'd forgotten how to walk. He teetered back and sat on the cot, hugging himself with crossed arms. Ginny took a step toward him, keeping a wary eye on Dulaine. She hardly thought he'd try anything stupid in the middle of a police station, but if he did, she was damn well going to put him down.

"He hired someone to try to kill me," Ginny told LeGrand, still watching the banker. "And what's worse, he killed his own son."

That finally got a rise out of him. "Don't listen to her," Dulaine said. "She's a damned liar."

She turned to the priest. "Just because Paula told you the baby was yours doesn't make it true. She was sleeping with half the men in town. And one of them killed her."

The priest flinched, like her words had slapped him across the face. Even with his lined forehead and graying hair, he reminded her of a lost child. She sat next to him on the cot and put a hand on his knee.

"I can only think of one reason why Dulaine would have risked trying to dig up Paula's body," she said. "Eighteen years ago he wouldn't have worried about the baby's DNA." LeGrand gasped, eyes darting around the room but seeing nothing. "But now, with the construction on the lake—"

"Shut your mouth," Dulaine snapped.

Ginny ignored him. "Sonya said her sister had come into some money before she disappeared. I doubt you were the one who gave it to her." LeGrand shook his head, almost imperceptibly, and bit his bottom lip. "She couldn't hold down a job. So where does a girl like that get money? From a rich boyfriend."

A snide expression had taken up residence on Dulaine's face. LeGrand, on the other hand, was starting to look like he was only half there.

"How dare you accuse me of consorting with that slut?" Dulaine hissed at her. "I have no idea what happened to Paula and her bastard brat, but she deserved whatever she got."

Ginny had been on guard against Dulaine. It hadn't occurred to her to worry about the priest—to imagine that this agonized, guilt-ridden shade of a man might try to overpower her as she sat there comforting him.

She should have known better; fury can be more potent than steroids. Still, she wasn't prepared for the priest to shove her forward onto the floor, knocking her off balance and grabbing the revolver from the small of her back.

The next thing Ginny knew, Father LeGrand had leaped to his feet, with more agility than she would've thought he possessed. He stood there, the .38 surprisingly firm in his grip, aimed directly at Dulaine.

Then, with the dexterity of someone who knew just how to handle a gun, he slid the safety off.

48

Father," she said, "give me the gun."

He ignored her.

"Stop waving that thing around," Dulaine said. "You don't even know what you're doing."

"My father taught me," LeGrand said.

Dulaine didn't look impressed. "You know you couldn't hurt a fly." When the priest didn't answer, Dulaine yelled, "Officer!"

No one came. There were only two cops on duty in the station, and neither of them was in earshot.

"Be quiet!" LeGrand shouted at him. "And don't move."

His tone was near hysterical, totally at odds with his steady grip on the gun. Dulaine looked at the weapon, his face suddenly revealing a healthy respect for its ability to do harm.

"What are you going to do, Pierre?" he asked in a voice still tinged with condescension. "Shoot me? You're a *priest*."

"And you're a deacon," LeGrand said. "How could you?"

Arrogance overtook fear. "Be careful," Dulaine said. "You can't violate the confessional."

LeGrand cocked the revolver. "How dare you hide behind the church? For years I've watched you throw your weight around, like you were the only one holy enough to tell right from wrong. But you're nothing but a hypocrite."

"*Officer!*"

Dulaine's second cry for help was no more successful than the first, but it did an excellent job of infuriating the priest. LeGrand moved closer, pressing the barrel against Dulaine's forehead. Ginny stepped forward, approaching him with an outstretched hand.

"Father," she said, "please give me the gun."

"Take one more step," the priest said, "and I'll kill him right now. I swear it."

Ginny let her arm drop. "Nobody has to get hurt," she said. "Dulaine will pay for what he did. I promise."

He ignored her, turning back to Dulaine. "Get on your knees," he said.

The banker raised his hands in a posture of surrender. "Take it easy, Pierre. You don't—"

"Get on your knees!"

Dulaine did as he was told, arms still raised.

"Now," the priest said, "pray for forgiveness."

LeGrand took a step back, gun still aimed at Dulaine's head. The banker brought his palms together, diamond pinkie ring glinting in the light of the single bulb.

"I'm sorry," Dulaine said in a voice finally devoid of bravado. "Please forgive me."

"Now tell her what you did. Tell her how you killed that poor girl."

Dulaine turned a pair of pleading eyes to Ginny. "You can't just let him—"

"Tell her!"

Something in the priest's voice scared Dulaine even more than before. He squeezed his eyes shut, hands pressed together in supplication, immaculate coat getting sullied with dust.

"Pierre asked me for help," Dulaine whimpered, eyes still closed. "One day I found him crying in the rectory, and he told me everything. How Paula was pregnant and she wanted him to go away with her." He opened his eyes, again appealing to Ginny. "Please, you can't just stand there and—"

"I said tell her!"

The priest stood over him, eyes filled with fury. Dulaine drew in a quick, terrified breath.

"Pierre didn't know I was seeing her, too. I'd been seeing her for years. She promised to stop her whoring and put her bastard son up for adoption and be faithful to me. So I gave her money, and I said I'd set her up in an apartment." He turned back to Ginny in a pathetic bid for understanding. "I loved her. I was obsessed with her. You have no idea how beautiful she was, how incredibly sensual. She made me feel so *alive*. My wife will only have relations with the lights off, like making love to a corpse—"

"Arthur."

It was one word, but it contained enough malice to make Dulaine squeeze his eyes shut again, like LeGrand and his gun were too terrible to behold.

"I was jealous," he said. "I was crazy with it. I planned the whole thing. Paula had told Pierre to meet her at the Fish Pond. I told him I'd meet her instead—I'd talk some sense into her and put her on a bus out of town. When she got there, she was so excited about running off with another man. When she saw it was me, she was confused. I told her she had no right. No right to bleed me dry and make a fool of me—to take my money and then cuckold me with a *priest*."

Dulaine's speech had come out in a torrent, one word slamming into the next, spittle raining onto the floor in front of him and the priest opposite. He was hyperventilating, shirtfront heaving beneath his necktie and coat.

"Finish," LeGrand said.

His voice scared Dulaine into raising his hands again in surrender. When he realized what he'd done, he clasped his palms back together—desperately, like he hoped the priest hadn't noticed.

"I strangled her," he said. "I didn't even give her the chance to explain. Nothing she could've said would've made any difference. I'd brought a shovel and some garbage bags. I came prepared. I dug a hole and buried her with her suitcase. I told Pierre everything had gone just as planned. Which was the truth."

The priest's eyes had filled with tears. They were running down his face, but Ginny could tell that he didn't even notice. His grip on the gun was starting to falter.

"Come on, Father," she said. "It's over. He admitted what he did. Now it's time to put the gun down."

She stepped closer, trying to gauge whether she could disarm him before he shot Dulaine. But the priest seemed to sense that she was about to act, and he tightened his grip. She eyed the distance between them; she was quick, but she wasn't that quick.

In the momentary silence she listened for any sign that one of the cops might be coming. But there was a heavy door between the cellblock and the rest of the station, and no reason for Rolly's men to check on LeGrand anytime soon. Frankly, Ginny hoped they stayed away; add a couple of inexperienced, trigger-happy cops into the mix, and somebody was going to end up dead.

"Tell me about Daniel," the priest said.

Dulaine looked confused at first, as though he wasn't sure

whom LeGrand was talking about. He coughed and cleared his throat. When he spoke again, it was in a monotone, like a man under hypnosis.

"He was looking for his mother," Dulaine said to the cell floor. "He kept asking around. I couldn't have him find out what had happened between me and Paula—what if someone remembered seeing us together? So I had my nephew Lance—"

"Nephew?"

Ginny spat the word out without thinking. It seemed to startle Dulaine, like he'd momentarily forgotten she was there.

"My wife's sister's son. He'd done . . . favors for me in the past. I knew he wasn't above getting his hands dirty. And he was willing to help, once I promised to get his house back. But I swear, I never wanted him to hurt the Markowicz boy—just rough him up, convince him to leave it alone. But he wouldn't listen."

He looked up at LeGrand, eyes pleading for understanding; he didn't get it. A long pause, several intakes of breath, and he stared back down at the floor.

"Then the city sold the land where Paula was buried. I knew it was only a matter of time until her body was found. Once construction started on those lakefront condos, they'd be sure to dig her up, and the baby, too. I knew the child had to be mine. We'd been together so many times. How could it not be mine? So she had to be disposed of. But it was so long ago. I couldn't remember exactly where I buried her."

He lifted his gaze to Ginny. "And then you came home. I knew you'd see everything. You had to be stopped. Not killed, just stopped. I had Lance tamper with your car, but you still wouldn't go away. So I told him to take care of you, but you got the better of him. And then I saw you with Jimmy Griffin. Everyone knew you'd been together all through high school. I thought if something happened to him, you'd stop." He shook his head. "But you wouldn't. You even found Paula, when I couldn't find her myself."

Dulaine shook his head again, but this time he looked like he was snapping out of something, coming to his senses. "None of it matters," he said. "A confession obtained at gunpoint. No judge would allow it in court."

"You're not finished," she said. "Tell me what you did to Danny." The banker shook his head yet again, his jaw firmly set. "Tell me how you beat him to death. How you killed Geoffrey Dobson when he tried to blackmail you."

Dulaine didn't answer. LeGrand, for his part, had regained a firmer grip on the gun, now fixed on the banker's chest.

"A pregnant woman," the priest said. "An innocent child. I sent them to you like lambs to the slaughter."

The banker's mouth curled up into the barest suggestion of a smile. Dulaine was starting to get his groove back. "There's no need to be so dramatic, Pierre," he said. "Paula was anything but innocent. Who knows how many men I saved from her?"

The gun started to waver again, and the priest brought up his left hand to steady his right. Ginny thought his arm must be getting tired. She was going to have to make her move.

"She was only nineteen years old," LeGrand said.

"I saved you, Pierre," Dulaine said. "I saved us both. How many good men have been corrupted by—"

LeGrand shot him. The sound was deafening inside the tiny cell, the explosion bouncing off the walls, seeming to grow louder instead of fading away.

Dulaine stared down at his shirtfront, at the stain widening across the pristine white linen. Then, without a word, he crumpled forward.

The priest turned toward her, gun still extended; for a half second she thought she was in trouble. But then he turned the

revolver around and handed it to her butt-forward, like his father must have taught him.

He sat down on the cot and looked up at Ginny, a surprisingly placid expression on his face.

"An eye for an eye," he said.

Father LeGrand didn't want a lawyer; Ginny got him one,
anyway. Although defense attorneys drove her as crazy as
the next cop, she figured if anybody could make a convincing
case for extreme emotional disturbance, it was him. So she
called one of Jimmy's older sisters, who'd gone to law school in
Boston and come home to hang out a shingle and was willing to
represent the priest for the right price, which was nothing.

There was an itchy moment when Rolly wanted to know
where LeGrand had gotten the .38—even the local cops knew
enough to search somebody before they locked him up—and
Ginny thought she was going to be in hot water for carrying an
unlicensed handgun. But the priest, who probably figured one
little lie was nothing on top of all the sins he was shouldering,
covered for her by saying it had belonged to Dulaine. Ginny was
in no hurry to contradict him.

Three days after Dulaine's death Sonya still hadn't allowed
Pete back into the house—not even to get a change of under-
wear. He'd started sleeping on the couch at his parents' place,
since they'd turned his childhood bedroom into a den. Ginny

wasn't sure if Sonya was going to stay mad forever, but her friend did go so far as to ask if Jimmy's sister handled divorce cases.

Ginny was over at Sonya's, helping her cram her husband's clothes into garbage bags for Ginny to drop off at his parents' house, when the phone rang. They let the machine get it: Sonya was in no mood to take another call from Rhonda, who'd been phoning every fifteen minutes to tell her she was making the biggest mistake of her life.

"Detective Lavoie, this is Matt Zeigler from the M.E.'s office in Pittsfield. I—"

Ginny scooped up the phone.

"I'm here," she said.

"I hear you've been having some excitement in your neck of the woods."

"Just a little," she said. "You do the post on Dulaine?"

"Yeah," he said. "I probably shouldn't say this, but that priest was a pretty good shot. Right through the heart."

Though she knew it was horrible of her, Ginny smiled; she couldn't resist the symbolism.

"The reason I called," he said, "is that the results finally came back on that DNA test you asked me for. Paula's fetus and Danny Markowicz did not have the same father."

"Really?"

"Really."

"Wow. So Dulaine didn't father the baby she was carrying, after all."

"Actually," Zeigler said, "he did. The D.A.'s office asked me to put a rush on the—"

"Wait a minute," Ginny interrupted. "Are you saying that Dulaine was not *Danny's* father?"

"He couldn't possibly have been. The blood types don't work. Markowicz was A-positive, and Dulaine—"

"Oh my God," Ginny said. "Are you sure?"

Zeigler made a harrumphing sound; Ginny realized he must think she was quite the nut job. "Of course I'm sure," he said.

She thanked him, apologized for coming off like a maniac, and got off the phone. Sonya took one look at her and knew something wasn't right.

"What is it?"

Ginny's brain cells were playing connect-the-dots. "Dulaine," she said.

"What about him?"

Ginny repeated what Zeigler had told her. Sonya took it all in, then sat down on the edge of the bed she no longer shared with her husband.

"He didn't kill Danny, after all," Sonya said. "That's what you're telling me, isn't it? Because we know Danny's father's blood was in the mill. But I thought Dulaine confessed to you."

Ginny sat down next to Sonya, replaying the scene in her head. "He never admitted to killing him, or Dobson, either. But I thought it was just that Father LeGrand shot him before he had the chance."

"But he didn't," Sonya said. "He couldn't have—not if Danny's father's blood was there. Isn't that right?"

"It's the only thing that makes sense," Ginny said. "Believe me, I've thought about other scenarios, like his father was trying to defend him or something. But they all seem pretty absurd."

Ginny got up and went to the kitchen, throat suddenly gone dry. Sonya had made a pitcher of iced tea, and Ginny poured herself a glass. Her friend followed, watching in silence as Ginny leaned against the kitchen counter and tried to figure out what the hell was going on.

"Paula always said she didn't know who his father was," Sonya said. "I really think she was telling the truth."

Ginny put her glass on the counter and went out to the enclosed side porch. When she came back in, she was carrying the Wisk box filled with Paula's trophies. "Do you think," Ginny asked, "that something in here might belong to him?"

Sonya nodded, looking very solemn. "I guess it's possible," she said.

They sifted through the box again, that collection of junk representing Paula's feeble attempts to feel loved. Ginny had never been a fan of Sonya's older sister, but after hearing about her death at Dulaine's hands she couldn't help but pity her.

She lifted the items out of the box and laid them on the bed, as she had the day Sonya realized that her husband had slept with her sister. The paperback bore Pete's name, but the rest of the stuff seemed impossible to trace. How could you find out which Rotarian lost a membership pin eighteen years ago? Or who liked to go to the dog races? Or who won first place in some long-forgotten wrestling match?

She paused, the wrestling trophy in her hand. Maybe she could trace it, and the winner of the second-place swimming medal, too. Didn't schools keep records about that kind of thing? She kept going through the box, suddenly feeling like she was on a roll. Maybe she could find out who was in the Rotary Club back then—could look up the annual group photo in the *Transcript* and see if any of the men looked like Danny. The graduation tassel was green and gold, the colors of the vocational high school, with the number '85 attached to it; she could track down the yearbook and do the same thing. It was a long shot, but it was better than nothing.

"Do you see something in here?" Sonya asked. "'Cause I sure don't."

Ginny told her what she'd been thinking. Unfortunately, when she said it out loud, it sounded a lot less promising than it had in her head.

They finished gathering up Pete's clothes, and Ginny delivered them to the Markowiczes' house. Pete was at work, but his parents were home; she was on the receiving end of Rhonda's latest lecture about how it wasn't right for Sonya to be so unforgiving. Pete Senior, who'd clearly heard it all before, sat at the kitchen table looking as though he wished he could drink his lunch.

She went from there to Café des Artistes, where a one-armed Jimmy was taking measurements and trying to figure out how he was going to get the smell of cigarettes out of the walls. Topher hadn't wasted any time unloading the place; it was a lot easier to exorcise tobacco smoke than bad memories.

They had lunch at Angelina's, their old high school hangout, where Ginny indulged in a sub loaded with onions and three kinds of meat. She kissed him good-bye, well aware she had the breath of a dragon but pretty sure he wouldn't mind, and walked over to the public library.

The building used to be a mansion, home to a local bigwig back when the mills were churning out cloth as fast as the trains could shoot it through the Hoosac Tunnel and off to market. The library was a five-minute walk from Ginny's childhood home, and she'd always done her homework there; anything to get out of the house, so she didn't have to hear her dad talk to her mom like she was dirt on the carpet.

She shrugged off the memories and went straight to the reference room, where she scrutinized Rotary Club photos on microfilm until she got motion sickness. Then she found the old vocational school yearbooks and looked through the Class of '85 photos, hoping to see Danny's eyes staring back at her. No such luck.

She consulted the notes she'd made about the items in the box. There were those two sports awards, the Western Mass wrestling trophy and the medal for second place in something called the Tunnel City Tunas Tenth Annual Swimathon. She consulted the reference librarian, who had no idea about the wrestling but pointed out that there were only two competition-quality pools in town: one at the state college, the other at the YMCA.

She tried the college first, because it was just down the street, but the lady in the athletic department office said the Tunnel City Tunas didn't sound familiar. So she went to the Y and was told that, yes, a club by that name used to swim there, but it dissolved ages ago—and why would anybody care who won a race back then, anyway?

Kicking herself, Ginny went back to the library; she should've thought about looking up old sports pages in the first place. She sat down in front of the microfilm machine, lamenting that she hadn't picked up some Dramamine, and dove back in.

And finally, there it was: under the headline LOCAL SWIMMERS SWEEP TUNA TOURNEY. There was a group photo of the hometown medal winners, young people with wet hair and lean bodies. And staring back at her in black and white was a face so familiar she scarcely needed to read the caption beneath it. And her reaction was the same as Sonya's a few days before:

Oh, no.

50

She called him at work, but she'd just missed him; he'd already left for the day. She said she'd try him at home, but the voice at the other end of the phone told her that he wasn't there: he wanted to get some exercise, so he was hiking up to Trinity Falls.

Ginny snapped her cell phone shut and ran to the truck. How could she not have seen it? The resemblance was there once she opened her eyes and really *looked*. She drove with her attention only half on the road, got to the trailhead faster than she would've thought the laws of physics would allow. She parked on the packed dirt of the turnoff, wide enough for four cars but containing only one other.

Her track team had run up this trail a few times, but that was years ago. The route was no longer familiar, and she had to follow the blazes. Good shape or not, trotting straight uphill left her winded, and she had to stop every half mile to catch her breath.

She was almost to the top when she heard the waterfall, gurgling above her on the mountain's other face. Maybe it was just because she was half-zonked with exertion, but she could swear that under the sound of the cascade was an accusation. *It was right in front of your eyes,* it said. *Right in front of all of you, but somehow you couldn't see.*

She made it to the top, leaned over and rested her palms on her thighs, and waited for her heart rate to drop back to normal. A stream ran off to her right—a deceptively gentle thing, but it soon turned into a rush that ran to the edge of the rocks and off the mountain in a suicidal leap.

After a minute or so she straightened up. He was just a few dozen yards away, standing at the overlook to the falls.

"Ginny?"

She wasn't afraid of him. The local cops had confiscated her .38, but she couldn't imagine he'd ever want to hurt her. Still, after what he'd done to Danny, there had to be something vicious lurking beneath the surface. She felt for Pete's hunting knife, made sure it was accessible in her back pocket, and walked toward him.

"Coach Hank."

"Funny running into you up here. Beautiful afternoon, huh?"

"I was looking for you," she said. "The school said you'd gone hiking."

They were close enough to look each other in the eye. Hank's expression was still placid and friendly; once he saw the look on Ginny's face, though, everything changed. He'd been closing the distance between them, but he stopped dead.

"Looking for me?"

She nodded. "I think you know why."

He took off his day pack and unzipped it. For a half second Ginny thought he might actually be going for a weapon, but he was pulling out a Nalgene bottle. He took a drink and extended it to her. She was plenty thirsty, but she shook her head.

"You ought to know better than to hike up here with no water," Hank said.

He sounded genuinely concerned for her, odd at the present moment but perfectly at home with the previous twenty years. Could she be wrong about him? She sure as hell *wanted* to be wrong about him. But something told her that, finally, she was absolutely right.

She accepted the bottle and took a drink. Then she handed it back and said, "I can't believe I never saw the resemblance."

Hank put the bottle back in the pack and dropped it at his feet. "Nobody did," he said. "Not even me."

Ginny pushed her sweaty bangs away from her forehead. The whole situation was goddamn surreal. "How did you figure it out?"

Hank's lips formed a tight smile. "I could ask you the same thing."

"Your blood was at the crime scene," she said. "Danny's father's blood."

He nodded. It wasn't the whole explanation, but at the moment it seemed to be enough. He turned and walked a few steps toward the falls, then stopped and faced her again.

"I only slept with her once, you know. Just one time. But like I tell my kids, that's all it takes."

Ginny followed. "You were Danny's coach for four years," she said. "Are you telling me you never realized you were his father?"

Hank shrugged, a gesture that struck Ginny as indescribably sad. "I've asked myself that a thousand times," he said. "All I can figure is, we never really look at the things we see every day. You know? Then one time we were at an away game, some team we'd never played before. The other coach saw Danny and he asked me, 'Is that your son?' He said we had exactly the same eyes. It wasn't like he was the spitting image of me—except for the eyes. And as God is my witness, that was the first time it ever occurred to me. Paula and I had only hooked up that one time. She was a student and I was a teacher—and Lucie and I were already engaged, for chrissake. One time was bad enough."

"How did Danny figure it out?"

Hank shook his head. "He didn't. I swiped a sweaty towel from his locker and sent it off to one of those labs, along with a swab from inside my cheek. And of course the test came back positive. But I never meant to tell him." He shook his head, took another step toward the falls. "I sure as hell never meant to hurt him."

A wild look had taken up residence behind his eyes. When he took yet another step toward the overlook, Ginny instinctively grabbed his arm and held on. He seemed startled, and she realized that all he'd intended to do was sit down on the few steps leading up to the platform.

"I kept waiting for you to figure it out," he said. "I heard rumors that you were in trouble with the NYPD, but I still knew you must be good at your job. When you told me that Sonya asked you to find out who killed Danny, I knew it was just a matter of time."

She sat down next to him. "What happened?"

"Once I found out Danny was mine, I started taking an interest in him—you know, even more than before. He wasn't just one of my athletes anymore. He was my son. My *only* son."

Ginny thought of those five golden-haired daughters, recalled Hank's lighthearted tale about trying for a boy and winding up with twin girls. But that wished-for son had been right in front of him all along.

"After he graduated I didn't see him much," Hank went on. "But I'd go into the Skillet on the weekends sometimes just to keep an eye on him, find out how he was doing. All that stuff I told you about him asking after his mom was true. And then one time I ran into Pete pumping gas, and he said that something with Danny wasn't right. He was hanging around with those guys from New York City, and Pete thought they'd put some bad ideas in his head. Pete hadn't said anything to Sonya, but he was afraid Danny had gotten into drugs.

"Coaching at the high school, I've seen plenty. One of my runners OD'd on crystal and nearly died. I'd heard that café where Danny was working was bad news, that if you wanted to get your hands on something, this Dobson was the guy to see. I knew Danny needed to make money for college. I was afraid those city people had sucked him in."

She took it all in, not interrupting. Coming from opposite directions, she and Hank had arrived at exactly the same conclusion.

"I started following him," Hank said. "I know it sounds crazy, but I felt like it was my responsibility to look after him. Finally, one night I trailed him to the Fish Pond. I was sure he and Dobson were hatching some drug deal and if I caught them in the act, it'd scare him straight."

Hank had turned his gaze to the dirt, as though he couldn't tell the story and look her in the eye. He was quiet for so long Ginny couldn't stand it anymore.

"But it wasn't about drugs," she said. "Was it?"

Hank shook his head, reluctant to traverse the minefield of memory. He took a deep breath, closed his eyes, then exhaled and opened them again.

"I'm sure a more sophisticated man would've been clued in by the steamed-up windows," he said. "But I'm not a sophisticated man. I yanked open the door of Danny's truck expecting to see them counting their dope."

He was quiet again, for even longer this time. Finally, Ginny said, "But they were having sex."

Hank's jaw tightened. "Danny's pants were down and Dobson was . . . behind him. And I went insane. I pulled Danny out of there and threw him in my car and just *drove*. I asked him what the hell he was doing, and Danny said something ridiculous about how Dobson was helping him look for his mother and they'd gone up to the Fish Pond because that was the last place she'd been seen and one thing led to another.

"That's when I told him I was his father. I was so *angry*. I

wasn't thinking straight. I said no son of mine was going to be-
have like some dirty—" He choked on the words. "Like some
dirty—" He gave up and raised his gaze to her. "When I first realized Danny was mine, I was *happy*. I was so proud of him—that
he'd turned out so smart and strong and good. And then to see
him like that, bent over for some drug dealer. I lost my mind."

"How did you end up at the mill?"

Another helpless shrug. "It was like the car drove itself. And
when Danny asked what we were doing there, I realized why I'd
done it. I dragged him inside to show him—to show him where
he was conceived. How his mother and I had screwed like ani-
mals on that floor, surrounded by all that garbage. I wanted him
to see where his life started, to warn him that if he didn't
straighten up, he'd wind up just like his mother—a miserable
human being who was right at home in all that filth.

"And he screamed at me not to talk about her like that. And
then he hit me, bloodied my nose, and after that I can barely remember anything.

"I know I picked up something off the floor and hit him
with it, and he was on the ground, and I saw my own eyes staring back up at me. And the next thing I knew I was standing
over him, and the sight of what I'd done made me puke. I threw
the pipe in the river behind the mill, and when I saw that my
clothes were covered in blood, I threw them away and put on
some sweats I had in my car.

"And then," he said, "I went home."

Coach Hank's eyes were dry, as though the story were its
own anesthetizing drug. The murder had been so much like
Ginny had envisioned—only never in a million years would she
have imagined that this sweet, protective man was the one who
did it.

"What about Geoffrey Dobson?"

Hank seemed startled, like the name was a word from a foreign language. But then he blinked a few times and said, "I kept waiting for the police to show up on my doorstep. Dobson had seen me pull Danny out of the truck, and Danny had used my name. Then he called me, said he wanted my help or he was going to the cops."

"Your help?"

"Selling his poison. He knew I'd been trying like hell to keep my students clean. But he didn't just want me to get out of the way—he wanted me to mule for him, make deliveries when the team went on the road. I couldn't goddamn believe it. But I said I would. Meeting at the Fish Pond was his idea—the bastard had a flair for the dramatic. So I stole the van. I'm sure you already know the rest."

Ginny looked at him. Something had changed, and it took her a minute to figure out that unlike Danny's murder, Hank described killing Dobson with an utter lack of regret.

"The second murder," she said, "is always easier than the first."

Hank whirled on her, brow furrowed in anger. "Dobson was scum—a drug dealer. He sure as hell didn't care that he was ruining Danny's life. And you know something? If he'd called the cops, I might have confessed. But he saw Danny's death as just another chance to make a buck. He deserved exactly what he got."

Arthur Dulaine had used the same words when he talked about killing Danny's mother. Moral superiority was a slippery slope.

"And what," she asked, "do you deserve?"

He smiled at her, the last thing she'd expected. Then he cocked his head in the direction of the falls.

"A second ago you thought I was going to jump. If I wanted to do it now, you wouldn't try to stop me, would you?"

Ginny thought about it. "I'd have to," she said.

Her answer seemed to surprise him. "But why?"

"Sonya deserves to look her son's killer in the eye. To watch when a jury calls him guilty and a judge sentences him to prison."

"What about my girls? They don't deserve to grow up disgraced. Do they?"

"Some people might say that's part of your punishment," she said. "Maybe the worst part of all."

"And you?"

"I guess I'd have to agree."

He digested that, eyes moving from Ginny to the railing and back again. "You think you could stop me?"

"Maybe not," she said. "But I think I could promise you that even if you took the easy way out, I could put together enough evidence to prove what you did. Maybe not in a court of law, but in the court of public opinion. Then your kids would have all the disgrace and a dead father, to boot."

His eyes narrowed. "You'd do that? You wouldn't just tell Sonya the truth and leave it be?"

"I'm not some kind of vigilante," she said. "I'm a cop."

She stood up. She'd pushed him too far, and his mood had shifted so fast it was scary. There was something dangerous in his eyes, and for the first time she could see him as the person who'd beaten Danny to death. Before, that man had been an abstraction. Lulled into complacency by Hank's confession and twenty years of friendship, Ginny had thought he was no longer a danger to anyone but himself. But threatening his family's future had awakened something elemental in him—just like the sight of his only son in the embrace of another man.

Hank lunged for her. Ginny jumped the three stairs from the overlook to the ground and started sprinting for the trail. But

Hank was too fast for her; she was ten years younger, but he'd taught her everything she knew about running, and he'd apparently kept a few secrets to himself. He caught up with her and grabbed her arm, and though she managed to pop him once in the jaw, he just shook it off.

She aimed a knee at his groin, but Hank was a lot more agile than Lance Pecor; he shifted to one side and the blow hit his thigh. He grabbed for her throat, and she managed to head-butt him, but since it seemed to daze her as much as him, it was probably a mistake. He made another grab for her throat, and this time she punched him hard in the stomach; he hadn't tensed up for it, and it knocked the wind out of him.

Ginny whirled around, grabbed Hank's right arm, and pulled him over her in a judo toss she'd learned at the gym but never once tried on the street. He landed on the ground; she barely had time to congratulate herself for flipping him, because he bounced right back up and came at her again. He tried a right cross, but she dodged him; Hank was athletic, but when it came to fighting, he was an amateur.

What he lacked in training, though, he more than made up in desperation. He came at her again, rammed her with his whole body, knocked her flat, and landed on top of her. He tried to grab her hands, to pin her to the ground, and she flailed to elude his grasp. She felt the hunting knife—hard against her right butt cheek and very much out of reach. In desperation she leaned up and bit him, practically tearing off his earlobe, and the pain was enough to make him cry out and clutch the side of his head.

She used her freed right hand to push against the ground and shove him off her. The look in his eyes had shifted from unhinged to something worse, and as he clutched his bleeding ear, she kneed him directly in the nuts. It wasn't original, but it got the job done. Hank doubled over in pain, and she reached for the first rock she could find and whacked him a good one on the head. His eyes rolled back, and he was quiet.

Then, because she was no idiot, she yanked off her sneakers and used the laces to tie his hands behind his back. Quickly, in case he came to, she cut the knots on his hiking boots and used their laces to secure his feet. She grabbed his day pack and emptied its contents on the ground, finding a first-aid kit; inside was a roll of white athletic tape. It wasn't ideal, but it was all she had. She dragged Coach Hank's limp body over to the nearest sturdy tree and taped his hands to it, wrapping it around and around until the roll ran out.

She opened the Nalgene bottle and took a long drink; when she was done, she saw it was tinted pink with a backwash of blood. Hank still hadn't made a sound. She hefted the pack onto her back, spared a final glance for his motionless body, and headed back down the mountain. Her unlaced sneakers flopped as she walked, but she managed to keep them on her feet.

EPILOGUE

Coach Hank was still there when the state police found him, that side of the mountain being mercifully out of Rolly's jurisdiction. After what he'd tried to do to her, Ginny had no idea what to expect, but in the end the desire to spare his family the agony of a trial won out and he confessed. His wife and five daughters put their house on the market and fled, pulling up stakes from the town their family had called home for four generations on both sides.

They'd gone before the bruises had even faded from Ginny's face; amazing how fast things could change.

Take Sonya, who'd always seemed to Ginny the picture of domesticity and moderation. Her anger at Pete's refusal to own up to his indiscretion with her sister was outdone only by her utter fury when he finally admitted it.

One night, when she and Ginny were drinking coffee on the front porch bundled up against the November chill, Sonya told her that maybe she wouldn't be so mad if he had come clean from the beginning. She could see how Paula could have seduced him, a red-blooded young man whose girlfriend was saving herself for their wedding night. But the lies on top of the betrayal: that's what Sonya couldn't stomach. Maybe she'd forgive him in the long run. But for now she couldn't stand the sight of him.

Neither could she figure out why Monique kept showing up on her front porch, with casseroles or bunches of flowers or offers to help with the housework. Sonya thought it was probably because she was Monique's last connection to Danny, to the fantasy she'd had of their perfect life as grown-up versions of the king and queen of the prom. Ginny recalled Monique's raw, makeup-smeared face the day she'd admitted to flattening Danny's tires, to saying she wanted him dead only to have her awful wish come true. Maybe Monique's devotion to Danny's mother was her idea of atonement.

Jimmy was hard at work on his new café—lightening the place up by painting it bright yellow and replacing the dark furniture with pale wood and cheery floral cushions. Whether or not the two of them had a chance was an open question. But he was right: after fifteen years neither of them had found anybody else who drove them half as crazy, and that had to tell you something.

The weekend after Coach Hank was arrested, Ginny finally went to Sunday dinner at her Aunt Lisette's. The pot roast was just as good as she remembered, the emotional bullying just as bad. But for once, Ginny didn't mind so much. That afternoon she'd called her father, just to say hello. It wasn't good to let things fester; bad feelings had a way of multiplying over time. Maybe she'd even go down to Florida for a visit—especially if he sprang for the ticket.

She knew one thing for sure: sooner or later she was going to have to go back to the city and deal with the mess that was her life. Finally, she felt strong enough to face it. But for now, for these few waning days of fall, she couldn't make herself go. Manhattan seemed a lifetime away. And for the first time in forever, her hometown felt like home.

About the Author

Elizabeth Bloom is the author of the highly praised mystery *See Isabelle Run* and a journalist, playwright, and film critic who has worked for a variety of publications. An associate editor at the Cornell alumni magazine, she lives in Ithaca, New York, with her dogs, Nancy Drew and Mr. Jane Austen.